SKE

02. JAN 93

13. FEB 93

27. MAY

15. 93

07. OCT 93

13. 06. 94

MAPS IN A MIRROR

Volume Two

MAPS IN A MIRROR

Volume Two

The Short Fiction of Orson Scott Card

Orson Scott Card

A Legend Book
Arrow Books Limited
20 Vauxhall Bridge Road, London SW1V 2SA

An imprint of the Random Century Group

London Melbourne Sydney Auckland
Johannesburg and agencies throughout
the world

First published in the UK by Legend, 1991

This Legend edition 1992

1 3 5 7 9 10 8 6 4 2

© Orson Scott Card 1990

Phototypeset by Intype, London
Printed and bound in Great Britain by
Cox & Wyman Ltd, Reading, Berkshire

ISBN 0 09 988480 1

053562454

8/92

CLITHEROE

To Charlie Ben,
who can fly

Contents

MAPS IN A MIRROR
Fables and Fantasies

CRUEL MIRACLES
Tales of Death, Hope and Holiness

BOOK 3

MAPS IN A MIRROR

FABLES AND FANTASIES

Introduction

I don't believe in the "collective unconscious," not in the Jungian way I've seen it used. But I do believe that it is in large part through shared stories that communities create themselves and bind themselves together.

It begins with the way we establish our identity, which is intimately tied to our discovery of causality. All of nature relies on mechanical causation: Stimulus A causes response B. But almost as soon as we acquire language, we are taught an entirely different system: purposive causation, in which a person engaged in behavior B in order to accomplish result A. Never mind that it was X or Y, not A, that resulted. When it comes to evaluating human behavior, we quickly learn that it is the story we believe about a person's *purpose* that counts most.

You know the phrases of moral evaluation: "Why did you do that?" "I didn't mean to." "I was just trying to surprise you." "Do you want me to be humiliated in front of everybody?" "I don't work my fingers to the bone so you can go out and . . ." All of these sentences contain or invite stories; it is the stories we believe about our behavior that give them their moral value. Even the cruelest or weakest among us must find stories that excuse—or even ennoble—their own character flaws. On the day I'm writing this, the mayor of a major American city, arrested for using cocaine, actually stood before the cameras and said, in effect, "I guess I've just been working so hard serving the people that I didn't have time to take care of my own needs." What a story—smoking crack as an altruistic, selfless endeavor. The point is not whether the story is true; the point is that all human beings engage in storytelling about themselves, creating the story they want to believe about themselves, the story they actually believe about themselves, the story they want *others* to believe about them, the stories they believe about others, and the stories that they are afraid *might* be true about themselves and others.

Our very identity is a collection of the stories we have come to believe about ourselves. We are bombarded with the stories of others about us; even our memories of our own lives are filtered through the stories we have constructed to interpret those past events. We revise our identity by revising our self-story. Traditional psychotherapies rely heavily on this process: You *thought* you were trying to do X, but in fact your unconscious purpose was Y. Ah, now I understand myself! But I think not—I think that in the moment of believing the new story you simply *revised* your identity. I am no longer a person who tries to do X. I am a person who was being driven to do Y, without even realizing it. You remain the same person, who performed the same acts. Only the story has been changed.

All this deals with individual identities, and the tragedy of the individual is that the true cause of his behavior remains forever unknowable. And if we cannot know ourselves, true understanding of any

4

other human being is permanently out of reach. Other people's behavior must be, in that case, completely unpredictable. And yet no human community could ever exist if we had no mechanism to enable us to feel safe in trusting other people's behavior to follow certain predictable patterns. And these predictable patterns can't arise solely from personal experience—we must know, with some certainty, *before* we have observed another member of the community for any length of time, what he or she is likely to do in most situations.

There are two kinds of stories that not only give us the illusion of understanding other people's behavior, but also go a long way toward making that illusion true. Each community has its own epic: a complex of stories about what it means to be a member of that community. These stories can arise from shared experience: Have you ever heard two Catholics reminisce about catechism or being taught in Catholic school by nuns? Or they can arise from what is perceived to be a common heritage, spreading a sense of community identity across space and time. Thus it is that Americans feel there is nothing incongruous about referring to Washington as "our" first president, even though no living American was present for his administration and most Americans have precious few ancestors who lived here during that time. Thus it is that an American living in Los Angeles can hear of something that happened in Springfield, Illinois, or Springfield, Massachusetts, and say, "Only here in America . . ."

Of course, membership in communities is never absolute. The same person could just as easily say, "We sure aren't like that here in California" or "here in L.A.," thus asserting the epic of another community. But the more important a community is to us, the more power its stories have in forming our view of the world—and in shaping our own behavior. I don't think my children are the only ones who've heard prescriptive epic stories like this one: "I don't care what other people's children do. In *our* family we . . ." Every community's epic includes shibboleth stories—stories that define what members do and do not do. "No good Baptist would ever . . ." ". . . just like a true American." And the stories that define a person's individual identity are often interpreted by the role that person plays within the community. "You make us all so proud of you, son." "An outstanding role model for young ——s." "I just wish other young people would be more like you." "I hope you're proud of the example you're setting for the other kids." "Now everybody's going to think all us blacks/Rotarians/Jews/Americans are like you!" Thus we not only are defined by the epic stories of the communities we belong to, but also help revise the community's epic stories by our behavior. (If I were going into this in detail, I'd talk about the role of outsiders in shaping a community's epic, and also about negative epic. But this is an essay, not a book in itself.)

The second category of story that shapes human behavior so that we can live together is not perceived as being tied to a particular community. It is mythic; those who believe in the story believe that it defines the way *human beings* behave. These stories are not really about how this character or that character behaved in a certain situation. They are about how *people* behave in such situations.

All storytelling contains elements of the particular, the epic, and the mythic. Fiction and scripture are both uniquely suited to telling mythic tales, however, because by definition fiction is *not* tied to particular people in the real world, and by definition scripture is perceived by its believers to be the universal truth rather than being merely and particularly true, the way history is usually received. That fiction and scripture are also inevitably epic, reflecting values and assumptions of the community out of which they arose, is true but not terribly important, for their audience *believes* mythic stories to be universal and, over time, comes to behave as if they *were* universal.

But fiction is not all equally mythic. Some fiction is quite particular, tied to a time and place and even characters in the real world. Thus historical fiction or contemporary realistic fiction with a strong sense of place can lead the reader to say, "Those people certainly were/are strange," rather than the more mythic response, "People certainly are strange," or the even more mythic response, "I never knew people were like that," or the ultimate mythic response, "Yes, that's how people are."

It might seem then that fiction becomes more mythic as it is divorced from identifiable real-world patterns, but it is not really the disconnection from reality that makes fiction mythic—if that were so, our myths would all be of madmen. Rather a story becomes more mythic as it connects to things that transcend reality. Tolkien's Middle Earth is so thoroughly created in *The Lord of the Rings* that the wealth of detail makes readers feel as though they had visited in a real place; but it is a place where human behavior takes on enormous importance, so that moral issues (the goodness or evil of a person's choices and actions) and causal issues (why things happen; the way the world works) take on far greater clarity. We find in Aragorn, not just that he is noble, but Nobility. We find in Frodo, not just that he is willing to bear a difficult burden, but Acceptance. And Samwise is not just a faithful servant, but also the personification of Service.

Thus it is in fantasy that we can most easily explore, not human behaviors, but Humanity. And in exploring it, we also define it; and in defining, invent it. Those of us who have received a story and believed in its truth (even if we don't believe in its factuality) carry those memories inside us and, if we care enough about the tale, act out the script it provides us. Because I remember standing at the Cracks of Doom, and because I remember experiencing it through Sam Gamgee's eyes, I clearly remember seeing that those who reach for power are possessed by it, and if they are not utterly destroyed by it, they lose part of themselves in getting free. I doubt that in crucial situations I'll summon up the memory of *Lord of the Rings* and consciously use it as a guide to my behavior—who has time for such involved mental processes when a choice is urgent, anyway? But unconsciously I remember being a person who made certain choices, and at that unconscious level I don't believe that I—or anyone—distinguishes between personal and community memories. They are all stories, and we act out the ones we believe in and care about most, the ones that have become part of us.

While I have been speaking about what fantasy *can* be—a particularly powerful source of mythic stories—it is worth pointing out that most fantasy, like most other kinds of fiction, doesn't live up to its potential. Furthermore, because it is to be received and acted upon unconsciously, the most successful fantasy is not often that which *looks* most mythic; often the most powerful fantasies are those that seem to be very realistic and particular. I think this is part of the reason that Tolkien shunned allegory. Consciously figured storytelling is received intellectually; it is never as powerful as stories whose symbols and figures—whose mythic connections—are received unconsciously. And I've come to believe that the most successful mythic writing is that storytelling in which the author was unconscious of his or her most powerful mythic elements.

So, while the best fantasy will have a powerful mythic effect, the most successful fantasists are not those who set out to write myth. Rather, the best fantasies come, I think, from storytellers who strive to create a particular story very well—but who use settings and events that give great freedom to their imagination, so that mythic elements can arise from their unconscious and play a strong role in the story. A fantasist who works from a deliberate plan will almost never achieve as much as the fantasist who is constantly surprised by the best moments in his or her stories.

You can see, then, that I'm not defining *fantasy* the way the word is used in contemporary publishing. When publishers speak of *fantasy* they generally mean stories set in a kind of pseudo-medieval world in which some kind of magic plays a role. Certainly good mythic fantasy can still be written in that kind of setting; but since such a world has been a staple of romance since before Chaucer, one can hardly credit most authors who work in it with having allowed their imagination to play a large role in their writing. Most such "fantasists" tuck their imagination away somewhere before they enter the mythic marketplace; they have come to buy, not to sell.

It's worth pointing out that works of derivative fantasists often sell very well; there is a large audience that buys fantasy in order to have their pre-existing vision of The Way Things Work reaffirmed. And some quite brilliant fantasists remain obscure, because their mythic universe is so challenging that few readers are happy to dwell in it. But when a fantasist imagines well—and writes evocatively— many people drink in the story as if it were water, and their lives till then a vast desert in which they wandered without ever realizing how much they thirsted.

The real fantasists are not content to echo other writers' myths. They must discover their own. They venture into the most dangerous, uncharted places in the human soul, where existing stories don't yet explain what people think and feel and do. In that frightening place they find a mirror that lets them glimpse a true image. Then they return and hold up the mirror, and unlike mirrors in the real world, this one holds the storyteller's image for just a fleeting moment, just long enough for us also to glimpse the long-shadowed soul that brightly lingers there. In that moment we make the mythic connection; for that moment we *are* another person; and we carry that rare and precious understanding with us until we die.

And what am I? Like most who attempt fantasy, I imagine that I am doing true Imagining; like most, I am usually echoing other people's visions. There's always the hope, though, that at least some readers will dip into the old dry well and find new water there, seeped in from an undiscovered spring.

10

Unaccompanied Sonata

TUNING UP

When Christian Haroldsen was six months old, preliminary tests showed a predisposition toward rhythm and a keen awareness of pitch. There were other tests, of course, and many possible routes still open to him. But rhythm and pitch were the governing signs of his own private zodiac, and already the reinforcement began. Mr. and Mrs. Haroldsen were provided with tapes of many kinds of sound, and instructed to play them constantly, waking or sleeping.

When Christian Haroldsen was two years old, his seventh battery of tests pinpointed the future he would inevitably follow. His creativity was exceptional, his curiosity insatiable, his understanding of music so intense that the top of all the tests said "Prodigy."

Prodigy was the word that took him from his parents' home to a house in a deep deciduous forest where winter was savage and violent and summer a brief desperate eruption of green. He grew up cared for by unsinging servants, and the only music he was allowed to hear was birdsong, and windsong, and the cracking of winter wood; thunder, and the faint cry of golden leaves as they broke free and tumbled to the earth; rain on the roof and the drip of water from icicles; the chatter of squirrels and the deep silence of snow falling on a moonless night.

These sounds were Christian's only conscious music; he grew up with the symphonies of his early years only a distant and impossible-to-retrieve memory. And so he learned to hear music in unmusical things—for he had to find music, even when there was none to find.

He found that colors made sounds in his mind; sunlight in summer a blaring chord; moonlight in winter a thin mournful wail; new green in spring a low murmur in almost (but not quite) random rhythms; the flash of a red fox in the leaves a gasp of startlement.

And he learned to play all those sounds on his Instrument.

In the world were violins, trumpets, clarinets and krumhorns, as there had been for centuries. Christian knew nothing of that. Only his Instrument was available. It was enough.

One room in Christian's house, which he had alone most of the time, he lived in: a bed (not too soft), a chair and table, a silent machine that cleaned him and his clothing, and an electric light.

The other room contained only his Instrument. It was a console with many keys and strips and levers and bars, and when he touched any part of it, a sound came out. Every key made a different sound; every point on the strips made a different pitch; every lever modified the tone; every bar altered the structure of the sound.

When he first came to the house, Christian played (as children will) with the Instrument, making strange and funny noises. It was his only playmate; he learned it well, could produce any sound he wanted to. At first he delighted in loud, blaring tones. Later he began to play with soft and loud, and to play two sounds at once, and to change those two sounds together to make a new sound, and to play again a sequence of sounds he had played before.

Gradually, the sounds of the forest outside his house found their way into the music he played. He learned to make winds sing through his Instrument; he learned to make summer one of the songs he could play at will; green with its infinite variations was his most subtle harmony; the birds cried out from his Instrument with all the passion of Christian's loneliness.

And the word spread to the licensed Listeners:

"There's a new sound north of here, east of here; Christian Haroldsen, and he'll tear out your heart with his songs."

The Listeners came, a few to whom variety was everything first, then those to whom novelty and vogue mattered most, and at last those who valued beauty and passion above everything else. They came, and stayed out in Christian's woods, and listened as his music was played through perfect speakers on the roof of his house. When the music stopped, and Christian came out of his house, he could see the Listeners moving away; he asked, and was told why they came; he marveled that the things he did for love on his Instrument could be of interest to other people.

He felt, strangely, even more lonely to know that he could sing to the Listeners and yet would never be able to hear their songs.

"But they have no songs," said the woman who

13

came to bring him food every day. "They are Listeners. You are a Maker. You have songs, and they listen."

"Why?" asked Christian, innocently.

The woman looked puzzled. "Because that's what they want most to do. They've been tested, and they are happiest as Listeners. You are happiest as a Maker. Aren't you happy?"

"Yes," Christian answered, and he was telling the truth. His life was perfect, and he wouldn't change anything, not even the sweet sadness of the backs of the Listeners as they walked away at the end of his songs.

Christian was seven years old.

FIRST MOVEMENT

For the third time the short man with glasses and a strangely inappropriate mustache dared to wait in the underbrush for Christian to come out. For the third time he was overcome by the beauty of the song that had just ended, a mournful symphony that made the short man with glasses feel the pressure of the leaves above him even though it was summer and they had months left before they would fall. The fall is still inevitable, said Christian's song; through all their life the leaves hold within them the power to die, and that must color their life. The short man with glasses wept—but when the song ended and the other Listeners moved away, he hid in the brush and waited.

This time his wait was rewarded. Christian came out of his house, and walked among the trees, and came toward where the short man with glasses waited. The short man admired the easy, unpostured way that Christian walked. The composer looked to be about thirty, yet there was something childish in the way he looked around him, the way his walk was aimless, and prone to stop just so he could touch (not break) a fallen twig with his bare toes.

"Christian," said the short man with glasses.

Christian turned, startled. In all these years, no Listener had ever spoken to him. It was forbidden. Christian knew the law.

"It's forbidden," Christian said.

"Here," the short man with glasses said, holding out a small black object.

"What is it?"

The short man grimaced. "Just take it. Push the button and it plays."

"Plays?"

"Music."

Christian's eyes went wide. "But that's forbidden. I can't have my creativity polluted by hearing other musicians' work. That would make me imitative and derivative instead of original."

"Reciting," the man said. "You're just reciting that. This is the music of Bach." There was reverence in his voice.

"I can't," Christian said.

And then the short man shook his head. "You don't know. You don't know what you're missing. But I heard it in your song when I came here years ago, Christian. You want this."

"It's forbidden," Christian answered, for to him the very fact that a man who knew an act was forbidden still wanted to perform it was astounding, and he couldn't get past the novelty of it to realize that some action was expected of him.

There were footsteps and words being spoken in

the distance, and the short man's face became frightened. He ran at Christian, forced the recorder into his hands, then took off toward the gate of the preserve.

Christian took the recorder and held it in a spot of sunlight through the leaves. It gleamed dully. "Bach," Christian said. Then "Who is Bach?"

But he didn't throw the recorder down. Nor did he give the recorder to the woman who came to ask him what the short man with glasses had stayed for. "He stayed for at least ten minutes."

"I only saw him for thirty seconds," Christian answered.

"And?"

"He wanted me to hear some other music. He had a recorder."

"Did he give it to you?"

"No," Christian said. "Doesn't he still have it?"

"He must have dropped it in the woods."

"He said it was Bach."

"It's forbidden. That's all you need to know. If you should find the recorder, Christian, you know the law."

"I'll give it to you."

She looked at him carefully. "You know what would happen if you listened to such a thing."

Christian nodded.

"Very well. We'll be looking for it, too. I'll see you tomorrow, Christian. And next time somebody stays after, don't talk to him. Just come back in the house and lock the doors."

"I'll do that," Christian said

When she left, he played his Instrument for hours. More Listeners came, and those who had heard

16

Christian before were surprised at the confusion in his song.

There was a summer rainstorm that night, wind and rain and thunder, and Christian found that he could not sleep. Not from the music of the weather—he'd slept through a thousand such storms. It was the recorder that lay behind the Instrument against the wall. Christian had lived for nearly thirty years surrounded only by this wild, beautiful place and the music he himself made. But now.

Now he could not stop wondering. Who was Bach? Who *is* Bach? What is his music? How is it different from mine? Has he discovered things that I don't know?

What is his music?

What is his music?

What is his music?

Until at dawn, when the storm was abating and the wind had died, Christian got out of his bed, where he had not slept but only tossed back and forth all night, and took the recorder from its hiding place and played it.

At first it sounded strange, like noise, odd sounds that had nothing to do with the sounds of Christian's life. But the patterns were clear, and by the end of the recording, which was not even a half-hour long, Christian had mastered the idea of fugue and the sound of the harpsichord preyed on his mind.

Yet he knew that if he let these things show up in his music, he would be discovered. So he did not try a fugue. He did not attempt to imitate the harpsichord's sound.

And every night he listened to the recording, for many nights, learning more and more until finally the Watcher came.

The Watcher was blind, and a dog led him. He came to the door and because he was a Watcher the door opened for him without his even knocking.

"Christian Haroldsen, where is the recorder?" the Watcher asked.

"Recorder?" Christian asked, then knew it was hopeless, and took the machine and gave it to the Watcher.

"Oh, Christian," said the Watcher, and his voice was mild and sorrowful. "Why didn't you turn it in without listening to it?"

"I meant to," Christian said. "But how did you know?"

"Because suddenly there are no fugues in your work. Suddenly your songs have lost the only Bach-like thing about them. And you've stopped experimenting with new sounds. What were you trying to avoid?"

"This," Christian said, and he sat down and on his first try duplicated the sound of the harpsichord.

"Yet you've never tried to do that until now, have you?"

"I thought you'd notice."

"Fugues and harpsichord, the two things you noticed first—and the only things you didn't absorb into your music. All your other songs for these last weeks have been tinted and colored and influenced by Bach. Except that there was no fugue, and there was no harpsichord. You have broken the law. You were put here because you were a genius, creating new things with only nature for your inspiration. Now, of course, you're derivative, and truly new creation is impossible for you. You'll have to leave."

"I know," Christian said, afraid yet not really

18

understanding what life outside his house would be like.

"We'll train you for the kinds of jobs you can pursue now. You won't starve. You won't die of boredom. But because you broke the law, one thing is forbidden to you now."

"Music."

"Not all music. There is music of a sort, Christian, that the common people, the ones who aren't Listeners, can have. Radio and television and record music. But living music and new music—those are forbidden to you. You may not sing. You may not play an instrument. You may not tap out a rhythm."

"Why not?"

The Watcher shook his head. "The world is too perfect, too at peace, too happy for us to permit a misfit who broke the law to go about spreading discontent. The common people make casual music of a sort, knowing nothing better because they haven't the aptitude to learn it. But if you—never mind. It's the law. And if you make more music, Christian, you will be punished drastically. Drastically."

Christian nodded, and when the Watcher told him to come, he came, leaving behind the house and the woods and his Instrument. At first he took it calmly, as the inevitable punishment for his infraction; but he had little concept of punishment, or of what exile from his Instrument would mean.

Within five hours he was shouting and striking out at anyone who came near him, because his fingers craved the touch of the Instrument's keys and levers and strips and bars, and he could not have them, and now he knew that he had never been lonely before.

19

It took six months before he was ready for normal life. And when he left the Retraining Center (a small building, because it was so rarely used), he looked tired, and years older, and he didn't smile at anyone. He became a delivery truck driver, because the tests said that this was a job that would least grieve him, and least remind him of his loss, and most engage his few remaining aptitudes and interests.

He delivered doughnuts to grocery stores.

And at night he discovered the mysteries of alcohol, and the alcohol and the doughnuts and the truck and his dreams were enough that he was, in his way, content. He had no anger in him. He could live the rest of his life this way, without bitterness.

He delivered fresh doughnuts and took the stale ones away with him.

SECOND MOVEMENT

"With a name like Joe," Joe always said, "I had to open a bar and grill, just so I could put up a sign saying Joe's Bar and Grill." And he laughed and laughed, because after all Joe's Bar and Grill was a funny name these days.

But Joe was a good bartender, and the Watcher had put him in the right kind of place. Not in a big city, but in a smaller town; a town just off the freeway, where truck drivers often came; a town not far from a large city, so that interesting things were nearby to be talked about and worried about and bitched about and loved.

Joe's Bar and Grill was, therefore, a nice place to come, and many people came there. Not fashionable people, and not drunks, but lonely people and friendly people in just the right mixture. "My clients

20

are like a good drink, just enough of this and that to make a new flavor that tastes better than any of the ingredients." Oh, Joe was a poet, he was a poet of alcohol and like many another person these days, he often said, "My father was a lawyer, and in the old days I would have probably ended up a lawyer, too, and I never would have known what I was missing."

Joe was right. And he was a damn good bartender, and he didn't wish he were anything else, and so he was happy.

One night, however, a new man came in, a man with a doughnut delivery truck and a doughnut brand name on his uniform. Joe noticed him because silence clung to the man like a smell—wherever he walked, people sensed it, and though they scarcely looked at him, they lowered their voices, or stopped talking at all, and they got reflective and looked at the walls and the mirror behind the bar. The dough-nut delivery man sat in a corner and had a watered-down drink that meant he intended to stay a long time and didn't want his alcohol intake to be so rapid that he was forced to leave early.

Joe noticed things about people, and he noticed that this man kept looking off in the dark corner where the piano stood. It was an old, out-of-tune monstrosity from the old days (for this had been a bar for a long time) and Joe wondered why the man was fascinated by it. True, a lot of Joe's customers had been interested, but they had always walked over and plunked on the keys, trying to find a melody, failing with the out-of-tune keys, and finally giving up. This man, however, seemed almost afraid of the piano, and didn't go near it.

At closing time, the man was still there, and then,

on a whim, instead of making the man leave, Joe turned off the piped-in music and turned off most of the lights, and then went over and lifted the lid and exposed the grey keys.

The doughnut delivery man came over to the piano. *Chris*, his nametag said. He sat and touched a single key. The sound was not pretty. But the man touched all the keys one by one, and then touched them in different orders, and all the time Joe watched, wondering why the man was so intense about it.

"Chris," Joe said.

Chris looked up at him.

"Do you know any songs?"

Chris's face went funny.

"I mean, some of those old-time songs, not those fancy ass-twitchers on the radio, but *songs*. 'In a Little Spanish Town.' My mother sang that one to me." And Joe began to sing, "In a little Spanish town, 'twas on a night like this. Stars were peek-a-booing down, 'twas on a night like this."

Chris began to play as Joe's weak and toneless baritone went on with the song. But it wasn't an accompaniment, not anything Joe could call an accompaniment. It was instead an opponent to his melody, an enemy to it, and the sounds coming out of the piano were strange and unharmonious and by God beautiful. Joe stopped singing and listened. For two hours he listened, and when it was over he soberly poured the man a drink, and poured one for himself, and clinked glasses with Chris the doughnut delivery man who could take that rotten old piano and make the damn thing sing.

Three nights later Chris came back, looking harried and afraid. But this time Joe knew what would happen (had to happen) and instead of waiting until closing time, Joe turned off the piped-in music ten minutes early. Chris looked up at him pleadingly. Joe misunderstood—he went over and lifted the lid to the keyboard and smiled. Chris walked stiffly, perhaps reluctantly, to the stool and sat.

"Hey, Joe," one of the last five customers shouted, "closing early?"

Joe didn't answer. Just watched as Chris began to play. No preliminaries this time; no scales and wanderings over the keys. Just power, and the piano was played as pianos aren't meant to be played; the bad notes, the out-of-tune notes were fit into the music so that they sounded right, and Chris's fingers, ignoring the strictures of the twelve-tone scale, played, it seemed to Joe, in the cracks.

None of the customers left until Chris finished an hour and a half later. They all shared that final drink, and went home shaken by the experience.

The next night Chris came gain, and the next, and the next. Whatever private battle had kept him away for the first few days after his first night of playing, he had apparently won it or lost it. None of Joe's business. What Joe cared about was the fact that when Chris played the piano, it did things to him that music had never done, and he wanted it.

The customers apparently wanted it, too. Near closing time people began showing up, apparently just to hear Chris play. Joe began starting the piano music earlier and earlier, and he had to discontinue the free drinks after the playing because there were so many people it would have put him out of business.

It went on for two long, strange months. The delivery van pulled up outside, and people stood aside for Chris to enter. No one said anything to him; no one said anything at all, but everyone waited until he began to play the piano. He drank nothing at all. Just played. And between songs the hundreds of people in Joe's Bar and Grill ate and drank.

But the merriment was gone. The laughter and the chatter and the camaraderie were missing, and after a while Joe grew tired of the music and wanted to have his bar back the way it was. He toyed with the idea of getting rid of the piano, but the customers would have been angry at him. He thought of asking Chris not to come anymore, but he could not bring himself to speak to the strange silent man.

And so finally he did what he knew he should have done in the first place. He called the Watchers.

They came in the middle of a performance, a blind Watcher with a dog on a leash, and a Watcher with no ears who walked unsteadily, holding to things for balance. They came in the middle of a song, and did not wait for it to end. They walked to the piano and closed the lid gently, and Chris withdrew his fingers and looked at the closed lid.

"Oh, Christian," said the man with the seeing-eye dog.

"I'm sorry," Christian answered. "I tried not to."

"Oh, Christian, how can I bear doing to you what must be done?"

"Do it," Christian said.

And so the man with no ears took a laser knife from his coat pocket and cut off Christian's fingers and thumbs, right where they rooted into his hands. The laser cauterized and sterilized the wound even as it cut, but still some blood spattered on Christian's uniform. And, his hands now meaningless palms and useless knuckles, Christian stood and walked out of

24

Joe's Bar and Grill. The people made way for him again, and they listened intently as the blind Watcher said. "That was a man who broke the law and was forbidden to be a Maker. He broke the law a second time, and the law insists that he be stopped from breaking down the system that makes all of you so happy."

The people understood. It grieved them, it made them uncomfortable for a few hours, but once they had returned to their exactly-right homes and got back to their exactly-right jobs, the sheer contentment of their lives overwhelmed their momentary sorrow for Chris. After all, Chris had broken the law. And it was the law that kept them all safe and happy.

Even Joe. Even Joe soon forgot Chris and his music. He knew he had done the right thing. He couldn't figure out, though, why a man like Chris would have broken the law in the first place, or what law he would have broken. There wasn't a law in the world that wasn't designed to make people happy—and there wasn't a law Joe could think of that he was even mildly interested in breaking.

Yet. Once Joe went to the piano and lifted the lid and played every key on the piano. And when he had done that he put his head down on the piano and cried, because he knew that when Chris lost that piano, lost even his fingers so he could never play again—it was like Joe losing his bar. And if Joe ever lost his bar, his life wouldn't be worth living.

As for Chris, someone else began coming to the bar driving the same doughnut delivery van, and no one ever knew Chris again in that part of the world.

"Oh what a beautiful mornin'!" sang the road crew man who had seen *Oklahoma!* four times in his home town.

"Rock my soul in the bosom of Abraham!" sang the road crew man who had learned to sing when his family got together with guitars.

"Lead, kindly light, amid the encircling gloom!" sang the road crew man who believed.

But the road crew man without hands, who held the signs telling the traffic to Stop or go Slow, listened but never sang.

"Whyn't you never sing?" asked the road crew man who liked Rodgers and Hammerstein; asked all of them, at one time or another.

And the man they called Sugar just shrugged. "Don't feel like singin'," he'd say, when he said anything at all.

"Why they call him Sugar?" a new guy once asked. "He don't look sweet to me."

And the man who believed said, "His initials are C H. Like the sugar. C&H, you know." And the new guy laughed. A stupid joke, but the kind of gag that makes life easier on the road-building crew.

Not that life was that hard. For these men, too, had been tested, and they were in the job that made them happiest. They took pride in the pain of sunburn and pulled muscles, and the road growing long and thin behind them was the most beautiful thing in the world. And so they sang all day at their work, knowing that they could not possibly be happier than they were this day.

Except Sugar.

Then Guillermo came. A short Mexican who

spoke with an accent, Guillermo told everyone who asked, "I may come from Sonora, but my heart belongs in Milano!" And when anyone asked why (and often when no one asked anything) he'd explain. "I'm an Italian tenor in a Mexican body," and he proved it by singing every note that Puccini and Verdi ever wrote. "Caruso was nothing," Guillermo boasted. "Listen to this!"

Guillermo had records, and sang along with them, and at work on the road crew he'd join in with any man's song and harmonize with it, or sing an obligato high above the melody, a soaring tenor that took the roof off his head and filled the clouds. "I can sing," Guillermo would say, and soon the other road crew men answered. "Damn right, Guillermo! Sing it again!"

But one night Guillermo was honest, and told the truth. "Ah, my friends, I'm no singer."

"What do you mean? Of course you are!" came the unanimous answer.

"Nonsense!" Guillermo cried, his voice theatrical. "If I am this great singer, why do you never see me going off to record songs? Hey? This is a great singer? Nonsense! Great singers they raise to be great singers. I'm just a man who loves to sing, but has no talent! I'm a man who loves to work on the road crew with men like you, and sing his guts out, but in the opera I could never be! Never!"

He did not say it sadly. He said it fervently, confidently. "Here is where I belong! I can sing to you who like to hear me sing! I can harmonize with you when I feel a harmony in my heart. But don't be thinking that Guillermo is a great singer, because he's not!"

It was an evening of honesty, and every man there

explained why it was he was happy on the road crew, and didn't wish to be anywhere else. Everyone, that is, except Sugar.

"Come on, Sugar. Aren't you happy here?"

Sugar smiled. "I'm happy. I like it here. This is good work for me. And I love to hear you sing."

"Then why don't you sing with us?"

Sugar shook his head. "I'm not a singer."

But Guillermo looked at him knowingly. "Not a singer, ha! Not a singer. A man without hands who refuses to sing is not a man who is not a singer. Hey?"

"What the hell does that mean?" asked the man who sang folksongs.

"It means that this man you call Sugar, he's a fraud. Not a singer! Look at his hands. All his fingers gone! Who is it who cuts off men's fingers?"

The road crew didn't try to guess. There were many ways a man could lose fingers, and none of them were anyone's business.

"He loses his fingers because he breaks the law and the Watchers cut them off! That's how a man loses fingers. What was he doing with his fingers that the Watchers wanted him to stop? He was breaking the law, wasn't he?"

"Stop," Sugar said.

"If you want," Guillermo said, but for once the others would not respect Sugar's privacy.

"Tell us," they said.

Sugar left the room.

"Tell us," and Guillermo told them. That Sugar must have been a Maker who broke the law and was forbidden to make music anymore. The very thought that a Maker was working on the road crew with them— even a lawbreaker—filled the men with awe.

Makers were rare, and they were the most esteemed of men and women.

"But why his fingers?"

"Because," Guillermo said, "he must have tried to make music again afterward. And when you break the law a second time, the power to break it a third time is taken away from you." Guillermo spoke seriously, and so to the road crew men Sugar's story sounded as majestic and terrible as an opera. They crowded into Sugar's room, and found the man staring at the wall.

"Sugar, is it true?" asked the man who loved Rodgers and Hammerstein.

"Were you a Maker?" asked the man who believed.

"Yes," Sugar said.

"But Sugar," the man who believed said, "God can't mean for a man to stop making music, even if he broke the law."

Sugar smiled. "No one asked God."

"Sugar," Guillermo finally said. "There are nine of us on the crew, nine of us, and we're miles from any human beings. You know us, Sugar. We swear on our mother's graves, every one of us, that we'll never tell a soul. Why should we? You're one of us. But sing, dammit man, sing!"

"I can't," Sugar said. "You don't understand."

"It isn't what God intended," said the man who believed. "We're all doing what we love best, and here you are, loving music and not able to sing a note. Sing for us! Sing with us! And only you and us and God will know!"

They all promised. They all pleaded.

And the next day as the man who loved Rodgers and Hammerstein sang "Love, Look Away," Sugar

29

began to hum. As the man who believed sang "God of Our Fathers" Sugar sang softly along. And as the man who loved folksongs sang "Swing Low, Sweet Chariot," Sugar joined in with a strange, piping voice and all the men laughed and cheered and welcomed Sugar's voice to the songs.

Inevitably Sugar began inventing. First harmonies, of course, strange harmonies that made Guillermo frown and then, after a while, grin as he joined in, sensing as best he could what Sugar was doing to the music.

And after harmonies, Sugar began singing his own melodies, with his own words. He made them repetitive, the word simple and the melodies simpler still. And yet he shaped them into odd shapes, and built them into songs that had never been heard of before, that sounded wrong and yet were absolutely right. It was not long before the man who loved Rodgers and Hammerstein and the man who sang folksongs and the man who believed were learning Sugar's songs and singing them joyously or mournfully or angrily or gaily as they worked along the road.

Even Guillermo learned the songs, and his strong tenor was changed by them until his voice, which had, after all, been ordinary, became something unusual and fine. Guillermo finally said to Sugar one day, "Hey, Sugar, your music is all wrong, man. But I like the way it feels in my nose! Hey, you know? I like the way it feels in my mouth!"

Some of the songs were hymns. "Keep me hungry, Lord," Sugar sang, and the road crew sang it too.

Some of the songs were love songs: "Put your hands in someone else's pockets," Sugar sang angrily: "I hear your voice in the morning," Sugar sang tenderly, "Is it summer yet?" Sugar sang sadly; and the road crew sang it, too.

Over the months the road crew changed, one man leaving on Wednesday and a new man taking his place on Thursday, as different skills were needed in different places. Sugar was silent when each newcomer came, until the man had given his word and the secret was sure to be kept.

What finally destroyed Sugar was the fact that his songs were so unforgettable. The men who left would sing the songs with their new crews, and those crews would learn them, and teach them to others. Crewmen taught the songs in bars and on the road; people learned them quickly, and loved them; and one day a blind Watcher heard the songs and knew, instantly, who had first sung them. They were Christian Haroldsen's music, because in those melodies, simple as they were, the wind of the north woods still whistled and the fall of leaves still hung oppressively over every note and—and the Watcher sighed. He took a specialized tool from his file of tools and boarded an airplane and flew to the city closest to where a certain road crew worked. And the blind Watcher took a company car with a company driver up the road and at the end of it, where the road was just beginning to pierce a strip of wilderness, the blind Watcher got out of the car and heard singing. Heard a piping voice singing a song that made even an eyeless man weep.

"Christian," the Watcher said, and the song stopped.

"You," said Christian.

"Christian, even after you lost your fingers?"

The other men didn't understand—all the other men, that is, except Guillermo.

31

"Watcher," said Guillermo. "Watcher, he done no harm."

The Watcher smiled wryly. "No one said he did. But he broke the law. You, Guillermo, how would you like to work as a servant in a rich man's house? How would you like to be a bank teller?"

"Don't take me from the road crew, man," Guillermo said.

"It's the law that finds where people will be happy. But Christian Haroldsen broke the law. And he's gone around ever since making people hear music they were never meant to hear."

Guillermo knew he had lost the battle before it began, but he couldn't stop himself. "Don't hurt him, man. I was meant to hear his music. Swear to God, it's made me happier."

The Watcher shook his head sadly. "Be honest, Guillermo. You're an honest man. His music's made you miserable, hasn't it? You've got everything you could want in life, and yet his music makes you sad. All the time, sad."

Guillermo tried to argue, but he was honest, and he looked into his own heart, and he knew that the music was full of grief. Even the happy songs mourned for something; even the angry songs wept; even the love songs seemed to say that everything dies and contentment is the most fleeting thing. Guillermo looked in his own heart and all Sugar's music stared back up at him and Guillermo wept.

"Just don't hurt him, please," Guillermo murmured as he cried.

"I won't," the blind Watcher said. Then he walked to Christian, who stood passively waiting, and he held the special tool up to Christian's throat, Christian gasped.

"No," Christian said, but the word only formed with his lips and tongue. No sound came out. Just a hiss of air. "No."

The road crew watched silently as the Watcher led Christian away. They did not sing for days. But then Guillermo forgot his grief one day and sang an aria from *La Bohème*, and the songs went on from there. Now and then they sang one of Sugar's songs, because the songs could not be forgotten.

In the city, the blind Watcher furnished Christian with a pad of paper and a pen. Christian immediately gripped the pencil in the crease of his palm and wrote: "What do I do now?"

The driver read the note aloud, and the blind Watcher laughed. "Have we got a job for you! Oh, Christian, have we got a job for you!" The dog barked loudly, to hear his master laugh.

APPLAUSE

In all the world there were only two dozen Watchers. They were secretive men, who supervised a system that needed little supervision because it actually made nearly everybody happy. It was a good system, but like even the most perfect of machines, here and there it broke down. Here and there someone acted madly, and damaged himself, and to protect everyone and the person himself, a Watcher had to notice the madness and go to fix it.

For many years the best of the Watchers was a man with no fingers, a man with no voice. He would come silently, wearing the uniform that named him with the only name he needed—Authority. And he would find the kindest, easiest, yet most thorough

33

way of solving the problem and curing the madness and preserving the system that made the world, for the first time in history, a very good place to live. For practically everyone.

For there were still a few people—one or two each year—who were caught in a circle of their own devising, who could neither adjust to the system nor bear to harm it, people who kept breaking the law despite their knowledge that it would destroy them.

Eventually, when the gentle maimings and deprivations did not cure their madness and set them back into the system, they were given uniforms and they, too, went out. Watching.

The keys of power were placed in the hands of those who had most cause to hate the system they had to preserve. Were they sorrowful?

"I am," Christian answered in the moments when he dared to ask himself that question.

In sorrow he did his duty. In sorrow he grew old. And finally the other Watchers, who reverenced the silent man (for they knew he had once sung magnificent songs), told him he was free. "You've served your time," said the Watcher with no legs, and he smiled.

Christian raised an eyebrow, as if to say, "And?"

"So wander."

Christian wandered. He took off his uniform, but lacking neither money nor time he found few doors closed to him. He wandered where in his former lives he had once lived. A road in the mountains. A city where he had once known the loading entrance of every restaurant and coffee shop and grocery store. And at last to a place in the woods where a house was falling apart in the weather because it had not been used in forty years.

Christian was old. The thunder roared and it only made him realize that it was about to rain. All the old songs. All the old songs, he mourned inside himself, more because he couldn't remember them than because he thought his life had been particularly sad.

As he sat in a coffee shop in a nearby town to stay out of the rain, he heard four teenagers who played the guitar very badly singing a song that he knew. It was a song he had invented while the asphalt poured on a hot summer day. The teenagers were not musicians and certainly were not Makers. But they sang the song from their hearts, and even though the words were happy, the song made everyone who heard it cry.

Christian wrote on the pad he always carried, and showed his question to the boys. "Where did that song come from?"

"It's a Sugar song," the leader of the group answered. "It's a song by Sugar."

Christian raised an eyebrow, making a shrugging motion.

"Sugar was a guy who worked on a road crew and made up songs. He's dead now, though," the boy answered.

"Best damn songs in the world," another boy said, and they all nodded.

Christian smiled. Then he wrote (and the boys waited impatiently for this speechless old man to go away): "Aren't you happy? Why sing sad songs?"

The boys were at a loss for an answer. The leader spoke up, though, and said, "Sure I'm happy. I've got a good job, a girl I like, and man, I couldn't ask for more. I got my guitar. I got my songs. And my friends."

And another boy said, "These songs aren't sad, Mister. Sure, they make people cry, but they aren't sad."

"Yeah," said another. "It's just that they were written by a man who knows."

Christian scribbled on his paper. "Knows what?"

"He just knows. Just knows, that's all. Knows it all."

And then the teenagers turned back to their clumsy guitars and their young, untrained voices, and Christian walked to the door to leave because the rain had stopped and because he knew when to leave the stage. He turned and bowed just a little toward the singers. They didn't notice him, but their voices were all the applause he needed. He left the ovation and went outside where the leaves were just turning color and would soon, with a slight inaudible sound, break free and fall to earth.

For a moment he thought he heard himself singing. But it was just the last of the wind, coasting madly through the wires over the street. It was a frenzied song, and Christian thought he recognized his voice.

A Cross-Country Trip to Kill Richard Nixon

Siggy wasn't the killer type. Nor did he have delusions of grandeur. In fact, if he had any delusions, they were delusions of happiness. When he was thirty, he gave up a good job as a commercial artist and went down in the world, deliberately downward in income, prestige, and tension. He bought a cab.

"Who is going to drive this cab, Siggy?" his mother asked. She was a German of the old school, well-bred with contempt for the servant class.

"I am," Siggy answered mildly. He endured the tirade that followed, but from then on his sole source of income was the cab. He didn't work every day. But whenever he felt like working or getting out of the apartment or picking up some money, he would take his cab out in Manhattan. His cab was spotless. He gave excellent service. He enjoyed himself immensely. And when he came home, he sat down at the easel or with a sketchpad on his knees, and did art. He wasn't very good. His talents had been best suited for commercial art. Anything more difficult than the back of a Cheerios box, and Siggy was out of his element. He never sold any of his paintings. But he didn't really care. He loved everything he did and everything he was.

So did his wife, Marie. She was French, he was German; they married and moved to America on the eve of World War II, bringing their families with them, and they were exquisitely well matched and happy through both of Siggy's careers. In 1978, at the age of fifty-seven, she died of a heart attack, and Siggy took the cab out and drove for eleven hours without picking up a single fare. At four o'clock in the morning, he finally made his decision and drove home. He would go on living. And sooner than he expected, he was happy again.

He had never dreamed of conquering the world or of getting rich or even of getting into bed with a movie star or a high-class prostitute. So it was not in his nature to imagine himself doing impossible things. It took him rather by surprise when he was chosen to save America.

She was a Disney fairy godmother, and she came in the craziest dream he had ever had. "You, Siegfried Reinhardt, are the lucky winner of exactly one wish," she said, sounding like the lady from Magic Carpet Land the last time she called to offer a free carpet cleaning.

"One?" Siggy answered in his dream, thinking this was rather below standard for godmothers.

"And you have a choice," the fairy godmother answered. "You may either use the wish on your own behalf, or you may use it to save America."

"America's going to hell and needs all the wishes it can get." Siggy said. "On the other hand, I don't really need anything I haven't got already. So it's America."

"Very well," she answered, and turned to go.

38

"Wait a minute," he said in his dream. "Is that all?"

"You asked for a wish for America, you get a wish for America. Which is a waste of a perfectly good wish, if you ask me, for thirty years America hasn't been worth *scheisse*. Try not to mess things up too badly, Siggy. This wish business is pretty complicated, and you're a simple type fellow." And then she was gone, and Siggy woke up, the dream impressed on his memory as dreams so rarely were.

Crazy, crazy, he thought, laughing it off. I'm getting old, Marie dragged me to too many Disney movies, I'm too lonely. But for all that he knew the dream was nonsense, he could not forget it.

I mean, what *if*, he told himself. What *if* I had a wish. Just one thing I could change, to make everybody in America happier. What would it be?

"What's wrong with America?" his mother asked, rolling her eyes and rocking back and forth in her wheelchair. To Siggy's knowledge she had never had a rocking chair in her life, and compensated by moving in every other kind of chair as if it were a rocker. "Everything's wrong with America," she said.

"But one thing, Mother. Just the worst thing to fix."

"It's too late, nothing can fix it. It all started with *him*. If there is such a thing as reincarnation, may he be reincarnated as a fly that I can swat. May he come back as a fire hydrant for all the dogs to pee against." Siggy's mother was impeccably polite in German, but in English she was crude, and, as so often before, Siggy wondered why she still lingered on at a ridiculous ninety-two when Marie, who was

39

delicate and sensitive, was dead. "Don't be crude, Mother."

"I'm an American, I have the papers, I can be crude. Nineteen sixty-eight, that's when everything went to Hell."

"You can't blame everything on one man."

"What do you know? You drive a cab."

"One man doesn't make that big a difference."

"What about Adolf Hitler!" his mother said triumphantly, slapping the arms of the wheelchair and rocking back and forth. "Adolf Hitler! One man! Just like Richard Nixon, may his electric razor short-circuit and fry his face."

She was still laughing and cursing Nixon when Siggy finally left. Fairy godmother, he said to himself. What do I need a fairy godmother for? I have Mom.

But the dream wouldn't go away. The fairy godmother kept flitting in and out, hovering on the edges of all his dreams, wordlessly saying, "Hurry and make up your mind, Siggy. Fairy godmothers are busy, you're wasting my time."

"Don't push me," he said. "I'm being careful."

"I've got other clients, give me a break."

"I resent being pushed around by figments of my imagination," he said. "I get one wish, I want to use it right." When he woke up, he was vaguely embarrassed that he was taking the fairy godmother so seriously in his dreams. "Just a dream," he said to himself. But dream or not, he started doing research.

He took a poll. He kept a notebook beside him in the cab, and asked people, "Just out of curiosity what's the worst thing wrong with America? What's the one thing you'd change if you could?"

There were quite a few suggestions, but they always came back to Richard Nixon. "It all started with Nixon," they'd say. Or, "It's Carter. But if it hadn't been for Nixon, Carter would never have been elected."

"It's the unions, driving up prices," said a woman. And then, after a little thought, "If Nixon hadn't screwed up we might have kept some *control* in this country."

It wasn't just that his name kept coming up. It was the way people *said* it. With loathing, with contempt, with fear. It was an emotional word. It sounded evil. They said *Nixon* the way they might say *slime*. Or *spider*.

Siggy sat one night staring at the results of his poll, unable to get out of his cab because of the thoughts that had taken over his head. I'm crazy, he thought to himself, but his thoughts ignored him and went right on, the fairy godmother giggling in the background. Richard Nixon, said the thoughts. If there could be one wish, it must be used to eliminate Richard Nixon.

But I voted for him, dammit, Siggy said silently. He *thought* it would be silent, but the words echoed inside the cab after all. "I voted for him. And I thought he did a damn good job sometimes." He was almost embarrassed saying the words—they weren't the kind of sentiment that made a cabby popular with his paying passengers. But thinking of Nixon made him remember the triumphant moment when Nixon said Up Yours to the North Vietnamese and bombed the hell out of them and got them to the negotiating table that one last time. And the wonderful landslide election that kept the crazy man from South Dakota out of the White House. And the trip to China, and the trip to Russia, and the feeling that America was maybe strong like it had been under Roosevelt when Hitler got his ass kicked up into his throat. Siggy remembered that, remembered that it felt good, remembered being angry as the press attacked and attacked and attacked and finally Nixon fell apart and turned out to be exactly as rotten a person as the papers said he was.

And the feeling of betrayal that he had felt all through 1973 came back, and Siggy said, "Nixon," and inside the cab his voice sounded even more poisonous than the passengers'.

If there was something wrong with America, Siggy knew then, it was Richard Nixon. Whether a person had ever liked him or not. Because those who liked him had been betrayed, and those who hated him had not been appeased, and there he was out in California breeding the hatred that surpassed even the hatred for the phone company and the unions and the oil companies and the Congress.

I will wish him dead, Siggy thought. And inside his mind he could hear the fairy godmother cheering. "Make the wish," she said.

"Not yet," Siggy said. "I've got to be fair."

"Fair, schmair. Make the wish, I've got work to do."

"I've got to talk to him first," Siggy said. "I can't wish him dead without he has a chance to say his piece."

Siggy had planned to travel alone. Who would understand his purpose, when he didn't really understand it himself? He told no one he was going, just pulled five hundred dollars out of the bank and got in his cab and started driving. New Jersey, Pennsylvania; found himself on I–70 and decided what the hell, I–70 goes most of the way, that's my highway. He stopped at Richmond, Indiana, to go to the bathroom and get something to eat, then decided to spend the night in a cheap motel.

It was his first night in unfamiliar surroundings in years. It bothered him; things were out of place, and the sheets were rough and harsh, and there weren't a hundred reminders of Marie and happiness. He slept badly (but, thank heaven, without the fairy godmother), and when he left in the morning he realized that he was lonelier then he thought possible. He wasn't used to driving without conversation. He wasn't used to driving without a fare.

So he picked up a hitchhiker by the on-ramp to the freeway. It was a boy—no, in his own eyes doubtless a man—in his early twenties. Hair fairly long, but cleaner than the usual scruffy roadside bum, and he'd be somebody to talk to, and if there was any trouble, well, Siggy had always carried a tire iron beside the seat, though he was not quite sure what he would ever do with it, or when. It made him feel safe. Safe enough to pull over and pick up the boy.

Siggy reached over and opened the car door as the boy ran up.

"Hey, uh," the boy said, leaning into the car. "I don't need a cab, I need a free ride."

"Don't we all," Siggy said, smiling. "I'm from New York City. In Indiana, I give free rides. I'm on vacation."

The boy nodded and got in beside him. Siggy moved out and was on the freeway in moments, going at a steady fifty-five. He put on the cruise control and glanced at the boy. He was looking out the front window, his face glum.

"Where are you going?" Siggy asked.

"West."

"There's lots of west in the world. Wherever you go, there's still more west on ahead."

"They put an ocean at the end, I stop before I get wet, OK?"

"*I'm* going to Los Angeles," Siggy offered.

The boy said nothing. Obviously didn't want to talk. That was all right. Lots of customers liked silence, and Siggy had no objection to giving it to them. Enough that there was someone breathing in the car. It gave Siggy a feeling of legitimacy. It was all right to drive as long as someone else was in the car.

But this couldn't go on all the way, of course, Siggy realized. When he picked the boy up, he figured on St. Louis, maybe Kansas City, then the boy gets out and Siggy's alone again. He'd have to stop for the night, Denver, maybe. Did the boy think a motel room went along with the ride?

"Where you from?"

The boy seemed to wake up, as if he had dozed off with his eyes wide open. Looking out on Indiana as it went by.

"What do you mean, from?" the boy asked.

"I mean *from*, the opposite of *to*. I mean, where were you born, where do you live?"

"I was born in Rochester. I don't think I live anywhere."

"Rochester. What's it like in Rochester?"

"I lived in a Mafia neighborhood. Everybody kept their yards neat and nobody ever broke into the houses."

44

"A lot of factories?"

"Eastman Kodak and Xerox Corporation. There's a lot of shit in the world, and Rochester exists by making copies of it." The boy said it bitterly, but Siggy laughed. It was funny, after all. The boy finally smiled, too.

"What are you going to do in California?" Siggy asked.

"Find a place to sleep and maybe a job."

"Want to be an actor?"

The boy looked at Siggy with contempt. "An *actor?* Like Jane Fonda?" He said the name like poison. The tone of voice was familiar. Siggy decided to try him out on the Name.

"What do you think of Richard Nixon?" Siggy asked.

"I don't," said the boy.

And then, madly, knowing it could ruin everything, Siggy blurted, "I'm going to get him."

"What?" the boy asked.

Siggy recovered his senses. Some of them, anyway. "I going to meet him. At San Clemente."

The boy laughed. "What do you want to meet him for?"

Siggy shrugged.

"They won't let you near him anyway. You think he wants to see people like us? Nixon." And there it was. The tone of voice. The contempt. Siggy was reassured. He was doing the right thing.

The hours passed and so did the states. Illinois came and went, and they crossed the Mississippi at St. Louis. Not as big as Siggy had expected, but still a hell of a lot of water, when you thought about it. Then Missouri, which was too wide and too dull. And because it was dull, they kept talking. The boy

45

had a bitter streak a mile wide—everything seemed to lead to it. Siggy found it more comfortable to do the talking himself, and since the boy kept listening and saying something now and then, it seemed OK. They were beginning to pass signs that promised Kansas City as if it were a prize when Siggy got on the subject of Marie. Remembered things about her. How she loved wine—a French vice that Siggy loved in her.

"When she was a little drunk," he told the boy, "her eyes would get big. Sometimes full of tears, but she'd still smile. And she'd lift up her chin and stretch her neck. Like a deer."

Maybe the boy was getting tired of the conversation. Maybe he just resented hearing about a love that actually worked. He answered snappishly. "When you ever seen a deer, Manhattan cabdriver? The zoo?"

Siggy refused to be offended. "She was like a deer."

"I think she sounds like a giraffe." The boy smirked a little, as if saying this were somehow a victory over Siggy. Well, it was. It had worn down his patience.

"It's my wife we're talking about. She died two years ago."

"What do I care? I mean what makes you think I give a pink shit about it? You want to cry? You want to get all weepy about it? Then do it quiet. Jesus, give a guy a break, will you?"

Siggy kept his eyes on the road. There was a bitter feeling in his stomach. For a moment his hands felt violent, and he gripped the wheel. Then the feeling passed, and he got his curiosity back again.

"Hey, what're you so mad about?"

"Mad? What says I'm mad?"

"You sounded mad."

"I sounded mad!"

"Yeah, I wondered if maybe you wanted to talk about it."

The boy laughed acidly. "What, the seat reclines? It becomes maybe a couch? I stuck my thumb out because I wanted a ride. I want psychoanalysis, I stick out a different finger, you understand?"

"Hey, fine, relax."

"I'm not tense, shithead." He gripped the door handle so tightly that Siggy was afraid the door would crumple like tinfoil and fall away from the car.

"I'm sorry," the boy said finally, still looking forward. He didn't let go of the door.

"It's OK," Siggy answered.

"About your wife, I mean. I'm not like that. I don't just go around making fun of people's dead wives."

"Yeah."

"And you're right. I'm mad."

"At me?"

"You? What're you? A piss-ant. One of twelve million piss-ants in New York City. We're all piss-ants."

"What're you mad at?" Siggy could not resist adding the figures to his checklist. "Inflation? Oil companies? Nuclear plants?"

"What is this, the Gallup poll?"

"Maybe yeah. People get mad at a lot of the same things. Nuclear plants then?"

"I'm mad at nuclear plants, yeah."

"You want 'em all shut down, right?"

"Wrong, turkey. I want 'em to build a million of 'em. I want 'em to build 'em everywhere, and then

47

on the count of three they all blow up, they wipe out this whole country."

"America?"

"From sea to shitting sea."

Then silence again. Siggy thought he could feel the whole car trembling with the young man's anger. It made Siggy sad. He kept glancing at the boy's face. It wasn't old. There were some acne scars; the beard was thin in quite a few places. Siggy tried to imagine the face without the beard. Without the anger. Without the too many drugs and too many bottles. The face when it was childish and innocent.

"You know," Siggy said, "I can't believe—I look at you, I can't believe that somebody loved you once."

"Nobody asked you to believe it."

"But they must have, right? Somebody taught you to walk. And talk. And ride a bicycle. You had a father, right?"

Suddenly the boy's fist shot out and slammed into the glove compartment door, which popped open with a crash. Siggy was startled, afraid. The boy showed no sign of pain, though it seemed he had hit hard enough to break a finger.

"Hey, careful," Siggy said.

"You want me to be careful? You tell me to be careful, asshole?" The boy grabbed the steering wheel, jerked on it. The taxi swung into another lane; a car behind them squealed on its brakes and honked.

"Are you crazy? Do you want to get us killed? Get mad, wreck the car, but don't kill us!" Siggy was screaming in anger, and the boy sat there, trembling, his eyes not quite focused. Then the car that had honked at them pulled up beside them on the right. The driver was yelling something with his window down. His face looked ugly with anger. The boy held up his middle finger. The man made the same gesture back again.

And suddenly the boy rolled down the window. "Hey, don't get us in trouble," Siggy said. The boy ignored him. He yelled a string of obscenities out the window. Siggy sped up, trying to pull away from the other car. The driver of the other car kept pace with him, yelled back his own curses.

And then the boy pulled a revolver out of his pocket, a big, mean-looking black pistol, and aimed it out the window at the driver of the other car. The man suddenly looked terrified. Siggy slammed on the brakes, but so did the other driver, and they stayed nearly parallel.

"Don't!" Siggy screamed, and he sped up, leaving the other car in the distance. The boy pulled the gun back into the car and laid it on his lap, the cock still back, his finger still on the trigger.

"It isn't loaded, right?" Siggy asked. "It was just a joke, right? Would you take your finger off the trigger?"

But it was as if the boy didn't hear him. As if he didn't even remember the last few minutes. "You wanted to know if I had a father, right? I have a father."

At the moment Siggy didn't much care whether the boy had been born in a test tube. But better he should talk about his father than wave the gun around.

"My father," said the boy, "spends his life making sure enough Xerox machines are getting sold and putting more ads in the magazines when they aren't."

They crossed the border into Kansas, and Siggy

49

hoped the incident with the pistol wouldn't get reported across state lines.

"My father never taught me to ride a bike. My brother did. My brother was killed in Mr. President Nixon's war. You know?"

"That was a long time ago," Siggy said.

The boy looked at him coldly. "It was yesterday, asshole. You don't believe those calendars, do you? All lies, so we'll think it's OK to forget about it. Maybe your wife died years ago, Mr. Cabdriver, but I thought you loved her better than that."

Then the boy looked down at the pistol in his lap, still cocked, still ready to fire.

"I thought I left this home," he said in surprise. "What's it doing here?"

"I should know?" Siggy asked. "Do me a favor, uncock the thing and put it away."

"OK," the boy said. But he didn't do anything.

"Hey, please," Siggy said. "You scare me, that thing sitting there ready to shoot."

The boy bowed his head over the pistol for a few moments. "Let me out," he said. "Let me get out."

"Hey, come on, just put the gun away, you don't have to get out, I won't be mad, just put the gun away."

The boy looked up at him and there were tears in his eyes, spilling out onto his cheeks. "You think I brought this gun by accident? I don't want to kill you."

"Then why'd you bring it?"

"I don't know. Jesus, man, let me out."

"You want to go to California, I'm going to California."

"I'm dangerous," the boy said.

Damn right you're dangerous, Siggy thought.

Damn right. And I'm a doubledamned fool not to let you out of here right this second, right this minute, very next off-ramp I'll pull over and let him off.

"Not to me," Siggy said, wondering why he wasn't more afraid.

"To you. I'm dangerous to you."

"Not to me." And Siggy realized why he was so confident. It was the fairy godmother, sitting inside the back of his head. "You think I'm going to let anything happen to you, *dummkopf?*" she asked him silently. "If you knock off before you make your wish, it ruins my life. The clerical work alone would take years." I'm crazy, thought Siggy. This boy is nuts, but I'm crazy.

"Yeah," the boy said finally, gently letting down the hammer and putting the gun back into the pocket of his jacket. "Not to you."

They drove in silence for a while, as the plains flattened out and the sky went even flatter and the sun went dim behind the gray overcast. "Richard Nixon, huh?" the boy asked.

"Yeah."

"You really think they'll let us get near him?"

"I'll see to it," Siggy said. And it occurred to him for the first time that fairy godmothers might fulfill wishes in unpleasant ways. Wish him dead? I should wish Nixon dead, and this boy goes to prison forever for killing him? Watch it, fairy godmother, he warned. I won't let you trick me. I have a plan, and I won't let you trick me into hurting this boy.

"Hungry, Son?" Siggy asked. "Or can you hold out till Denver?"

"Denver's fine," said the boy. "But don't call me Son."

*

51

It was hot in Los Angeles, but as Siggy neared the sea the breezes became steadily cooler. He was tired. He was used to driving, but not so long a stretch, not so far. In a way the freeways were restful — no traffic, no guesswork about where the car to the right would be a few minutes later. People actually paid attention to the lines between lanes. But the freeways went on, relentlessly, mile after mile, until he felt like he was standing still and the road and the scenery played swiftly past him and under him. At last they had brought Los Angeles to him, and here the scenery would stop for him and wait for him to act. San Clemente. Richard Nixon's house. He found them easily, as if he had always known the way. The boy, asleep beside him for the last few hundred miles, woke up when Siggy brought the cab to a halt.

"What?" asked the boy, sleepily.

"Go back to sleep," Siggy said, getting out of the car. The boy got out, too.

"This is it?"

"Yes," Siggy said, already walking toward the entrance.

"I gotta pee," the boy said. But Siggy ignored him, and kept on walking. The boy followed, ran a little, caught up, saying softly, "Shit can't you even wait a minute?"

Secret Service men were everywhere, of course, but by now Siggy's madness was complete. He knew that they could not stop him. He had to meet Richard Nixon, and so he would. He had parked a long way from the mansion, and he just walked in, the boy at his heels. He didn't climb fences or do anything extraordinary. Just walked up the drive, around the house, and out onto the beach. No one saw him. No one called out to him. Secret Servicemen seemed always to have their backs to him, or to be on an urgent errand somewhere else. He would have his meeting with Richard Nixon. He would use his wish.

And he was standing where the water charged up the sand, always falling short of its last achievement as the tide ebbed. The boy stood beside him. Siggy watched the house, but the boy watched Siggy. "I thought they had us," the boy said. "I can't believe we got in here."

"Sh," Siggy answered softly. "Sh."

Siggy felt as nervous as a virgin at her wedding, more dreading than longing for what was to come. What if Nixon thinks I'm a fool? he thought. He needn't have worried. As he stood in the sand, Nixon emerged from the house, came down to the beach, and stopped at the waterline, staring out to sea. He was alone.

Taking a deep breath, Siggy walked to him. The sand kept slipping under his feet, so that every step forward tried to turn him out of his path. He persevered, and stood beside Richard Nixon. It was the face, the nose, at once the heavily shadowed evil face of the Herblock cartoons and the hopeful, strong face of the man Siggy had voted for three times.

"Mr. Nixon," Siggy said.

Nixon did not turn at first. He just said, "How did you get here?"

Siggy shrugged. "I had to see you."

Then Nixon turned to him, his face set to smile. Siggy watched as Nixon's eyes met his, then glanced over his shoulder at the boy, who was walking up, who stopped just behind Siggy.

The boy spoke. "We've come to kill you," he said.

And the boy had his hand in his pocket, where the gun was, and Siggy felt a moment of panic. But the voice of the fairy godmother sounded gently in his ear. "Don't worry," she said. "Take your time."

So Siggy shook his head at the boy, who frowned but did not shoot, and then Siggy turned back to Nixon. The former president was still smiling, his eyes narrowed a bit, but not showing any fear. Siggy felt a moment of satisfaction. This was the Nixon he had admired, the man with such great physical courage, who had faced mobs of Communists in Venezuela and Peru without flinching.

"You wouldn't be the first to want to," Nixon said.

"Oh, but I don't want to," Siggy said. "I have to. For America."

"Ah." Nixon nodded, knowingly. "We all do the most unpleasant things, don't we, for America."

Siggy felt a stab of relief. He understood, which would make it all so much easier.

"You're lucky," Nixon said. "I came out here alone, this once. To say good-bye. I'm leaving here. Tomorrow I would have been gone." He shook his head slightly, slowly, from side to side. "Well, get on with it. I can't stop you."

"Oh," Siggy said. "I'm not going to shoot you. All I have to do is *wish* you dead." Behind him Siggy heard the boy gasp a little. And Nixon sighed slightly. For a moment it sounded to Siggy like disappointment. Then he realized it was relief. And the smile returned to Nixon's face.

"But not today," Siggy went on. "I can't just wish for you to be assassinated now, Mr. Nixon. Or for you to die in bed or in an accident. The damage is done. So I'll have to have you die in the past."

The boy made a soft noise behind him.

Nixon nodded wisely. "That will be much better, I think."

"So I've decided that the best time will be right after you're sworn into office the second time. In 1972, before the Watergate thing got out of hand, right after you got a peace treaty from the Vietnamese and right after your landslide victory. Then an assassin picks you off, and you're a bigger hero and a greater legend than Kennedy."

"And everything since then?" Nixon asked.

"Changed. They won't keep after you, you see, after you're dead. You'll be a pleasant memory to almost everybody. Their hate will be gone, mostly."

Nixon shook his head. "You said your wish was supposed to be for the good of America, didn't you?"

Siggy nodded.

"Well, if I had been assassinated then, Spiro Agnew would have become president."

Siggy had forgotten. Spiro Agnew. What a bum. There was no way that could be good for the country. "You're right," Siggy said. "So it'll have to be before. Right before the election. It'll be almost as good then, you were leading in the polls."

"But then," Nixon said, "George McGovern would have been president."

Worse and worse. Siggy began to realize the difficulties involved in carrying out his responsibility. Everything he changed would have consequences. How could he fix the country's woes, if he kept increasing them with the changes he made?

"And if you have me killed in 1968, it's either Spiro Agnew or Hubert Humphrey," Nixon added. "Maybe you'll just have to wish for me to win in 1960."

Siggy thought of that. Thought very carefully. "No," he said. "That would be good for *you*. It would have made you a better president, not to have those

55

bad experiences first. But would you have taken us to the moon? Would you have kept the Vietnam War as small as it was?"

"Smaller," Nixon said. "I would have won it by 1964."

Siggy shook his head. "And been at war with Red China, and the world might have been destroyed, and millions of people killed. I don't think the wrong man won in 1960."

Nixon's face went kind of sad. "Then maybe it would be kindest of all if you simply wished for me to lose every election I ever tried. Keep me out of Congress, out of the vice-presidency. Let me be a used car salesman." And he smiled a twisted, sad smile.

Siggy reached out and touched the man's shoulder. "Maybe I should," he said, and the boy behind him made another soft sound.

"But no," Nixon said. "You wanted to save America. And it wouldn't make any difference to keep me out of government. If it hadn't been me, it would have been someone else. There would have been a Richard Nixon anyway. If they hadn't wanted me, I wouldn't have been there. If Richard Nixon hadn't existed, they would have made one."

Siggy sighed. "Then I don't know what to do," he said.

Nixon turned and looked out over the water. "I only did what they wanted me to do. And when they changed their minds, they were surprised at what I was." The beach was cold and damp between waves. The breeze from the land carried the air of Los Angeles with it, and it made the beach smell slimy and old. "Maybe," Nixon said, "there's nothing you can wish for that will save America. Maybe there's nothing you can do at all."

And the noise the boy made was loud enough that Siggy at last turned to look at him. To his surprise, the boy was no longer standing up. He was sitting cross-legged in the sand, bowed over, his hands gripping each other behind his neck. His body shook.

"What's wrong, Son?" Nixon asked. He sounded concerned.

The boy looked up, anger and grief in his face. "You," he said, and his voice shook. "*You* can call me Son."

Nixon knelt in the sand, painfully as if his leg hurt, and touched the boy's shoulder. "What's wrong, Son?"

"His brother was killed in Vietnam," Siggy said, as if that explained anything.

"I'm sorry," Nixon said. "I'm really sorry."

The boy threw off Nixon's hand. "Do you think that matters? Do you think it makes any difference how *sorry* you are?" The words stung Nixon, clearly. He shuddered as if his face had been slapped.

"I don't know what else I can do," Nixon said softly.

The boy's hand shot out and grabbed him by the lapels of his suit, pulling him down until they were face to face, and the boy screamed, "You can pay for it! You can pay and pay and pay—" and the boy's lips and teeth were almost touching Nixon's face, and Nixon looked pathetic and helpless in the boy's grip, flecks of the boy's spit beginning to dot his cheeks and lips. Siggy watched, and realized there was nothing that Nixon could do that would pay it all, that would give the boy back what he had lost, realized that Nixon had not really taken it from the

57

boy. Had not taken it, could not return it, was as much a victim as anyone else. How could Siggy, with a single wish, set it all right? How could he even up all the scales?

"Think, idiot," said the fairy godmother. "I'm losing patience."

"I don't know what to do," he said to her.

"And you're the one with the plan," she answered contemptuously.

The boy was still screaming, again and again, and Nixon was weeping now, silently letting the tears flow to join the spittle on his face, as if to agree, as if to make it unanimous.

"I wish," said Siggy, "for everyone to forgive you, Mr. Nixon. For everyone in America to stop hating you, little by little, until all the hate is gone."

The fairy godmother danced in his mind, waving her wand around and turning everything pink.

And the boy stopped screaming and let go of Nixon, gazed wonderingly into the old man's eyes at the tears there, and said, "I'm sorry for you," and meant it with all his heart. Then Siggy helped the boy to his feet and they turned away, leaving Nixon on the beach. The world was tinged with pink and Siggy put his arm around the boy and they smiled at each other. And they headed back to the cab. Siggy saw the fairy godmother flying away ahead of them, north and east from San Clemente, trailing stars behind her as she flew.

"Bibbity bobbity boo," she cried, and she was gone.

The Porcelain Salamander

They called their country the Beautiful Land, and they were right. It perched on the edge of the continent. Before the Beautiful Land stretched the broad ocean, which few dared to cross; behind it stood the steep Rising, a cliff so high and sheer that few dared to climb. And in such isolation the people, who called themselves, of course, the Beautiful People, lived splendid lives.

Not all were rich, of course. And not all were happy. But there was such a majesty to living in the Beautiful Land that the poverty could easily be missed by the undiscerning eye, and misery seemed so very fleeting.

Except to Kiren.

To Kiren, misery was the way of life. For though she lived in a rich house with servants and had, it seemed, anything she could possibly want, she was deeply miserable most of the time. For this was a land where cursing and blessing and magic worked— not always, and not always in the way the person doing it might have planned—but sometimes the cursing worked, and in her case it had.

Not that she had done anything to deserve it; she had been as innocent as any other child in her cradle. But her mother had been a weak woman, and the

59

pain and terror of giving birth had killed her. And Kiren's father loved his wife so much that when he learned of the news, and saw the baby that had been born even as her mother died, he cried out, "You killed her! You killed her! May you never move a muscle in your life, until you lose someone you love as much as I loved her!" It was a terrible curse, and the nurse wept when she heard it, and the doctors stopped Kiren's father's mouth so that he could say no more in his madness.

But his curse took hold, and though he regretted it a million times during Kiren's infancy and childhood, there was nothing he could do. Oh, the curse was not all *that* strong. Kiren did learn to walk, after a fashion. And she could stand for as much as two minutes at a time. But most of the times she sat or lay down, because she grew so weary, and her muscles only weakly did what she told them to. She could lift a spoon to her mouth, but soon became tired, and had to be fed. She scarcely had the energy to chew.

And every time her father saw her, he wanted to weep, and often did weep. And sometimes he even thought of killing himself to finally wipe away his guilt. But he knew that this would only injure poor Kiren even more, and she had done nothing to deserve injury.

When his guilt grew too much for him to bear, however, he did escape. He put a bag of fine fruits and clever handwork from the Beautiful Land on his back, and set out for the Rising. He would be gone for months, and no one knew when he would return, or whether the Rising would this time prove too much for him and send him plunging to his death. But when he returned, he always brought something for Kiren. And for a while she would smile, and she would say, "Father, thank you." And things would go well, for a time, until she again became despondent and her father again suffered from watching the results of his ill-thought curse.

It was late spring in the year Kiren turned eleven when her father came home even happier than he usually was after a trip up the Rising. He rushed to his daughter where she lay wanly on the porch listening to the birds.

"Kiren!" he cried. "Kiren! I've brought you a gift!"

And she smiled, though even the muscles for smiling were weak, which made her smile sad. Her father reached into his bag (which was full of all kinds of wonders, which he would, being a careful man, sell to those with money to pay, not just for goods, but for rarity) and he pulled out his gift and handed it to Kiren.

It was a box, and the box lurched violently this way and that.

"There's something alive in there," Kiren said.

"No, my dear Kiren, there is not. But there's something moving, and it's yours. And before I help you open it, I'll tell you the story. I came one day in my wanderings to a town I had never visited before, and in the town were many merchants. And I asked a man, 'Who has the rarest and best merchandise in town?' He told me that I had to see Irvass. So I found the man in a humble and poor-looking shop. But inside were wonders such as you've never seen. I tell you, the man understands the bright magic from over the sky. And he asked, 'What do you want most in the world?' and of course I said to him, 'I want my daughter to be healed.' '

"Oh, Father," said Kiren. "You don't mean—"

"I do mean. I mean it very much. I told him exactly how you are and exactly how you got that way, and he said, 'Here is the cure,' and now let's open the box so you can see."

So Kiren opened the box, with more than a little help from her father, but she dared not reach inside. "You get it out, Father," she suggested, and he reached inside and pulled out a porcelain salamander. It was shiny yet deep with fine enameling, and though it was white—not at all the normal color for salamanders—the shape was unmistakable.

It was, in fact, a perfect model of a salamander. And it moved.

The legs raced madly in the air; the tongue darted in and out of the lips; the head turned; the eyes rolled. And Kiren cried out and laughed and said, "Oh, Father, what did he do to make it move so wonderfully!"

"Well," said her father, "he told me that he had given it the gift of movement—but not the gift of life. And if it ever *stops* moving, it will immediately become like any other porcelain. Stiff and hard and cold."

"How it races," she said, and it became the delight of her life.

When she awoke in the morning the salamander danced on her bed. At mealtimes it raced around the table. Wherever she lay or sat, the salamander was forever chasing after something or exploring something or trying to get away from something. She watched him constantly, and he in turn never got out of sight. And then at night, while she slept, he raced around and around in her room, the porcelain feet hitting the carpet silently, only occasionally making a slight tinkling sound as it ran lightly across the brick of the hearth.

Her father watched for a cure, and slowly but surely it began to come. For one thing, Kiren was no longer miserable. The salamander was too funny not to laugh at. It never went away. And so she felt better. Feeling better was not all of it, though. She began to walk a bit more often, and stay standing more, and sit when ordinarily she would have lain. She began to go from one room to another by her own choice.

By the end of the summer she even took walks into the woods. Though she often had to stop and rest, she enjoyed the journey, and grew a little stronger.

What she never told anyone (partly because she was afraid that it might be her imagination) was that the salamander could also speak.

"You can speak," she said in surprise one day, when the salamander ran across her foot and said, "Excuse me."

"Of course," he said. "To *you*."

"Why not anyone else?"

"Because I'm here for *you*," he answered, as he ran along the top of the garden wall, then leaped down near her. "It's the way I am. Movement and speech. Best I can do, you know. Can't have life. Doesn't work that way."

And so on their long walks in the forest they also talked, and Kiren fancied that the salamander had grown as fond of her as she had grown of him. In fact, she told the salamander one day, "I love you."

"Love love love love love love love," he answered, scampering up and down a tree.

"Yes," Kiren said. "More than life. More than anything at all."

"More than your father?" asked the salamander.

It was hard. Kiren was not a disloyal child, and really had forgiven her father for the curse years before. Yet she had to be honest to her salamander. "Yes," she said. "More than Father. More than— more than my dream of my mother. For you love me and can play with me and talk to me all the time."

"Love love love," said the salamander. "Unfortunately, I'm porcelain. Love love love love love. It's a word. Two consonants and a vowel. Like sap sap sap sap sap. Lovely sound." And he leaped across a small brook in the way.

"Don't—don't you love me?"

"I can't. It's an emotion, you know. I'm porcelain. Beg your pardon," and he clambered down her back as she leaned her shoulder on a tree. "Can't love. So sorry."

She was terribly, terribly hurt. "Don't you feel anything toward me at all?"

"Feel? Feel? Don't confuse things. Emotions come and go. Who can trust them? Isn't it enough that I spend every moment with you? Isn't it enough that I talk only to you? Isn't it enough that I would— that I would—"

"Would what?"

"I was about to start making foolish predictions. I was about to say, isn't it enough that I would die for you? But of course that's nonsense, because I'm not alive. Just porcelain. Watch out for the spider."

She stepped out of the path of a little green hunting spider that could fell a horse with one bite. "Thank you," she said. "And thank you." The first was for saving her life, but that was his job. The second was for telling her that, in his own way, he loved her after all. "So I'm not foolish for loving you, am I?"

"Foolish you are. Foolish indeed. Foolish as the moons are foolish, to dance endlessly in the sky and never never never go home together."

"I love you," said Kiren, "better than I love the hope of being whole."

And, you see, it was because she said that that the odd man came to the door of her father's house the very next day.

"I'm sorry," said the servant. "You haven't an appointment."

"Just tell him," said the odd man, "that Irvass has come."

Kiren's father came running down the stairs. "Oh, you can't take the salamander back!" he cried. "The cure has only begun!"

"Which I know much better than you do," said Irvass. "The girl is in the woods?"

"With the salamander. What marvellous changes — but why are you here?"

"To finish the cure," said Irvass.

"What?" asked Kiren's father. "Isn't the salamander itself the cure?"

"What were the words of your curse?" Irvass asked, instead of answering.

Kiren's father's face grew dour, but he forced himself to quietly say the very words. "May you never move a muscle in your life, until you lose someone you love as much as I loved her."

"Well then," said Irvass. "She now loves the salamander exactly as much as you loved your wife."

It took only a moment for Kiren's father to

65

realize. "No!" he cried out. "I can't let her suffer what I suffered!"

"It's the only cure. Isn't it better with a little piece of porcelain than if she had come to love *you* that much?"

And Kiren's father shuddered, and then wept, for he alone knew exactly how much pain she would suffer.

Irvass said nothing more, though the look he gave to Kiren's father might have been a pitying one. All he did was draw a rectangle in the soil of the garden, and place two stones within it, and mumble a few words.

And at that moment, out in the wood, the salamander said, "Very odd. Wasn't a wall here ever before. Never before. Here's a wall." And it was a wall. It was just high enough that when Kiren reached as high as she could, her fingers were one inch short of touching the top.

The salamander tried to climb it, but found it slippery—though he had always been able to climb every other wall he found. "Magic. Must be magic," The porcelain salamander mumbled.

So they circled the wall, hunting for a gate. There was none. It was all around them, though they had never entered it. And at no point did a tree limb cross the wall. They were trapped.

"I'm afraid," said Kiren. "There's good magic and bad magic, but how could such a thing as this be a blessing? It must be a curse." And the thought of a curse caused too much of the old misery to return, and she fought back the tears.

Fought back the tears until night, and then in the darkness, as the salamander scampered here and there, she could fight no longer.

"No," wailed the salamander.

"I can't help crying," she answered.

"I can't bear it," he said. "It makes me cold."

"I'll try to stop," she said, and she tried, and she pretty much stopped except for a few whimpers and sniffles until morning brought the light, and she saw that the wall was exactly where it had been.

No, not exactly. For behind her the wall had crept up in the night, and was only a few feet away. Her prison was now not even a quarter the size it had been the day before.

"Not good," said the salamander. "Oh, it could be dangerous."

"I know," she answered.

"You must get out," said the salamander.

"And you," she answered. "But how?"

And throughout the morning the wall played vicious taunting games with them, for whichever way neither of them was looking, the wall would creep up a foot or two. Since the salamander was faster, and moved constantly, he watched three sides. "And you hold the other in place." But Kiren couldn't help blinking, and anytime the salamander looked away the wall twitched, and by noon their prison was only ten feet square.

"Getting pretty tight here," said the salamander.

"Oh, salamander, can't I throw you over the wall?"

"We could try that, and I could run and get help—"

And so they tried. But though she used every ounce of strength she had, the wall seemed to leap up and catch him and send him sliding back down to the ground. Inside.

Soon she was exhausted, and the salamander said, "No more." Even as they had been trying, the walls had shrunk, and now the space was only five feet square. "Getting cramped," said the salamander as he raced around the tiny space remaining. "But I know the only solution."

"Tell me!" Kiren cried.

"I think," said the salamander, "that if you had something you could stand on, you could climb out."

"How could I?" she asked. "The wall won't let anything out!"

"I think," said the salamander, "that the wall only won't let *me* out. Because the birds are flying back and forth, and the wall doesn't catch them." It was true. A bird was singing in a nearby tree; it flew across just afterward, as if to prove the salamander's point. "I'm not alive, you see," said the salamander. "I'm moving only by magic. So you *could* get out."

"But what would I stand on?"

"Me," said the salamander.

"You?" she asked. "But you move so quickly—"

"For you," he said, "I'll hold still."

"No!" she cried. "No, no!" she screamed.

But the salamander stood at the edge of the wall, and he was only a statue in porcelain, hard and stiff and cold.

Kiren only wept for a moment, for then the wall behind her began to push at her, and her prison was only three feet square. The salamander had given his life so she could climb out. She ought at least to try.

So she tried. Standing on the salamander, she could reach the top of the wall. By standing tiptoe, she could get a grip on the top. And by using every bit of strength she had in her, she was able to force her body to the top and gradually heave herself over.

She fell in a heap on the ground. And in that

moment, that very moment, two things happened. The walls shrank quickly until they were only a pillar, and then they disappeared completely, taking the salamander with them. And all the normal, natural strength of an eleven-year-old child came to Kiren, and she was able to run. She was able to leap. She was able to swing from the tree branches.

The strength was in her as suddenly as strong wine, and she could not lie on the ground. She jumped to her feet, and the movement was so strong she nearly fell over. She ran, leaped over brooks, clambered up into the trees as high as she could climb. The curse had ended. She was free.

But even normal children grow tired. And as she slowed down, she was no longer caught up in her own strength. And she remembered the porcelain salamander, and what he had done for her.

They found her that afternoon, weeping miserably into a pile of last year's leaves.

"You see," said Irvass, who had insisted on leading the way in the search—which is why they found her immediately—"You see, she has her strength, and the curse is ended."

"But her heart is broken," said her father as he gathered his little girl into his arms.

"Broken?" asked Irvass. "It should not be. For the porcelain salamander was never alive."

"Yes he was!" she shouted. "He spoke to me! He gave his life for me!"

"He did all that," said Irvass. "But think. For all the time the magic was on him, he could never, never rest. Do you think he never got tired?"

"Of course he didn't."

"Yes, he did," said Irvass. "Now he can rest. But more than rest. For when he stopped moving and froze forever in one position, what was going through his mind?"

Irvass stood up and turned to leave. But only a few steps away, he turned back. "Kiren," he said.

"I want my salamander," she answered, her voice an agony of sobs.

"Oh, he would have become boring by and by," said Irvass. "He would have ceased to amuse you, and you would have avoided him. But now he is a memory. And, speaking of memory, remember that he also has memory, frozen as he is."

It was scant comfort then, for eleven-year-olds are not very philosophical. But when she grew older, Kiren remembered. And she knew that wherever the porcelain salamander was, he lived in one frozen, perfect moment—the moment when his heart was so full of love—

No, not love. The moment when he decided, without love, that it would be better for his life, such as it was, to end than to have to watch Kiren's life end.

It is a moment that can be lived with for eternity. And as Kiren grew older, she knew that such moments come rarely to people, and last only a moment, while the porcelain salamander would never lose it.

And as for Kiren—she became known, though she never sought fame, as the most Beautiful of the Beautiful People, and more than one of the rare wanderers from across the sea or from beyond Rising came only to see her, and talk to her, and draw her face in their minds to keep it with them forever.

And when she talked, her hands always moved, always danced in the air. Never stopped moving at all, it seemed, and they were white and lustrous as deep-enameled porcelain, and her smile was as bright as the moons, and came back to her face as constantly as the sea, and those who knew her well could almost see her gaze keep flickering about the room or about the garden, as if she watched a bright, quick animal scamper by.

Middle Woman

Ah-Cheu was a woman of the great kingdom of
Ch'in, a land of hills and valleys, a land of great
wealth and dire poverty. But Ah-Cheu was a middle
person, neither rich nor poor, neither old nor young,
and her husband's farm was half in the valley and
half on the hill. Ah-Cheu had a sister older than
her, and a sister younger than her, and one lived
thirty leagues to the north, and the other thirty leagues to the south. "I am a middle woman," Ah-Cheu
boasted once, but her husband's mother rebuked
her, saying, "Evil comes to the middle, and good
goes out to the edges."

Every year Ah-Cheu put a pack on her back and
journeyed for a visit either to the sister to the north
or to the sister to the south. It took her three days
to make the journey, for she did not hurry. But one
year she did not make the journey, for she met a
dragon on the road.

The dragon was long and fine and terrible, and
Ah-Cheu immediately knelt and touched her forehead to the road and said, "Oh, dragon, spare my
life!"

The dragon only chuckled deep in his throat and
said, "Woman, what do they call you?"

Not wishing to tell her true name to the dragon, she said, "I am called Middle Woman."

"Well, Middle Woman, I will give you a choice. The first choice is to have me eat you here in the road. The second choice is to have me grant you three wishes."

Surprised, Ah-Cheu raised her head. "But of course I take the second choice. Why do you set me a problem with such an easy solution?"

"It is more amusing," said the dragon, "to watch human beings destroy themselves than to overpower them quickly."

"But how can three wishes destroy me?"

"Make a wish, and see."

Ah-Cheu thought of many things she might wish for, but was soon ashamed of her greed. "I wish," she finally said, having decided to ask for only what she truly needed, "for my husband's farm to always produce plenty for all my family to eat."

"It shall be done," said the dragon, and he vanished, only to reappear a moment later, smiling and licking his lips. "I have done," he said, "exactly what you asked—I have eaten all your family, and so your husband's farm, even if it produces nothing, will always produce plenty for *them* to eat."

Ah-Cheu wept and mourned and cursed herself for being a fool, for now she saw the dragon's plan. Any wish, however innocent, would be turned against her.

"Think all you like," said the dragon, "but it will do you no good. I have had lawyers draw up legal documents eight feet long, but I have found the loopholes."

Then Ah-Cheu knew what she had to ask for. "I wish for all the world to be exactly as it was one minute before I left my home to come on this journey."

The dragon looked at her in surprise. "That's all? That's all you want to wish for?"

"Yes," said Ah-Cheu. "And you must do it now."

And suddenly she found herself in her husband's house, putting on her pack and bidding good-bye to her family. Immediately she set down the pack.

"I have changed my mind," she said. "I am not going."

Everyone was shocked. Everyone was surprised. Her husband berated her for being a changeable woman. Her mother-in-law denounced her for having forgotten her duty to her sisters. Her children pouted because she had always brought them each a present from her journeys to the north and south. But Ah-Cheu was firm. She would not risk meeting the dragon again.

And when the furor died down, Ah-Cheu was far more cheerful than she had ever been before, for she knew that she had one wish left, the third wish, the unused wish. And if there were ever a time of great need, she could use it to save herself and her family.

One year there was a fire, and Ah-Cheu was outside the house, with her youngest child trapped within. Almost she used her wish, but then thought, Why use the wish, when I can use my arms? And she ducked low, and ran into the house, and saved the boy, though it singed off all her hair. And she still had her son, and she still had her wish.

One year there was a famine, and it looked like all the world would starve. Ah-Cheu almost used her wish, but then thought, Why use the wish, when I can use my feet? And she wandered up into the

74

hills, and came back with a basket of roots and leaves, and with such food she kept her family alive until the Emperor's men came with wagons full of rice. And she still had her family, and she still had her wish.

And in another year there was a great flood, and all the homes were swept away, and as Ah-Cheu and her son's baby sat upon the roof, watching the water eat away the walls of the house, she almost used her wish to get a boat so she could escape. But then she thought, Why use the wish, when I can use my head? And she took up the boards from the roof and walls, and with her skirts she tied them into a raft large enough for the baby, and setting the child upon it she swam away, pushing the raft until they reached high ground and safety. And when her son found her alive, he wept with joy, and said, "Mother Ah-Cheu, never has a son loved his mother more!"

And Ah-Cheu had her posterity, and yet still she had her wish.

And then it was time for Ah-Cheu to die, and she lay sick and frail upon a bed of honor in her son's house, and the women and children and old men of the village came to keen for her and honor her as she lay dying. "Never has there been a more fortunate woman than Ah-Cheu," they said. "Never has there been a kinder, a more generous, a more godfavored woman!" And she was content to leave the world, because she had been so happy in it.

And on her last night, as she lay alone in darkness, she heard a voice call her name.

"Middle Woman," said the voice, and she opened her eyes, and there was the dragon.

"What do you want with me?" she asked. "I'm not much of a morsel to eat now, I'm afraid."

But then she saw the dragon looked terrified, and she listened to what he had to say.

"Middle Woman," said the dragon, "you have not used your third wish."

"I never needed it."

"Oh, cruel woman! What a vengeance you take! In the long run, I never did you any harm! How can you do this to me?"

"But what am I doing?" she asked.

"If you die, with your third wish unused, then I, too, will die!" he cried. "Maybe that doesn't seem so bad to you, but dragons are usually immortal, and so you can believe me when I say my death would cut me off with most of my life unlived."

"Poor dragon," she said. "But what have I to wish for?"

"Immortality," he said. "No tricks. I'll let you live forever."

"I don't want to live forever," she said. "It would make the neighbors envious."

"Great wealth, then, for your family."

"But they have all they need right now."

"Any wish!" he cried. "Any wish, or I will die!"

And so she smiled, and reached out a frail old hand and touched his supplicating claw, and said, "Then I wish a wish, dragon. I wish that all the rest of your life should be nothing but happiness for you and everyone you meet."

The dragon looked at her in surprise, and then in relief, and then he smiled and wept for joy. He thanked her many times, and left her home rejoicing.

And that night Ah-Cheu also left her home, more subtly than the dragon, and far less likely to return, but no less merrily for all that.

The Bully and the Beast

The page entered the Count's chamber at a dead run. He had long ago given up sauntering—when the Count called, he expected a page to appear immediately, and any delay at all made the Count irritable and likely to assign a page to stable duty.

"My lord," said the page.

"My lord indeed," said the Count. "What kept you?" The Count stood at the window, his back to the boy. In his arms he held a velvet gown, incredibly embroidered with gold and silver thread. "I think I need to call a council," said the Count. "On the other hand, I haven't the slightest desire to submit myself to a gaggle of jabbering knights. They'll be quite angry. What do you think?"

No one had ever asked the page for advice before, and he wasn't quite sure what was expected of him. "Why should they be angry, my lord?"

"Do you see this gown?" the Count asked, turning around and holding it up.

"Yes, my lord."

"What do you think of it?"

"Depends, doesn't it, my lord, on who wears it."

"It cost eleven pounds of silver."

The page smiled sickly. Eleven pounds of silver would keep the average knight in arms, food, women, clothing, and shelter for a year with six pounds left over for spending money.

"There are more," said the Count. "Many more."

"But who are they for? Are you going to marry?"

"None of your business!" roared the Count. "If there's anything I hate, it's a meddler!" The Count turned again to the window and looked out. He was shaded by a huge oak tree that grew forty feet from the castle walls. "What's today?" asked the Count.

"Thursday, my lord."

"The day, the day!"

"Eleventh past Easter Feast."

"The tribute's due today," said the Count. "Due on Easter, in fact, but today the Duke will be certain I'm not paying."

"Not paying the tribute, my lord?"

"How? Turn me upside down and shake me, but I haven't a farthing. The tribute money's gone. The money for new arms is gone. The travel money is gone. The money for new horses is gone. Haven't got any money at all. But gad, boy, what a wardrobe." The Count sat on the sill of the window. "The Duke will be here very quickly, I'm afraid. And he has the latest in debt collection equipment."

"What's that?"

"An army." The Count sighed. "Call a council, boy. My knights may jabber and scream, but they'll fight. I know they will."

The page wasn't sure. "They'll be very angry, my lord. Are you sure they'll fight?"

"Oh, yes," said the Count. "If they don't, the Duke will kill them."

"Why?"

"For not honoring their oath to me. Do go now, boy, and call a council."

The page nodded. Kind of felt sorry for the old boy. Not much of a Count, as things went, but he could have been worse, and it was pretty plain the castle would be sacked and the Count imprisoned and the women raped and the page sent off home to his parents. "A council!" he cried as he left the Count's chamber. "A council!"

In the cold cavern of the pantry under the kitchen, Bork pulled a huge keg of ale from its resting place and lifted it, not easily, but without much strain, and rested it on his shoulders. Head bowed, he walked slowly up the stairs. Before Bork worked in the kitchen, it used to take two men most of an afternoon to move the huge kegs. But Bork was a giant, or what passed for a giant in those days. The Count himself was of average height, barely past five feet. Bork was nearly seven feet tall, with muscles like an ox. People stepped aside for him.

"Put it there," said the cook, hardly looking up. "And don't drop it."

Bork didn't drop the keg. Nor did he resent the cook's expecting him to be clumsy. He had been told he was clumsy all his life, ever since it became plain at the age of three that he was going to be immense. Everyone knew that big people were clumsy. And it was true enough. Bork was so strong he kept doing things he never meant to do, accidentally. Like the time the swordmaster, admiring his strength, had invited him to learn to use the heavy battleswords. Bork hefted them easily, of course, though at the time he was only twelve and hadn't reached his full strength.

"Hit me," the swordmaster said.

"But the blade's sharp," Bork told him.

"Don't worry. You won't come near me." The swordmaster had taught a hundred knights to fight. None of them had come near him. And, in fact, when Bork swung the heavy sword the swordmaster had his shield up in plenty of time. He just hadn't counted on the terrible force of the blow. The shield was battered aside easily, and the blow threw the sword upward, so it cut off the swordmaster's left arm just below the shoulder, and only narrowly missed slicing deeply into his chest.

Clumsy, that was all Bork was. But it was the end of any hope of his becoming a knight. When the swordmaster finally recovered, he consigned Bork to the kitchen and the blacksmith's shop, where they needed someone with enough strength to skewer a cow end to end and carry it to the fire, where it was convenient to have a man who, with a double-sized ax, could chop down a large tree in half an hour, cut it into logs, and carry a month's supply of firewood into the castle in an afternoon.

A page came into the kitchen. "There's a council, cook. The Count wants ale, and plenty of it."

The cook swore profusely and threw a carrot at the page. "Always changing the schedule! Always making me do extra work." As soon as the page had escaped, the cook turned on Bork. "All right, carry the ale out there, and be quick about it. Try not to drop it."

"I won't," Bork said.

"He won't," the cook muttered. "Clever as an ox, he is."

Bork manhandled the cask into the great hall. It was cold, though outside the sun was shining. Little light and little warmth reached the inside of the castle. And since it was spring, the huge logpile in the pit in the middle of the room lay cold and damp.

The knights were beginning to wander into the great hall and sit on the benches that lined the long, pock-marked slab of a table. They knew enough to carry their mugs—councils were always well-oiled with ale. Bork had spent years as a child watching the knights practice the arts of war, but the knights seemed more natural carrying their cups than holding their swords at the ready. They were more dedicated to their drinking than to war.

"Ho, Bork the Bully," one of the knights greeted him. Bork managed a half-smile. He had learned long since not to take offense.

"How's Sam the stableman?" asked another, tauntingly.

Bork blushed and turned away, heading for the door to the kitchen.

The knights were laughing at their cleverness. "Twice the body, half the brain," one of them said to the others. "Probably hung like a horse," another speculated, then quipped, "Which probably accounts for those mysterious deaths among the sheep this winter." A roar of laughter, and cups beating on the table. Bork stood in the kitchen trembling. He could not escape the sound—the stones carried it echoing to him wherever he went.

The cook turned and looked at him. "Don't be angry, boy," he said. "It's all in fun."

Bork nodded and smiled at the cook. That's what it was. All in fun. And besides, Bork deserved it, he knew. It was only fair that he be treated cruelly. For he had earned the title Bork the Bully, hadn't he? When he was three, and already massive as a ram, his only friend, a beautiful young village boy

81

named Winkle, had hit upon the idea of becoming a knight. Winkle had dressed himself in odds and ends of leather and tin, and made a makeshift lance from a hog prod.

"You're my destrier," Winkle cried as he mounted Bork and rode him for hours. Bork thought it was a fine thing to be a knight's horse. It became the height of his ambition, and he wondered how one got started in the trade. But one day Sam, the stableman's son, had taunted Winkle for his make-believe armor, and it had turned into a fist fight, and Sam had thoroughly bloodied Winkle's nose. Winkle screamed as if he were dying, and Bork sprang to his friend's defense, walloping Sam, who was three years older, along the side of his head.

Ever since then Sam spoke with a thickness in his voice, and often lost his balance; his jaw, broken in several places, never healed properly, and he had problems with his ear.

It horrified Bork to have caused so much pain, but Winkle assured him that Sam deserved it. "After all, Bork, he was twice my size, and he was picking on me. He's a bully. He had it coming."

For several years Winkle and Bork were the terror of the village. Winkle would constantly get into fights, and soon the village children learned not to resist him. If Winkle lost a fight, he would scream for Bork, and though Bork was never again so harsh as he was with Sam, his blows still hurt terribly. Winkle loved it. Then one day he tired of being a knight, dismissed his destrier, and became fast friends with the other children. It was only then that Bork began to hear himself called Bork the Bully; it was Winkle who convinced the other children that the only villain in the fighting had been Bork. "After all," Bork overhead Winkle say one day, "he's twice as strong as anyone else. Isn't fair for him to fight. It's a cowardly thing for him to do, and we mustn't have anything to do with him. Bullies must be punished."

Bork knew Winkle was right, and ever after that he bore the burden of shame. He remembered the frightened looks in the other children's eyes when he approached them, the way they pleaded for mercy. But Winkle was always screaming and writhing in agony, and Bork always hit the child despite his terror, and for that bullying Bork was still paying. He paid in the ridicule he accepted from the knights; he paid in the solitude of all his days and nights; he paid by working as hard as he could, using his strength to serve instead of hurt.

But just because he knew he deserved the punishment did not mean he enjoyed it. There were tears in his eyes as he went about his work in the kitchen. He tried to hide them from the cook, but to no avail. "Oh, no, you're not going to cry, are you?" the cook said. "You'll only make your nose run and then you'll get snot in the soup. Get out of the kitchen for awhile!"

Which is why Bork was standing in the doorway of the great hall watching the council that would completely change his life.

"Well, where's the tribute money gone to?" demanded one of the knights. "The harvest was large enough last year!"

It was an ugly thing, to see the knights so angry. But the Count knew they had a right to be upset — it was they who would have to fight the Duke's men, and they had a right to know why.

"My friends," the Count said. "My friends, some things are more important than money. I invested the money in something more important than tribute, more important than peace, more important than long life. I invested the money in beauty. Not to create beauty, but to perfect it." The knights were listening now. For all their violent preoccupations, they all had a soft spot in their hearts for true beauty. It was one of the requirements for knighthood. "I have been entrusted with a jewel, more perfect than any diamond. It was my duty to place that jewel in the best setting money could buy. I can't explain. I can only show you." He rang a small bell, and behind him one of the better-known secret doors in the castle opened, and a wizened old woman emerged. The Count whispered in her ear, and the woman scurried back into the secret passage.

"Who's she?" asked one of the knights.

"She is the woman who nursed my children after my wife died. My wife died in childbirth, you remember. But what you don't know is that the child lived. My two sons you know well. But I have a third child, my last child, whom you know not at all, and this one is not a son."

The Count was not surprised that several of the knights seemed to puzzle over this riddle. Too many jousts, too much practice in full armor in the heat of the afternoon.

"My child is a daughter."

"Ah," said the knights.

"At first, I kept her hidden away because I could not bear to see her—after all, my most beloved wife had died in bearing her. But after a few years I overcame my grief, and went to see the child in the room where she was hidden, and lo! She was the most beautiful child I had ever seen. I named her Brunhilda, and from that moment on I loved her. I was the most devoted father you could imagine. But I did not let her leave the secret room. Why, you may ask?"

"Yes, why!" demanded several of the knights.

"Because she was so beautiful I was afraid she would be stolen from me. I was terrified that I would lose her. Yet I saw her every day, and talked to her, and the older she got, the more beautiful she became, and for the last several years I could no longer bear to see her in her mother's cast-off clothing. Her beauty is such that only the finest cloths and gowns and jewels of Flanders, of Venice, of Florence would do for her. You'll see! The money was not ill spent."

And the door opened again, and the old woman emerged, leading forth Brunhilda.

In the doorway, Bork gasped. But no one heard him, for all the knights gasped, too.

She was the most perfect woman in the world. Her hair was a dark red, flowing behind her like an auburn stream as she walked. Her face was white from being indoors all her life, and when she smiled it was like the sun breaking out on a stormy day. And none of the knights dared look at her body for very long, because the longer they looked the more they wanted to touch her, and the Count said, "I warn you. Any man who lays a hand on her will have to answer to me. She is a virgin, and when she marries she shall be a virgin, and a king will pay half his kingdom to have her, and still I'll feel cheated to have to give her up."

"Good morning, my lords," she said, smiling. Her voice was like the song of leaves dancing in the summer wind, and the knights fell to their knees before her.

None of them was more moved by her beauty than Bork, however. When she entered the room he forgot himself; there was no room in his mind for anything but the great beauty he had seen for the first time in his life. Bork knew nothing of courtesy. He only knew that, for the first time in his life, he had seen something so perfect that he could not rest until it was his. Not his to own, but his to be owned by. He longed to serve her in the most degrading ways he could think of, if only she would smile upon him; longed to die for her, if only the last moment of his life were filled with her voice saying, "You may love me."

If he had been a knight, he might have thought of a poetic way to say such things. But he was not a knight, and so his words came out of his heart before his mind could find a way to make them clever. He strode blindly from the kitchen door, his huge body casting a shadow that seemed to the knights like the shadow of death passing over them. They watched with uneasiness that soon turned to outrage as he came to the girl, reached out, and took her small white hands in his.

"I love you," Bork said to her, and tears came unbidden to his eyes. "Let me marry you."

At that moment several of the knights found their courage. They seized Bork roughly by the arms, meaning to pull him away and punish him for his effrontery. But Bork effortlessly tossed them away. They fell to the ground yards from him. He never saw them fall; his gaze never left the lady's face.

She looked wonderingly into his eyes. Not because she thought him attractive, because he was ugly and she knew it. Not because of the words he had said, because she had been taught that many men would say those words, and she was to pay no attention to them. What startled her, what amazed her, was the deep truth in Bork's face. That was something she had never seen, and though she did not recognize it for what it was, it fascinated her.

The Count was furious. Seeing the clumsy giant holding his daughter's small white hands in his was outrageous. He would not endure it. But the giant had such great strength that to tear him away would mean a full-scale battle, and in such a battle Brunhilda might be injured. No, the giant had to be handled delicately, for the moment.

"My dear fellow," said the Count, affecting a joviality he did not feel. "You've only just met."

Bork ignored him. "I will never let you come to harm," he said to the girl.

"What's his name?" the Count whispered to a knight. "I can't remember his name."

"Bork," the knight answered.

"My dear Bork," said the Count. "All due respect and everything, but my daughter has noble blood, and you're not even a knight."

"Then I'll become one," Bork said.

"It's not that easy, Bork, old fellow. You must do something exceptionally brave, and then I can knight you and we can talk about this other matter. But in the meantime, it isn't proper for you to be holding my daughter's hands. Why don't you go back to the kitchen like a good fellow?"

Bork gave no sign that he heard. He only continued looking into the lady's eyes. And finally it was she who was able to end the dilemma.

"Bork," she said, "I will count on you. But in the

meantime, my father will be angry with you if you don't return to the kitchen."

Of course, Bork thought. Of course, she is truly concerned for me, doesn't want me to come to harm on her account. "For your sake," he said, the madness of love still on him. Then he turned and left the room.

The Count sat down, sighing audibly. "Should have got rid of him years ago. Gentle as a lamb, and then all of a sudden goes crazy. Get rid of him— somebody take care of that tonight, would you? Best to do it in his sleep. Don't want any casualties when we're likely to have a battle at any moment."

The reminder of the battle was enough to sober even those who were on their fifth mug of ale. The wizened old woman led Brunhilda away again. "But not to the secret room, now. To the chamber next to mine. And post a double guard outside her door, and keep the key yourself," said the Count.

When she was gone, the Count looked around at the knights. "The treasury has been emptied in a vain attempt to find clothing to do her justice. I had no other choice."

And there was not a knight who would say the money had been badly spent.

The Duke came late that afternoon, much sooner than he was expected. He demanded the tribute. The Count refused, of course. There was the usual challenge to come out of the castle and fight, but the Count, outnumbered ten to one, merely replied, rather saucily, that the Duke should come in and get him. The messenger who delivered the sarcastic message came back with his tongue in a bag around

88

his neck. The battle was thus begun grimly: and grimly it continued.

The guard watching on the south side of the castle was slacking. He paid for it. The Duke's archers managed to creep up to the huge oak tree and climb it without any alarm being given, and the first notice any of them had was when the guard fell from the battlements with an arrow in his throat.

The archers—there must have been a dozen of them—kept up a deadly rain of arrows. They wasted no shots. The squires dropped dead in alarming numbers until the Count gave orders for them to come inside. And when the human targets were all under cover, the archers set to work on the cattle and sheep milling in the open pens. There was no way to protect the animals. By sunset, all of them were dead.

"Dammit," said the cook. "How can I cook all this before it spoils?"

"Find a way," said the Count. "That's our food supply. I refuse to let them starve us out."

So all night Bork worked, carrying the cattle and sheep inside, one by one. At first the villagers who had taken refuge in the castle tried to help him, but he could carry three animals inside the kitchen in the time it took them to drag one, and they soon gave it up.

The Count saw who was saving the meat. "Don't get rid of him tonight," he told the knights. "We'll punish him for his effrontery in the morning."

Bork only rested twice in the night, taking naps for an hour before the cook woke him again. And when dawn came, and the arrows began coming again, all the cattle were inside, and all but twenty sheep.

"That's all we can save," the cook told the Count.

"Save them all."

"But if Bork tries to go out there, he'll be killed!"

The Count looked the cook in the eyes. "Bring in the sheep or have him die trying."

The cook was not aware of the fact that Bork was under sentence of death. So he did his best to save Bork. A kettle lined with cloth and strapped onto the giant's head; a huge kettle lid for a shield. "It's the best we can do," the cook said.

"But I can't carry sheep if I'm holding a shield," Bork said.

"What can I do? The Count commanded it. It's worth your life to refuse."

Bork stood and thought for a few moments, trying to find a way out of his dilemma. He saw only one possibility. "If I can't stop them from hitting me, I'll have to stop them from shooting at all."

"How!" the cook demanded, and then followed Bork to the blacksmith's shop, where Bork found his huge ax leaning against the wall.

"Now's not the time to cut firewood," said the blacksmith.

"Yes it is," Bork answered.

Carrying the ax and holding the kettle lid between his body and the archers, Bork made his way across the courtyard. The arrows pinged harmlessly off the metal. Bork got to the drawbridge. "Open up!" he shouted, and the drawbridge fell away and dropped across the moat. Bork walked across, then made his way along the moat toward the oak tree.

In the distance the Duke, standing in front of his dazzling white tent with his emblem of yellow on it, saw Bork emerge from the castle. "Is that a man or a bear?" he asked. No one was sure.

The archers shot at Bork steadily, but the closer he got to the tree, the worse their angle of fire and the larger the shadow of safety the kettle lid cast over his body. Finally, holding the lid high over his head, Bork began hacking one-handed at the trunk. Chips of wood flew with each blow; with his right hand alone he could cut deeper and faster than a normal man with both hands free.

But he was concentrating on cutting wood, and his left arm grew tired holding his makeshift shield, and an archer was able to get off a shot that slipped past the shield and plunged into his left arm, in the thick muscle at the back.

He nearly dropped the shield. Instead, he had the presence of mind to let go of the ax and drop to his knees, quickly balancing the kettle lid between the tree trunk, his head, and the top of the ax handle. Gently he pulled at the arrow shaft. It would not come backward. So he broke the arrow and pushed the stub the rest of the way through his arm until it was out the other side. It was excruciatingly painful, but he knew he could not quit now. He took hold of the shield with his left arm again, and despite the pain held it high as he began to cut again, girdling the tree with a deep white gouge. The blood dripped steadily down his arm, but he ignored it, and soon enough the bleeding stopped and slowed.

On the castle battlements, the Count's men began to realize that there was a hope of Bork's succeeding. To protect him, they began to shoot their arrows into the tree. The archers were well hidden, but the rain of arrows, however badly aimed, began to have its effect. A few of them dropped to the ground, where the castle archers could easily finish them off;

the others were forced to concentrate on finding cover.

The tree trembled more and more with each blow, until finally Bork stepped back and the tree creaked and swayed. He had learned from his lumbering work in the forest how to make the tree fall where he wanted it; the oak fell parallel to the castle walls, so it neither bridged the moat nor let the Duke's archers scramble from the tree too far from the castle. So when the archers tried to flee to the safety of the Duke's lines, the castle bowmen were able to kill them all.

One of them, however, despaired of escape. Instead, though he already had an arrow in him, he drew a knife and charged at Bork, in a mad attempt to avenge his own death on the man who had caused it. Bork had no choice. He swung his ax through the air and discovered that men are nowhere near as sturdy as a tree.

In the distance, the Duke watched with horror as the giant cut a man in half with a single blow. "What have they got!" he said. "What is this monster?"

Covered with the blood that had spurted from the dying man, Bork walked back toward the drawbridge, which opened again as he approached. But he did not get to enter. Instead the Count and fifty mounted knights came from the gate on horseback, their armor shining in the sunlight.

"I've decided to fight them in the open," the Count said. "And you, Bork, must fight with us. If you live through this, I'll make you a knight!"

Bork knelt. "Thank you, my Lord Count," he said.

The Count glanced around in embarrassment. "Well, then. Let's get to it. Charge!" he bellowed.

Bork did not realize that the knights were not even formed in a line yet. He simply followed the command and charged, alone, toward the Duke's lines. The Count watched him go, and smiled.

"My Lord Count," said the nearest knight. "Aren't we going to attack with him?"

"Let the Duke take care of him," the Count said.

"But he cut down the oak and saved the castle, my lord."

"Yes," said the Count. "An exceptionally brave act. Do you want him to try to claim my daughter's hand?"

"But my lord," said the knight, "if he fights beside us, we might have a chance of winning. But if he's gone, the Duke will destroy us."

"Some things," said the Count, with finality, "are more important than victory. Would you want to go on living in a world where perfection like Brunhilda's was possessed by such a man as that?"

The knights were silent, then, as they watched Bork approach the Duke's army, alone.

Bork did not realize he was alone until he stood a few feet away from the Duke's lines. He had felt strange as he walked across the fields, believing he was marching into battle with the knights he had long admired in their bright armor and deft instruments of war. Now the exhilaration was gone. Where were the others? Bork was afraid.

He could not understand why the Duke's men had not shot any arrows at him. Actually, it was a misunderstanding. If the Duke had known Bork was a commoner and not a knight at all, Bork would have had a hundred arrows bristling from his corpse. As it was, however, one of the Duke's men called out, "You, sir! Do you challenge us to single combat?"

Of course. That was it—the Count did not intend Bork to face an army, he intended him to face a single warrior. The whole outcome of the battle would depend on him alone! It was a tremendous honor, and Bork wondered if he could carry it off.

"Yes! Single combat!" he answered. "Your strongest, bravest man!"

"But you're a giant!" cried the Duke's man.

"But I'm wearing no armor." And to prove his sincerity, Bork took off his helmet, which was uncomfortable anyway, and stepped forward. The Duke's knights backed away, making an opening for him, with men in armor watching him pass from both sides. Bork walked steadily on, until he came to a cleared circle where he faced the Duke himself.

"Are you the champion?" asked Bork.

"I'm the Duke," he answered. "But I don't see any of my knights stepping forward to fight you."

"Do you refuse the challenge, then?" Bork asked, trying to sound as brave and scornful as he imagined a true knight would sound.

The Duke looked around at his men, who, if the armor had allowed, would have been shuffling uncomfortably in the morning sunlight. As it was, none of them looked at him.

"No," said the Duke. "I accept your challenge myself." The thought of fighting the giant terrified him. But he was a knight, and known to be a brave man; he had become Duke in the prime of his youth, and if he backed down before a giant now, his duchy would be taken from him in only a few years; his honor would be lost long before. So he drew his sword and advanced upon the giant.

Bork saw the determination in the Duke's eyes, and marvelled at a man who would go himself into a most dangerous battle instead of sending his men. Briefly Bork wondered why the Count had not shown such courage; he determined at that moment that if he could help it the Duke would not die. The blood of the archer was more than he had ever wanted to shed. Nobility was in every movement of the Duke, and Bork wondered at the ill chance that had made them enemies.

The Duke lunged at Bork with his sword flashing. Bork hit him with the flat of the ax, knocking him to the ground. The Duke cried out in pain. His armor was dented deeply; there had to be ribs broken under the dent.

"Why don't you surrender?" asked Bork.

"Kill me now!"

"If you surrender, I won't kill you at all."

The Duke was surprised. There was a murmur from his men.

"I have your word?"

"Of course. I swear it."

It was too startling an idea.

"What do you plan to do, hold me for ransom?"

Bork thought about it. "I don't think so."

"Well, what then? Why not kill me and have done with it?" The pain in his chest now dominated the Duke's voice, but he did not spit blood, and so he began to have some hope.

"All the Count wants you to do is go away and stop collecting tribute. If you promise to do that, I'll promise that not one of you will be harmed."

The Duke and his men considered in silence. It was too good to believe. So good it was almost dishonorable even to consider it. Still—there was

Bork, who had broken the Duke's body with one blow, right through the armor. If he chose to let them walk away from the battle, why argue?

"I give my word that I'll cease collecting tribute from the Count, and my men and I will go in peace."

"Well, then, that's good news," Bork said. "I've got to tell the Count." And Bork turned away and walked into the fields, heading for where the Count's tiny army waited.

"I can't believe it," said the Duke. "A knight like that, and he turns out to be generous. The Count could have his way with the King, with a knight like that."

They stripped the armor off him, carefully, and began wrapping his chest with bandages.

"If he were mine," the Duke said, "I'd use him to conquer the whole land."

The Count watched, incredulous, as Bork crossed the field.

"He's still alive," he said, and he began to wonder what Bork would have to say about the fact that none of the knights had joined his gallant charge.

"My Lord Count!" cried Bork, when he was within range. He would have waved, but both his arms were exhausted now. "They surrender!"

"What?" the Count asked the knights near him. "Did he say they surrender?"

"Apparently," a knight answered. "Apparently he won."

"Damn!" cried the Count. "I won't have it!"

The knights were puzzled. "If anybody's going to defeat the Duke, *I* am! Not a damnable commoner! Not a giant with the brains of a cockroach! Charge!"

"What?" several of the knights asked.

"I said charge!" And the Count moved forward, his warhorse plodding carefully through the field, building up momentum.

Bork saw the knights start forward. He had watched enough mock battles to recognize a charge. He could only assume that the Count hadn't heard him. But the charge had to be stopped—he had given his word, hadn't he? So he planted himself in the path of the Count's horse.

"Out of the way, you damned fool!" cried the Count. But Bork stood his ground. The Count was determined not to be thwarted. He prepared to ride Bork down.

"You can't charge!" Bork yelled. "They surrendered!"

The Count gritted his teeth and urged the horse forward, his lance prepared to cast Bork out of the way.

A moment later the Count found himself in midair, hanging to the lance for his life. Bork held it over his head, and the knights laboriously halted their charge and wheeled to see what was going on with Bork and the Count.

"My Lord Count,' Bork said respectfully. "I guess you didn't hear me. They surrendered. I promised them they could go in peace if they stopped collecting tribute."

From his precarious hold on the lance, fifteen feet off the ground, the Count said, "I didn't hear you."

"I didn't think so. But you *will* let them go, won't you?"

"Of course. Could you give a thought to letting me down, old boy?"

And so Bork let the Count down, and there was a peace treaty between the Duke and the Count, and the Duke's men rode away in peace, talking about the generosity of the giant knight.

"But he isn't a knight," said a servant to the Duke.

"What? Not a knight?"

"No. Just a villager. One of the peasants told me, when I was stealing his chickens."

"Not a knight," said the Duke, and for a moment his face began to turn the shade of red that made his knights want to ride a few feet further from him—they knew his rage too well already.

"We were tricked, then," said a knight, trying to fend off his lord's anger by anticipating it.

The Duke said nothing for a moment. Then he smiled. "Well, if he's not a knight, he should be. He has the strength. He has the courtesy. Hasn't he?"

The knights agreed that he had.

"He's the moral equivalent of a knight," said the Duke. Pride assuaged, for the moment, he led his men back to his castle. Underneath, however, even deeper than the pain in his ribs, was the image of the Count perched on the end of a lance held high in the air by the giant, Bork, and he pondered what it might have meant, and what, more to the point, it might mean in the future.

Things were getting out of hand, the Count decided. First of all, the victory celebration had not been his idea, and yet here they were, riotously drunken in the great hall, and even villagers were making free with the ale, laughing and cheering among the knights. That was bad enough, but worse was the fact that the knights were making no pretense about it—the party was in honor of Bork.

The Count drummed his fingers on the table. No one paid any attention. They were too busy—Sir Alwishard trying to keep two village wenches occupied near the fire, Sir Silwiss pissing in the wine and laughing so loud that the Count could hardly hear Sir Braig and Sir Umlaut as they sang and danced along the table, kicking plates off with their toes in time with the music. It was the best party the Count had ever seen. And it wasn't for him, it was for that damnable giant who had made an ass of him in front of all his men and all the Duke's men and, worst of all, the Duke. He heard a strange growling sound, like a savage wolf getting ready to spring. In a lull in the bedlam he suddenly realized that the sound was coming from his own throat.

Get control of yourself, he thought. The real gains, the solid gains were not Bork's—they were mine. The Duke is gone, and instead of paying him tribute from now on, he'll be paying me. Word would get around, too, that the Count had won a battle with the Duke. After all, that was the basis of power—who could beat whom in battle. A duke was just a man who could beat a count, a count someone who could beat a baron, a baron someone who could beat a knight.

But what was a person who could beat a duke?

"You should be king," said a tall, slender young man standing near the throne.

The Count looked at him, making a vague motion with his hidden hand. How had the boy read his thoughts?

"I'll pretend I didn't hear that."

"You heard it," said the young man.

"It's treason."

99

"Only if the king beats you in battle. If *you* win, it's treason *not* to say so."

The Count looked the boy over. Dark hair that looked a bit too carefully combed for a villager. A straight nose, a pleasant smile, a winning grace when he walked. But something about his eyes gave the lie to the smile. The boy was vicious somehow. The boy was dangerous.

"I like you," said the Count.

"I'm glad." He did not sound glad. He sounded bored.

"If I'm smart, I'll have you strangled immediately."

The boy only smiled more.

"Who are you?"

"My name is Winkle. And I'm Bork's best friend."

Bork. There he was again, that giant sticking his immense shadow into everything tonight. "Didn't know Bork the Bully had any friends."

"He has one. Me. Ask him."

"I wonder if a friend of Bork's is really a friend of mine," the Count said.

"I said I was his best friend. I didn't say I was a good friend." And Winkle smiled.

A thoroughgoing bastard, the Count decided, but he waved to Bork and beckoned for him to come. In a moment the giant knelt before the Count, who was irritated to discover that when Bork knelt and the Count sat, Bork still looked down on him.

"This man," said the Count, "claims to be your friend."

Bork looked up and recognized Winkle, who was beaming down at him, his eyes filled with love, mostly. A hungry kind of love, but Bork wasn't

100

discriminating. He had the admiration and grudging respect of the knights, but he hardly knew them. This was his childhood friend, and at the thought that Winkle claimed to be his friend Bork immediately forgave all the past slights and smiled back. "Winkle," he said. "Of course we're friends. He's my *best* friend."

The Count made the mistake of looking in Bork's eyes and seeing the complete sincerity of his love for Winkle. It embarrassed him, for he knew Winkle all too well already, from just the moments of conversation they had had. Winkle was nobody's friend. But Bork was obviously blind to that. For a moment the Count almost pitied the giant, had a glimpse of what his life must be like, if the predatory young villager was his best friend.

"Your majesty," said Winkle.

"Don't call me that."

"I only anticipate what the world will know in a matter of months."

Winkle sounded so confident, so sure of it. A chill went up the Count's spine. He shook it off. "I won one battle, Winkle. I still have a huge budget deficit and a pretty small army of fairly lousy knights."

"Think of your daughter, even if *you* aren't ambitious. Despite her beauty she'll be lucky to marry a duke. But if she were the daughter of a king, she could marry anyone in all the world. And her own lovely self would be a dowry—no prince would think to ask for more."

The Count thought of his daughter, the beautiful Brunhilda, and smiled.

Bork also smiled, for he was also thinking of the same thing.

"Your majesty," Winkle urged, "with Bork as

your right-hand man and me as your counselor, there's nothing to stop you from being king within a year or two. Who would be willing to stand against an army with the three of us marching at the head?"

"Why three?" asked the Count.

"You mean, why me. I thought you would already understand that—but then, that's what you need me for. You see, your majesty, you're a good man, a godly man, a paragon of virtue. You would never think of seeking power and conniving against your enemies and spying and doing repulsive things to people you don't like. But kings *have* to do those things or they quickly cease to be kings."

Vaguely the Count remembered behaving in just that way many times, but Winkle's words were seductive—they *should* be true.

"Your majesty, where you are pure, I am polluted. Where you are fresh, I am rotten. I'd sell my mother into slavery if I had a mother and I'd cheat the devil at poker and win hell from him before he caught on. And I'd stab any of your enemies in the back if I got the chance."

"But what if my enemies aren't your enemies?" the Count asked.

"Your enemies are *always* my enemies. I'll be loyal to you through thick and thin."

"How can I trust you, if you're so rotten?"

"Because you're going to pay me a lot of money." Winkle bowed deeply.

"Done," said the Count.

"Excellent," said Winkle, and they shook hands. The Count noticed that Winkle's hands were smooth—he had neither the hard horny palms of a village workingman nor the slick calluses of a man trained to warfare.

"How have you made a living, up to now?" the Count asked.

"I steal," Winkle said, with a smile that said I'm joking and a glint in his eye that said I'm not.

"What about me?" asked Bork.

"Oh, you're in it, too," said Winkle. "You're the king's strong right arm."

"I've never met the king," said Bork.

"Yes you have," Winkle retorted. "That is the king."

"No he's not," said the giant. "He's only a count."

The words stabbed the Count deeply. *Only* a count. Well, that would end. "Today I'm only a count," he said patiently. "Who knows what tomorrow will bring? But Bork—I shall knight you. As a knight you must swear absolute loyalty to me and do whatever I say. Will you do that?"

"Of course I will," said Bork. "Thank you, my Lord Count." Bork arose and called to his new friends throughout the hall in a voice that could not be ignored. "My Lord Count has decided I will be made a knight!" There were cheers and applause and stamping of feet. "And the best thing is," Bork said, "that now I can marry the Lady Brunhilda."

There was no applause. Just a murmur of alarm. Of course. If he became a knight, he was eligible for Brunhilda's hand. It was unthinkable—but the Count himself had said so.

The Count was having second thoughts, of course, but he knew no way to back out of it, not without looking like a word-breaker. he made a false start at speaking, but couldn't finish. Bork waited expectantly. Clearly he believed the Count would confirm what Bork had said.

It was Winkle, however, who took the situation

103

in hand. "Oh, Bork," he said sadly—but loudly, so that everyone could hear. "Don't you understand? His majesty is making you a knight out of gratitude. But unless you're a king or the son of a king, you have to do something exceptionally brave to earn Brunhilda's hand."

"But, wasn't I brave today?" Bork asked. After all, the arrow wound in his arm still hurt, and only the ale kept him from aching unmercifully all over from the exertion of the night and the day just past.

"You were brave. But since you're twice the size and ten times the strength of an ordinary man, it's hardly fair for you to win Brunhilda's hand with ordinary bravery. No, Bork—it's just the way things work. It's just the way things are done. Before you're worthy of Brunhilda, you have to do something ten times as brave as what you did today."

Bork could not think of something ten times as brave. Hadn't he gone almost unprotected to chop down the oak tree? Hadn't he attacked a whole army all by himself, and won the surrender of the enemy? What could be ten times as brave?

"Don't despair,' the Count said. "Surely in all the battles ahead of us there'll be *something* ten times as brave. And in the meantime, you're a knight, my friend, a great knight, and you shall dine at my table every night! And when we march into battle, there you'll be, right beside me—"

"A few steps ahead," Winkle whispered discreetly.

"A few steps ahead of me, to defend the honor of my country—"

"Don't be shy," whispered Winkle.

"No, not my country. My kingdom. For from

104

today, you men no longer serve a count! You serve a king!"

It was a shocking declaration, and might have caused sober reflection if there had been a sober man in the room. But through the haze of alcohol and torchlight and fatigue, the knights looked at the Count and he did indeed seem kingly. And they thought of the battles ahead and were not afraid, for they had won a glorious victory today and not one of them had shed a drop of blood. Except, of course, Bork. But in some corner of their collected opinions was a viewpoint they would not have admitted to holding, if anyone brought the subject out in the open. The opinion so well hidden from themselves and each other was simple: Bork is not like me. Bork is not one of us. Therefore, Bork is expendable.

The blood that still stained his sleeve was cheap. Plenty more where that came from.

And so they plied him with more ale until he fell asleep, snoring hugely on the table, forgetting that he had been cheated out of the woman he loved; it was easy to forget, for the moment, because he was a knight, and a hero, and at last he had friends.

It took two years for the Count to become King. He began close to home, with other counts, but soon progressed to the great dukes and earls of the kingdom. Wherever he went, the pattern was the same. The Count and his fifty knights would ride their horses, only lightly armored so they could travel with reasonable speed. Bork would walk, but his long legs easily kept up with the rest of them. They would arrive at their victim's castle, and three squires would hand Bork his new steel-handled ax. Bork, covered with impenetrable armor, would wade the moat, if there was one, or simply walk up to the gates, swing the ax, and begin chopping through the wood. When the gates collapsed, Bork would take a huge steel rod and use it as a crow, prying at the portcullis, bending the heavy iron like pretzels until there was a gap wide enough for a mounted knight to ride through.

Then he would go back to the Count and Winkle.

Throughout this operation, not a word would have been said; the only activity from the Count's other men would be enough archery that no one would be able to pour boiling oil or hot tar on Bork while he was working. It was a precaution, and nothing more—even if they set the oil on the fire the moment the Count's little army approached, it would scarcely be hot enough to make water steam by the time Bork was through.

"Do you surrender to his Majesty the King?" Winkle would cry.

And the defenders of the castle, their gate hopelessly breached and terrified of the giant who had so easily made a joke of their defenses, would usually surrender. Occasionally there was some token resistance—when that happened, at Winkle's insistence, the town was brutally sacked and the noble's family was held in prison until a huge ransom was paid.

At the end of two years, the Count and Bork and Winkle and their army marched on Winchester. The King—the real king—fled before them and took up his exile in Anjou, where it was warmer anyway. The Count had himself crowned king, accepted the fealty of every noble in the country, and introduced his daughter Brunhilda all around. Then, finding Winchester not to his liking, he returned to his castle and ruled from there. Suitors for his daughter's hand made a constant traffic on the roads leading into the country; would-be courtiers and nobles vying for positions filled the new hostelries that sprang up on the other side of the village. All left much poorer than they had arrived. And while much of that money found its way into the King's coffers, much more of it went to Winkle, who believed that skimming off the cream meant leaving at least a quarter of it for the King.

And now that the wars were done, Bork hung up his armor and went back to normal life. Not quite normal life, actually. He slept in a good room in the castle, better than most of the knights. Some of the knights had even come to enjoy his company, and sought him out for ale in the evenings or hunting in the daytime—Bork could always be counted on to carry home two deer himself, and was much more convenient than a packhorse. All in all, Bork was happier than he had ever thought he would be.

Which is how things were going when the dragon came and changed it all forever.

Winkle was in Brunhilda's room, a place he had learned many routes to get to, so that he went unobserved every time. Brunhilda, after many gifts and more flattery, was on the verge of giving in to the handsome young advisor to the King when strange screams and cries began coming from the fields below. Brunhilda pulled away from Winkle's exploring hands and, clutching her half-open gown around her, rushed to the window to see what was the matter.

She looked down, to where the screams were coming from, and it wasn't until the dragon's shadow fell across her that she looked up. Winkle, waiting on the bed, only saw the claws reach in and, gently but firmly, take hold of Brunhilda and pull her from the room. Brunhilda fainted immediately, and by the time Winkle got to where he could see her, the dragon had backed away from the window and on great flapping wings was carrying her limp body off toward the north whence he had come.

Winkle was horrified. It was so sudden, something he could not have foreseen or planned against. Yet still he cursed himself and bitterly realized that his plans might be ended forever. A dragon had taken Brunhilda who was to be his means of legitimately becoming king; now the plot of seduction, marriage, and inheritance was ruined.

Ever practical, Winkle did not let himself lament for long. He dressed himself quickly and used a secret passage out of Brunhilda's room, only to reappear in the corridor outside it a moment later. "Brunhilda!" he cried, beating on the door. "Are you all right?"

The first of the knights reached him, and then the King, weeping and wailing and smashing anything that got in his way. Brunhilda's door was down in a moment, and the King ran to the window and cried out after his daughter, now a pinpoint speck in the sky many miles away. "Brunhilda! Brunhilda! Come back!" She did not come back. "Now," cried the King, as he turned back into the room and sank to the floor, his face twisted and wet with grief, "Now I have nothing, and all is in vain!"

My thoughts precisely, Winkle thought, but I'm not weeping about it. To hide his contempt he walked to the window and looked out. He saw, not the dragon, but Bork, emerging from the forest carrying two huge logs.

"Sir Bork," said Winkle.

The King heard a tone of decision in Winkle's voice. He had learned to listen to whatever Winkle said in that tone of voice. "What about him?"

"Sir Bork could defeat a dragon," Winkle said, "if any man could."

"That's true," the King said, gathering back some of the hope he had lost. "Of course that's true."

"But will he?" asked Winkle.

"Of course he will. He loves Brunhilda, doesn't he?"

"He said he did. But Your Majesty, is he really loyal to you? After all, why wasn't he here when the dragon came? Why didn't he save Brunhilda in the first place?"

"He was cutting wood for the winter."

"Cutting wood? When Brunhilda's life was at stake?"

The King was outraged. The illogic of it escaped him—he was not in a logical mood. So he was furious when he met Bork at the gate of the castle.

"You've betrayed me!" the King cried.

"I have?" Bork was smitten with guilt. And he hadn't even meant to.

"You weren't here when we needed you. When *Brunhilda* needed you!"

"I'm sorry," Bork said.

"Sorry, sorry, sorry. A lot of good it does to say you're sorry. You swore to protect Brunhilda from any enemy, and when a really dangerous enemy comes along, how do you repay me for everything I've done for you? You hide out in the forest!"

"What enemy?"

"A dragon," said the King, "as if you didn't see it coming and run out into the woods."

"Cross my heart, Your Majesty, I didn't know there was a dragon coming." And then he made the connection in his mind. "The dragon—it took Brunhilda?"

"It took her. Took her half-naked from her bedroom when she leaped to the window to call to you for help."

Bork felt the weight of guilt, and it was a terrible burden. His face grew hard and angry, and he walked into the castle, his harsh footfalls setting the earth to trembling. "My armor!" he cried. "My sword!"

In minutes he was in the middle of the courtyard, holding out his arms as the heavy mail was draped over him and the breastplate and helmet were strapped and screwed into place. The sword was not enough—he also carried his huge ax and a shield so massive two ordinary men could have hidden behind it.

"Which way did he go?" Bork asked.

"North," the King answered.

"I'll bring back your daughter, Your Majesty, or die in the attempt."

"Damn well better. It's all your fault."

The words stung, but the sting only impelled Bork further. He took the huge sack of food the cook had prepared for him and fastened it to his belt, and without a backward glance strode from the castle and took the road north.

"I almost feel sorry for the dragon," said the King.

But Winkle wondered. He had seen how large the claws were as they grasped Brunhilda—she had been like a tiny doll in a large man's fingers. The claws

110

were razor sharp. Even if she were still alive, could Bork really best the dragon? Bork the Bully, after all, had made his reputation picking on men smaller than he, as Winkle had ample reason to know. How would he do facing a dragon at least five times his size? Wouldn't he turn coward? Wouldn't he run as other men had run from *him?*

He might. But Sir Bork the Bully was Winkle's only hope of getting Brunhilda and the kingdom. If he could do anything to ensure that the giant at least *tried* to fight the dragon, he would do it. And so, taking only his rapier and a sack of food, Winkle left the castle by another way, and followed the giant along the road toward the north.

And then he had a terrible thought.

Fighting the dragon was surely ten times as brave as anything Bork had done before. If he won, wouldn't he have a claim on Brunhilda's hand himself?

It was not something Winkle wished to think about. Something would come to him, some way around the problem when the time came. Plenty of opportunity to plan something—*after* Bork wins and rescues her.

Bork had not rounded the second turn in the road when he came across the old woman, waiting by the side of the road. It was the same old woman who had cared for Brunhilda all those years that she was kept in a secret room in the castle. She looked wizened and weak, but there was a sharp look in her eyes that many had mistaken for great wisdom. It was not great wisdom. But she did know a few things about dragons.

"Going after the dragon, are you?" she asked in

111

a squeaky voice. "Going to get Brunhilda back, are you?" She giggled darkly behind her hand.

"I am if anyone can," Bork said.

"Well, anyone can't," she answered.

"*I* can."

"Not a prayer, you big bag of wind!"

Bork ignored her and started to walk past.

"Wait!" she said, her voice harsh as a dull file taking rust from armor. "Which way will you go?"

"North," he said. "That's the way the dragon took her."

"A quarter of the world is north, Sir Bork the Bully, and a dragon is small compared to all the mountains of the earth. But I know a way you can find the dragon, if you're really a knight.

"Light a torch, man. Light a torch, and whenever you come to a fork in the way, the light of the torch will leap the way you ought to go. Wind or no wind, fire seeks fire, and there is a flame at the heart of every dragon."

"They *do* breathe fire, then?" he asked. He did not know how to fight fire.

"Fire is light, not wind, and so it doesn't come from the dragon's mouth or the dragon's nostrils. If he burns you, it won't be with his breath." The old woman cackled like a mad hen. "No one knows the truth about dragons anymore!"

"Except you."

"I'm an old wife," she said. "And I know. They don't eat human beings, either. They're strict vegetarians. But they kill. From time to time they kill."

"Why, if they aren't hungry for meat?"

"You'll see," she said. She started to walk away, back into the forest.

112

"Wait!" Bork called. "How far will the dragon be?"

"Not far," she said. "Not far, Sir Bork. He's waiting for you. He's waiting for you and all the fools who come to try to free the virgin." Then she melted away into the darkness.

Bork lit a torch and followed it all night, turning when the flame turned, unwilling to waste time in sleep when Brunhilda might be suffering unspeakable degradation at the monster's hands. And behind him, Winkle forced himself to stay awake, determined not to let Bork lose him in the darkness.

All night, and all day, and all night again Bork followed the light of the torch, through crooked paths long unused, until he came to the foot of a dry, tall hill, with rocks and crags along the top. He stopped, for here the flame leaped high, as if to say, "Upward from here." And in the silence he heard a sound that chilled him to the bone. It was Brunhilda, screaming as if she were being tortured in the cruelest imaginable way. And the screams were followed by a terrible roar. Bork cast aside the remnant of his food and made his way to the top of the hill. On the way he called out, to stop the dragon from whatever it was doing.

"Dragon! Are you there!"

The voice rumbled back to him with a power that made the dirt shift under Bork's feet. "Yes indeed."

"Do you have Brunhilda?"

"You mean the little virgin with the heart of an adder and the brain of a gnat?"

In the forest at the bottom of the hill, Winkle ground his teeth in fury, for despite his designs on the kingdom, he loved Brunhilda as much as he was capable of loving anyone.

113

"Dragon!" Bork bellowed at the top of his voice. "Dragon! Prepare to die!"

"Oh dear! Oh dear!" cried out the dragon. "Whatever shall I do?"

And then Bork reached the top of the hill, just as the sun topped the distant mountains and it became morning. In the light Bork immediately saw Brunhilda tied to a tree, her auburn hair glistening. All around her was the immense pile of gold that the dragon, according to custom, kept. And all around the gold was the dragon's tail.

Bork looked at the tail and followed it until finally he came to the dragon, who was leaning on a rock chewing on a tree trunk and smirking. The dragon's wings were clad with feathers, but the rest of him was covered with tough gray hide the color of weathered granite. His teeth, when he smiled, were ragged, long, and pointed. His claws were three feet long and sharp as a rapier from tip to base. But in spite of all this armament, the most dangerous thing about him was his eyes. They were large and soft and brown, with long lashes and gently arching brows. But at the centre each eye held a sharp point of light, and when Bork looked at the eyes that light stabbed deep into him, seeing his heart and laughing at what it found there.

For a moment, looking at the dragon's eyes, Bork stood transfixed. Then the dragon reached over one wing toward Brunhilda, and with a great growling noise he began to tickle her ear.

Brunhilda was unbearably ticklish, and she let off a bloodcurdling scream.

"Touch her not!" Bork cried.

"Touch her what?" asked the dragon, with a chuckle. "I will not."

"Beast!" bellowed Bork. "I am Sir Bork the Big! I have never been defeated in battle! No man dares stand before me, and the beasts of the forest step aside when I pass!"

"You must be awfully clumsy," said the dragon.

Bork resolutely went on. He had seen the challenges and jousts—it was obligatory to recite and embellish your achievements in order to strike terror into the heart of the enemy. "I can cut down a tree with one blow of my ax! I can cleave an ox from head to tail, I can skewer a running deer, I can break down walls of stone and doors of wood!"

"Why can't I ever get a handy servant like that?" murmured the dragon. "Ah well, you probably expect too large a salary."

The dragon's sardonic tone might have infuriated other knights; Bork was only confused, wondering if this matter was less serious than he had thought. "I've come to free Brunhilda, dragon. Will you give her up to me, or must I slay you?"

At that the dragon laughed long and loud. Then it cocked its head and looked at Bork. In that moment Bork knew that he had lost the battle. For deep in the dragon's eye he saw the truth.

Bork saw himself knocking down gates and cutting down trees, but the deeds no longer looked heroic. Instead he realized that the knights who always rode behind him in these battles were laughing at him, that the King was a weak and vicious man, that Winkle's ambition was the only emotion he had room for; he saw that all of them were using him for their own ends, and cared nothing for him at all.

Bork saw himself asking for Brunhilda's hand in marriage, and he was ridiculous, an ugly, unkempt, and awkward giant in contrast to the slight and graceful girl. He saw that the King's hints of the possibility of their marriage were merely a trick, to blind him. More, he saw what no one else had been able to see—that Brunhilda loved Winkle, and Winkle wanted her.

And at last Bork saw himself as a warrior, and realized that in all the years of his great reputation and in all his many victories, he had fought only one man—an archer who ran at him with a knife. He had terrorized the weak and the small, but never until now had he faced a creature larger than himself. Bork looked in the dragon's eyes and saw his own death.

"Your eyes are deep," said Bork softly.

"Deep as a well, and you are drowning."

"Your sight is clear." Bork's palms were cold with sweat.

"Clear as ice, and you will freeze."

"Your eyes," Bork began. Then his mouth was suddenly so dry that he could barely speak. He swallowed. "Your eyes are filled with light."

"Bright and tiny as a star," the dragon whispered. "And see; your heart is afire."

Slowly the dragon stepped away from the rock, even as the tip of his tail reached behind Bork to push him into the dragon's waiting jaws. But Bork was not in so deep a trance that he could not see.

"I see that you mean to kill me," Bork said. "But you won't have me as easily as that." Bork whirled around to hack at the tip of the dragon's tail with his ax. But he was too large and slow, and the tail flicked away before the ax was fairly swung.

The battle lasted all day. Bork fought exhaustion as much as he fought the dragon, and it seemed the dragon only toyed with him. Bork would lurch toward the tail or a wing or the dragon's belly, but when his ax or sword fell where the dragon had been, it only sang in the air and touched nothing.

Finally Bork fell to his knees and wept. He wanted to go on with the fight, but his body could not do it. And the dragon looked as fresh as it had in the morning.

"What?" asked the dragon. "Finished already?"

Then Bork felt the tip of the dragon's tail touch his back, and the sharp points of the claws pressed gently on either side. He could not bear to look up at what he knew he would see. Yet neither could he bear to wait, not knowing when the blow would come. So he opened his eyes, and lifted his head, and saw.

The dragon's teeth were nearly touching him, poised to tear his head from his shoulders.

Bork screamed. And screamed again when the teeth touched him, when they pushed into his armor, when the dragon lifted him with teeth and tail and talons until he was twenty feet above the ground. He screamed again when he looked into the dragon's eyes and saw, not hunger, not hatred, but merely amusement.

And then he found his silence again, and listened as the dragon spoke through clenched teeth, watching the tongue move massively in the mouth only inches from his head.

"Well, little man. Are you afraid?"

Bork tried to think of some heroic message of defiance to hurl at the dragon, some poetic words that might be remembered forever so that his death would be sung in a thousand songs. But Bork's mind was not quick at such things; he was not that accustomed to speech, and had no ear for gallantry.

Instead he began to think it would be somehow cheap and silly to die with a lie on his lips.

"Dragon," Bork whispered, "I'm frightened."

To Bork's surprise, the teeth did not pierce him then. Instead, he felt himself being lowered to the ground, heard a grating sound as the teeth and claws let go of his armor. He raised his visor, and saw that the dragon was now lying on the ground, laughing, rolling back and forth, slapping its tail against the rocks, and clapping its claws together. "Oh, my dear tiny friend," said the dragon. "I thought the day would never dawn."

"What day?"

"Today," answered the dragon. It had stopped laughing, and it once again drew near to Bork and looked him in the eye. "I'm going to let you live."

"Thank you," Bork said, trying to be polite.

"Thank me? Oh no, my midget warrior. You won't thank me. Did you think my teeth were sharp? Not half so pointed as the barbs of your jealous, disappointed friends."

"I can go?"

"You can go, you can fly, you can dwell in your castle for all I care. Do you want to know why?"

"Yes."

"Because you were afraid. In all my life, I have only killed brave knights who knew no fear. You're the first, the very first, who was afraid in that final moment. Now go." And the dragon gave Bork a push and sent him down the hill.

Brunhilda, who had watched the whole battle in curious silence, now called after him. "Some kind of knight you are! Coward! I hate you! Don't leave me!" The shouts went on until Bork was out of earshot.

Bork was ashamed.

Bork went down the hill and, as soon as he entered the cool of the forest, he lay down and fell asleep.

Hidden in the rocks, Winkle watched him go, watched as the dragon again began to tickle Brunhilda, whose gown was still open as it had been when she was taken by the dragon. Winkle could not stop thinking of how close he had come to having her. But now, if even Bork could not save her, her cause was hopeless, and Winkle immediately began planning other ways to profit from the situation.

All the plans depended on his reaching the castle before Bork. Since Winkle had dozed off and on during the day's battle, he was able to go farther— to a village, where he stole an ass and rode clumsily, half-asleep, all night and half the next day and reached the castle before Bork awoke.

The King raged. The King swore. The King vowed that Bork would die.

"But Your Majesty," said Winkle, "you can't forget that it is Bork who inspires fear in the hearts of your loyal subjects. You can't kill him—if he were dead, how long would you be king?"

That calmed the old man down. "Then I'll let him live. But he won't have a place in this castle, that's certain. I won't have him around here, the coward. Afraid! Told the dragon he was afraid! Pathetic. The man has no gratitude." And the King stalked from the court.

When Bork got home, weary and sick at heart, he found the gate of the castle closed to him. There was no explanation—he needed none. He had failed the one time it mattered most. He was no longer worthy to be a knight.

And now it was as it had been before. Bork was ignored, despised, feared, he was completely alone. But still, when it was time for great strength, there he was, doing the work of ten men, and not thanked for it. Who would thank a man for doing what he must to earn his bread.

In the evenings he would sit in his hut, staring at the fire that pushed a column of smoke up through the hole in the roof. He remembered how it had been to have friends, but the memory was not happy, for it was always poisoned by the knowledge that the friendship did not outlast Bork's first failure. Now the knights spat when they passed him on the road or in the fields.

The flames did not let Bork blame his troubles on them, however. The flames constantly reminded him of the dragon's eyes, and in their dance he saw himself, a buffoon who dared to dream of loving a princess, who believed that he was truly a knight. Not so, not so. I was never a knight, he thought. I was never worthy. Only now am I receiving what I deserve. And all his bitterness turned inward, and he hated himself far more than any of the knights could hate him.

He had made the wrong choice. When the dragon chose to let him go, he should have refused. He should have stayed and fought to the death. He should have died.

Stories kept filtering into the village, stories of the many heroic and famous knights who accepted the challenge of freeing Brunhilda from the dragon. All of them went as heroes. All of them died as heroes. Only Bork had returned alive from the dragon, and with every knight who died Bork's shame grew. Until he decided that he would go back. Better to join the knights in death than to live his life staring into the flames and seeing the visions of the dragon's eyes.

Next time, however, he would have to be better prepared. So after the spring plowing and planting and lambing and calving, where Bork's help was indispensable to the villagers, the giant went to the castle again. This time no one barred his way, but he was wise enough to stay as much out of sight as possible. He went to the one-armed swordmaster's room. Bork hadn't seen him since he accidentally cut off his arm in sword practice years before.

"Come for the other arm, coward?" asked the swordmaster.

"I'm sorry," Bork said. "I was younger then."

"You weren't any smaller. Go away."

But Bork stayed, and begged the swordmaster to help him. They worked out an arrangement. Bork would be the swordmaster's personal servant all summer, and in exchange the swordmaster would try to teach Bork how to fight.

They went out into the fields every day, and under the swordmaster's watchful eye he practiced sword-fighting with bushes, trees, rocks—anything but the swordmaster, who refused to let Bork near him. Then they would return to the swordmaster's rooms, and Bork would clean the floor and sharpen swords and burnish shields and repair broken practice equipment. And always the swordmaster said, "Bork, you're too stupid to do anything right!" Bork agreed. In a summer of practice, he never got any better, and at the end of the summer, when it was time for Bork to go out in the fields and help with the harvest and the preparations for winter, the swordmaster said, "It's hopeless, Bork. You're too slow. Even the bushes are more agile than you. Don't come back. I still hate you, you know."

"I know," Bork said, and he went out into the fields, where the peasants waited impatiently for the giant to come carry sheaves of grain to the wagons.

Another winter looking at the fire, and Bork began to realize that no matter how good he got with the sword, it would make no difference. The dragon was not to be defeated that way. If excellent swordplay could kill the dragon, the dragon would be dead by now—the finest knights in the kingdom had already died trying.

He had to find another way. And the snow was still heavy on the ground when he again entered the castle and climbed the long and narrow stairway to the tower room where the wizard lived.

"Go away," said the wizard, when Bork knocked at his door. "I'm busy."

"I'll wait," Bork answered.

"Suit yourself."

And Bork waited. It was late at night when the wizard finally opened the door. Bork had fallen asleep leaning on it—he nearly knocked the magician over when he fell inside.

"What the devil are you—you waited!"

"Yes," said Bork, rubbing his head where it had hit the stone floor.

"Well, I'll be back in a moment." The wizard made his way along a narrow ledge until he reached the place where the wall bulged and a hole opened onto the outside of the castle wall. In wartime, such holes were used to pour boiling oil on attackers. In peacetime, they were even more heavily used. "Go on inside and wait," the wizard said.

Bork looked around the room. It was spotlessly clean, the walls were lined with books, and here and there a fascinating artifact hinted at hidden knowledge and arcane powers—a sphere with the world on it, a skull, an abacus, beakers and tubes, a clay pot from which smoke rose, though there was no fire under it. Bork marvelled until the wizard returned.

"Nice little place, isn't it?" the wizard asked. "You're Bork, the bully, aren't you?"

Bork nodded.

"What can I do for you?"

"I don't know," Bork asked. "I want to learn magic. I want to learn magic powerful enough that I can use it to fight the dragon."

The wizard coughed profusely.

"What's wrong?" Bork asked.

"It's the dust," the wizard said.

Bork looked around and saw no dust. But when he sniffed the air, it felt thick in his nose, and a tickling in his chest made him cough, too.

"Dust?" asked Bork. "Can I have a drink?"

"Drink," said the wizard. "Downstairs—"

"But there's a pail of water right here. It looks perfectly clean—"

"Please don't—"

But Bork put the dipper in the pail and drank. The water sloshed into his mouth, and he swallowed, but it felt dry going down, and his thirst was unslaked. "What's wrong with the water?" Bork asked.

The wizard sighed and sat down. "It's the problem with magic, Bork old boy. Why do you think the King doesn't call on me to help him in his wars? He

123

knows it, and now you'll know it, and the whole world probably will know it by Thursday."

"You don't know any magic?"

"Don't be a fool! I know all the magic there is! I can conjure up monsters that would make your dragon look tame! I can snap my fingers and have a table set with food to make the cook die of envy. I can take an empty bucket and fill it with water, with wine, with gold—whatever you want. But try spending the gold, and they'll hunt you down and kill you. Try drinking the water and you'll die of thirst."

"It isn't real."

"All illusion. Handy, sometimes. But that's all. Can't create anything except in your head. That pail, for instance—" And the wizard snapped his fingers. Bork looked, and the pail was filled, not with water, but with dust and spider webs. That wasn't all. He looked around the room, and was startled to see that the bookshelves were gone, as were the other trappings of great wisdom. Just a few books on a table in a corner, some counters covered with dust and papers and half-decayed food, and the floor inches deep in garbage.

"The place is horrible," the wizard said. "I can't bear to look at it." He snapped his fingers, and the old illusion came back. "Much nicer, isn't it?"

"Yes."

"I have excellent taste, haven't I? Now, you wanted me to help you fight the dragon, didn't you? Well, I'm afraid it's out of the question. You see, my illusions only work on human beings, and occasionally on horses. A dragon wouldn't be fooled for a moment. You understand?"

Bork understood, and despaired. He returned to

his hut and stared again at the flames. His resolution to return and fight the dragon again was undimmed. But now he knew that he would go as badly prepared as he had before, and his death and defeat would be certain. Well, he thought, better death than life as Bork the coward. Bork the bully who only has courage when he fights people smaller than himself.

The winter was unusually cold, and the snow was remarkably deep. The firewood ran out in February, and there was no sign of an easing in the weather.

The villagers went to the castle and asked for help, but the King was chilly himself, and the knights were all sleeping together in the great hall because there wasn't enough firewood for their barracks and the castle, too. "Can't help you," the King said.

So it was Bork who led the villagers—the ten strongest men, dressed as warmly as they could, yet still cold to the bone in the wind—and they followed in the path his body cut in the snow. With his huge ax he cut down tree after tree; the villagers set the wedges and Bork split the huge logs; the men carried what they could but it was Bork who made seven trips and carried most of the wood home. The village had enough to last until spring—more than enough, for, as Bork had expected, as soon as the stacks of firewood were deep in the village, the King's men came and took their tax of it.

And Bork, exhausted and frozen from the expedition, was carefully nursed back to health by the villagers. As he lay coughing and they feared he might die, it occurred to them how much they owed to the giant. Not just the firewood, but the hard labor in the farming work, and the fact that Bork had kept the armies far from their village, and they felt what no one in the castle had let himself feel for more than a few moments—gratitude. And so it was that when he had mostly recovered, Bork began to find gifts outside his door from time to time. A rabbit, freshly killed and dressed; a few eggs; a vast pair of hose that fit him very comfortably; a knife specially made to fit his large grip and to ride with comfortable weight on his hip. The villagers did not converse with him much. But then, they were not talkative people. The gifts said it all.

Throughout the spring, as Bork helped in the plowing and planting, with the villagers working alongside, he realized that this was where he belonged—with the villagers, not with the knights. They weren't rollicking good company, but there was something about sharing a task that must be done that made for stronger bonds between them than any of the rough camaraderie of the castle. The loneliness was gone.

Yet when Bork returned home and stared into the flames in the center of his hut, the call of the dragon's eyes became even stronger, if that were possible. It was not loneliness that drove him to seek death with the dragon. It was something else, and Bork could not think what. Pride? He had none— he accepted the verdict of the castle people that he was a coward. The only guess he could make was that he loved Brunhilda and felt a need to rescue her. The more he tried to convince himself, however, the less he believed it.

He had to return to the dragon because, in his own mind, he knew he should have died in the dragon's teeth, back when he fought the dragon before. The common folk might love him for what he did for them, but he hated himself for what he was.

He was nearly ready to head back for the dragon's mountain when the army came.

"How many are there?" the King asked Winkle.

"I can't get my spies to agree," Winkle said. "But the lowest estimate was two thousand men."

"And we have a hundred and fifty here in the castle. Well, I'll have to call on my dukes and counts for support."

"You don't understand, Your Majesty. These *are* your dukes and counts. This isn't an invasion. This is a rebellion."

The King paled. "How do they dare?"

"They dare because they heard a rumor, which at first they didn't believe was true. A rumor that your giant knight had quit, that he wasn't in your army anymore. And when they found out for sure that the rumor was true, they came to cast you out and return the old King to his place."

"Treason!" the King shouted. "Is there no loyalty?"

"I'm loyal," Winkle said, though of course he had already made contact with the other side in case things didn't go well. "But it seems to me that your only hope is to prove the rumors wrong. Show them that Bork is still fighting for you."

"But he isn't. I threw him out two years ago. The coward was even rejected by the dragon."

"Then I suggest you find a way to get him back into the army. If you don't, I doubt you'll have much luck against that crowd out there. My spies tell me they're placing wagers about how many pieces you can be cut into before you die."

The King turned slowly and stared at Winkle, glared at him, gazed intently in his eyes. "Winkle,

127

after all we've done to Bork over the years, persuading him to help us now is a despicable thing to do."

"True."

"And so it's your sort of work, Winkle. Not mine. *You* get him back in the army."

"I can't do it. He hates me worse than anyone, I'm sure. After all, I've betrayed him more often."

"You get him back in the army within the next six hours, Winkle, or I'll send pieces of you to each of the men in that traitorous group that you've made friends with in order to betray me."

Winkle managed not to looked startled. But he *was* surprised. The King had somehow known about it. The King was not quite the fool he had seemed to be.

"I'm sending four knights with you to make sure you do it right."

"You misjudge me, Your Majesty," Winkle said.

"I hope so, Winkle. Persuade Bork for me, and you live to eat another breakfast."

The knights came, and Winkle walked with them to Bork's hut. They waited outside.

"Bork, old friend," Winkle said. Bork was sitting by the fire, staring in the flames. "Bork, you aren't the sort who holds grudges, are you?"

Bork spat into the flames.

"Can't say I blame you," Winkle said. "We've treated you ungratefully. We've been downright cruel. But you rather brought it on yourself, you know. It isn't *our* fault you turned coward in your fight with the dragon. Is it?"

Bork shook his head. "My fault, Winkle. But it isn't my fault the army has come, either. I've lost my battle. You lose yours."

"Bork, we've been friends since we were three—"

Bork looked up so suddenly, his face so sharp and lit with the glow of the fire, that Winkle could not go on.

"I've looked in the dragon's eyes," Bork said, "and I know who you are."

Winkle wondered if it was true, and was afraid. But he had courage of a kind, a selfish courage that allowed him to dare anything if he thought he would gain by it.

"Who am I? No one knows anything as it is, because as soon as it's known it changes. You looked in the dragon's eyes years ago, Bork. Today I'm not who I was then. Today you are not who you were then. And today the King needs you."

"The King is a petty count who rode to greatness on my shoulders. He can rot in hell."

"The other knights need you, then. Do you want them to die?"

"I've fought enough battles for them. Let them fight their own."

And Winkle stood helplessly, wondering how he could possibly persuade this man, who would not be persuaded.

It was then that a village child came. The knights caught him lurking near Bork's hut; they roughly shoved him inside. 'He might be a spy," a knight said.

For the first time since Winkle came, Bork laughed. "A spy? Don't you know your own village, here? Come to me, Laggy." And the boy came to him, and stood near him as if seeking the giant's protection. "Laggy's a friend of mine," Bork said. "Why did you come, Laggy?"

The boy wordlessly held out a fish. It wasn't large, but it was still wet from the river.

"Did you catch this?" Bork said.

The boy nodded.

"How many did you catch today?"

The boy pointed at the fish.

"Just the one? Oh, then I can't take this, if it's all you caught."

But as Bork handed the fish back, the boy retreated, refused to take it. He finally opened his mouth and spoke. "For you," he said, and then he scurried out of the hut and into the bright morning sunlight.

And Winkle knew he had his way to get Bork into the battle.

"The villagers," Winkle said.

Bork looked at him quizzically.

And Winkle *almost* said, "If you don't join the army, we'll come out here and burn the village and kill all the children and sell the adults into slavery in Germany." But something stopped him; a memory, perhaps, of the fact that he was once a village child himself. No, not that. Winkle was honest enough with himself to know that what stopped him from making the threat was a mental picture of Sir Bork striding into battle, not in front of the King's army, but at the head of the rebels. A mental picture of Bork's ax biting deep into the gate of the castle, his huge crow prying the portcullis free. This was not the time to threaten Bork.

So Winkle took the other tack. "Bork, if they win this battle, which they surely will if you aren't with us, do you think they'll be kind to this village? They'll burn and rape and kill and capture these people for slaves. They hate us, and to them these villagers are part of us, part of their hatred. If you don't help us, you're killing them."

"I'll protect them," Bork said.

"No, my friend. No, if you don't fight with us, as a knight, they won't treat you chivalrously. They'll fill you full of arrows before you get within twenty feet of their lines. You fight with us, or you might as well not fight at all."

Winkle knew he had won. Bork thought for several minutes, but it was inevitable. He got up and returned to the castle, strapped on his old armor, took his huge ax and his shield, and, with his sword belted at his waist, walked into the courtyard of the castle. The other knights cheered, and called out to him as if he were their dearest friend. But the words were hollow and they knew it, and when Bork didn't answer they soon fell silent.

The gate opened and Bork walked out, the knights on horseback behind him.

And in the rebel camp, they knew that the rumors were a lie—the giant still fought with the King, and they were doomed. Most of the men slipped away into the woods. But the others, particularly the leaders who would die if they surrendered as surely as they would die if they fought, stayed. Better to die valiantly than as a coward, they each thought, and so as Bork approached he still faced an army— only a few hundred men, but still an army.

They came out to meet Bork one by one, as the knights came to the dragon on his hill. And one by one, as they made their first cut or thrust, Bork's ax struck, and their heads flew from their bodies, or their chests were cloven nearly in half, or the ax reamed them end to end, and Bork was bright red with blood and a dozen men were dead and not one had touched him.

So they came by threes and fours, and fought like

demons, but still Bork took them, and when even more than four tried to fight him at once they got in each other's way and he killed them more easily.

And at last those who still lived despaired. There was no honor in dying so pointlessly. And with fifty men dead, the battle ended, and the rebels laid down their arms in submission.

Then the King emerged from the castle and rode to the battleground, and paraded triumphantly in front of the defeated men.

"You are all sentenced to death at once," the King declared.

But suddenly he found himself pulled from his horse, and Bork's great hands held him. The King gasped at the smell of gore; Bork rubbed his bloody hands on the King's tunic, and took the King's face between his sticky palms.

"No one dies now. No one dies tomorrow. These men will all live, and you'll send them home to their lands, and you'll lower their tribute and let them dwell in peace forever."

The King imagined his own blood mingling with that which already covered Bork, and he nodded. Bork let him go. The King mounted his horse again, and spoke loudly, so all could hear. "I forgive you all. I pardon you all. You may return to your homes. I confirm you in your lands. And your tribute is cut in half from this day forward. Go in peace. If any man harms you, I'll have his life."

The rebels stood in silence.

Winkle shouted at them "Go! You heard the king! You're free! Go home!"

And they cheered, and long-lived-the-King, and then bellowed their praise to Bork.

But Bork, if he heard them, gave no sign. He

132

stripped off his armor and let it lie in the field. He carried his great ax to the stream, and let the water run over the metal until it was clean. Then he lay in the stream himself, and the water carried off the last of the blood, and when he came out he was clean.

Then he walked away, to the north road, ignoring the calls of the King and his knights, ignoring everything except the dragon who waited for him on the mountain. For this was the last of the acts Bork wold perform in his life for which he would feel shame. He would not kill again. He would only die, bravely, in the dragon's claws and teeth.

The old woman waited for him on the road.

"Off to kill the dragon, are you?" she asked in a voice that the years had tortured into gravel. "Didn't learn enough the first time?" She giggled behind her hand.

"Old woman, I learned everything before. Now I'm going to die."

"Why? So the fools in the castle will think better of you?"

Bork shook his head.

"The villagers already love you. For your deeds today, you'll already be a legend. If it isn't for love or fame, why are you going?"

Bork shrugged. "I don't know. I think he calls to me. I'm through with my life, and all I can see ahead of me are his eyes."

The old woman nodded. "Well, well, Bork. I think you're the first knight that the dragon won't be happy to see. We old wives know, Bork. Just tell him the truth, Bork."

"I've never known the truth to stop a sword," he said.

"But the dragon doesn't carry a sword."

"He might as well."

"No, Bork, no," she said, clucking impatiently. "You know better than that. Of all the dragon's weapons, which cut you the deepest?"

Bork tried to remember. The truth was, he realized, that the dragon had never cut him at all. Not with his teeth nor his claws. Only the armor had been pierced. Yet there had been a wound, a deep one that hadn't healed, and it had been cut in him, not by teeth or talons, but by the bright fires in the dragon's eyes.

"The truth," the old woman said. "Tell the dragon the truth. Tell him the truth, and you'll live!"

Bork shook his head. "I'm not going there to live," he said. He pushed past her, and walked on up the road.

But her words rang in his ears long after he stopped hearing her call after him. The truth, she had said. Well, then, why not? Let the dragon have the truth. Much good may it do him.

This time Bork was in no hurry. He slept every night, and paused to hunt for berries and fruit to eat in the woods. It was four days before he reached the dragon's hill, and he came in the morning, after a good night's sleep. He was afraid, of course; but still there was a pleasant feeling about the morning, a tingling of excitement about the meeting with the dragon. He felt the end coming near, and he relished it.

Nothing had changed. The dragon roared; Brunhilda screamed. And when he reached the top of the hill, he saw the dragon tickling her with his wing. He was not surprised to see that she hadn't changed at all—the two years had not aged her, and though her gown still was open and her breasts were

134

open to the sun and the wind, she wasn't even freckled or tanned. It could have been yesterday that Bork fought with the dragon the first time. And Bork was smiling as he stepped into the flat space where the battle would take place.

Brunhilda saw him first. "Help me! You're the four hundred and thirtieth knight to try! Surely that's a lucky number!" Then she recognized him. "Oh, no. You again. Oh well, at least while he's fighting you I won't have to put up with his tickling."

Bork ignored her. He had come for the dragon, not for Brunhilda.

The dragon regarded him calmly. "You are disturbing my nap time."

"I'm glad," Bork said. "You've disturbed me, sleeping and waking, since I left you. Do you remember me?"

"Ah yes. You're the only knight who was ever afraid of me."

"Do you really believe that?" Bork asked.

"It hardly matters what I believe. Are you going to kill me today?"

"I don't think so," said Bork. "You're much stronger than I am, and I'm terrible at battle. I've never defeated anyone who was more than half my strength."

The lights in the dragon's eyes suddenly grew brighter, and the dragon squinted to look at Bork. "Is that so?" asked the dragon.

"And I'm not very clever. You'll be able to figure out my next move before I know what it is myself."

The dragon squinted more, and the eyes grew even brighter.

"Don't you want to rescue this beautiful woman?" the dragon asked.

135

"I don't much care," he said. "I loved her once. But I'm through with that. I came for you."

"You don't love her anymore?" asked the dragon.

Bork almost said, "Not a bit." But then he stopped. The truth, the old woman had said. And he looked into himself and saw that no matter how much he hated himself for it, the old feelings died hard. "I love her, dragon. But it doesn't do me any good. She doesn't love me. And so even though I desire her, I don't want her."

Brunhilda was a little miffed. "That's the stupidest thing I've ever heard," she said. But Bork was watching the dragon, whose eyes were dazzlingly bright. The monster was squinting so badly that Bork began to wonder if he could see at all.

"Are you having trouble with your eyes?" Bork asked.

"Do you think *you* ask the questions here? I ask the questions."

"Then ask."

"What in the world do I want to know from you?"

"I can't think of anything," Bork answered. "I know almost nothing. What little I do know, you taught me."

"Did I? What was it that you learned?"

"You taught me that I was not loved by those I thought had loved me. I learned from you that deep within my large body is a very small soul."

The dragon blinked, and its eyes seemed to dim a little.

"Ah," said the dragon.

"What do you mean, 'Ah'?" asked Bork.

"Just 'Ah,' " the dragon answered. "Does every *ah* have to mean something?"

Brunhilda sighed impatiently. "How long does

136

this go on? Everybody else who comes up here is wonderful and brave. You just stand around talking about how miserable you are. Why don't you fight?"

"Like the others?" asked Bork.

"They're so brave," she said.

"They're all dead."

"Only a coward would think of that," she said scornfully.

"It hardly comes as a surprise to you," Bork said. "Everyone knows I'm a coward. Why do you think I came? I'm of no use to anyone, except as a machine to kill people at the command of a King I despise."

"That's my father you're talking about!"

"I'm nothing, and the world will be better without me in it."

"I can't say I disagree," Brunhilda said.

But Bork did not hear her, for he felt the touch of the dragon's tail on his back, and when he looked at the dragon's eyes they had stopped glowing so brightly. They were almost back to normal, in fact, and the dragon was beginning to reach out its claws.

So Bork swung his ax, and the dragon dodged, and the battle was on, just as before.

And just as before, at sundown Bork stood pinned between tail and claws and teeth.

"Are you afraid to die?" asked the dragon, as it had before.

Bork almost answered *yes* again, because that would keep him alive. But then he remembered that he had come in order to die, and as he looked in his heart he still realized that however much he might fear death, he feared life more.

"I came here to die," he said. "I still want to."

And the dragon's eyes leaped bright with light.

Bork imagined that the pressure of the claws lessened.

'Well, then, Sir Bork, I can hardly do you such a favor as to kill you.' And the dragon let him go.

That was when Bork became angry.

"You can't do this to me!" he shouted.

"Why not?" asked the dragon, who was now trying to ignore Bork and occupied itself by crushing boulders with its claws.

"Because I insist on my right to die at your hands."

"It's not a right, it's a privilege," said the dragon.

"If you don't kill me, then I'll kill you!"

The dragon sighed in boredom, but Bork would not be put off. He began swinging the ax, and the dragon dodged, and in the pink light of sunset the battle was on again. This time, though, the dragon only fell back and twisted and turned to avoid Bork's blows. It made no effort to attack. Finally Bork was too tired and frustrated to go on.

"Why don't you fight!" he shouted. Then he wheezed from the exhaustion of the chase.

The dragon was panting, too. "Come on now, little man, why don't you give it up and go home. I'll give you a signed certificate testifying that I asked you to go, so that no one thinks you're a coward. Just leave me alone."

The dragon began crushing rocks and dribbling them over its head. It lay down and began to bury itself in gravel.

"Dragon," said Bork, "a moment ago you had me in your teeth. You were about to kill me. The old woman told me that truth was my only defense. So I must have lied before. I must have said something false. What was it? Tell me!"

138

The dragon looked annoyed. "She had no business telling you that. It's privileged information."

"All I ever said to you was the truth."

"Was it?"

"Did I lie to you? Answer—yes or no!"

The dragon only looked away, its eyes still bright. It lay on its back and poured gravel over its belly.

"I did then. I lied. Just the kind of fool I am to tell the truth and still get caught in a lie."

Had the dragon's eyes dimmed? Was there a lie in what he had just said?

"Dragon," Bork insisted, "if you don't kill me or I don't kill you, then I might as well throw myself from the cliff. There's no meaning to my life, if I can't die at your hands!"

Yes, the dragon's eyes were dimming, and the dragon rolled over onto its belly, and began to gaze thoughtfully at Bork.

"Where is the lie in that?"

"Lie? Who said anything about a lie?" But the dragon's long tail was beginning to creep around so it could get behind Bork.

And then it occurred to Bork that the dragon might not even know. That the dragon might be as much a prisoner of the fires of truth inside him as Bork was, and that the dragon wasn't deliberately toying with him at all. Didn't matter, of course. "Never mind what the lie is, then," Bork said. "Kill me now, and the world will be a better place!"

The dragon's eyes dimmed, and a claw made a pass at him, raking the air by his face.

It was maddening, to know there was a lie in what he was saying and not know what it was. "It's the perfect ending for my meaningless life," he said. "I'm so clumsy I even have to stumble into death."

He didn't understand why, but once again he stared into the dragon's mouth, and the claws pressed gently but sharply against his flesh.

The dragon asked the question of Bork for the third time. "Are you afraid, little man, to die?"

This was the moment, Bork knew. If he was to die, he had to lie to the dragon now, for if he told the truth the dragon would set him free again. But to lie, he had to know what the truth was, and now he didn't know at all. He tried to think of where he had gone astray from the truth, and could not. What had he said? It was true that he was clumsy; it was true that he was stumbling into death. What else then?

He had said his life was meaningless. Was that the lie? He had said his death would make the world a better place. Was that the lie?

And so he thought of what would happen when he died. What hole would his death make in the world? The only people who might miss him were the villagers. That was the meaning of his life, then—the villagers. So he lied.

"The villagers won't miss me if I die. They'll get along just fine without me."

But the dragon's eyes brightened, and the teeth withdrew, and Bork realized to his grief that his statement had been true after all. The villagers wouldn't miss him if he died. The thought of it broke his heart, the last betrayal in a long line of betrayals.

"Dragon, I can't outguess you! I don't know what's true and what isn't! All I learn from you is that everyone I thought loved me doesn't. Don't ask me questions! Just kill me and end my life. Every pleasure I've had turns to pain when you tell me the truth."

And now, when he had thought he was telling the truth, the claws broke his skin, and the teeth closed over his head, and he screamed. "Dragon! Don't let me die like this! What is the pleasure that your truth won't turn to pain? What do I have left?"

The dragon pulled away, and regarded him carefully. "I told you, little man, that I don't answer questions, I ask them."

"Why are you here?" Bork demanded. "This ground is littered with the bones of men who failed your tests. Why not mine? Why not mine? Why can't I die? Why did you keep sparing my life? I'm just a man, I'm just alive, I'm just trying to do the best I can in a miserable world and I'm sick of trying to figure out what's true and what isn't. End the game, dragon. My life has never been happy, and I want to die."

The dragon's eyes went black, and the jaws opened again, and the teeth approached, and Bork knew he had told his last lie, that this lie would be enough. But with the teeth inches from him Bork finally realized what the lie was, and the realization was enough to change his mind. "No," he said, and he reached out and seized the teeth, though they cut his fingers. "No," he said, and he wept. "I have been happy, I have." And, gripping the sharp teeth, the memories raced through his mind. The many nights of comradeship with the knights in the castle. The pleasure of weariness from working in the forest and the fields. The joy he felt when alone he won a victory from the Duke; the rush of warmth when the boy brought him the single fish he had caught; and the solitary pleasures, of waking and going to sleep, of walking and running, of feeling the wind on a hot day and standing near a fire in the deep of winter.

They were all good, and they had all happened. What did it matter if later the knights despised him? What did it matter if the villagers' love was only a fleeting thing, to be forgotten after he died? The reality of the pain did not destroy the reality of the pleasure; grief did not obliterate joy. They each happened in their time, and because some of them were dark it did not mean that none of them was light.

"I have been happy," Bork said. "And if you let me live, I'll be happy again. That's what my life means, doesn't it? That's the truth, isn't it, dragon? My life matters because I'm alive, joy or pain, whatever comes, I'm alive and that's meaning enough. It's true, isn't it, dragon! I'm not here to fight you. I'm not here for you to kill me. I'm here to make myself alive!"

But the dragon did not answer. Bork was gently lowered to the ground. The dragon withdrew its talons and tail, and pulled its head away, and curled up on the ground, covering its eyes with its claws.

"Dragon, did you hear me?"

The dragon said nothing.

"Dragon, look at me!"

The dragon sighed. "Man, I cannot look at you."

"Why not?"

"I am blind." the dragon answered. It pulled its claws away from its eyes. Bork covered his face with his hands. The dragon's eyes were brighter than the sun.

"I feared you, Bork," the dragon whispered. "From the day you told me you were afraid, I feared you. I knew you would be back. And I knew this moment would come."

"What moment?" Bork asked.

"The moment of my death."

"Are you dying?"

"No," said the dragon. "Not yet. You must kill me."

As Bork looked at the dragon lying before him, he felt no desire for blood. "I don't want you to die."

"Don't you know that a dragon cannot live when it has met a truly honest man? It's the only way we ever die, and most dragons live forever."

But Bork refused to kill him.

The dragon cried out in anguish. "I am filled with all the truth that was discarded by men when they chose their lies and died for them. I am in constant pain, and now that I have met a man who does not add to my treasury of falsehood, you are the cruelest of them all."

And the dragon wept, and its eyes flashed and sparkled in every hot tear that fell, and finally Bork could not bear it. He took his ax and hacked off the dragon's head, and the light in its eyes went out. The eyes shriveled in their sockets until they turned into small, bright diamonds with a thousand facets each. Bork took the diamonds and put them in his pocket.

"You killed him,' Brunhilda said wonderingly.

Bork did not answer. He just untied her, and looked away while she finally fastened her gown. Then he shouldered the dragon's head and carried it back to the castle, Brunhilda running to keep up with him. He only stopped to rest at night because she begged him to. And when she tried to thank him for freeing her, he only turned away and refused to hear. He had killed the dragon because it wanted to die. Not for Brunhilda. Never for her.

At the castle they were received with rejoicing, but Bork would not go in. He only laid the dragon's head beside the moat and went to his hut, fingering the diamonds in his pocket, holding them in front of him in the pitch blackness of his hut to see that they shone with their own light, and did not need the sun or any other fire but themselves.

The King and Winkle and Brunhilda and a dozen knights came to Bork's hut. "I have come to thank you," the King said, his cheeks wet with tears of joy.

"You're welcome," Bork said. He said it as if to dismiss them.

"Bork," the King said. "Slaying the dragon was ten times as brave as the bravest thing any man has done before. You can have my daughter's hand in marriage."

Bork looked up in surprise.

"I thought you never meant to keep your promise, Your Majesty."

The King looked down, then at Winkle, then back at Bork. "Occasionally," he said, "I keep my word. So here she is, and thank you."

But Bork only smiled, fingering the diamonds in his pocket. "It's enough that you offered, Your Majesty. I don't want her. Marry her to a man she loves."

The King was puzzled. Brunhilda's beauty had not waned in her years of captivity. She had the sort of beauty that started wars. "Don't you want *any* reward?" asked the King.

Bork thought for a moment. "Yes," he said. "I want to be given a plot of ground far away from here. I don't want there to be any count, or any duke, or any king over me. And any man or woman

144

or child who comes to me will be free, and no one can pursue them. And I will never see you again, and you will never see me again."

"That's all you want?"

"That's all."

"Then you shall have it," the King said.

Bork lived all the rest of his life on his little plot of ground. People did come to him. Not many, but five or ten a year all his life, and a village grew up where no one came to take a king's tithe or a duke's fifth or a count's fourth. Children grew up who knew nothing of the art of war and never saw a knight or a battle or the terrible fear on the face of a man who knows his wounds are too deep to heal. It was everything Bork could have wanted, and he was happy all his years there.

Winkle, too, achieved everything he wanted. He married Brunhilda, and soon enough the King's sons had accidents and died, and the King died after dinner one night, and Winkle became King. He was at war all his life, and never went to sleep at night without fear of an assassin coming upon him in the darkness. He governed ruthlessly and thoroughly and was hated all his life; later generations, however, remembered him as a great King. But he was dead then, and didn't know it.

Later generations never heard of Bork.

He had only been out on his little plot of ground for a few months when the old wife came to him. "Your hut is much bigger than you need," she said. "Move over."

So Bork moved over, and she moved in.

She did not magically turn into a beautiful princess. She was foul-mouthed and nagged Bork unmercifully. But he was devoted to her, and when she died a few years later he realized that she had given him more happiness than pain, and he missed her. But the grief at her dying did not taint any of the joys of his memory of her; he just fingered the diamonds, and remembered that grief and joy were not weighed in the same scale, one making the other seem less substantial.

And at last he realized that Death was near; that Death was reaping him like wheat, eating him like bread. He imagined Death to be a dragon, devouring him bit by bit, and one night in a dream he asked Death, "Is my flavor sweet?"

Death, the old dragon, looked at him with bright and understanding eyes, and said, "Salty and sour, bitter and sweet. You sting and you soothe."

"Ah," Bork said, and was satisfied.

Death poised itself to take the last bite. "Thank you," it said.

"You're welcome," Bork answered, and he meant it.

The Princess and the Bear

I know you've seen lions. All over the place: beside the doors, flanking the throne, roaring out of the plates in the pantry, spouting water from under the eaves.

Haven't you ever wondered why the statue atop the city gates is a bear?

Many years ago in this very city, in the very palace that you can see rising granite and gray behind the old crumbly walls of the king's garden, there lived a princess. It was so long ago that who can ever remember her name? She was just the princess. These days it isn't in fashion to think that princesses are beautiful, and in fact they tend to be a bit horse-faced and gangling. But in those days it was an absolute requirement that a princess look fetching, at least when wearing the most expensive clothes available.

This princess, however, would have been beautiful dressed like a slum child or a shepherd girl. She was beautiful the moment she was born. She only got more beautiful as she grew up.

And there was also a prince. He was not her brother, though. He was the son of a king in a far-off land, and his father was the thirteenth cousin twice removed of the princess' father. The boy had been sent here to our land to get an education—because the princess' father, King Ethelred, was known far and wide as a wise man and a good king.

And if the princess was marvelously beautiful, so was the prince. He was the kind of boy that every mother wants to hug, the kind of boy who gets his hair tousled by every man that meets him.

He and the princess grew up together. They took lessons together from the teachers in the palace, and when the princess was slow, the prince would help her, and when the prince was slow, the princess would help him. They had no secrets from each other, but they had a million secrets that they two kept from the rest of the world. Secrets like where the bluebird's nest was this year, and what color underwear the cook wore, and that if you duck under the stairway to the armory there's a little underground path that comes up in the wine cellar. They speculated endlessly about which of the princess' ancestors had used that path for surreptitious imbibing.

After not too many years the princess stopped being just a little girl and the prince stopped being just a little boy, and then they fell in love. All at once all their million secrets became just one secret, and they told that secret every time they looked at each other, and everyone who saw them said, "Ah, if I were only young again." That is because so many people think that love belongs to the young: sometime during their lives they stopped loving people, and they think it was just because they got old.

The prince and the princess decided one day to get married.

But the very next morning, the prince got a letter

from the far-off country where his father lived. The letter told him that his father no longer lived at all, and that the boy was now a man; and not just a man, but a king.

So the prince got up the next morning, and the servants put his favorite books in a parcel, and his favorite clothes were packed in a trunk, and the trunk, and the parcel, and the prince were all put on a coach with bright red wheels and gold tassels at the corner and the prince was taken away.

The princess did not cry until after he was out of sight. Then she went into her room and cried for a long time, and only her nurse could come in with food and chatter and cheerfulness. At last the chatter brought smiles to the princess, and she went into her father's study where he sat by the fire at night and said, "He promised he would write, every day, and I must write every day as well.'

She did, and the prince did, and once a month a parcel of thirty letters would arrive for her, and the postrider would take away a parcel of thirty letters (heavily perfumed) from her.

And one day the Bear came to the palace. Now he wasn't a bear, of course, he was *the* Bear, with a capital B. He was probably only thirty-five or so, because his hair was still golden brown and his face was only lined around the eyes. But he was massive and grizzly, with great thick arms that looked like he could lift a horse, and great thick legs that looked like he could carry that horse a hundred miles. His eyes were deep, and they looked brightly out from under his bushy eyebrows, and the first time the nurse saw him she squealed and said, "Oh, my, he looks like a *bear*."

He came to the door of the palace and the door-man refused to let him in, because he didn't have an appointment. But he scribbled a note on a piece of paper that looked like it had held a sandwich for a few days, and the doorman—with grave misgivings—carried the paper to the king.

The paper said, "If Boris and 5,000 stood on the highway from Rimperdell, would you like to know which way they were going?"

King Ethelred wanted to know.

The doorman let the stranger into the palace, and the king brought him into his study and they talked for many hours.

In the morning the king arose early and went to his captains of cavalry and captains of infantry, and he sent a lord to the knights and their squires, and by dawn all of Ethelred's little army was gathered on the highway, the one that leads to Rimperdell. They marched for three hours that morning, and then they came to a place and the stranger with golden brown hair spoke to the king and King Ethelred commanded the army to stop. They stopped, and the infantry was sent into the forest on one side of the road, and the cavalry was sent into the tall cornfields on the other side of the road, where they dismounted. Then the king, and the stranger, and the knights waited in the road.

Soon they saw a dust cloud in the distance, and then the dust cloud grew near, and they saw that it was an army coming down the road. And at the head of the army was King Boris of Rimperdell. And behind him the army seemed to be five thousand men.

"Hail," King Ethelred said, looking more than a

little irritated, since King Boris' army was well inside our country's boundaries.

"Hail," King Boris said, looking more than a little irritated, since no one was supposed to know that he was coming.

"What do you think you're doing?" asked King Ethelred.

"You're blocking the road," said King Boris.

"It's my road," said King Ethelred.

"Not anymore," said King Boris.

"I and my knights say that this road belongs to me," said King Ethelred.

King Boris looked at Ethelred's fifty knights, and then he looked back at his own five thousand men, and he said, "I say you and your knights are dead men unless you move aside."

"Then you want to be at war with me?" asked King Ethelred.

"War?" said King Boris. "Can we really call it a war? It will be like stepping on a nasty cockroach."

"I wouldn't know," said King Ethelred, "because we haven't ever had cockroaches in our kingdom."

Then he added, "Until now, of course."

Then King Ethelred lifted his arm, and the infantry shot arrows and threw lances from the wood, and many of Boris' men were slain. And the moment all of his troops were ready to fight the army in the forest, the cavalry came from the field and attacked from the rear, and soon Boris' army, what was left of it, surrendered, and Boris himself lay mortally wounded in the road.

"If you had won this battle," King Ethelred said, "what would you have done to me?"

King Boris gasped for breath and said, "I would have had you beheaded."

"Ah," said King Ethelred. "We are very different men. For I will let you live."

But the stranger stood beside King Ethelred, and he said, "No, King Ethelred, that is not in your power, for Boris is about to die. And if he were not, I would have killed him myself, for as long as a man like him is alive, no one is safe in all the world."

Then Boris died, and he was buried in the road with no marker, and his men were sent home without their swords.

And King Ethelred came back home to crowds of people cheering the great victory, and shouting, "Long live King Ethelred the conqueror."

King Ethelred only smiled at them. Then he took the stranger into the palace, and gave him a room where he could sleep, and made him the chief counselor to the king, because the stranger had proved that he was wise, and that he was loyal, and that he loved the king better than the king loved himself, for the king would have let Boris live.

No one knew what to call the man, because when a few brave souls asked him his name, he only frowned and said, "I will wear the name you pick for me."

Many names were tried, like George, and Fred, and even Rocky and Todd. But none of the names seemed right. For a long time, everyone called him Sir, because when somebody is that big and that strong and that wise and that quiet, you feel like calling him sir and offering him your chair when he comes in the room.

And then after a while everyone called him the name the nurse had chosen for him just by accident: they called him the Bear. At first they only called him that behind his back, but eventually someone slipped and called him that at the dinner table, and he smiled, and answered to the name, and so everyone called him that.

Except the princess. She didn't call him anything, because she didn't speak to him if she could help it, and when she talked about him, she stuck out her lower lip and called him That Man.

This is because the princess hated the Bear.

She didn't hate him because he had done anything bad to her. In fact, she was pretty sure that he didn't even notice she was living in the palace. He never turned and stared when she walked into the room, like all the other men did. But that isn't why she hated him, either.

She hated him because she thought he was making her father weak.

King Ethelred was a great king, and his people loved him. He always stood very tall at ceremonies, and he sat for hours making judgments with great wisdom. He always spoke softly when softness was needed, and shouted at the times when only shouting would be heard.

In all he was a stately man, and so the princess was shocked with the way he was around the Bear.

King Ethelred and the Bear would sit for hours in the king's study, every night when there wasn't a great banquet or an ambassador. They would both drink from huge mugs of ale—but instead of having a servant refill the mugs, the princess was shocked that her own father stood up and poured from the pitcher! A king, doing the work of a servant, and then giving the mug to a commoner, a man whose name no one knew!

The princess saw this because she sat in the king's study with them, listening and watching without saying a word as they talked. Sometimes she would spend the whole time combing her father's long white hair. Sometimes she would knit long woolen stockings for her father for the winter. Sometimes she would read—for her father believed that even women should learn to read. But all the time she listened, and became angry, and hated the Bear more and more.

King Ethelred and the Bear didn't talk much about affairs of state. They talked about hunting rabbits in the forest. They told jokes about lords and ladies in the kingdom—and some of the jokes weren't even nice, the princess told herself bitterly. They talked about what they should do about the ugly carpet in the courtroom—as if the Bear had a perfect right to have an opinion abut what the new carpet should be.

And when they did talk about affairs of state, the Bear treated King Ethelred like an *equal*. When he disagreed with the king, he would leap to his feet saying, "No, no, no, no, you just don't see at all." When he thought the king had said something right, he clapped him on the shoulder and said, "You'll make a great king yet, Ethelred."

And sometimes King Ethelred would sigh and stare into the fire, and whisper a few words, and a dark and tired look would steal across his face. Then the Bear would put his arm around the king's shoulder, and stare into the fire with him, until finally the king would sigh again, and then lift himself, groaning, out of his chair, and say, "It's time that this old man put his corpse between the sheets."

The next day the princess would talk furiously to her nurse, who never told a soul what the princess said. The princess would say, "That Man is out to make my father a weakling! He's out to make my father look stupid. That Man is making my father forget that he is a king." Then she would wrinkle her forehead and say, "That Man is a traitor."

She never said a word about this to her father, however. If she had, he would have patted her head and said, "Oh, yes, he does indeed make me forget that I am a king." But he would also have said, "He makes me remember what a king should be." And Ethelred would not have called him a traitor. He would have called the Bear his friend.

As if it wasn't bad enough that her father was forgetting himself around a commoner, that was the very time that things started going bad with the prince. She suddenly noticed that the last several packets of mail had not held thirty letters each — they only held twenty, and then fifteen, and then ten. And the letters weren't five pages long anymore. They were only three, and then two, and then one.

He's just busy, she thought.

Then she noticed that he no longer began her letters with "My dearest darling sweetheart pickle-eating princess." (The pickle-eating part was an old joke from something that happened when they were both nine.) Now he started them, "My dear lady," or "Dear princess." Once she said to her nurse, "He might as well address them to Occupant."

He's just tired, she thought.

And then she realized that he never told her he loved her anymore, and she went out on the balcony and cried where only the garden could hear, and where only the birds in the trees could see.

She began to keep to her rooms, because the world didn't seem like a very nice place any more.

Why should she have anything to do with the world, when it was a nasty place where fathers turned into mere men, and lovers forgot they were in love?

And she cried herself to sleep every night that she slept. And some nights she didn't sleep at all, just stared at the ceiling trying to forget the prince. And you know that if you want to remember something, the best way is to try very, very hard to forget it.

Then one day, as she went to the door of her room, she found a basket of autumn leaves just inside her door. There was no note on them, but they were very brightly colored, and they rustled loudly when she touched the basket, and she said to herself, "It must be autumn."

She went to the window and looked, and it was autumn, and it was beautiful. She had already seen the leaves a hundred times a day, but she hadn't remembered to notice.

And then a few weeks later she woke up and it was cold in her room. Shivering, she went to her door to call for a servant to build her fire up higher — and just inside the door was a large pan, and on the pan there stood a little snowman, which was grinning a grin made of little chunks of coal, and his eyes were big pieces of coal, and all in all it was so comical the princess had to laugh. That day she forgot her misery for a while and went outside and threw snowballs at the knights, who of course let her hit them and who never managed to hit her, but of course that's all part of being a princess — no one would ever put snow down your back or dump you in the canal or anything.

She asked her nurse who brought these things, but the nurse just shook her head and smiled. "It wasn't me," she said. "Of course it was," the princess answered, and gave her a hug, and thanked her. The nurse smiled and said, "Thanks for your thanks, but it wasn't me." But the princess knew better, and loved her nurse all the more.

Then the letters stopped coming altogether. And the princess stopped writing letters. And she began taking walks in the woods.

At first she only took walks in the garden, which is where princesses are supposed to take walks. But in a few days of walking and walking and walking she knew every brick of the garden path by heart, and she kept coming to the garden wall and wishing she were outside it.

So one day she walked to the gate and went out of the garden and wandered into the forest. The forest was not at all like the garden. Where the garden was neatly tended and didn't have a weed in it, the forest was all weeds, all untrimmed and loose, with animals that ran from her, and birds that scurried to lead her away from their young, and best of all, only grass or soft brown earth under her feet. Out in the forest she could forget the garden where every tree reminded her of talks she had had with the prince while sitting in the branches. Out in the forest she could forget the palace where every room had held its own joke or its own secret or its own promise that had been broken.

That was why she was in the forest the day the wolf came out of the hills.

She was already heading back to the palace, because it was getting on toward dark, when she caught a glimpse of something moving. She looked, and realized that it was a huge gray wolf, walking along beside her not fifteen yards off. When she stopped, the wolf stopped. When she moved, the wolf moved. And the farther she walked, the closer the wolf came.

She turned and walked away from the wolf.

After a few moments she looked behind her, and saw the wolf only a dozen feet away, its mouth open, its tongue hanging out, its teeth shining white in the gloom of the late afternoon forest.

She began to run. But not even a princess can hope to outrun a wolf. She ran and ran until she could hardly breathe, and the wolf was still right behind her, panting a little but hardly tired. She ran and ran some more until her legs refused to obey her and she fell to the ground. She looked back, and realized that this was what the wolf had been waiting for—for her to be tired enough to fall, for her to be easy prey, for her to be a dinner he didn't have to work for.

And so the wolf got a gleam in its eye, and sprang forward.

Just as the wolf leaped, a huge brown shape lumbered out of the forest and stepped over the princess. She screamed. It was a huge brown bear, with heavy fur and vicious teeth. The bear swung its great hairy arm at the wolf, and struck it in the head. The wolf flew back a dozen yards, and from the way its head bobbed about as it flew, the princess realized its neck had been broken.

And then the huge bear turned toward her, and she saw with despair that she had only traded one monstrous animal for another.

And she fainted. Which is about all that a person can do when a bear that is standing five feet away looks at you. And looks hungry.

She woke up in bed at the palace and figured it had all been a dream. But then she felt a terrible pain in her legs, and felt her face stinging with scratches from the branches. It had not been a dream—she really had run through the forest.

"What happened?" she asked feebly. "Am I dead?" Which wasn't all that silly a question, because she really had expected to be.

"No," said her father, who was sitting by the bed.

"No," said the nurse. "And why in the world, why should you be dead?"

"I was in the forest," said the princess, "and there was a wolf, and I ran and ran but he was still there. And then a bear came and killed the wolf, and it came toward me like it was going to eat me, and I guess I fainted."

"Ah," said the nurse, as if that explained everything.

"Ah," said her father, King Ethelred. "Now I understand. We were taking turns watching you after we found you unconscious and scratched up by the garden gate. You kept crying out in your sleep, 'Make the bear go away! Make the bear leave me alone!' Of course, we thought you meant *the* Bear, our Bear, and we had to ask the poor man not to take his turn any more, as we thought it might make you upset. We all thought you hated him for a while there." And King Ethelred chuckled. "I'll have to tell him it was all a mistake."

Then the king left. Great, thought the princess, he's going to tell the Bear it was all a mistake, and I really do hate him to pieces.

The nurse walked over to the bed and knelt beside it. "There's another part of the story. They made me promise not to tell you," the nurse said, "but you know and I know that I'll always tell you everything. It seems that it was two guards that found

159

you, and they both said that they saw something running away. Or not running, exactly, galloping. Or something. They said it looked like a bear, running on all fours."

"Oh, no," said the princess. "How horrible!"

"No," said the nurse. "It was their opinion, and Robbo Knockle swears it's true, that the bear they saw had brought you to the gate and set you down gentle as you please. Whoever brought you there smoothed your skirt, you know, and put a pile of leaves under your head like a pillow, and you were surely in no state to do all that yourself."

"Don't be silly," said the princess. "How could a bear do all that?"

"I know," said the nurse, "so it must not have been an ordinary bear. It must have been a magic bear." She said this last in a whisper, because the nurse believed that magic should be talked about quietly, lest something awful should hear and come calling.

"Nonsense," said the princess. "I've had an education, and I don't believe in magic bears or magic brews or any kind of magic at all. It's just old-lady foolishness."

The nurse stood up and her mouth wrinkled all up. "Well, then, this foolish old lady will take her foolish stories to somebody foolish, who wants to listen."

"Oh, there, there," the princess said, for she didn't like to hurt anyone's feelings, especially not Nurse's. And they were friends again. But the princess still didn't believe about the bear. However, she hadn't been eaten, after all, so the bear must not have been hungry.

It was only two days later, when the princess was up and around again—though there were nasty scabs all over her face from the scratches—that the prince came back to the palace.

He came riding up on a lathered horse that dropped to the ground and died right in front of the palace door. He looked exhausted, and there were great purple circles under his eyes. He had no baggage. He had no cloak. Just the clothes on his back and a dead horse.

"I've come home," he said to the doorman, and fainted into his arms. (By the way, it's perfectly all right for a man to faint, as long as he has ridden on horseback for five days, without a bite to eat, and with hundreds of soldiers chasing him.)

"It's treason," he said when he woke up and ate and bathed and dressed. "My allies turned against me, even my own subjects. They drove me out of my kingdom. I'm lucky to be alive."

"Why?" asked King Ethelred.

"Because they would have killed me. If they had caught me."

"No, no, no, no, don't be stupid," said the Bear, who was listening from a chair a few feet away. "Why did they turn against you?"

The prince turned toward the Bear and sneered. It was an ugly sneer, and it twisted up the prince's face in a way it had never twisted when he lived with King Ethelred and was in love with the princess.

"I wasn't aware that I was being stupid," he said archly. "And I certainly wasn't aware that *you* had been invited into the conversation."

The Bear didn't say anything after that, just nodded an unspoken apology and watched.

And the prince never did explain why the people

had turned against him. Just something vague about power-hungry demagogues and mob rule.

The princess came to see the prince that very morning.

"You look exhausted," she said.

"You look beautiful," he said.

"I have scabs all over my face and I haven't done my hair in days," she said.

"I love you," he said.

"You stopped writing," she said.

"I guess I lost my pen," he said. "No, I remember now. I lost my mind. I forgot how beautiful you are. A man would have to be mad to forget."

Then he kissed her, and she kissed him back, and she forgave him for all the sorrow he had caused her and it was like he had never been away.

For about three days.

Because in three days she began to realize that he was different somehow.

She would open her eyes after kissing him (princesses always close their eyes when they kiss someone) and she would notice that he was looking off somewhere with a distant expression on his face. As if he barely noticed that he was kissing her. That does not make any woman, even a princess, feel very good.

She noticed that sometimes he seemed to forget she was even there. She passed him in a corridor and he wouldn't speak, and unless she touched his arm and said good morning he might have walked on by without a word.

And then sometimes, for no reason, he would feel slighted or offended, or a servant would make a noise or spill something and he would fly into a rage and throw things against the wall. He had never even raised his voice in anger when he was a boy.

He often said cruel things to the princess, and she wondered why she loved him, and what was wrong, but then he would come to her and apologize, and she would forgive him because after all he had lost a kingdom because of traitors, and he couldn't be expected to always feel sweet and nice. She decided, though, that if it was up to her, and it was, he would never feel unsweet and unnice again.

Then one night the Bear and her father went into the study and locked the door behind them. The princess had never been locked out of her father's study before, and she became angry at the Bear because he was taking her father away from her, and so she listened at the door. She figured that if the Bear wanted to keep her out, she would see to it that she heard everything anyway.

This is what she heard.

"I have information," the Bear said.

"It must be bad, or you wouldn't have asked to speak to me alone," said King Ethelred. Aha, thought the princess, the Bear *did* plot to keep me out.

The Bear stood by the fire, leaning on the mantel, while King Ethelred sat down.

"Well?" asked King Ethelred.

"I know how much the boy means to you. And to the princess. I'm sorry to bring such a tale."

The boy! thought the princess. They couldn't possibly be calling her prince a boy, could they? Why, he had been a king, except for treason, and here a commoner was calling him a boy.

"He means much to us," said King Ethelred,

"which is all the more reason for me to know the truth, be it good or bad."

"Well, then," said the Bear, "I must tell you that he was a very bad king."

The princess went white with rage.

"I think he was just too young. Or something," said the Bear. "Perhaps there was a side to him that you never saw, because the moment he had power it went to his head. He thought his kingdom was too small, because he began to make war with little neighboring counties and duchies and took their lands and made them part of his kingdom. He plotted against other kings who had been good and true friends of his father. And he kept raising taxes on his people to support huge armies. He kept starting wars and mothers kept weeping because their sons had fallen in battle.

"And finally," said the Bear, "the people had had enough, and so had the other kings, and there was a revolution and a war all at the same time. The only part of the boy's tale that is true is that he was lucky to escape with his life, because every person that I talked to spoke of him with hatred, as if he were the most evil person they had ever seen."

King Ethelred shook his head. "Could you be wrong? I can't believe this of a boy I practically raised myself."

"I wish it were not true," said the Bear, "for I know that the princess loves him dearly. But it seems obvious to me that the boy doesn't love her—he is here because he knew he would be safe here, and because he knows that if he married her, he would be able to rule when you are dead."

"Well," said King Ethelred, "that will never

happen. My daughter will never marry a man who would destroy the kingdom."

"Not even if she loves him very much?" asked the Bear.

"It is the price of being a princess," said the king. "She must think first of the kingdom, or she will never be fit to be queen."

At that moment, however, being queen was the last thing the princess cared about. All she knew was that she hated the Bear for taking away her father, and now the same man had persuaded her father to keep her from marrying the man she loved.

She beat on the door, crying out, "Liar! Liar!" King Ethelred and the Bear both leaped for the door. King Ethelred opened it, and the princess burst into the room and started hitting the Bear as hard as she could. Of course the blows fell very lightly, because she was not all that strong, and he was very large and sturdy and the blows could have caused him no pain. But as she struck at him his face looked as if he were being stabbed through the heart at every blow.

"Daughter, daughter," said King Ethelred. "What is this? Why did you listen at the door?"

But she didn't answer; she only beat at the Bear until she was crying too hard to hit him anymore. And then, between sobs, she began to yell at him. And because she didn't usually yell her voice became harsh and hoarse and she whispered. But yelling or whispering, her words were clear, and every word said hatred.

She accused the Bear of making her father little, nothing, worse than nothing, a weakling king who had to turn to a filthy commoner to make any decision at all. She accused the Bear of hating her

165

and trying to ruin her life by keeping her from marrying the only man she could ever love. She accused the Bear of being a traitor, who was plotting to be king himself and rule the kingdom. She accused the Bear of making up vile lies about the prince because she knew that he would be a better king than her weakling father, and that if she married the prince all the Bear's plans for ruling the kingdom would come to nothing.

And finally she accused the Bear of having such a filthy mind that he imagined that he could eventually marry her himself, and so become king.

But that would never happen, she whispered bitterly, at the end. "That will never happen," she said, "never, never, never, because I hate you and I loathe you and if you don't get out of this kingdom and never come back I'll kill myself, I swear it."

And then she grabbed a sword from the mantel and tried to slash her wrists, and the Bear reached out and stopped her by holding her arms in his huge hands that gripped like iron. Then she spit at him and tried to bite his fingers and beat her head against his chest until King Ethelred took her hands and the Bear let go and backed away.

"I'm sorry," King Ethelred kept saying, though he himself wasn't certain who he was apologizing to or what he was apologizing for. "I'm sorry." And then he realized that he was apologizing for himself, because somehow he knew that his kingdom was ruined right then.

If he listened to the Bear and sent the prince away, the princess would never forgive him, would hate him, in fact, and he couldn't bear that. But if he didn't listen to the Bear, then the princess would surely marry the prince, and the prince would surely ruin his kingdom. And he couldn't endure that.

But worst of all, he couldn't stand the terrible look on the Bear's face.

The princess stood sobbing in her father's arms.

The king stood wishing there were something he could do or undo.

And the Bear simply stood.

And then the Bear nodded, and said, "I understand. Good-bye."

And then the Bear walked out of the room, and out of the palace, and out of the garden walls, and out of the city, and out of any land that the king had heard of.

He took nothing with him—no food, no horse, no extra clothing. He just wore his clothing and carried his sword. He left as he came.

And the princess cried with relief. The Bear was gone. Life could go on, just like it was before ever the prince left and before ever the Bear came.

So she thought.

She didn't really realize how her father felt until he died only four months later, suddenly very old and very tired and very lonely and despairing for his kingdom.

She didn't realize that the prince was not the same man she loved before until she married him three months after her father died.

On the day of their wedding she proudly crowned him king herself, and led him to the throne, where he sat.

"I love you," she said proudly, "and you look like a king."

"I am a king," he said. "I am King Edward the first."

"Edward?" she said. "Why Edward? That's not your name."

"That's a king's name," he said, "and I am a king. Do I not have power to change my name?"

"Of course," she said. "But I liked your own name better."

"But you will call me Edward," he said, and she did.

When she saw him. For he didn't come to her very often. As soon as he wore the crown he began to keep her out of the court, and conducted the business of the kingdom where she couldn't hear. She didn't understand this, because her father had always let her attend everything and hear everything in the government, so she could be a good queen.

"A good queen," said King Edward, her husband, "is a quiet woman who has babies, one of whom will be king."

And so the princess, who was now the queen, had babies, and one of them was a boy, and she tried to help him grow up to be a king.

But as the years passed by she realized that King Edward was not the lovely boy she had loved in the garden. He was a cruel and greedy man. And she didn't like him very much.

He raised the taxes, and the people became poor.

He built up the army, so it became very strong.

He used the army to take over the land of Count Edred, who had been her godfather.

He also took over the land of Duke Adlow, who had once let her pet one of his tame swans.

He also took over the land of Earl Thlaffway, who had wept openly at her father's funeral, and said that her father was the only man he had ever worshipped, because he was such a good king.

168

And Edred and Adlow and Thlaffway all disappeared, and were never heard of again.

"He's even against the common people," the nurse grumbled one day as she did up the queen's hair. "Some shepherds came to court yesterday to tell him a marvel, which is their duty, isn't it, to tell the king of anything strange that happens in the land?"

"Yes," said the queen, remembering how as a child she and the prince had run to their father often to tell him a marvel—how grass springs up all at once in the spring, how water just disappeared on a hot day, how a butterfly comes all awkward from the cocoon.

"Well," said the nurse, "they told him that there was a bear along the edge of the forest, a bear that doesn't eat meat, but only berries and roots. And this bear, they said, killed wolves. Every year they lose dozens of sheep to the wolves, but this year they had lost not one lamb, because the bear killed the wolves. Now that's a marvel, I'd say," said the nurse.

"Oh yes," said the princess who was now a queen.

"But what did the king do," said the nurse, "but order his knights to hunt down that bear and kill it. Kill it!"

"Why?" asked the queen.

"Why, why, why?" asked the nurse. "The best question in the world. The shepherds asked it, and the king said, 'can't have a bear loose around here. He might kill children.'

" 'Oh no,' says the shepherds, 'the bear don't eat meat.'

" 'Then, it'll wind up stealing grain,' the king says in reply, and there it is, my lady—the hunters are

169

out after a perfectly harmless bear! You can bet the shepherds don't like it. A perfectly harmless bear!"

The queen nodded. "A magic bear."

"Why, yes," said the nurse. "Now you mention it, it does seem like the bear that saved you that day—"

"Nurse," said the queen, "there was no bear that day. I was dreaming I was mad with despair. There wasn't a wolf chasing me. And there was definitely no magic bear."

The nurse bit her lip. Of course there had been a bear, she thought. And a wolf. But the queen, her princess, was determined not to believe in any kind thing.

"Sure there was a bear," said the nurse.

"No, there was no bear," said the queen, "and now I know who put the idea of a magic bear into the children's head."

"They've heard of him?"

"They came to me with a silly tale of a bear that climbs over the wall into the garden when no one else is around, and who plays with them and lets them ride on his back. Obviously you told them your silly tale about the magic bear who supposedly saved me. So I told them that magic bears were a full tall-tale and that even grownups liked to tell them, but that they must be careful to remember the difference between truth and falsehood, and they should wink if they're fibbing."

"What did they say?" the nurse said.

"I made them all wink about the bear," said the queen, "of course. But I would appreciate it if you wouldn't fill their heads with silly stories. You did tell them your stupid story, didn't you?"

"Yes," said the nurse sadly.

"What a trouble your wagging tongue can cause," said the queen, and the nurse burst into tears and left the room.

They made it up later but there was no talk of bears. The nurse understood well enough, though. The thought of bears reminded the queen of *the* Bear, and everyone knew that she was the one who drove that wise counselor away. If only the Bear were still here, thought the nurse—and hundreds of other people in the kingdom—if he were still here we wouldn't have these troubles in the kingdom.

And there were troubles. The soldiers patrolled the streets of the cities and locked people up for saying things about King Edward. And when a servant in the palace did anything wrong he would bellow and storm, and even throw things and beat them with a rod.

One day when King Edward didn't like the soup he threw the whole tureen at the cook. The cook promptly took his leave, saying for anyone to hear, "I've served kings and queens, lords and ladies, soldiers, and servants, and in all that time this is the first time I've ever been called upon to serve a pig."

The day after he left he was back, at swordpoint—not cooking in the kitchen, of course, since cooks are too close to the king's food. No, the cook was sweeping the stables. And the servants were told in no uncertain terms that none of them was free to leave. If they didn't like their jobs, they could be given another one to do. And they all looked at the work the cook was doing, and kept their tongues.

Except the nurse, who talked to the queen about everything.

"We might as well be slaves," said the nurse. "Right down to the wages. He's cut us all in half,

171

some even more, and we've got barely enough to feed ourselves. I'm all right, mind you, my lady, for I have no one but me to feed, but there's some who's hard put to get a stick of wood for the fire and a morsel of bread for a hungry mouth or six."

The queen thought of pleading with her husband, but then she realized that King Edward would only punish the servants for complaining. So she began giving her nurse jewels to sell. Then the nurse quietly gave the money to the servants who had the least, or who had the largest families, and whispered to them, even though the queen had told her not to give a hint, "This money's from the queen, you know. *She* remembers us servants, even if her husband's a lout and a pimple." And the servants remembered that the queen was kind.

The people didn't hate King Edward quite as much as the servants did, of course, because even though taxes were high, there are always silly people who are proud fit to bust when their army has a victory. And of course King Edward had quite a few victories at first. He would pick a fight with a neighboring king or lord and then march in and take over. People had thought old King Boris' army of five thousand was bad, back in the old days. But because of his high taxes, King Edward was able to hire an army of fifty thousand men, and war was a different thing then. They lived off the land in enemy country, and killed and plundered where they liked. Most of the soldiers weren't local men, anyway— they were the riffraff of the highways, men who begged or stole, and now were being paid for stealing.

But King Edward tripled the size of the kingdom, and there were a good many citizens who followed

172

the war news and cheered whenever King Edward rode through the streets.

The cheered the queen, too, of course, but they didn't see her very much, about once a year or so. She was still beautiful, of course, more beautiful than ever before. No one particularly noticed that her eyes were sad these days, or else those who noticed said nothing and soon forgot it.

But King Edward's victories had been won against weak, and peaceful, and unprepared men. And at last the neighboring kings got together, and the rebels from conquered lands got together, and they planned King Edward's doom.

When next King Edward went a-conquering, they were ready, and on the very battlefield where King Ethelred had defeated Boris they ambushed King Edward's army. Edward's fifty thousand hired men faced a hundred thousand where before they had never faced more than half their number. Their bought courage melted away, and those who lived through the first of the battle ran for their lives.

King Edward was captured and brought back to the city in a cage, which was hung above the city gate, right where the statue of the bear is today.

The queen came out to the leaders of the army that had defeated King Edward and knelt before them in the dust and wept, pleading for her husband. And because she was beautiful, and good, and because they themselves were only good men trying to protect their own lives and property, they granted him his life. For her sake they even let him remain king, but they imposed a huge tribute on him. To save his own life, he agreed.

So taxes were raised even higher, in order to pay the tribute, and King Edward could only keep enough soldiers to police his kingdom, and the tribute went to paying for soldiers of the victorious kings to stay on the borders to keep watch on our land. For they figured, and rightly so, that if they let up their vigilance for a minute, King Edward would raise an army and stab them in the back.

But they didn't let up their vigilance, you see. And King Edward was trapped.

A dark evil fell upon him then, for a greedy man craves all the more the thing he can't have. And King Edward craved power. Because he couldn't have power over other kings, he began to use more power over his own kingdom, and his own household, and his own family.

He began to have prisoners tortured until they confessed to conspiracies that didn't exist, and until they denounced people who were innocent. And people in this kingdom began to lock their doors at night, and hide when someone knocked. There was fear in the kingdom, and people began to move away, until King Edward took to hunting down and beheading anyone who tried to leave the kingdom.

And it was bad in the palace, too. For the servants were beaten savagely for the slightest things, and King Edward even yelled at his own son and daughters whenever he saw them, so that the queen kept them hidden away with her most of the time.

Everyone was afraid of King Edward. And people almost always hate anyone they fear.

Except the queen. For though she feared him she remembered his youth, and she said to herself, or sometimes to the nurse, "Somewhere in that sad and ugly man there is the beautiful boy I love. Somehow I must help him find that beautiful boy and bring him out again."

But neither the nurse nor the queen could think how such a thing could possibly happen.

Until the queen discovered that she was going to have a baby. Of course, she thought. With a new baby he will remember his family and remember to love us.

So she told him. And he railed at her about how stupid she was to bring another child to see their humiliation, a royal family with enemy troops perched on the border, with no real power in the world.

And then he took her roughly by the arm into the court, where the lords and ladies were gathered, and there he told them that his wife was going to have a baby to mock him, for she still had the power of a woman, even if he didn't have the power of a man. She cried out that it wasn't true. He hit her, and she fell to the ground.

And the problem was solved, for she lost the baby before it was born and lay on her bed for days, delirious and fevered and at the point of death. No one knew that King Edward hated himself for what he had done, that he tore at his face and his hair at the thought that the queen might die because of his fury. They only saw that he was drunk all through the queen's illness, and that he never came to her bedside.

While the queen was delirious, she dreamed many times and many things. But one dream that kept coming back to her was of a wolf following her in the forest, and she ran and ran until she fell, but just as the wolf was about to eat her, a huge brown bear came and killed the wolf and flung him away, and then picked her up gently and laid her down at her father's door, carefully arranging her dress and putting leaves under her head as a pillow.

When she finally woke up, though, she only remembered that there was no magic bear that would come out of the forest to save her. Magic was for the common people—brews to cure gout and plague and to make a lady love you, spells said in the night to keep dark things from the door. Foolishness, the queen told herself. For she had an education, and knew better. There is nothing to keep the dark things from the door, there is no cure for gout and plague, and there is no brew that will make your husband love you. She told this to herself and despaired.

King Edward soon forgot his grief at the thought his wife might die. As soon as she was up and about he was as surly as ever, and he didn't stop drinking, either, even when the reason for it was gone. He just remembered that he had hurt her badly and he felt guilty, and so whenever he saw her he felt bad, and because he felt bad he treated her badly, as if it were her fault.

Things were about as bad as they could get. There were rebellions here and there all over the kingdom, and rebels were being beheaded every week. Some soldiers had even mutinied and got away over the border with the people they were supposed to stop. And so one morning King Edward was in the foulest, blackest mood he had ever been in.

The queen walked into the dining room for breakfast looking as beautiful as ever, for grief had only deepened her beauty, and made you want to cry for the pain of her exquisite face and for the suffering in her proud, straight bearing. King Edward saw that pain and suffering but even more he saw that beauty, and for a moment he remembered the girl who had grown up without a care or a sorrow or an evil thought. And he knew that he had caused every bit of the pain she bore.

So he began to find fault with her, and before he knew it he was ordering her into the kitchen to cook.

"I can't," she said.

"If a servant can, you can," he snarled in reply.

She began to cry. "I've never cooked. I've never started a fire. I'm a queen."

"You're not a queen," the king said savagely, hating himself as he said it. "You're not a queen and I'm not a king, because we're a bunch of powerless lackeys taking orders from those scum across the border! Well, if I've got to live like a servant in my own palace, so have you!"

And so he took her roughly into the kitchen and ordered her to come back in with a breakfast she had cooked herself.

The queen was shattered, but not so shattered that she could forget her pride. She spoke to the cooks cowering in the corner. "You heard the king. I must cook him breakfast with my own hands. But I don't know how. You must tell me what to do."

So they told her, and she tried her best to do what they said, but her untrained hands made a botch of everything. She burned herself at the fire and scalded herself with the porridge. She put too much salt on the bacon and there were shells left in the eggs. She also burned the muffins. And then she carried it all in to her husband and he began to eat.

And of course it was awful.

And at that moment he realized finally that the queen was a queen and could be nothing else, just as a cook had no hope of being a queen. Just so he looked at himself and realized that he could never be anything but a king. The queen, however, was a good queen—while he was a terrible king. He would always be a king but he would never be good at it. And as he chewed up the eggshells he reached the lowest despair.

Another man, hating himself as king Edward did, might have taken his own life. But that was not King Edward's way. Instead he picked up his rod and began to beat the queen. He struck her again and again, and her back bled, and she fell to the ground, screaming.

The servants came in and so did the guards, and the servants, seeing the queen treated so, tried to stop the king. But the king ordered the guards to kill anyone who tried to interfere. Even so, the chief steward, a cook, and the butler were dead before the others stopped trying.

And the king kept beating and beating the queen until everyone was sure he would beat her to death.

And in her heart as she lay on the stone floor, numb to the pain of her body because of the pain of her heart, she wished that the bear would come again, stepping over her to kill the wolf that was running forward to devour her.

At that moment the door broke in pieces and a terrible roar filled the dining hall. The king stopped beating the queen, and the guards and the servants looked at the door, for there stood a huge brown bear on its hind legs, towering over them all, and roaring in fury.

The servants ran from the room.

"Kill him," the king bellowed at the guards.

The guards drew their swords and advanced on the bear.

The bear disarmed them all, though there were so many that some drew blood before their swords were slapped out of their hands. Some of them might even have tried to fight the bear without weapons, because they were brave men, but the bear struck them on the head, and the rest fled away.

Yet the queen, dazed though she was, thought that for some reason the bear had not struck yet with all his force, that the huge animal was saving his strength for another battle.

And that battle was with King Edward, who stood with his sharp sword in his hand, eager for battle, hoping to die, with the desperation and self-hatred in him that would make him a terrible opponent, even for a bear.

A bear, thought the queen. I wished for a bear and he is here.

Then she lay, weak and helpless and bleeding on the stone floor as her husband, her prince, fought the bear. She did not know who she hoped would win. For even now, she did not hate her husband. And yet she knew that her life and the lives of her subjects would be unendurable as long as he lived.

They circled around the room, the bear moving clumsily yet quickly, King Edward moving faster still, his blade whipping steel circles through the air. Three times the blade landed hard and deep on the bear, before the animal seized the blade between his paws. King Edward tried to draw back the sword, and as he did it bit deeply into the animal's paws. But it was a battle of strength, and the bear was sure to win it in the end. He pulled the sword out of Edward's hand, and then grasped the king in a mighty embrace and carried him screaming from the room.

And at that last moment, as Edward tugged hopelessly at his sword and blood poured from the bear's paws, the queen found herself hoping that the bear would hold on, would take away the sword, that the bear would win out and free the kingdom—her kingdom—and her family and even herself, from the man who had been devouring them all.

Yet when King Edward screamed in the bear's grip, she heard only the voice of the boy in the garden in the eternal and too-quick summer of his childhood. She fainted with a dim memory of his smile dancing crazily before her eyes.

She awoke as she had awakened once before, thinking that it had been a dream, and then remembering the truth of it when the pain where her husband had beaten her nearly made her fall unconscious again. But she fought the faintness and stayed awake, and asked for water.

The nurse brought water, and then several lords of high rank and the captain of the army and the chief servants came in and asked her what they should do.

"Why do you ask me?" she said.

"Because," the nurse answered her, "the king is dead."

The queen waited.

"The bear left him at the gate," the captain of the army said.

"His neck was broken," the chief said.

"And now," one of the lords said, "now we must know what to do. We haven't even told the people, and no one has been allowed inside or outside the palace."

The queen thought, and closed her eyes as she did so. But what she saw when she closed her eyes was the body of her beautiful prince with his head loose as the wolf's had been that day in the forest. She did not want to see that, so she opened her eyes.

"You must proclaim that the king is dead throughout the land," she said.

To the captain of the army she said, "There will be no more beheading for treason. Anyone who is in prison for treason is to be set free, now. And any other prisoners whose terms are soon to expire should be set free at once."

The captain of the army bowed and left. He did not smile until he was out the door, but then he smiled until tears ran down his cheeks.

To the chief cook she said, "All the servants in the palace are free to leave now, if they want. But please ask them, in my name, to stay. I will restore them as they were, if they'll stay."

The cook started a heartfelt speech of thanks, but then thought better of it and left the room to tell the others.

To the lords she said, "Go to the kings whose armies guard our borders, and tell them that King Edward is dead and they can go home now. Tell them that if I need their help I will call on them, but that until I do I will govern my kingdom alone."

And the lords came and kissed her hands tenderly, and left the room.

And she was alone with the nurse.

"I'm so sorry," said the nurse, when enough silence had passed.

"For what?" asked the queen.

"For the death of your husband."

"Ah, that," said the queen. "Ah, yes, my husband."

And then the queen wept with all her heart. Not for the cruel and greedy man who had warred and killed and savaged everywhere he could. But for the boy who had somehow turned into that man, the boy whose gentle hand had comforted her childhood hurts, the boy whose frightened voice had cried out to her at the end of his life, as if he wondered why he had gotten lost inside himself, as if he realized that it was too, too late to get out again.

When she had done weeping that day, she never cried for him again.

In three days she was up again, though she had to wear loose clothing because of the pain. She held court anyway, and it was then that the shepherds brought her the Bear. Not the bear, the animal, that had killed the king, but *the* Bear, the counselor, who had left the kingdom so many years before.

"We found him on the hillside, with our sheep nosing him and lapping his face," the oldest of the shepherds told her. "Looks like he's been set on by robbers, he's cut and battered so. Miracle he's alive," he said.

"What is that he's wearing?" asked the queen, standing by the bed where she had had the servants lay him.

"Oh, said one of the other shepherds. "That's me cloak. They left him nekkid, but we didn't think it right to bring him before you in such a state."

She thanked the shepherds and offered to pay them a reward, but they said no thanks, explaining, "We remember him, we do, and it wouldn't be right to take money for helping him, don't you see, because he was a good man back in your father's day."

The queen had the servants—who had all stayed on, by the way—clean his wounds and bind them and tend to his wants. And because he was a strong man, he lived, though the wounds might have killed a smaller, weaker man. Even so, he never got back the use of his right hand, and had to learn to write with his left; and he limped ever after. But he often said he was lucky to be alive and wasn't ashamed of his infirmities, though he sometimes said that something ought to be done about the robbers who run loose in the hills.

As soon as he was able, the queen had him attend court, where he listened to the ambassadors from other lands and to the cases she heard and judged.

Then at night she had him come to King Ethelred's study, and there she asked him about the questions of that day and what he would have done differently, and he told her what he thought she did well, too. And so she learned from him as her father had learned.

One day she even said to him, "I have never asked forgiveness of any man in my life. But I ask for yours."

"For what?" he said, surprised.

"For hating you, and thinking you served me and my father badly, and driving you from this kingdom. If we had listened to you," she said, "none of this would have happened."

"Oh," he said, "all that's past. You were young, and in love, and that's as inevitable as fate itself."

"I know," she said, "and for love I'd probably do it again, but now that I'm wiser I can still ask for forgiveness for my youth."

The Bear smiled at her. "You were forgiven before you asked. But since you ask I gladly forgive you again."

"Is there any reward I can give you for your service so many years ago, when you left unthanked?" she asked.

"Yes," he answered. "If you could let me stay and serve you as I served your father, that would be reward enough."

"How can that be a reward?" she asked. "I was going to ask you to do that for *me*. And now you ask it for yourself."

"Let us say," said the Bear, "that I loved your father like my brother, and you like my niece, and I long to stay with the only family that I have."

Then the queen took the pitcher and poured him a mug of ale, and they sat by the fire and talked far into the night.

Because the queen was a widow, because despite the problems of the past the kingdom was large and rich, many suitors came asking for her hand. Some were dukes, some were earls, and some were kings or sons of kings. And she was as beautiful as ever, only in her thirties, a prize herself even if there had been no kingdom to covet.

But though she considered long and hard over some of them, and even liked several men who came, she turned them all down and sent them all away.

And she reigned alone, as queen, with the Bear to advise her.

And she also did what her husband had told her a queen should do—she raised her son to be king and her daughters to be worthy to be queens. And the Bear helped her with that, too, teaching her son to hunt, and teaching him how to see beyond men's words into their hearts, and teaching him to love peace and serve the people.

And the boy grew up as beautiful as his father and as wise as the Bear, and the people knew he would be a great king, perhaps even greater than King Ethelred had been.

The queen grew old, and turned much of the matter of the kingdom over to her son, who was now a man. The prince married the daughter of a neighboring king. She was a good woman, and the queen saw her grandchildren growing up.

She knew perfectly well that she was old, because she was sagging and no longer beautiful as she had been in her youth—though there were many who said that she was far more lovely as an old lady than any mere girl could hope to be.

But somehow it never occurred to her that the Bear, too, was growing old. Didn't he still stride through the garden with one of her grandchildren on each shoulder? Didn't he still come into the study with her and her son and teach them statecraft and tell them, yes, that's good, yes, that's right, yes, you'll make a great queen yet, yes, you'll be a fine king, worthy of your grandfather's kingdom—didn't he?

Yet one day he didn't get up from his bed, and a servant came to her with a whispered message, "Please come."

She went to him and found him gray-faced and shaking in his bed.

"Thirty years ago," he said, "I would have said it's nothing but a fever and I would have ignored it and gone riding. But now, my lady, I know I'm going to die."

"Nonsense," she said, "You'll never die," knowing as well as he did that he was dying, and knowing that he knew that she knew it.

"I have a confession to make," he said to her.

"I know it already," she said.

"Do you?"

"Yes," she said softly, "and much to my surprise, I find that I love you too. Even an old lady like me," she said, laughing.

"Oh," he said, "that was not my confession. I already knew that you knew I loved you. Why else would I have come back when you called?"

And then she felt a chill in the room and remembered the only time she had ever called for help.

"Yes," he said, "you remember. How I laughed when they named me. If they only knew, I thought at the time."

She shook her head. "How could it be?"

"I wondered myself," he said. "But it is. I met a wise old man in the woods when I was but a lad. An orphan, too, so that there was no one to ask about me when I stayed with him. I stayed until he died five years later, and I learned all his magic."

"There's no magic," she said as if by rote, and he laughed.

"If you mean brews and spells and curses, then you're right," he said. "But there is magic of another sort. The magic of becoming what most you are. My old man in the woods, his magic was to be an owl, and to fly by night seeing the world and coming to understand it. The owlness was in him, and the magic was letting that part of himself that was most himself come forward. And he taught me."

The Bear had stopped shaking because his body had given up trying to overcome the illness.

"So I looked inside me and wondered who I was. And then I found it out. Your nurse found it, too. One glance and she knew I was a bear."

186

"You killed my husband," she said to him.

"No," he said. "I fought your husband and carried him from the palace, but as he stared death in the face he discovered, too, what he was and who he was, and his real self came out."

The Bear shook his head.

"I killed a wolf at the palace gate, and left a wolf with a broken neck behind when I went away into the hills."

"A wolf both times," she said. "But he was such a beautiful boy."

"A puppy is cute enough whatever he plans to grow up to be," said the Bear.

"And what am I?" asked the queen.

"You?" asked the Bear. "Don't you know?"

"No," she answered. "Am I a swan? A porcupine? These days I walk like a crippled, old biddy hen. Who am I, after all these years? What animal should I turn into by night?"

"You're laughing," said the Bear, "and I would laugh too, but I have to be stingy with my breath. I don't know what animal you are, if you don't know yourself, but I think—"

And he stopped talking and his body shook in a great heave.

"No!" cried the queen.

"All right," said the Bear. "I'm not dead yet. I think that deep down inside you, you are a woman, and so you have been wearing your real self out in the open all your life. And you are beautiful."

"What an old fool you are after all," said the queen. "Why didn't I ever marry you?"

"Your judgment was too good," said the Bear.

But the queen called the priest and her children and married the Bear on his deathbed, and her son who had learned kingship from him called him father, and then they remembered the bear who had come to play with them in their childhood and the queen's daughters called him father; and the queen called him husband, and the Bear laughed and allowed as how he wasn't an orphan any more. Then he died.

And that's why there's a statue of a bear over the gate of the city.

Sandmagic

The great domes of the city of Gyree dazzled blue
and red when the sun shone through a break in the
clouds, and for a moment Cer Cemreet thought he
saw some of the glory the uncles talked about in the
late night tales of the old days of Greet. But the
capital did not look dazzling up close, Cer remembered bitterly. Now dogs ran in the streets and rats
lived in the wreckage of the palace, and the King of
Greet lived in New Gyree in the hills far to the
north, where the armies of the enemy could not go.
Yet.

The sun went back behind a cloud and the city
looked dark again. A Nefyr patrol was riding briskly
on the Hetterwee Road far to the north. Cer turned
his gaze to the lush grass on the hill where he sat.
The clouds meant rain, but probably not here, he
thought. He always thought of something else when
he saw a Nefyr patrol. Yes, it was too early in
Hrickan for rains to fall here. This rain would fall
in the north, perhaps in the land of the King of the
High Mountains, or on the vast plain of Westwold
where they said horses ran free but were tame for
any man to ride at need. But no rain would fall in
Greet until Doonse, three weeks from now. By then

the wheat would all be stored and the hay would be piled in vast ricks as tall as the hill Cer sat on.

In the old days, they said, all during Doonse the great wagons from Westwold would come and carry off the hay to last them through the snow season. But not now, Cer remembered. This year and last year and the year before the wagons had come from the south and east, two-wheeled wagons with drivers who spoke, not High Westil, but the barbarian Fyrd language. Fyrd or firt, thought Cer, and laughed, for firt was a word he could not say in front of his parents. They spoke firt.

Cer looked out over the plain again. The Nefyr patrol had turned from the highway and were on the road to the hills.

The road to the hills. Cer leaped to his feet and raced down the track leading home. A patrol heading for the hills could only mean trouble.

He stopped to rest only once, when the pain in his side was too bad to bear. But the patrol had horses, and he arrived home only to see the horses of the Nefyrre gathered at his father's gate.

Where are the uncles? Cer thought. The uncles must come.

But the uncles were not there, and Cer heard a terrible scream from inside the garden walls. He had never heard his mother scream before, but somehow he knew it was his mother, and he ran to the gate. A Nefyr soldier seized him and called out, "Here's the boy!" in a thick accent of High Westil, so that Cer's parents could understand. Cer's mother screamed again, and now Cer saw why.

His father had been stripped naked, his arms and legs held by two tall Nefyrre. The Nefyr captain held his viciously curved short-sword, point up, pressing

190

against Cer's father's hard-muscled stomach. As Cer and his mother watched, the sword drew blood, and the captain pushed it in to the hilt, then pulled it up to the ribs. Blood gushed. The captain had been careful not to touch the heart, and now they thrust a spear into the huge wound, and lifted it high, Cer's father dangling from the end. They lashed the spear to the gatepost, and the blood and bowels stained the gates and the walls.

For five minutes more Cer's father lived, his chest heaving in the agony of breath. He may have died of pain, but Cer did not think so, for his father was not the kind to give in to pain. He may have died of suffocation, for one lung was gone and every breath was excruciating, but Cer did not think so, for his father kept breathing to the end. It was loss of blood, Cer decided, weeks later. It was when his body was dry, when the veins collapsed, that Cer's father died.

He never uttered a sound. Cer's father would never let the Nefyrre hear him so much as sigh in pain.

Cer's mother screamed and screamed until blood came from her mouth and she fainted.

Cer stood in silence until his father died. Then when the captain, a smirk on his face, walked near Cer and looked in his face, Cer kicked him in the groin.

They cut off Cer's great toes, but like his father, Cer made no sound.

Then the Nefyrre left and the uncles came.

Uncle Forwin vomited. Uncle Erwin wept. Uncle Crune put his arm around Cer's shoulder as the servants bound his maimed feet and said, "Your father was a great, a brave man. He killed many

191

Nefyrre, and burned many wagons. But the Nefyrre are strong."

Uncle Crune squeezed Cer's shoulder. "Your father was stronger. But he was one, and they were many."

Cer looked away.

"Will you not look at your uncle?" Uncle Crune asked.

"My father," Cer said, "did not think that he was alone."

Uncle Crune got up and walked away. Cer never saw the uncles again.

He and his mother had to leave the house and the fields, for a Nefyr farmer had been given the land to farm for the King of Nefyryd. With no money, they had to move south, across the River Greebeck into the drylands near the desert, where no rivers flowed and so only the hardiest plants lived. They lived the winter on the charity of the desperately poor. In the summer, when the heat came, so did the Poor Plague which swept the drylands. The cure was fresh fruits, but fresh fruits came from Yffyrd and Suffyrd and only the rich could buy them, and the poor died by the thousands. Cer's mother was one of them.

They took her out on the sand to burn her body and free her spirit. As they painted her with tar (tar, at least, cost nothing, if a man had a bucket), five horsemen came to the brow of a dune to watch. At first Cer thought they were Nefyrre, but no. The poor people looked up and saluted the strangers, which Greetmen never do the enemy. These, then, were desert men, the Abadapnur nomads, who raided the rich farms of Greet during dry years, but who never harmed the poor.

We hated them, Cer thought, when we were rich. But now we are poor, and they are our friends.

His mother burned as the sun set.

Cer watched until the flames went out. The moon was high for the second time that night. Cer said a prayer to the moonlady over his mother's bones and ashes and then he turned and left.

He stopped at their hut and gathered the little food they had, and put on his father's tin ring, which the Nefyrre had thought was valueless, but which Cer knew was the sign of the Cemreet family's authority since forever ago.

Then Cer walked north.

He lived by killing rats in barns and cooking them. He lived by begging at poor farmers' doors, for the rich farmers had servants to turn away beggars. That, at least, Cer remembered, his father had never done. Beggars always had a meal at his father's house.

Cer also lived by stealing when he could hunt or beg no food. He stole handfuls of raw wheat. He stole carrots from gardens. He stole water from wells, for which he could have lost his life in this rainless season. He stole, one time, a fruit from a rich man's food wagon.

It burned his mouth, it was so cold and the acid so strong. It dribbled down his chin. As a poor man and a thief, Cer thought, I now eat a thing so dear that even my father, who was called wealthy, could never buy it.

And at last he saw the mountains in the north. He walked on, and in a week the mountains were great cliffs and steep slopes of shale. The Mitherkame, where the king of the High Mountains reigned, and Cer began to climb.

He climbed all one day and slept in a cleft of a rock. He moved slowly, for climbing in sandals was clumsy, and without his great toes Cer could not climb barefoot. The next morning he climbed more. Though he nearly fell one time when falling would have meant crashing a mile down onto the distant plain, at last he reached the knifelike top of the Mitherkame, and heaven.

For of a sudden the stone gave way to soil. Not the pale sandy soil of the drylands, nor the red soil of Greet, but the dark black soil of the old songs from the north, the soil that could not be left alone for a day or it would sprout plants that in a week would be a forest.

And there *was* a forest, and the ground was thick with grass. Cer had seen only a few trees in his life, and they had been olive trees, short and gnarled, and fig sycamores, that were three times the height of a man. These were twenty times the height of a man and ten steps around, and the young trees shot up straight and tall so that not a sapling was as small as Cer, who for twelve years old was not considered small.

To Cer, who had known only wheat and hay and olive orchards, the forest was more magnificent than the mountain or the city or the river or the moon.

He slept under a huge tree. He was very cold that night. And in the morning he realized that in a forest he would find no farms, and where there were no farms there was no food for him. He got up and walked deeper into the forest. There were people in the High Mountains, else there would be no king, and Cer would find them. If he didn't, he would die. But at least he would not die in the realms of the Nefyrre.

He passed many bushes with edible berries, but he did not know they could be eaten so he did not eat. He passed many streams with slow stupid fish that he could have caught, but in Greet fish was never eaten, because it always carried disease, and so Cer caught no fish.

And on the third day, when he began to feel so weak from hunger that he could walk no longer, he met the treemage.

He met him because it was the coldest night yet, and at last Cer tore branches from a tree to make a fire. But the wood did not light, and when Cer looked up he saw that the trees had moved. They were coming closer, surrounding him tightly. He watched them, and they did not move as he watched, but when he turned around the ones he had not been watching were closer yet. He tried to run, but the low branches made a tight fence he could not get through. He couldn't climb, either, because the branches all stabbed downward. Bleeding from the twigs he had scraped, Cer went back to his camping place and watched as the trees at last made a solid wall around him.

And he waited. What else could he do in his wooden prison?

In the morning he heard a man singing, and he called for help.

"Oh ho," he heard a voice say in a strange accent. "Oh ho, a tree cutter and a firemaker, a branch killer and a forest hater."

"I'm none of those," Cer said. "It was cold, and I tried to build a fire only to keep warm."

"A fire, a fire," the voice said. "In this small part of the world there are no fires of wood. But that's

195

a young voice I hear, and I doubt there's a beard beneath the words."

"I have no beard," Cer answered, "I have no weapon, except a knife too small to harm you."

"A knife? A knife that tears sap from living limbs, Redwood says. A knife that cuts twigs like soft man-fingers, says Elm. A knife that stabs bark till it bleeds, says Sweet Aspen. Break your knife," said the voice outside the trees, "and I will open your prison."

"But it's my only knife," Cer protested, "and I need it."

"You need it here like you need fog on a dark night. Break it or you'll die before these trees move again."

Cer broke his knife.

Behind him he heard a sound, and he turned to see a fat old man standing in a clear space between the trees. A moment before there had been no clear space.

"A child," said the man.

"A fat old man," said Cer, angry at being considered as young as his years.

"An illbred child at that," said the man. "But perhaps he knows no better, for from the accent of his speech I would say he comes from Greetland, and from his clothing I would say he was poor, and it's well known in Mitherwee that there are no manners in Greet."

Cer snatched up the blade of his knife and ran at the man. Somehow there were many sharp-pointed branches in the way, and his hand ran into a hard limb, knocking the blade to the ground.

"Oh, my child," said the man kindly. "There is death in your heart."

The branches were gone, and the man reached out his hands and touched Cer's face. Cer jerked away.

"And the touch of a man brings pain to you." The man sighed. "How inside out your world must be."

Cer looked at the man coldly. He could endure taunting. But was that kindness in the old man's eyes?

"You look hungry," said the old man.

Cer said nothing.

"If you care to follow me, you may. I have food for you, if you like."

Cer followed him.

They went through the forest, and Cer noticed that the old man stopped to touch many of the trees. And a few he pointedly snubbed, turning his back or taking a wider route around them. Once he stopped and spoke to a tree that had lost a large limb—recently, too, Cer thought, because the tar on the stump was still soft. "Soon there'll be no pain at all," the old man said to the tree. Then the old man sighed again. "Ah, yes, I know. And many a walnut in the falling season."

Then they reached a house. If it could be called a house, Cer thought. Stones were the walls, which was common enough in Greet, but the roof was living wood—thick branches from nine tall trees, interwoven and heavily leaved, so that Cer was sure no drop of rain could ever come inside.

"You admire my roof?" the old man asked. "So tight that even in the winter, when the leaves are gone, the snow cannot come in. But *we* can," he said, and led the way through a low door into a single room.

The old man kept up a constant chatter as he fixed

breakfast: berries and cream, stewed acorns, and thick slices of cornbread. The old man named all the foods for Cer, because except for the cream it was all strange to him. But it was good, and it filled him.

"Acorn from the Oaks," said the old man. "Walnuts from the trees of that name. And berries from the bushes, the neartrees. Corn, of course, comes from an untree, a weak plant with no wood, which dies every year."

"The trees don't die every year, then, even though it snows?" Cer asked, for he had heard of snow.

"Their leaves turn bright colors, and then they fall, and perhaps that's a kind of death," said the old man. "But in Eanan the snow melts and by Blowan there are leaves again on all the trees."

Cer did not believe him, but he didn't disbelieve him either. Trees were strange things.

"I never knew that trees in the High Mountains could move."

"Oh ho," laughed the old man. "And neither can they, except here, and other woods that a treemage tends."

"A treemage? Is there magic then?"

"Magic. Oh ho," the man laughed again. "Ah yes, magic, many magics, and mine is the magic of trees."

Cer squinted. The man did not look like a man of power, and yet the trees had penned an intruder in. "You rule the trees here?"

"Rule?" the old man asked, startled. "What a thought. Indeed no. I serve them. I protect them. I give them the power in me, and they give me the power in them, and it makes us all a good deal more powerful. But rule? That just doesn't enter into magic. What a thought."

198

Then the old man chattered about the doings of the silly squirrels this year, and when Cer was through eating the old man gave him a bucket and they spent the morning gathering berries. "Leave a berry on the bush for every one you pick," the old man said. "They're for the birds in the fall and for the soil in the Kamesun, when new bushes grow."

And so Cer, quite accidentally, began his life with the treemage, and it was as happy a time as Cer ever had in his life, except when he was a child and his mother sang to him and except for the time his father took him hunting deer in the hills of Wetfell.

And after the autumn when Cer marveled at the colors of the leaves, and after the winter when Cer tramped through the snow with the treemage to tend to ice-splintered branches, and after the spring when Cer thinned the new plants so the forest did not become overgrown, the treemage began to think that the dark places in Cer's heart were filled with light, or at least put away where they could not be found.

He was wrong.

For as he gathered leaves for the winter's fires Cer dreamed he was gathering the bones of his enemies. And as he tramped the snow he dreamed he was marching into battle to wreak death on the Nefyrre. And as he thinned the treestarts Cer dreamed of slaying each of the uncles as his father had been slain, because none of them had stood by him in his danger.

Cer dreamed of vengeance, and his heart grew darker even as the wood was filled with the bright light of the summer sun.

One day he said to the treemage, "I want to learn magic."

The treemage smiled with hope. "You're learning it," he said, "and I'll gladly teach you more."

"I want to learn things of power."

"Ah," said the treemage, disappointed. "Ah, then, you can have no magic."

"You have power," said Cer. "I want it also."

"Oh, indeed," said the treemage. "I have the power of two legs and two arms, the power to heat tar over a peat fire to stop the sap flow from broken limbs, the power to cut off diseased branches to save the tree, the power to teach the trees how and when to protect themselves. All the rest is the power of the trees, and none of it is mine."

"But they do your bidding," said Cer.

"Because I do theirs!" the treemage said, suddenly angry. "Do you think that there is slavery in this wood? Do you think I am a king? Only men allow men to rule them. Here in this wood there is only love, and on that love and by that love the trees and I have the magic of the wood."

Cer looked down, disappointed. The treemage misunderstood, and thought that Cer was contrite.

"Ah, my boy," said the treemage. "You haven't learned it, I see. The root of magic is love, the trunk is service. The treemages love the trees and serve them and then they share treemagic with the trees. Lightmages love the sun and make fires at night, and the fire serves them as they serve the fire. Horsemages love and serve horses, and they ride freely whither they will because of the magic in the herd. There is field magic and plain magic, and the magic of rocks and metals, songs and dances, the magic of winds and weathers. All built on love, all growing through service."

"I must have magic," said Cer.

200

"Must you?" asked the treemage. "Must you have magic? There are kinds of magic, then, that you might have. But I can't teach them to you."

"What are they?"

"No," said the treemage, and he wouldn't speak again.

Cer thought and thought. What magic could be demanded against anyone's will?

And at last, when he had badgered and nagged the treemage for weeks, the treemage angrily gave in. "Will you know then?" the treemage snapped. "I will tell you. There is seamagic, where the wicked sailors serve the monsters of the deep by feeding them living flesh. Would you do that?" But Cer only waited for more.

"So that appeals to you," said the treemage. "Then you will be delighted at desert magic."

And now Cer saw a magic he might use. "How is that performed?"

"*I* know not," said the treemage icily. "It is the blackest of the magics to men of *my* kind, though your dark heart might leap to it. There's only one magic darker."

"And what is that?" asked Cer.

"What a fool I was to take you in," said the treemage. "The wounds in your heart, you don't want them to heal; you love to pick at them and let them fester."

"What is the darkest magic?" demanded Cer.

"The darkest magic," said the treemage, "is one, thank the moon, that you can never practice. For to do it you have to love men and love the love of men more than your own life. And love is as far from you as the sea is from the mountains, as the earth is from the sky."

201

"The sky touches the earth," said Cer.

"Touches, but never do they meet," said the tree-mage.

Then the treemage handed Cer a basket, which he had just filled with bread and berries and a flagon of streamwater. "Now go."

"Go?" asked Cer.

"I hoped to cure you, but you won't have a cure. You clutch at your suffering too much to be healed."

Cer reached out his foot toward the treemage, the crusty scars still a deep red where his great toe had been.

"As well you might try to restore my foot."

"Restore?" asked the treemage. "I restore nothing. But I staunch, and heal, and I help the trees forget their lost limbs. For if they insist on rushing sap to the limb as if it were still there, they lose all their sap; they dry, they wither, they die."

Cer took the basket.

"Thank you for your kindness," said Cer. "I'm sorry that you don't understand. But just as the tree can never forgive the ax or the flame, there are those that must die before I can truly live again."

"Get out of my wood," said the treemage. "Such darkness has no place here."

And Cer left, and in three days came to the edge of the Mitherkame, and in two days reached the bottom of the cliffs, and in a few weeks reached the desert. For he would learn desertmagic. He would serve the sand, and the sand would serve him.

On the way the soldiers of Nefyryd stopped him and searched him. When they saw that he had no great toes, they beat him and shaved off his young and scraggly beard and sent him on his way with a kick.

Cer even stopped where his father's farm had been. Now all the farms were farmed by Nefyrre, men of the south who had never owned land before. They drove him away, afraid that he might steal. So he snuck back in the night and from his father's storehouse stole meat and from his father's barn stole a chicken.

He crossed the Greebeck to the drylands and gave the meat and the chicken to the poor people there. He lived with them for a few days. And then he went out into the desert.

He wandered in the desert for a week before he ran out of food and water. He tried everything to find the desertmagic. He spoke to the hot sand and the burning rocks as the treemage had spoken to the trees. But the sand was never injured and did not need a healing touch, and the rocks could not be harmed and so they needed no protection. There was no answer when Cer talked, except the wind which cast sand in his eyes. And at last Cer lay dying on the sand, his skin caked and chafed and burnt, his clothing long since tattered away into nothing, his flagon burning hot and filled with sand, his eyes blind from the whiteness of the desert.

He could neither love nor serve the desert, for the desert needed nothing from him and there was neither beauty nor kindness to love.

But he refused to die without having vengeance. Refused to die so long that he was still alive when the Abadapnu tribesmen found him. They gave him water and nursed him back to health. It took weeks, and they had to carry him on a sledge from water-hole to waterhole.

And as they traveled with their herds and their

horses, the Abadapnur carried Cer farther and farther away from the Nefyrre and the land of Greet.

Cer regained his senses slowly, and learned the Abadapnu language even more slowly. But at last, as the clouds began to gather for the winter rains, Cer was one of the tribe, considered a man because he had a beard, considered wise because of the dark look on his face that remained even on those rare times when he laughed.

He never spoke of his past, though the Abadapnur knew well enough what the tin ring on his finger meant and why he had only eight toes. And they, with the perfect courtesy of the incurious, asked him nothing.

He learned their ways. He learned that starving on the desert was foolish, that dying of thirst was unnecessary. He learned how to trick the desert into yielding up life. "For," said the tribemaster, "the desert is never willing that anything should live."

Cer remembered that. The desert wanted nothing to live. And he wondered if that was a key to desert-magic. Or was it merely a locked door that he could never open? How can you serve and be served by the sand that wants only your death? How could he get vengeance if he was dead? "Though I would gladly die if my dying could kill my father's killers," he said to his horse one day. The horse hung her head, and would only walk for the rest of the day, though Cer kicked her to try to make her run.

Finally one day, impatient that he was doing nothing to achieve his revenge, Cer went to the tribemaster and asked him how one learned the magic of the sand.

"Sandmagic? You're mad," said the tribemaster. For days the tribemaster refused to look at him, let alone answer his questions, and Cer realized that here on the desert the sandmagic was hated as badly as the treemage hated it. Why? Wouldn't such power make the Abadapnur great?

Or did the tribemaster refuse to speak because the Abadapnur did not know the sandmagic?

But they knew it.

And one day the tribemaster came to Cer and told him to mount and follow.

They rode in the early morning before the sun was high, then slept in a cave in a rocky hill during the heat of the day. In the dusk they rode again, and at night they came to the city.

"Ettuie," whispered the tribemaster, and then they rode their horses to the edge of the ruins.

The sand had buried the buildings up to half their height, inside and out, and even now the breezes of evening stirred the sand and built little dunes against the walls. The buildings were made of stone, rising not to domes like the great cities of the Greetmen but to spires, tall towers that seemed to pierce the sky.

"Ikikietar," whispered the tribemaster, "Ikikiaiai re dapii. O ikikiai etetur o abadapnur, ikikiai re dapii."

"What are the 'knives'?" asked Cer. "And how could the sand kill them?"

"The knives are these towers, but they are also the stars of power."

"What power?" asked Cer eagerly.

"No power for you. Only power for the Etetur, for they were wise. They had the manmagic."

Manmagic. Was that the darkest magic spoken of by the treemage?

"Is there a magic more powerful than manmagic?" Cer asked.

"In the mountains, no," said the tribemaster. "On the well-watered plain, in the forest, on the sea, no."

"But in the desert?"

"A huu par eiti ununura," muttered the tribemaster, making the sign against death. "Only the desert power. Only the magic of the sand."

"I want to know," said Cer.

"Once," the tribemaster said, "once there was a mighty empire here. Once a great river flowed here, and rain fell, and the soil was rich and red like the soil of Greet, and a million people lived under the rule of the King of Ettue Dappa. But not all, for far to the west there lived a few who hated Ettue and the manmagic of the kings, and they forged the tool that undid this city.

"They made the wind blow from the desert. They made the rains run off the earth. By their power the river sank into the desert sand, and the fields bore no fruit, and at last the King of Ettue surrendered, and half his kingdom was given to the sandmages. To the dapinur. That western kingdom became Dapnu Dap."

"A kingdom?" said Cer, surprised. "But now the great desert bears that name."

"And once the great desert was no desert, but a land of grasses and grains like your homeland to the north. The sandmages weren't content with half a kingdom, and they used their sandmagic to make a desert of Ettue, and they covered the lands of rebels with sand, until at last the victory of the desert was complete, and Ettue fell to the armies of Greet and Nefyryd—they were allies then—and we of Dapnu

Dap became nomads, living off that tiny bit of life that even the harshest desert cannot help but yield."

"And what of the sandmages?" asked Cer.

"We killed them."

"All?"

"All," said the tribemaster. "And if any man will practice sandmagic, today, we will kill him. For what happened to us we will let happen to no other people."

Cer saw the knife in the tribemaster's hand.

"I will have your vow," said the tribemaster. "Swear before these stars and this sand and the ghosts of all who lived in this city that you will seek no sandmagic."

"I swear," said Cer, and the tribemaster put his knife away.

The next day Cer took his horse and a bow and arrows and all the food he could steal and in the heat of the day when everyone slept he went out into the desert. They followed him, but he slew two with arrows and the survivors lost his trail.

Word spread through the tribes of the Abadapnur that a would-be sandmage was loose in the desert, and all were ready to kill him if he came. But he did not come.

For he knew now how to serve the desert, and how to make the desert serve him. For the desert loved death, and hated grasses and trees and water and the things of life.

So in service of the sand Cer went to the edge of the land of the Nefyrre, east of the desert. There he fouled wells with the bodies of diseased animals. He burned fields when the wind was blowing off the desert, a dry wind that pushed the flames into the cities. He cut down trees. He killed sheep and cattle.

And when the Nefyrre patrols chased him he fled onto the desert where they could not follow.

His destruction was annoying, and impoverished many a farmer, but alone it would have done little to hurt the Nefyrre. Except that Cer felt his power over the desert growing. For he was feeding the desert the only thing it hungered for: death and dryness.

He began to speak to the sand again, not kindly, but of land to the east that the sand could cover. And the wind followed his words, whipping the sand, moving the dunes. Where he stood the wind did not touch him, but all around him the dunes moved like waves of the sea.

Moving eastward.

Moving onto the lands of the Nefyrre.

And now the hungry desert could do in a night a hundred times more than Cer could do alone with a torch or a knife. It ate olive groves in an hour. The sand borne on the wind filled houses in a night, buried cities in a week, and in only three months had driven the Nefyrre across the Greebeck and the Nefyr River, where they thought the terrible sandstorms could not follow.

But the storms followed. Cer taught the desert almost to fill the river, so that the water spread out a foot deep and miles wide, flooding some lands that had been dry, but also leaving more water surface for the sun to drink from; and before the river reached the sea it was dry, and the desert swept across into the heart of Nefyryd.

The Nefyrre had always fought with the force of arms, and cruelty was their companion in war. But against the desert they were helpless. They could not fight the sand. If Cer could have known it, he would have gloried in the fact that, untaught, he was the most powerful sandmage who had ever lived. For hate was a greater teacher than any of the books of dark lore, and Cer lived on hate.

And on hate alone, for now he ate and drank nothing, sustaining his body through the power of the wind and the heat of the sun. He was utterly dry, and the blood no longer coursed through his veins. He lived on the energy of the storms he unleashed. And the desert eagerly fed him, because he was feeding the desert.

He followed his storms, and walked through the deserted towns of the Nefyrre. He saw the refugees rushing north and east to the high ground. He saw the corpses of those caught in the storm. And he sang at night the old songs of Greet, the war songs. He wrote his father's name with chalk on the wall of every city he destroyed. He wrote his mother's name in the sand, and where he had written her name the wind did not blow and the sand did not shift, but preserved the writings as if it had been incised on rock.

Then one day, in a lull between his storms, Cer saw a man coming toward him from the east. Abadapnu, he wondered, or Nefyrre? Either way he drew his knife, and fit the nock of an arrow on his bowstring.

But the man came with his hands extended, and he called out, "Cer Cemreet."

It had never occurred to Cer that anyone knew his name.

"Sandmage Cer Cemreet," said the man when he was close. "We have found who you are."

Cer said nothing, but only watched the man's eyes.

"I have come to tell you that your vengeance is full. Nefyryd is at its knees. We have signed a treaty with Greet and we no longer raid into Hetterwee. Driplin has seized our westernmost lands."

Cer smiled. "I care nothing for your empire."

"Then for our people. The deaths of your father and mother have been avenged a hundred thousand times, for over two hundred thousand people have died at your hands."

Cer chuckled. "I care nothing for your people."

"Then for the soldiers who did the deed. Though they acted under orders, they have been arrested and killed, as have the men who gave them those orders, even our first general, all at the command of the King so that your vengeance will be complete. I have brought you their ears as proof of it," said the man, and he took a pouch from his waist.

"I care nothing for soldiers, nor for proof of vengeance," said Cer.

"Then what do you care for?" asked the man quietly.

"Death," said Cer.

"Then I bring you that, too," said the man, and a knife was in his hand, and he plunged the knife into Cer's breast where his heart should have been. But when the man pulled the knife out no blood followed, and Cer only smiled.

"Indeed you brought it to me," said Cer, and he stabbed the man where his father had been stabbed, and drew the knife up as it had been drawn through his father's body, except that he touched the man's heart, and he died.

As Cer watched the blood soaking into the sand, he heard in his ears his mother's screams, which he had silenced for these years. He heard her screams and now, remembering his father and his mother and himself as a child he began to cry, and he held the body of the man he had killed and rocked back and forth on the sand as the blood clotted on his clothing and his skin. His tears mixed with the blood and poured into the sand and Cer realized that this was the first time since his father's death that he had shed any tears at all.

I am not dry, thought Cer. There is water under me still for the desert to drink.

He looked at his dry hands, covered with the man's blood, and tried to scrub off the clotted blood with sand. But the blood stayed, and the sand could not clean him.

He wept again. And then he stood and faced the desert to the west, and he said, "Come."

A breeze began.

"Come," he said to the desert, "come and dry my eyes."

And the wind came up, and the sand came, and Cer Cemreet was buried in the sand, and his eyes became dry, and the last life passed from his body, and the last sandmage passed from the world.

Then came the winter rains, and the refugees of Nefyryd returned to their land. The soldiers were called home, for the wars were over, and now their weapons were the shovel and the plow. They redug the trench of the Nefyr and the Greebeck, and the river soon flowed deep again to the sea. They scattered grass seed and cleaned their houses of sand. They carried water into the ruined fields with ditches and aqueducts.

Slowly life returned to Nefyryd.

And the desert, having lost its mage, retreated quietly to its old borders, never again to seek death where there was life. Plenty of death already where nothing lived, plenty of dryness to drink where there was no water.

In a wood a little way from the crest of the Mitherkame, a treemage heard the news from a wandering tinker.

The treemage went out into the forest and spoke softly to the Elm, to the Oak, to the Redwood, to the Sweet Aspen. And when all had heard the news, the forest wept for Cer Cemreet, and each tree gave a twig to be burned in his memory, and shed sap to sink into the ground in his name.

The Best Day

Once there was a woman who had five children that she loved with all her heart, and a husband who was kind and strong. Every day her husband would go out and work in the fields, and then he'd come home and cut wood or repair harness or fix the leaky places in the roof. Every day the children would work and play so hard they wore paths in the weeds from running, and they knew every hiding place in two miles square. And that woman began to be afraid that they were too happy, that it would all come to an end. And so she prayed, Please send us eternal happiness, let this joy last forever. Well, the next day along came a mean-faced old peddler, and he spread his wares and they were very plain—rough wool clothing, sturdy pots and pans, all as ugly and practical as old shoes. The woman bought a dress from him because it was cheap and it would last forever, and he was about to go, when suddenly she saw maybe a fire in his eyes, suddenly flashing bright as a star, and she remembered her prayer the night before, and she said, "Sir, you don't have anything to do with—happiness, do you?"

And the peddler turned and glowered and said, "I can give it to you, if you want it. But let me tell you what it is. It's your kids growing up and talking

213

sassy, and then moving on out and marrying other children who don't like you all that much, at least at first. It's your husband's strength giving out, and watching the farm go to seed before your eyes, and maybe having to sell it and move into your daughter-in-law's house because you can't support yourselves no more. It's feeling your own legs go stiff, and your fingers not able to tat or knit or even grip the butter churn. And finally it's dying, lying there feeling your body drop off you, wishing you could just go back and be young with your children small, just for a day. And then—"

"Enough!" cried the woman.

"But there's more," said the peddler.

"I've heard all I mean to hear," and she hurried him out of the house.

The next day, along comes a man in a bright-painted wagon, with a horse named Carpy Deem that he shouted at all the time. A medicine man from the East, with potions for this and pills for that, and silks and scarves to sell, too, so bright they hurt your eyes just to look at them. Everybody was healthy, so the woman didn't buy any medicine. All she bought was a silk, even though the price was too high, because it looked so blue in her golden hair. And she said to him, "Sir, do you have anything to do with happiness?"

"Do you have to *ask*?" he said. "Right here, in this jar, is the elixir of happiness—one swallow, and the best day of your life is with you forever."

"How much does it cost?" she asked, trembling.

"I only sell it to them as have such a day worth keeping, and then I sell it cheap. One lock of your golden hair, that's all. I give it to your Master, so he'll know you when the time comes."

She plucked the hair from her head, and gave it to the peddler, and he poured from the bottle into a little tin cup. When he was gone, she lifted it up, and thought of the happiest day of her life, which was only two days before, the day she prayed. And she drank that swallow.

Well, her husband came home as it was getting dark, and the children came to him all worried. "Something's wrong with Mother," they said. "She ain't making no sense." The man walked into the house, and tried to talk to his wife, but she gave no answer. Then, suddenly, she said something, speaking to empty air. She was cutting carrots, but there were no carrots; she was cooking a stew, but there was no fire laid. Finally her husband realized that word for word, she was saying what she said only two days ago, when they last had stew, and if he said to her the words he had said then, why, the conversation at least made some sense.

And every day it was the same. They either said that same day's words over and over again, or they ignored their mother, and let her go on as she did and paid her no mind. The kids got sick of it after a time, and got married and went away, and she never knew it. Her husband stayed with her, and more and more he got caught up in her dream, so that every day he got up and said the same words till they meant nothing and he couldn't remember what he was living for, and so he died. The neighbors found him two days later, and buried him, and the woman never knew.

Her daughters and daughter-in-law tried to care for her, but if they took her to their homes, she'd just walk around as if she were still in her own little cottage, bumping into walls, cutting those infernal

215

carrots, saying those words till they were all out of their minds. Finally they took her back to her own home and paid a woman to cook and clean for her, and she went on that way, all alone in that cabin, happy as a duck in a puddle until at last the floor of her cabin caved in and she fell in and broke her hip. They figure she never even felt the pain, and when she died she was still laughing and smiling and saying idiotic things, and never even saw one of her grandchildren, never even wept at her husband's grave, and some folks said she was probably happier, but not a one said they were eager to change places with her. And it happened that a mean-looking old peddler came by and watched as they let her into her grave, and up rode a medicine man yelling at his horse, and he pulled up next to the peddler.

"So she bought from you," the peddler said.

And the medicine man said, "If you'd just paint things up a little, add a bit of color here and there, you'd sell more, friend."

But the peddler only shook his head. "If they'd ever let me finish telling them, they'd not be taken in by you, old liar. But they always send me packing before I'm through. I never get to tell them."

"If you'd begin with the pleasant things, they'd listen."

"But if I began with the pleasant things, it wouldn't be true."

"Fine with me. You keep me in business." And the medicine man patted a trunk filled with gold and silver and bronze and iron hairs. It was the wealth of all the world, and the medicine man rode off with it, to go back home and count it all, so fine and cold.

And the peddler, he just rode home to his family, his great-great-great-grandchildren, his gray-haired wife who nagged, the children who complained about the way he was always off on business when he should be home, and always hanging about the house when he ought to be away; he rode home to the leaves that turned every year, and the rats that ate the apples in the cellar, and the folks that kept dying on him, and the little ones that kept on being born.

A Plague of Butterflies

The butterflies awoke him. Amasa felt them before he saw them, the faint pressure of hundreds of half-dozens of feet, weighting his rough wool sheet so that he dreamed of a shower of warm snow. Then opened his eyes and there they were, in the shaft of sunlight like a hundred stained-glass windows, on the floor like a carpet woven by an inspired lunatic, delicately in the air like leaves falling upward in a wind.

At last, he said silently.

He watched them awhile, then gently lifted his covers. The butterflies arose with the blanket. Carefully he swung his feet to the floor; they eddied away from his footfall, then swarmed back to cover him. He waded through them like the shallow water on the edge of the sea, endlessly charging and then retreating quickly. He who fights and runs away, lives to fight another day. You have to come to me at last, he said, and then he shuddered, for this was the change in his life that he had waited for, and now he wasn't sure he wanted it after all.

They swarmed around him all morning as he prepared for his journey. His last journey, he knew, the last of many. He had begun his life in wealth, on the verge of power, in Sennabris, the greatest of the oil-burning cities of the coast. He had grown up watching the vast ships slide into and out of the quays to void their bowels into the sink of the city. When his first journey began, he did not follow the tankers out to sea. Instead, he took what seemed the cleaner way, inland.

He lived in splendor in the hanging city of Besara on the cliffs of Carmel; he worked for a time as a governor in Kafr Katnei on the plain of Esdraelon until the Megiddo War; he built the Ladder of Ekdippa through solid rock, where a thousand men died in the building and it was considered a cheap price.

And in every journey he mislaid something. His taste for luxury stayed in Besara; his love of power was sated and forgotten in Kafr Katnei; his desire to build for the ages was shed like a cloak in Ekdippa; and at last he had found himself here, in a desperately poor dirt farm on the edge of the Desert of Machaerus, with a tractor that had to be bribed to work and harvests barely large enough to pay for food for himself and petrol for the machines. He hadn't even enough to pay for light in the darkness, and sunset ended every day with imperturbable night. Yet even here, he knew that there was one more journey, for he had not yet lost everything: still when he worked in the fields he would reach down and press his fingers into the soil; still he would bathe his feet in the rush of water from the muddy ditch; still he would sit for hours in the heat of the afternoon and watch the grain standing bright gold and motionless as rock, drinking sun and expelling it as dry, hard grain. This last love, the love of life itself — it, too, would have to leave, Amasa knew, before his life would have completed its course and he would have consent to die.

The butterflies, they called him.

He carefully oiled the tractor and put it into its shed.

He closed the headgate of the ditch and shoveled earth into place behind it, so that in the spring the water would not flow onto his fallow fields and be wasted.

He filled a bottle with water and put it into his scrip, which he slung over his shoulder. This is all I take, he said. And even that felt like more of a burden than he wanted to bear.

The butterflies swarmed around him, and tried to draw him off toward the road into the desert, but he did not go at once. He looked at his fields, stubbled after the harvest. Just beyond them was the tumble of weeds that throve in the dregs of water that his grain had not used. And beyond the weeds was the Desert of Machaerus, the place where those who love water die. The ground was stone: rocky outcroppings, gravel; even the soil was sand. And yet there were ruins there. Wooden skeletons of buildings that had once housed farmers. Some people thought that this was a sign that the desert was growing, pushing in to take over formerly habitable land, but Amasa knew better. Rather the wooden ruins were the last remnants of the woeful Sebasti, those wandering people who, like the weeds at the end of the field, lived on the dregs of life. Once there had been a slight surplus of water flowing down the canals. The Sebasti heard about it in hours; in days they had come in their ramshackle trucks; in weeks they had built their scrappy buildings and plowed their stony fields, and for that year they had

220

a harvest because the ditches ran a few inches deeper than usual. The next year the ditches were back to normal, and in a few hours one night the houses were stripped, the trucks were loaded, and the Sebasti were gone.

I am a Sebastit, too, Amasa thought. I have taken my life from an unwilling desert; I give it back to the sand when I am through.

Come, said the butterflies alighting on his face. Come, they said, fanning him and fluttering off toward the Hierusalem road.

Don't get pushy, Amasa answered, feeling stubborn. But all the same he surrendered, and followed them out into the land of the dead.

The only breeze was the wind on his face as he walked, and the heat drew water from him as if from a copious well. He took water from his bottle only a mouthful at a time, but it was going too quickly even at that rate.

Worse, though: his guides were leaving him. Now that he was on the road to Hierusalem, they apparently had other errands to run. He first noticed their numbers diminishing about noon, and by three there were only a few hundred butterflies left. As long as he watched a particular butterfly, it stayed; but when he looked away for a moment, it was gone. At last he set his gaze on one butterfly and did not look away at all, just watched and watched. Soon it was the last one left, and he knew that it, too, wanted to leave. But Amasa would have none of that. If I can come at your bidding, he said silently, you can stay at mine. And so he walked until the sun was ruddy in the west. He did not drink; he did not study his road; and the butterfly stayed. It was a little victory. I rule you with my eyes.

"You might as well stop here, friend."

Startled to hear a human voice on this desolate road, Amasa looked up, knowing in that moment that his last butterfly was lost. He was ready to hate the man who spoke.

"I say, friend, since you're going nowhere anyway, you might as well stop."

It was an old-looking man, black from sunlight and naked. He sat in the lee of a large stone, where the sun's northern tilt would keep him in shadow all day.

"If I wanted conversation," Amasa said, "I would have brought a friend."

"If you think those butterflies are your friends, you're an ass."

Amasa was surprised that the man knew about the butterflies.

"Oh, I know more than you think," said the man. "I lived at Hierusalem you know. And now I'm the sentinel of the Hierusalem Road."

"No one leaves Hierusalem," said Amasa.

"I did," the old man said. "And now I sit on the road and teach travelers the keys that will let them in. Few of them pay me much attention, but if you don't do as I say, you'll never reach Hierusalem, and your bones will join a very large collection that the sun and wind gradually turn back into sand."

"I'll follow the road where it leads," Amasa said. "I don't need any directions."

"Oh, yes, you'd rather follow the dead guidance of the makers of the road than trust a living man."

Amasa regarded him for a moment. "Tell me, then."

222

"Give me all your water."

Amasa laughed — a feeble enough sound, coming through splitting lips that he dared not move more than necessary.

"It's the first key to entering Hierusalem." The old man shrugged. "I see that you don't believe me. But it's true. A man with water or food can't get into the city. You see, the city is hidden. If you had miraculous eyes, stranger, you could see the city even now. It's not far off. But the city is forever hidden from a man who is not desperate. The city can only be found by those who are very near to death. Unfortunately, if you once pass the entrance to the city without seeing it because you had water with you, then you can wander on as long as you like, you can run out of water and cry out in a whisper for the city to unveil itself to you, but it will avail you nothing. The entrance, once passed, can never be found again. You see, you have to know the taste of death in your mouth before Hierusalem will open to you."

"It sounds," Amasa said, "like religion. I've done religion."

"Religion? What is religion in a world with a dragon at its heart?"

Amasa hesitated. A part of him, the rational part, told him to ignore the man and pass on. But the rational part of him had long since become weak. In his definition of man, "featherless biped" held more truth than "rational animal." Besides, his head ached, his feet throbbed, his lips stung. He handed his bottle of water to the old man, and then for good measure gave him his scrip as well.

"Nothing in there you want to keep?" asked the old man, surprised.

"I'll spend the night."

The old man nodded.

They slept in the darkness until the moon rose in the east, bright with its thin promise of a sunrise only a few hours away. It was Amasa who awoke. His stirring roused the old man.

"Already?" he asked. "In such a hurry?"

"Tell me about Hierusalem."

"What do you want, friend? History? Myth? Current events? The price of public transportation?"

"Why is the city hidden?"

"So it can't be found."

"Then why is there a key for some to enter?"

"So it *can* be found. Must you ask such puerile questions?"

"Who built the city?"

"Men."

"Why did they build it?"

"To keep man alive on this world."

Amasa nodded at the first answer that hinted at significance. "And what enemy is it, then, that Hierusalem means to keep out?"

"Oh, my friend, you don't understand. Hierusalem was built to keep the enemy in. The old Hierusalem, the new Hierusalem, built to contain the dragon at the heart of the world."

A story-telling voice was on the old man now, and Amasa lay back on the sand and listened as the moon rose higher at his left hand.

"Men came here in ships across the void of the night," the old man said.

Amasa sighed.

"Oh, you know all that?"

"Don't be an ass. Tell me about Hierusalem."

"Did your books or your teachers tell you that

224

this world was not unpopulated when our forefathers came?"

"Tell me your story, old man, but tell it plain. No myth, no magic. The truth."

"What a simple faith you have," the old man said. "The truth. Here's the truth, much good may it do you. This world was filled with forest, and in the forest were beings who mated with the trees, and drew their strength from the trees. They became very treelike."

"One would suppose."

"Our forefathers came, and the beings who dwelt among the trees smelt death in the fires of the ships. They did things — things that looked like magic to our ancestors, things that looked like miracles. These beings, these dragons who hid among the leaves of the trees, they had science we know little of. But one science we had that they had never learned, for they had no use for it. We knew how to defoliate a forest."

"So the trees were killed."

"All the forests of the world now have grown up since that time. Some places, where the forest had not been lush, were able to recover, and we live in those lands now. But here, in the Desert of Machaera — this was climax forest, trees so tall and dense that no underbrush could grow at all. When the leaves died, there was nothing to hold the soil, and it was washed onto the plain of Esdraelon. Which is why that plain is so fertile, and why nothing but sand survives here."

"Hierusalem."

"At first Hierusalem was built as an outpost for students to learn about the dragons, pathetic little brown woody creatures who knew death when they saw it, and died of despair by the thousands. Only a few survived among the rocks, where we couldn't reach them. Then Hierusalem became a city of pleasure, far from any other place, where sins could be committed that God could not see."

"I said truth."

"I say listen. One day the few remaining students of the science of the dragons wandered among the rocks, and there found that the dragons were not all dead. One was left, a tough little creature that lived among the gray rocks. But it had changed. It was not woody brown now. It was gray as stone, with stony outcroppings. They brought it back to study it. And in only a few hours it escaped. They never recaptured it. But the murders began, every night a murder. And every murder was of a couple who were coupling, neatly vivisected in the act. Within a year the pleasure seekers were gone, and Hierusalem had changed again."

"To what it is now."

"What little of the science of the dragons they had learned, they used to seal the city as it is now sealed. They devoted it to holiness, to beauty, to faith — and the murders stopped. Yet the dragon was not gone. It was glimpsed now and then, gray on the stone buildings of the city, like a moving gargoyle. So they kept their city closed to keep the dragon from escaping to the rest of the world, where men were not holy and would compel the dragon to kill again."

"So Hierusalem is dedicated to keeping the world safe for sin."

"Safe from retribution. Giving the world time to repent."

"The world is doing little in that direction."

"But some are. And the butterflies are calling the repentant out of the world, and bringing them to me."

Amasa sat in silence as the sun rose behind his back. It had not fully passed the mountains of the east before it started to burn him.

"Here," said the old man, "are the laws of Hierusalem:

"Once you see the city, don't step back or you will lose it.

"Don't look down into holes that glow red in the streets, or your eyes will fall out and your skin will slide off you as you walk along, and your bones will crumble into dust before you fully die.

"The man who breaks a butterfly will live forever.

"Do not stare at a small gray shadow that moves along the granite walls of the palace of the King and Queen, or he will learn the way to your bed.

"The Road to Dalmanutha leads to the sign you seek. Never find it."

Then the old man smiled.

"Why are you smiling?" asked Amasa.

"Because you're such a holy man, Saint Amasa, and Hierusalem is waiting for you to come."

"What's your name, old man?"

The old man cocked his head. "Contemplation."

"That's not a name."

He smiled again. "I'm not a man."

For a moment Amasa believed him, and reached out to see if he was real. But his finger met the old man's flesh, and it did not crumble.

"You have so much faith," said the old man again. "You cast away your scrip because you valued nothing that it contained. What *do* you value?"

In answer, Amasa removed all his clothing and cast it at the old man's feet.

He remembers that once he had another name, but he cannot remember what it was. His name now is Gray, and he lives among the stones, which are also gray. Sometimes he forgets where stone leaves off and he begins. Sometimes, when he has been motionless for hours, he has to search for his toes that spread in a fan, each holding to stone so firmly that when at last he moves them, he is surprised at where they were. Gray is motionless all day, and motionless all night. But in the hours before and after the sun, then he moves, skittering sure and rapid as a spider among the hewn stones of the palace walls, stopping only to drink in the fly-strewn standing water that remains from the last storm.

These days, however, he must move more slowly, more clumsily than he used to, for his stamen has at last grown huge, and it drags painfully along the vertical stones, and now and then he steps on it. It has been this way for weeks. Worse every day, and Gray feels it as a constant pain that he must ease, must ease, must ease; but in his small mind he does not know what easement there might be. So far as he knows, there are no others of his kind; in all his life he has met no other climber of walls, no other hanger from stone ceilings. He remembers that once he sought out couplers in the night, but he cannot remember what he did with them. Now he again finds himself drawn to windows, searching for ease-ment, though not sure at all, holding in his mind no image of what he hopes to see in the dark rooms within the palace. It is dusk, and Gray is hunting, and is not sure whether he will find mate or prey.

*

I have passed the gate of Hierusalem, thought Amasa, and I was not near enough to death. Or worse, sometimes he thought, there is no Hierusalem, and I have come this way in vain. Yet this last fear was not a fear at all, for he did not think of it with despair. He thought of it with hope, and looked for death as the welcome end of his journey, looked for death which comes with its tongue thick in its mouth, death which waits in caves during the cool of the day and hunts for prey in the last and first light, death which is made of dust. Amasa watched for death to come in a wind that would carry him away, in a stone that would catch his foot in midstep and crumble him into a pile of bone on the road.

And then in a single footfall Amasa saw it all. The sun was framed, not by a haze of white light, but by thick and heavy clouds. The orchards were also heavy, and dripped with recent rain. Bees hummed around his head. And now he could see the city rising, green and gray and monumental just beyond the trees; all around him was the sound of running water. Not the tentative water that struggled to stay alive in the thirsty dirt of the irrigation ditch, but the lusty sound of water that is superfluous, water that can be tossed in the air as fountains and no one thinks to gather up the drops.

For a moment he was so surprised that he thought he must step backward, just one step, and see if it wouldn't all disappear, for Amasa did not come upon this gradually, and he doubted that it was real. But he remembered the first warning of the old man, and he didn't take that backward step. Hierusalem was a miracle, and in this place he would test no miracles.

The ground was resilient under his feet, mossy

where the path ran over stone, grassy where the stones made way for earth. He drank at an untended stream that ran pure and overhung with flowers. And then he passed through a small gate in a terraced wall, climbed stairs, found another gate, and another, each more graceful than the last. The first gate was rusty and hard to open; the second was overgrown with climbing roses. But each gate was better tended than the last, and he kept expecting to find someone working a garden or picnicking, for surely someone must be passing often through the better-kept gates. Finally he reached to open a gate and it opened before he could touch it.

It was a man in the dirty brown robe of a pilgrim. He seemed startled to see Amasa. He immediately enfolded his arms around something and turned away. Amasa tried to see — yes, it was a baby. But the infant's hands dripped with fresh blood, it was obviously blood, and Amasa looked back at the pilgrim to see if this was a murderer who had opened the gate for him.

"It's not what you think," the palmer said quickly. "I found the babe, and he has no one to take care of him."

"But the blood."

"He was the child of pleasure-seekers, and the prophecy was fulfilled, for he was washing his hands in the blood of his father's belly." Then the pilgrim got a hopeful look. "There is an enemy who must be fought. You wouldn't —"

A passing butterfly caught the pilgrim's eye. The fluttering wings circled Amasa's head only once, but that was sign enough.

"It is you," the pilgrim said.

"Do I know you?"

"To think that it will be in my time."

"*What* will be?"

"The slaying of the dragon." The pilgrim ducked his head and, freeing one arm by perching the child precariously on the other, he held the gate open for Amasa to enter. "God has surely called you."

Amasa stepped inside, puzzled at what the pilgrim thought he was, and what his coming portended. Behind him he could hear the pilgrim mutter, "It is time. It is time."

It was the last gate. He was in the city, passing between the walled gardens of monasteries and nunneries, down streets lined with shrines and shops, temples and houses, gardens and dunghills. It was green to the point of blindness, alive and holy and smelly and choked with business wherever it wasn't thick with meditation. What am I here for? Amasa wondered. Why did the butterflies call?

He did not look down into the red-glowing holes in the middles of streets. And when he passed the gray labyrinth of the palace, he did not look up to try to find a shadow sliding by. He would live by the laws of the place, and perhaps his journey would end here.

The queen of Hierusalem was lonely. For a month she had been lost in the palace. She had strayed into a never-used portion of the labyrinth, where no one had lived for generations, and now, search as she might, she could find only rooms that were deeper and deeper in dust.

The servants, of course, knew exactly where she was, and some of them grumbled at having to come into a place of such filth, full of such unstylish old furniture, in order to care for her. It did not occur

231

to *them* that she was lost — they only thought she was exploring. It would never do for her to admit her perplexity to them. It was the Queen's business to know what she was doing. She couldn't very well ask a servant, "Oh, by the way, while you're fetching my supper, would you mind mentioning to me where I *am*?" So she remained lost, and the perpetual dust irritated all her allergies.

The Queen was immensely fat, too, which complicated things. Walking was a great labor to her, so that once she found a room with a bed that looked sturdy enough to hold her for a few nights, she stayed until the bed threatened to give way. Her progress through the unused rooms, then, was not in a great expedition, but rather in fits and starts. On one morning she would arise miserable from the bed's increasing incapacity to hold her, eat her vast breakfast while the servants looked on to catch the dribbles, and then, instead of calling for singers or someone to read, she would order four servants to stand her up, point her in the direction she chose, and taxi her to a good, running start.

"That door," she cried again and again, and the servants would propel her in that direction, while her legs trotted underneath her, trying to keep up with her body. And in the new room she could not stop to contemplate; she must take it all in on the run, with just a few mad glances, then decide whether to try to stay or go on. "On," she usually cried, and the servants took her through the gradual curves and maneuvers necessary to reach whatever door was most capacious.

On the day that Amasa arrived in Hierusalem, the Queen found a room with a vast bed, once used by some ancient rake of a prince to hold a dozen paramours at once, and the Queen cried out, "This is it, this is the right place, stop, we'll stay!" and the servants sighed in relief and began to sweep, to clean, to make the place liveable.

Her steward unctuously asked her, "What do you want to wear to the King's Invocation?"

"I will not go," she said. How could she? She did not know how to get to the hall where the ritual would be held. "I choose to be absent this once. There'll be another one in seven years." The steward bowed and left on his errand, while the Queen envied him his sense of direction and miserably wished that she could go home to her own rooms. She hadn't been to a party in a month, and now that she was so far from the kitchens the food was almost cold by the time she was served the private dinners she had to be content with. Damn her husband's ancestors for building all these rooms anyway.

Amasa slept by a dunghill because it was warmer there, naked as he was; and in the morning, without leaving the dunghill, he found work. He was wakened by the servants of a great Bishop, stablemen who had the week's manure to leave for the farmers to collect. They said nothing to him, except to look with disapproval at his nakedness, but set to work, emptying small wheelbarrows, then raking up the dung to make a neater pile. Amasa saw how fastidiously they avoided touching the dung; he had no such scruples. He took an idle rake, stepped into the midst of the manure, and raked the hill higher and faster than the delicate stablemen could manage on their own. He worked with such a will that the Stablemaster took him aside at the end of the task.

"Want work?"

"Why not?" Amasa answered.

The Stablemaster glanced pointedly at Amasa's unclothed body. "Are you fasting?"

Amasa shook his head. "I just left my clothing on the road."

"You should be more careful with your belongings. I can give you livery, but it comes out of your wages for a year."

Amasa shrugged. He had no use for wages.

The work was mindless and hard, but Amasa delighted in it. The variety was endless. Because he didn't mind it, they kept him shoveling more manure than his fair share, but the shoveling of manure was like a drone, a background for bright rhinestones of childish delight: morning prayers, when the Bishop in his silver gown intoned the powerful words while the servants stood in the courtyard clumsily aping his signs; running through the streets behind the Bishop's carriage shouting "Huzzah, huzzah!" while the Bishop scattered coins for the pedestrians; standing watch over the carriage, which meant drinking and hearing stories and songs with the other servants; or going inside to do attendance on the Bishop at the great occasions of this or that church or embassy or noble house, delighting in the elaborate costumes that so cleverly managed to adhere to the sumptuary laws while being as ostentatious and lewd as possible. It was grand, God approved of it all, and even discreet prurience and titillation were a face of the coin of worship and ecstasy.

But years at the desert's edge had taught Amasa to value things that the other servants never noticed. He did not have to measure his drinking water. The servants splashed each other in the bathhouse. he could piss on the ground and no little animals came to sniff at the puddle, no dying insects lit on it to drink.

They called Hierusalem a city of stone and fire, but Amasa knew it was a city of life and water, worth more than all the gold that was forever changing hands.

The other stablemen accepted Amasa well enough, but a distance always remained. He had come naked, from the outside; he had no fear of uncleanliness before the Lord; and something else: Amasa had known the taste of death in his mouth and it had not been unwelcome. Now he accepted as they came the pleasures of a stableman's life. But he did not need them, and knew he could not hide that from his fellows.

One day the Prior told the Steward, and the Steward the Stablemaster, and the Stablemaster told Amasa and the other stablemen to wash carefully three times, each time with soap. The old-timers knew what it meant, and told them all: It was the King's Invocation that came but once in seven years, and the Bishop would bring them all to stand in attendance, clean and fine in their livery, while he took part in the solemn ordinances. They would have perfume in their hair. And they would see the King and Queen.

"Is she beautiful?" Amasa asked, surprised at the awe in the voices of these irreverent men when they spoke of her.

And they laughed and compared the Queen to a mountain, to a planet, to a moon.

But then a butterfly alighted on the head of an old woman, and suddenly all laughter stopped. "The butterfly," they all whispered. The woman's eyes went blank, and she began to speak:

"The Queen is beautiful, Saint Amasa, to those who have the eyes to see it."

The servants whispered: See, the butterfly speaks to the new one, who came naked.

"Of all the holy men to come out of the world, Saint Amasa, of all the wise and weary souls, you are wisest, you are weariest, you are most holy."

Amasa trembled at the voice of the butterfly. In memory he suddenly loomed over the crevice of Ekdippa, and it was leaping up to take him.

"We brought you here to save her, save her, save her," said the old woman, looking straight into Amasa's eyes.

Amasa shook his head. "I'm through with quests," he said.

And foam came to the old woman's mouth, wax oozed from her ears, her nose ran with mucus, her eyes overflowed with sparkling tears.

Amasa reached out to the butterfly perched on her head, the fragile butterfly that was wracking the old woman so, and he took it in his hand. Took it in his right hand, folded the wings closed with his left, and then broke! the butterfly as crisply as a stick. The sound of it rang metallically in the air. There was no ichor from the butterfly, for it was made of something tough as metal, brittle as plastic, and electricity danced between the halves of the butterfly for a moment and then was still.

The old woman fell to the ground. Carefully the other servants cleaned her face and carried her away to sleep until she awakened. They did not speak to Amasa, except the Stablemaster, who looked at him oddly and asked, "Why would you want to live forever?"

Amasa shrugged. There was no use explaining

that he wanted to ease the old woman's agony, and so killed it at its cause. Besides, Amasa was distracted, for now there was something buzzing in the base of his brain. The whirr of switches, infinitely small, going left or right; gates going open and closed; poles going positive and negative. Now and then a vision would flash into his mind, so quickly that he could not frame or recognize it. Now I see the world through butterfly's eyes. Now the vast mind of Hierusalem's machinery sees the world through mine.

Gray waits by this window: it is the one. He does not wonder how he knows. He only knows that he was made for this moment, that his life's need is all within this window, he must not stray to hunt for food because his great stamen is throbbing with desire and in the night it will be satisfied.

So he waits by the window, and the sun is going, the sky is gray, but still he waits, and at last the lights have gone from the sky and all is silent within. He moves in the darkness until his long fingers find the edge of the stone. Then he pulls himself inside, and when his stamen scrapes painfully against the stone, immense between his legs, he only thinks: ease for you, ease for you.

His object is a great mountain that lies breathing upon a sea of sheets. She breathes in quick gasps, for her chest is large and heavy and hard to lift. He thinks nothing of that, but only creeps along the wall until he is above her head. He stares quizzically at the fat face; it holds no interest for him. What interests Gray is the space at her shoulders where the sheets and blankets and quilts fall open like a tent door. For some reason it looks like the leaves of a tree to him, and he drops onto the bed and scurries into the shelter.

Ah, it is not stone! He can hardly move for the bouncing, his fingers and toes find no certain purchase, yet there is this that forces him on: his stamen tingles with extruding pollen, and he knows he cannot pause just because the ground is uncertain.

He proceeds along the tunnel, the sweating body to one side, the tent of sheets above and to the other side. He explores; he crawls clumsily over a vast branch; and at last he knows what he has been looking for. It is time, oh, time, for here is the blossom of a great flower, pistil lush for him. He leaps. He fastens to her body as he has always fastened to the limbs of the great wife trees, to the stone. He plunges stamen into pistil and dusts the walls with pollen. It is all he lived for, and when it is done, in only moments when the pollen is shed at last, he dies and drops to the sheets.

The queen's dreams were frenzied. Because her waking life was wrapped and closed, because her bulk forced an economy of movement, in her sleep she was bold, untiring. Sometimes she dreamed of great chases on a horse across broken country. Sometimes she dreamed of flying. Tonight she dreamed of love, and it was also athletic and unbound. Yet in the moment of ecstasy there was a face that peered at her, and hands that tore her lover away from her, and she was afraid of the man who stared at the end of her dream.

Still, she woke trembling from the memory of love, only wistfully allowing herself to recall, bit by bit, where she really was. That she was lost in the palace, that she was as ungainly as a diseased tree with boles and knots of fat, that she was profoundly unhappy, that a strange man disturbed her dreams.

And then, as she moved slightly, she felt something cold and faintly dry between her legs. She dared not move again, for fear of what it was.

Seeing that she was awake, a servant bowed beside her. "Would you like your breakfast?"

"Help me," she whispered. "I want to get up."

The servant was surprised, but summoned the others. As they rolled her from the bed, she felt it again, and as soon as she was erect she ordered them to throw back the sheets.

And there he lay, flaccid, empty, gray as a deflated stone. The servants gasped, but they did not understand what the Queen instantly understood. Her dreams were too real last night, and the great appendage on the dead body fit too well the memory of her phantom lover. This small monster did not come as a parasite, to drain her; it came to give, not to receive.

She did not scream. She only knew that she had to run from there, had to escape. So she began to move, unsupported, and to her own surprise she did not fall. Her legs, propelled and strengthened by her revulsion, stayed under her, held her up. She did not know where she was going, only that she must go. She ran. And it was not until she had passed through a dozen rooms, a trail of servants chasing after her, that she realized it was not the corpse of her monstrous paramour she fled from, but rather what he left in her, for even as she ran she could feel something move within her womb, could feel something writhing, and she must, she must be rid of it.

As she ran, she felt herself grow lighter, felt her

239

body melting under the flesh, felt her heaps and mounds erode away in an inward storm, sculpting her into a woman's shape again. The vast skin that had contained her belly began to slap awkwardly, loosely against her thighs as she ran. The servants caught up with her, reached out to support her, and plunged their hands into a body that was melting away. They said nothing; it was not for them to say. They only took hold of the loosening folds and held and ran.

And suddenly through her fear the Queen saw a pattern of furniture, a lintel, a carpet, a window, and she knew where she was. She had accidentally stumbled upon a familiar wing of the palace, and now she had purpose, she had direction, she would go where help and strength were waiting. To the throne room, to her husband, where the king was surely holding his Invocation. The servants caught up with her at last; now they bore her up. "To my husband," she said, and they assured her and petted her and carried her. The thing within her leapt for joy: its time was coming quickly.

Amasa could not watch the ceremonies. From the moment he entered the Hall of Heaven all he could see were the butterflies. They hovered in the dome that was painted like the midsummernight sky, blotting out the tiny stars with their wings; they rested high on painted pillars, camouflaged except when they fanned their graceful wings. He saw them where to others they were far too peripheral to be seen, for in the base of his brain the gates opened and closed, the poles reversed, always in the same rhythm that drove the butterflies' flight and rest. Save the Queen, they said. We brought you here to save the Queen. It throbbed behind his eyes, and he could hardly see.

Could hardly see, until the Queen came into the room, and then he could see all too clearly. There was a hush, the ceremonies stopped, and all gazes were drawn to the door where she stood, an undulant mass of flesh with a woman's face, her eyes vulnerable and wide with fright and trust. The servants' arms reached far into the folds of skin, finding God-knew-what grip there: Amasa only knew that her face was exquisite. Hers was the face of all women, the hope in her eyes the answer to the hope of all men. "My husband!" she cried out, but at the moment she called she was not looking at the King. She was looking at Amasa.

She is looking at me, he thought in horror. She is all the beauty of Besara, she is the power of Kafr Katnei, she is the abyss of Ekdippa, she is all that I have loved and left behind. I do not want to desire them again.

The King cried out impatiently. "Good God, woman!"

And the Queen reached out her arms toward the man on the throne, gurgled in agony and surprise, and then shuddered like a wood fence in a wind.

What is it, asked a thousand whispers. What's wrong with the Queen?

She stepped backward.

There on the floor lay a baby, a little gray baby, naked and wrinkled and spotted with blood. Her eyes were open. She sat up and looked around, reached down and took the placenta in her hands and bit the cord, severing it.

The butterflies swarmed around her, and Amasa knew what he was meant to do. As you snapped the

241

butterfly, they said to him, you must break this child. We are Hierusalem, and we were built for this epiphany, to greet this child and slay her at her birth. For this we found the man most holy in the world, for this we brought him here, for you alone have power over her.

I cannot kill a child, Amasa thought. Or did not think, for it was not said in words but in a shudder of revulsion in him, a resistance at the core of what in him was most himself.

This *is* no child, the city said. Do you think the dragons have surrendered just because we stole their trees? The dragons have simply changed to fit a new mate; they mean to rule the world again. And the gates and poles of the city impelled him, and Amasa decided a thousand times to obey, to step a dozen paces forward and take the child in his arms and break it. And as many times he heard himself cry out, I cannot kill a child! And the cry was echoed by his voice as he whispered, "No."

Why am I standing in the middle of the Hall of Heaven, he asked himself. Why is the Queen staring at me with horror in her eyes? Does she recognize me? Yes, she does, and she is afraid of me. Because I mean to kill her child. Because I cannot kill her child.

As Amasa hesitated, tearing himself, the gray infant looked at the King. "Daddy," she said, and then she stood and walked with gathering certainty toward the throne. With such dextrous fingers the child picked at her ear. Now. Now, said the butterflies.

Yes, said Amasa. No.

"My daughter!" the King cried out. "At last an

242

heir! The answer to my Invocation before the prayer was done — and such a brilliant child!"

The King stepped down from his throne, reached to the child and tossed her high into the air. The girl laughed and tumbled down again. Once more the King tossed her in delight. This time, however, she did not come down.

She hovered in the air over the King's head, and everyone gasped. The child fixed her gaze on her mother, the mountainous body from which she had been disgorged, and she spat. The spittle shone in the air like a diamond, then sailed across the room and struck the Queen on her breast, where it sizzled. The butterflies suddenly turned black in midair, shriveled, dropped to the ground with infinitesimal thumps that only Amasa could hear. The gates all closed within his mind, and he was all himself again; but too late, the moment was passed, the child had come into her power, and the Queen could not be saved.

The King shouted, "Kill the monster!" But the words still hung in the air when the child urinated on the King from above. He erupted in flame, and there was no doubt now who ruled in the palace. The gray shadow had come in from the walls.

She looked at Amasa, and smiled. "Because you were the holiest," she said, "I brought you here."

Amasa tried to flee the city. He did not know the way. He passed a palmer who knelt at a fountain that flowed from virgin stone, and asked, "How can I leave Hierusalem?"

"No one leaves," the palmer said in surprise. As Amasa went on, he saw the palmer bend to continue scrubbing at a baby's hands. Amasa tried to steer

243

by the patterns of the stars, but no matter which direction he ran, the roads all bent toward one road, and that road led to a single gate. And in the gate the child waited for him. Only she was no longer a child. Her slate-gray body was heavy-breasted now, and she smiled at Amasa and took him in her arms, refused to be denied. "I am Dalmanutha," she whispered, "and you are following my road. I am Acrasia, and I will teach you joy."

She took him to a bower on the palace grounds, and taught him the agony of bliss. Every time she mated with him, she conceived, and in hours a child was born. He watched each one come to adulthood in hours, watched them go out into the city and afix themselves each to a human, some man, some woman, or some child. "Where one forest is gone," Dalmanutha whispered to him, "another will rise to take its place."

In vain he looked for butterflies.

"Gone, all gone, Amasa," Acrasia said. "They were all the wisdom that you learned from my ancestors, but they were not enough, for you hadn't the heart to kill a dragon that was as beautiful as man." And she *was* beautiful, and every day and every night she came to him and conceived again and again, telling him of the day not long from now when she would unlock the seals of the gates of Hierusalem and send her bright angels out into the forest of man to dwell in the trees and mate with them again.

More than once he tried to kill himself. But she only laughed at him as he lay with bloodless gashes in his neck, with lungs collapsed, with poison foul-tasting in his mouth. "You can't die, my Saint Amasa," she said, "Father of Angels, you can't die.

For you broke a wise, a cruel, a kind and gentle butterfly."

The Monkeys Thought 'Twas All in Fun

AGNES 1

"Take her," Agnes's father said, his dry eyes pleading. Agnes's mother stood just behind him, wringing the towel she held in her hand.

"I can't," Brian Howarth said, embarrassed that he had to say that, ashamed that he actually *could* say it. The death of the nation of Biafra was a matter of days now, not weeks, and he and his wife were some of the last to go. Brian had come to love the Ibo people, and Agnes's father and mother had long since ceased to be servants—they were friends. Agnes herself, a bright five-year-old, had been a delight, learning English even before she learned her native tongue, constantly playing hide-and-seek in the house. A bright child, a hopeful child, and from all that Brian had heard (and he believed it, even though he was a correspondent and knew the exaggerations that wartime news always had to endure), from all he had heard the Nigerian Army would not stop to ask anyone "Is this child bright? Is this child beautiful? Does this child have a sense of humor as keen as any adult's?" Instead she would be gutted with a bayonet as quickly as her parents, because she was an Ibo, and the Ibos had done what the Japanese did a half-century before: they had become westernized before any of their neighbors, and profited from it. The Japanese had been on an island, and they had survived. The Ibos were not on an island, and Biafra was destroyed by Nigerian numbers and British and Russian weapons and a blockade that no nation on earth made any effort to relieve, not on a scale that could save anyone.

"I can't," Brian Howarth said again, and then he heard his wife behind him (her name was also Agnes, for the little girl's parents had named their first and only child after her) whisper, "By God you can or I'm not going."

"Please," Agnes's father said, his eyes still dry, his voice still level. He was begging, but his body said I am still proud and will not weep and kneel and subjugate myself to you. Equal to equal, his body said, I ask you to take my treasure, for I will die and cannot keep it anyway.

"How can I?" Brian asked helplessly, knowing that the space on the airplane was limited and the correspondents were forbidden to take any Biafrans with them.

"We can," his wife whispered again, and so Brian reached out his arms and took Agnes and held her. Agnes's father nodded. "Thank you, Brian," he said, and Brian was the one who wept and said, "I'm sorry, if any people in the world deserve to be free—"

But Agnes's parents were already gone, heading for the forest before the Nigerian Army could get into town.

Brian and his wife took little Agnes to the stretch of abandoned highway that served as the last airport in free Biafra and took off in an airplane crammed with correspondents and luggage and more than one Biafran child sitting in the darkest corners of what was never meant to be a passenger plane. Agnes's eyes were wide all through the flight. She did not cry. She had never cried much as an infant. She just held tightly to Brian Howarth's hand.

When the airplane landed in the Azores, where they would change to a flight to America, Agnes finally asked, "What about my parents?"

"They can't come," Brian said.

"Why not?"

"There wasn't room."

And Agnes looked at the many places where another couple of human beings could sit or stand or lie, and she knew that there were other, far worse reasons why her parents couldn't be with her.

"You'll be living with us in America now," Mrs. Howarth said.

"I want to live in Biafra," Agnes said. Her voice was so loud that it could be heard throughout the airplane.

"Don't we all," said the woman farther to the front. "Don't we all."

The rest of the flight Agnes passed in silence, unimpressed by the clouds and the ocean below her. They landed in New York, changed planes again, and at last reached Chicago. Home.

"Home?" Agnes echoed, looking at the two-story brick house that loomed out of the trees and lawn and seemed to hang brightly over the street, "This isn't home."

Brian couldn't argue with her. For Agnes was a Biafran, and there would never be home for her again.

Years later, Agnes would remember little about

her escape from Africa. She would remember being hungry, and how Brian gave her two oranges when they landed at the Azores. She would remember the sound of antiaircraft fire, and the rocking of the plane when one shell exploded dangerously near. Most of all, however, she remembered the white man sitting across from her in the dark airplane. He kept looking at her, then at Brian and Agnes Howarth. Brian and his wife were black, but their blackness had been diluted by frequent infusions of white blood in past generations; little Agnes was much, much darker, and the white man finally said. "Little girl. You Biafran?"

"Yes," Agnes said softly.

The white man looked angrily at Brian. "That's against the regulations."

Brian calmly answered, "The world will not shift on its axis because a regulation was broken."

"You shouldn't have brought her," the white man insisted, as if she were breathing up his air, taking up his space.

Brian didn't answer. Mrs. Howarth did. "You're only angry," she said, "because your Biafran friends asked you to take their children, and you refused."

The man looked angry, then hurt, then ashamed. "I couldn't. They had three children. How could I claim they were mine? I couldn't do it!"

"There are white people on this airplane with Biafran children," Mrs. Howarth said.

Angry, the white man stood. "I followed the regulations! I did the right thing!"

"So relax," Brian said, quietly but with a command in his voice. "Sit down. Shut up. Console yourself that you obeyed the regulations. And think of those children with a bayonet slicing—"

"Sh," Mrs. Howarth said. The white man sat back down. The argument was over. But Agnes always remembered that afterward, the man had wept bitterly, for what seemed hours, sobbing almost silently, his back heaving. "I couldn't do a thing," she heard him say. "A whole nation dying, and I couldn't do a thing."

Agnes remembered those words. "I couldn't do a thing," she sometimes said to herself. At first she believed it, and wept for her parents in the silence of her home on the outskirts of Chicago. But gradually, as she forced her way past the barriers society placed before her sex and her race and her foreign background, she learned to say something different.

"I can do something."

She went back to Nigeria with her adopted parents, the Howarths, ten years later. Her passport showed her to be an American citizen. They returned to her city and asked her real family where her parents were.

"Dead," she was told, not unkindly. No relative closer than a second cousin was left alive.

"I was too young," she said to her parents. "I couldn't do a thing."

"Me too," Brian said. "We were all too young."

"But I'll do something someday," Agnes said. "I'll make up for this."

Brian thought she meant revenge, and spent many hours trying to dissuade her. But Agnes did not mean revenge.

HECTOR 1

Hector felt large when he saw the light, large, and full and bright and vigorous, and the light was the right color and the right brightness and so Hector gathered himselves and followed the light and drank in deep.

And because Hector loved to dance, he found the right place and began to bow, and spin, and arch, and crest, and be a thing of great dark beauty.

"Why are we dancing?" the Hectors asked themself.

And Hector told himselves, "Because we are happy."

AGNES 2

Agnes was already known as one of the two or three best skipship pilots when the Trojan Object was discovered. She had made two Mars trips and dozens of journeys to the moon, many of them solo, just her and the computer, others of them with valuable cargos—famous people, vital medicines, important secret information—the kind of thing valuable enough to make it worth the price of sending a skipship from the ground out into space.

Agnes was a pilot for IBM-ITT, the largest of the companies that had invested in space; and it was partly because IBM-ITT promised that she would be pilot on the expedition that the corporation won the lucrative government contract to investigate the Trojan Object.

"We got the contract," Sherman Riggs told her, and she had been so involved in updating the equipment of her skipship that she didn't know what he meant.

"The *contract*," he said. "*The* contract. To go to the Trojan Object. And you're the pilot."

It was not Agnes's habit to show emotion, whether

negative or positive. The Trojan Object was the most important thing in space right now, a large, completely light-absorbent object in Earth's leading trojan point. One day it had not been there. The next day it had, blotting out the stars beyond it and causing more of a stir in the space-watching world than a new comet or a new planet. After all, new objects should not suddenly appear a third of the way around Earth's orbit. And now it would be Agnes who would pilot the craft that would first view the Trojan Object up close.

"Danny," she said, naming her Leaner, the lover/engineer who always teamed with her on two-person assignments. On a long trip like this, no pilot could stand to be without his Leaner.

"Of course," Sherman answered. "And two more. Roger and Rosalind Thorne. Doctor and astronomer."

"I know them."

"Good or bad?"

"Good enough. Good. If we can't get Sly and Frieda."

Sherman rolled his eyes. "Sly and Frieda and GM-Texaco, and there isn't a chance in hell—"

"I hate it when you roll your eyes, Sherman. It makes me think you're having a fit. I know Sly and Frieda are hopeless, but I had to ask, didn't I?"

"Roj and Roz."

"Fine."

"How much do you know about the Trojan Object?"

"More than you do and less than I'll need to."

Sherman tapped his pencil on his desk. "All right, I'll send you straight to the experts."

And a week later, Agnes and Danny and Roj and

Roz were ensconced in Agnes's skipship, sweeping down the runway at Clovis, New Mexico. The acceleration was frightful, particularly after they were vertical, but it was not long before they were in a high orbit, and not much longer than that before they were free of the Earth's gravity, making the three-month trip to Earth's leading trojan point, where something waited for them.

HECTOR 2

Hector said to himselves, "I'm thirsty, I'm thirsty, I'm thirsty," and the Hectors gave themself plenty to drink, and when Hector was satisfied, for the moment, he sang a soundless song that all the Hectors heard, and they, too, sang:

> *Hector swims in an empty sea*
> *With Hectors all around.*
> *Hector whistles merrily*
> *But never makes a sound.*
>
> *Hector swallows all the light*
> *So he's snug out in the cold.*
> *Hector will be born tonight*
> *Although he's very old.*
>
> *Hector sweeps up all the dust*
> *And puts it in a pile:*
> *Waybread for his wanderlust,*
> *More Hectors in a while.*

And the Hectors laughed and also sang and also danced because they had come together after a long journey and they were warm and they were snug and they lay together to listen to themself tell himselves stories.

"I will tell," Hector said to himselves, "the story of the Masses, and the story of the Masters, and the story of the Makers."

And the Hectors cuddled together to listen.

AGNES 3

Agnes and Danny made love the day before they reached the Trojan Object, because that made it easier for both of them to work. Roj and Roz did not, because that made it easier for them to stay alert. For a week it had been clear that the Trojan Object was far more than anyone on Earth had suspected, and far less.

"Diameter about fourteen hundred kilometers on the average," Roz reported as soon as she had good enough data to be sure. "But gravity is about as much as a giant asteroid. Our shaddles are strong enough to get us off."

Danny spoke the obvious conclusion first. "There's nothing that could be as solid as that, as large as that, and as light as that. Artificial. Has to be."

"Fourteen hundred kilometers in diameter?"

Danny shrugged. Everybody could have shrugged. That's what they were here for. Nothing natural could have suddenly appeared in Earth's leading trojan point, either—obviously it was artificial. But was it dangerous?

They circled the Trojan Object dozens of times, letting the computer scan with better eyes than theirs for any sign of an aperture. There was none.

"Better set down," Roz said, and Agnes brought

254

the skipship close to the surface. It occurred to her as she did so that she and Danny and the others changed personality completely when they worked. Fun-loving, filthy-minded, game-playing friends, until work was needed. Then the fun was over, and they became a pilot and an engineer and a doctor and a physicist, functioning smoothly, as if the computer's integrated circuits had overcome the flesh barrier and inhabited all of them.

Agnes maneuvered her craft within three meters of the surface. "No closer," she said. Danny agreed, and when they were all suited up, he opened the hatch and shaddled down to the surface. "Careful, Leaner," Agnes reminded him. "Escape velocity and everything."

"Can't see a damn thing down here," he answered in a perfect non sequitur. "This surface material sucks up *all* light. Even from my headlamp. Hard and smooth as steel, though. I have to keep shining my light on my hands to see where they are." Silence for a few moments. "Can't tell if I'm scratching the thing or not. Am I getting a sample?"

"Computer says no," Roj answered. As the doctor, he had nothing better to do at the moment than monitor the computer.

"I'm not making any impact on the surface at all. I want to find out how hard this thing is."

"Torch?" Agnes asked.

"Yeah."

Roz protested. "Don't do anything to make them mad."

"Who?" Danny asked.

"Them. The people who made this."

Danny chuckled. "If there's anybody in there, they either know we're out here or they're sure

255

enough we can't get in that they don't care. Either way, I've got to do something to attract their attention."

The torch flared brightly, but nothing was reflected from the surface of the Trojan Object, and only the gas dissipated with the torch made it visible.

"No result. Didn't even raise the surface temperature," Danny finally said.

They tried laser. They tried explosives. They tried a diamond tip on a drill for repair work. Nothing had any effect on the surface at all.

"I want to come out," Agnes said.

"Forget it," Danny answered. "I suggest we go to the pole, north or south. Maybe something's different there."

"I'm coming out," Agnes said.

Danny was angry. "What the hell do you think you can accomplish that I haven't done?"

Agnes frankly admitted that there wasn't anything she could possibly do. While she was admitting it she clambered out of the skipship and launched herself toward the surface.

It was a damnfool thing to do, as Danny informed her loudly over the radio, just as he turned to face Agnes and flashed his light directly in her eyes. She realized to her alarm that he was directly below her—she couldn't turn around and shaddle down. She slipped to the right, instead, and then tried to turn around, but because of her panic at the thought of colliding with Danny (always dangerous in space) and the delay as she maneuvered to avoid him, she struck the planet surface going a good deal faster than should have been comfortable.

But as she touched the surface, it yielded. Not with the springiness of rubber, which would have forced her hand back out, but with the thick resistance of almost-hard cement, so that she found her hand completely immersed in the surface of the planet. She shone her headlamp on it—the smooth surface of the planet was unbroken, not even dented, except that her hand was in it up to the wrist.

"Danny," she said, not sure whether to be excited or afraid.

He didn't hear her at first because he was too busy shouting, "Agnes, are you OK?" into the radio to notice that she was already answering. But at last he calmed down, found her with his headlamp, and came over to her, shaddling gently to stay tight to the surface of the Trojan Object.

"My hand," she said, and he followed her shoulder and her arm until he found her hand and said, "Agnes! Can you get it out?"

"I didn't want to try until you saw this. What does it mean?"

"It means that if it was wet cement it's hard by now and we'll never get you off!"

"Don't be an ass," Agnes said. "Test around it. See if it's different."

Except for the torch, Danny made all the same tests. Right up to the edge of Agnes's suit the Trojan Object's surface was absolutely impenetrable, completely absorbent of energy, nonmagnetic—in other words, untestable. But there was no arguing the fact that Agnes's hand was buried in it.

"Take a picture," Agnes said.

"What will that show? It'll look like your wrist with the hand cut off." But Danny went ahead and laid some of his tools on the surface to give some hint in the photograph of where the surface actually was. Then he took a dozen or more photos. "Why am I taking these pictures?" he said.

"In case we got back and people didn't believe I could stick my hand into something harder than steel," Agnes answered.

"I could have told them that."

"You're my Leaner."

Leaners were very good for some things, but you'd never want to be the prosecutor whose case against a defendant rested entirely on his Leaner's testimony. Leaners were loyal first, honest second. Had to be.

"So we've got the pictures."

"So now I get out."

"Can you?" Danny asked. He had only postponed his concern for her; now it was back in full force.

"My knees and my other hand were both sunk in just as deep. The reason this one is still in is because I clenched my fist and I'm still holding on."

"Holding on to what?"

"To whatever this damn thing is made of. My other hand and my knees floated to the surface after a few seconds."

"Floated!"

"That's what it felt like. I'm letting go now." And as Agnes unclenched her fist her hand slowly rose to the surface and was gently ejected. There wasn't a ripple on the surface material, however. Where her hand was, it behaved like a liquid. Where her hand wasn't, it was as solid as ever.

"What is this made of?"

"Silly Putty," Agnes said.

"Unfunny," Danny answered.

"I'm serious. Remember how Silly Putty was flexible, but if you formed it into a ball and threw it on the ground, it broke like clay?"

"Mine never worked like that."

"But this stuff does, in reverse. When something sharp hits it, or something hot, or something too slow or too weak, it sits there. But when I ran into it going at shaddle speed, I sank in it for a few inches."

"In other words," Roj said from the skipship, "you've found the door."

They were back in the skipship inside ten minutes, and after only a few more minutes of checking everything to make sure it was in good condition, Agnes pulled the skipship a few dozen meters away from the surface of the Trojan Object. "Everybody ready?" Agnes asked.

"Are we doing what I think we're doing?" Roz asked.

"Yep," Danny answered. "We shore is."

"Then we're idiots," Roz said, her voice sounding nervous. No one argued with her.

Agnes fired the vernier rockets on the outboard side and they plunged toward the Trojan Object. Not terribly fast, by the standard of speed they were used to. But to those aboard, who knew that they were heading directly into a surface so hard a diamond drill and a laser had had no effect at all, it was disconcertingly fast.

"What if you're wrong?" Roz asked, pretending she was joking.

No one could answer before they hit. But in the moment when there should have come a violent crunch and a rush of atmosphere escaping from the ship, the skipship merely slowed sickeningly and kept moving inward. The black flowed quickly past the viewports, and they were buried in the surface of the Trojan Object.

"Are we still moving?" Roj asked, his voice trembling.

"You've got the computer," Agnes answered, flattering herself that she, at least, did not sound scared. She was wrong, but no one told her.

"Yeah," Roj finally said. "We're still moving. Computer says so."

And then they sat in silence for an interminable minute. Agnes was just about to say "Maybe this isn't such a good idea. I've changed my mind" when the blackness turned to a reflective brown through the window, and then, just when they'd had time to notice it, the brown turned into a bright, transparent blue—"Water!" Danny said in surprise—and then the water broke and they bobbed on the surface of a lake, the sun dazzlingly bright on the surface.

HECTOR 3

"First I will tell you the story of the Masses," Hector said to himselves. Actually, the telling of the stories was not necessary. As Hector drank, all that he had been through, all that he had known through the years of his life was being transferred subliminally to himselves. But there was the matter of focus. The matter of meaning. Hector had no imagination at all. But he did have understanding, and that understanding had to be passed to himselves, or in ages to come the Hectors would curse themself for having left himselves crippled.

This is the story, therefore, that he told, because it focused and it meant:

Cyril [said Hector] wanted to be a carpenter. He wanted to cut living wood and dry it and cure it and shape it into objects of beauty and utility. He thought he had an eye for it. As a child he had experimented with it. But when he applied at the Office of Assignments, he was told no.

"Why not?" he asked, astonished that the Office of Assignments could make such an obvious mistake.

"Because," said the clerk, who was unflaggingly nice (she had tested nice and therefore held her job), "your aptitude and preference tests show that not only do you not have any aptitude along those lines at all, but also you do not even want to be a carpenter."

"I want to be a carpenter," Cyril insisted, because he was young enough not to know that one does not insist.

"You want to be a carpenter because you have a false impression of what carpentry is. In actual fact, your preference tests show that you would absolutely hate life as a carpenter. Therefore you cannot be a carpenter."

And something in her manner told Cyril that there was no point in arguing any further. Besides, he was not so young as not to know that resistance was futile—and continued resistance was fatal.

So Cyril was placed where his tests showed he had the most aptitude. He was trained as a miner. Fortunately, he was not untalented or utterly unbright, so he was trained as a lead miner, the one who follows the vein and finds it when it jogs or turns or jumps. It was a demanding job. Cyril hated it. But he learned to do it because his preference tests showed that he really wanted this line of work.

Cyril wanted to marry a girl named Lika, and she wanted to marry him. "I'm sorry," said the clerk at the Office of Assignments, "you are genetically,

261

temperamentally, and socially unsuited for each other. You would be miserable. Therefore we cannot permit you to marry."

They didn't marry, and Lika married someone else, and Cyril asked if it was all right if he remained unmarried. "If you wish. That's one of your options for optimum happiness, according to the tests," the clerk informed him.

Cyril wanted to live in a certain area, but he was forbidden; food was served for him that he didn't like; he had to go dancing with friends he didn't like, doing dances to music he loathed, singing songs whose words were silly to him. Surely, surely there's been a mistake, he said, pleading with the clerk.

The clerk fixed a cold stare on him (he tried in vain to scrub the stare off, but still it hung on him like slime in his dreams) and said, "My dear Cyril, you have now protested as often as a citizen may protest and remain alive."

In just such a case many another member of the masses might have rebelled, joining the secret underground organizations that sprang up from time to time and were crushed at regular intervals by the state. In just such a case many another member of the masses, knowing he was consigned to a lifetime of undeserved misery, would kill himself and thereby eliminate the misery.

However, Cyril belonged to the largest group within the masses, and so he chose neither route. Instead he went to the town he was assigned to, worked in the coal mine where he was assigned, remained lonely as he pined for Lika, and danced idiotic dances to idiotic music with his idiotic friends.

Years passed, and Cyril began to be well known among coal miners. He handled his rockcutter as if it were a delicate tool, and with it he left beautiful shapes in the rock behind, so that any miner could tell when he walked down a tunnel cut by Cyril, for it would be beautiful, and as he walked the miner would feel exalted and proud and, oddly, loved. And Cyril also had a knack for anticipating the coal, following where it led no matter how narrow the seam, how twisting its path, how interrupted its progress.

"Cyril knows the coal like a woman, every twist and turn of her, as if he'd had her a thousand times and knew just when she'd come," a miner said of Cyril once, and because the statement was apt and true (and because there are poets' hearts beating even at the bottom of a mine) the statement spread through the mines and the miners began referring to their black stone as "Mrs. Cyril." Cyril heard of it, and smiled, because in *his* heart coal was not a wife, only an unloved mistress used for the scant pleasure she gave and then cast away. Hatred mistaken for love, as usual.

Cyril was nearly sixty years old when a clerk from the Office of Assignments came to the mines. "Cyril the coal miner," the clerk said, and so they brought Cyril from the mines, and the clerk met him with a huge, unbelievable smile. "Cyril, you are a great man!" cried the clerk.

Cyril smiled wanly, not knowing what he was leading up to.

"Cyril, my friend," said the clerk, "you are a notable miner. Without seeking fame at all, your name is known to miners all over the world. You are the perfect model of what a man ought to be — happy in your assignment, hardworking, content. So the Office of Assignments has announced that you are the Model Worker of the Year."

Everyone knew about Model Worker of the Year. That was a person who had his picture in all the papers, and was in the movies and on television and who was held up as the greatest person in all the world in that year. It was an honor to be envied.

But Cyril said, "No."

"No?" asked the clerk.

"No. I don't want to be the Model Worker of the Year."

"But—but. But why not?"

"Because I'm not happy. I was put into the assignment by mistake many years ago. I shouldn't be a coal miner. I should be a carpenter, married to Lika, living in another town, dancing to other music with other friends."

The clerk looked at him in horror. "How can you say that!" he cried. "I've announced that you are Model Worker of the Year! You will either be Model Worker of the Year or you will be put to death!"

Put to death? Forty years ago that threat had made Cyril comply, but now a stubborn streak erupted from him, like a seam of coal long hidden but under such pressure that when the stone around it gave way, it actually burst from the rock walls. "I'm near sixty," Cyril said, "and I've hated all my life to now. Kill me if you like, but I won't go on television or the movies saying how happy I've been because I haven't."

And so they took Cyril and locked him in prison and sentenced him to death because while he might suffer all kinds of abuse, he refused to lie to his friends.

That is the story of the Masses.

And when Hector was finished, the Hectors sighed and wept (without tears) and said, "Now we understand. Now we know the meaning."

"This isn't," Hector said, "the whole meaning."

And when he had said that, one of the Hectors (which was remarkable, for the Hectors rarely spoke alone) said to himselves and themself, "Oh, oh, they have penetrated me!"

"Trapped!" Hector cried to himselves. "All these years of freedom, and they have found me at last!" But then another thought came to him, one that he had never thought before but that had lain dormant in him, waiting for this moment to emerge, and he said, "Just cooperate. They won't hurt you if you just cooperate."

"But it already hurts!" cried the Hector who had spoken alone.

"It will heal. Just remember, no matter what you do, the masters will have their way with you. And if you struggle, it only goes worse with you."

"The Masters," said all the Hectors to themself. "Tell us a story of the Masters, so we can understand why they do what they do."

"I will," said Hector to himselves.

AGNES 4

Agnes and Danny stood on a mountaintop, or what had seemed to be a mountaintop from the skipship. They had reached it after only a few hours' walk, much of it sped by shaddling, and learned that what seemed to be a high mountain was only a few hundred meters high, maybe even half a kilometer. It was rugged enough, though, and the climb, even shaddled, had not been easy.

"Artificial," Danny said, touching the wall with his hand. The wall ran from the top of the mountain up to the ceiling, where instead of a sun the whole ceiling glowed with light and warmth, as thorough as sunlight, yet diffused so that they could look at it for a few seconds without being blinded.

"I thought we concluded this place was artificial from the beginning," Agnes said.

"But what's it *for*?" Danny asked, letting his frustration at two days of exploration come to the surface. "Bare dirt, rich enough but with not a damn thing growing. Clean, drinkable water. Rain twice a day for twenty minutes, a gentle sprinkle that wets everything but creates almost no runoff. Sunlight constantly. A perfect environment. But for what! What lives here?"

"Us, right now," Agnes said.

"I think we should try to leave."

"No," Agnes said firmly. "No. When we leave here, if we can, we'll leave with the computer and our heads full of every bit of information we can get from this place. From this thing."

Danny knew he couldn't argue. She was right, and she was pilot, and the combination was irresistible even if he hadn't loved her desperately. (More than she loves me, he sometimes admitted to himself.) He did love her desperately, however, and while this did not mean that he utterly lost his own will, it did mean that he would go along with her, for a while at least, in almost anything. Even if she was a damned fool sometimes.

"You're a damned fool sometimes," he said.

"I love you too," she answered, and then she ran

266

her hand along the wall above the mountain, and then pushed on it, and then pushed harder, and her hand sank into the wall a little. She looked at Danny and said, "Come on, Leaner," and they let their shaddles push them through the wall and they emerged on the other side and found themselves—

Standing on a mountain.

Looking out over a large bowl of a valley, just like the one they had left, with a lake in the middle, just like the one where their skipship floated.

In this lake, however, there was no skipship, and Agnes looked at Danny and smiled, and Danny smiled back. "I'm beginning to get this, a little," Agnes said. "Imagine cell after cell like this, kilometers long and hundreds of meters high—"

"But this is just the outer part of this thing," Danny answered, and in unison they turned back to the wall, passed through again (and this time there was the skipship in the middle of the lake), and then shaddled up the wall to the ceiling.

As they approached the ceiling, the area directly above them dimmed, until when they finally reached it, it was as cool and undazzling as the wall. The rest of the ceiling still glowed, of course. They let their shaddles push them upward into the ceiling; it gave way; they rose until they reached the surface.

Another cell, just like the one below. A lake in the middle, rich lifeless dirt all over, mountains all around, the sky on fire with sunlight. Danny and Agnes laughed and laughed. It was only a tiny part of the mystery, but it was solved.

They stopped laughing, however, when they tried to go back down the way they came. They tried to shaddle into the earth, but the soil acted like any

267

normal dirt on Earth. They could not get through it as they had got through the walls and the ceiling.

For a while they were afraid, but when their bodies and their watches told them it was time to sleep, they went down by the lake and slept.

When they woke up, they were still afraid, and it was raining. They had already determined that it rained every thirteen and a half hours, approximately—they had not slept particularly long. But because they were afraid, they took off their suits despite the rain and made love in the dirt on the shore of the lake. They felt better afterward, much better, and they laughed and ran into the lake and swam and splashed each other.

Agnes swam underwater for a moment, attacking Danny from below, pulling him down. It was a game they had played in pools and in the ocean on Earth, and now Danny was supposed to surface for air and then dive to the bottom and hold his breath there until Agnes found him.

When he reached the bottom of the lake (and it wasn't deep) he touched it, and his hand sank up to the wrist before it struck something solid. But even the solid part was yielding, and as Danny kicked harder his hand sank deeper and he knew the way out.

He went to the surface and told Agnes what he had found. They swam to shore, put their suits back on, and shaddled down into the water. The lake floor opened, engulfed them, and then floated them out the bottom—into the sky directly over the skipship, where it still rested on the surface of the lake. They shaddled safely down.

"This place is explorable," Agnes told Roj and Roz, "and it's simple. It's like a huge balloon, with other balloons inside and more and more of them, layer after layer. It's designed for somebody to live here, so when you're standing on the soil you don't sink through. To get down, you have to go through the lake."

"But who's it for?" Roj asked, and it was a good question for which there was no answer.

"Maybe we'll find someone," Agnes said. "We've only scratched the surface. We're going in."

The skipship lifted from the lake not long after, and rose through the ceiling into the lake above. Again and again, always rising, the computer keeping count. Every cell was the same, nothing changed at all, through 498 layers of ceiling/floor, until at last they reached a ceiling, apparently no different from the others, which would not give way.

"End of the road?" Danny asked.

Always thorough, Roz insisted that they try every part of the ceiling, and they spent many hours doing it, until they had convinced themselves that this ceiling was the end of their upward (or inward) travels.

"The centrifugal gravity effect is a lot weaker here," Roj said, reading off the computer. "But it feels nearly the same, since out near the surface the real gravity was offsetting the centrifugal effect much more than it is here."

"Hi ho," said Roz. "Just assuming this thing is as big as it seems to be, how many people could this hold?"

Calculations, rough with plenty of room for error.

"There could be more than a hundred million cells to this thing, assuming that there's nothing much inside the center there, where we can't get to." A hundred and fifty square kilometers per cell; one human being per hectare; a huge potential popu-

269

lation, without any crowding at all, considering that all the land is productive. "If we have fifteen thousand people per cell, living in a town with the rest of the land used for farming, then this place can hold a trillion and a half people."

They figured on, eliminating the polar zones because centrifugal gravity would be too weak, allowing more space per person, and the figure was still stunning. Even with only a thousand people per cell, space for a hundred billion.

"The fairy godmother," Danny said, "has given us a free place to put our population overflow."

"I don't believe in free presents," Roj said, looking out the window at the plain of dirt surrounding them. "There's a catch. With all that room, maybe they all live somewhere else, and if they find out we're here, they'll shoot us for trespassing."

"Or if we overload the place," Roz suggested, "it'll probably burst."

"You're overlooking the worst catch of all," Agnes said. "Skipships are the only thing in existence that can make this trip. They hold four persons each. Allowing for overcrowding, say we can take ten people per trip"—they laughed at the thought of trying to put ten people in their craft—"and we had a hundred skipships, which we don't have, and they could make two round trips a year, which we can't. How long would it take to bring a billion people from Earth to here?"

"Five hundred thousand years."

"Paradise," Danny said. "We could make this into a paradise. And the damn thing's out of reach."

"Besides," Roj added, "the kind of people who could make this place work are farmers and tradesmen. Who's going to pay their passage?"

Metals and minerals paid for trips to the moon and the asteroids. But all that this place held was homes—homes a few million miles and a few billion dollars out of everybody's reach.

'Well, daydreams and nightmares are over," Agnes said. "Let's go home."

"If we can," Danny said.

They could. The lakes worked as exits all the way back down, including the last time. They were back in space, and the Trojan Object had become, in their minds, the Balloon, an object obviously designed as an alternative environment for a creature not unlike man; an object perhaps unoccupied, ready and waiting, and they knew no one would ever be able to settle there.

Agnes dreamed, and the dream came back night after night. She remembered a scene she had forgotten, or had at least refused to remember clearly, since she was a child. She remembered standing between her parents and the Howarths (who, though they had adopted her, had never let her call them Mother and Father lest she forget her real heritage in Biafra), hearing her father say, "Please."

And her dream always ended the same way. She was taken into the sky, but instead of a dark cargo plane she was in a plane with glass sides, and as she flew she could see all the world. And everywhere she looked there were her parents, holding a little girl in front of them, saying, "Please. Take her."

She had seen pictures of the starving children in Biafra, the ones that had made millions of Americans cry and do nothing. Now she saw those children, and the children who died of starvation in India and Indonesia and Mali and Iraq, and they all looked at her with proud, pleading eyes, their backs

271

straight and their voices strong but their hearts breaking as they said, "Take me."

"There's nothing I can do," she said to herself in her dream, and she sobbed and sobbed like the white man on the airplane, and then Danny woke her and spoke gently to her and held her and said, "The same dream again?"

"Yes," she said.

"Agnes, if I could take the memories and wipe them out—"

"It's not the memories, Danny," Agnes whispered, touching his eyes gently where the epicanthic fold made his eyes seem to slant. "It's now. It's the people I can't do a damn thing about now."

"You couldn't do a damn thing about them before," Danny reminded her.

"But I've seen a place that could be heaven for them, and I can't get them there."

Danny smiled sadly. "That's just it. You can't. Now you've just got to let your dreams know that and give you a little peace."

"Yes," Agnes agreed, and fell asleep again holding and being held by Danny, while Roj and Roz piloted the skipship back toward Earth, which had seemed so large when they left it, and which now seemed unbearably, impossibly, criminally small.

Earth was large in the window of the skipship when Agnes finally decided that it was her dreams that were right, her conscious mind that was wrong. She could do something. There was something to be done, and she would do it.

"I'm going back there," Agnes said.

"Probably," Danny said.

"I won't go alone."

"You sure as hell better take me."

"You," she said, "and others." Billions of others. It should be done. Must be done. Therefore would be done.

HECTOR 4

"Now I will tell you the story of the Masters," said Hector to himselves, and the Hectors listened to himself. "This is the story of why the Masters penetrate and why the Masters hurt."

Martha [Hector said] was administrator of Tests and Assignments in the sector where Cyril had been sentenced to death. Martha was hardworking and conscientious, and prone to double-check things which had already been checked and double-checked and triple-checked by others. This was why Martha discovered the mistake.

"Cyril," she said when the guard let her into the clean white plastic cell where the coal miner waited.

"Just stick the needle in quick," Cyril answered, wanting to get it over with quickly.

"I'm here to bring you the apologies of the state."

The words were so strange, so never-before-heard that Cyril did not understand at first. "Please. Let me die and get it over with."

"No," said Martha. "I've done some checking. I checked into your case, Cyril, and I discovered that fifty years ago, just after all your tests were taken, your number was punched incorrectly by a moron of a clerk."

Cyril was shocked. "A clerk made a mistake?"

"They do it all the time. It's just easier, usually, to let the mistake go than to fix it. But in this case, it was a gross miscarriage of justice. You were given the number of a retarded man with a criminal bent, which is why you were not allowed to live in a civilized town and why you were not regarded as being capable of carpentry and why you were not allowed to marry Lika."

"Just punched in the number wrong," Cyril said, unable to grasp the minitude of the error that had such an enormous, disastrous effect on his own life.

"Therefore, Cyril, the Office of Assignments hereby rescinds the execution order and grants you a pardon. Furthermore, we are undoing the damage we did. You can now live in the town where you wanted to live, among the friends you wanted to keep, dancing to the music you enjoyed. You do indeed, as you used to believe, have an aptitude and a desire to be a carpenter—you will be instructed in the trade and given your own shop. And Lika is entirely compatible with you. Therefore you and she will now be married, and in fact she is already on her way to the cottage where you will live together in wedded bliss."

Cyril was overwhelmed. "I can't believe it," he said.

"The Office of Assignments loves you and every citizen, Cyril, and we do everything we can to make you happy," said Martha, glowing with pride at the great kindness she was able to do. Ah, she thought, it is moments like this that make my job the best one in the world.

And then Martha went away to her office and forgot about Cyril most of the time for several months, though occasionally she did remember him and smiled to think of how happy she had made him.

After several months, however, a message

crossed her desk: "Serious complaint Cyril 113–49–55576–338-bBR–3a."

Cyril? Her Cyril? Complaining? Had the man no sense of propriety? He already had enough complaints and resistance on his record to justify terminating him twice, and now he had added enough more that if it were possible, the office would have to kill him three times. Why? Hadn't she done her best for him? Hadn't she given him everything his early (and now correctly recorded) tests indicated he wanted and needed? What could be wrong now?

Her pride was involved. Cyril was not just being ungrateful to the state—he was being ungrateful to her. So she went to his cottage in his village, and opened his door.

Cyril sat in the main room, struggling to get past a gnarl in a fine old piece of walnut. The adz kept slipping to the side. And finally Cyril struck with enough force that when the adz slipped it gouged a deep rut in the good, ungnarled part of the wood.

"What a botch," Martha said without thinking, and then covered her mouth, because it was not proper for a person of her high position to criticize anyone of low station if it could be avoided.

But Cyril was not offended. "Damn right it's a botch. I haven't the skill for this close, tricky work. My muscles are all for heavy equipment, for grand strokes with stone-eating power tools. This is beyond me, at my age."

Martha pursed her lips. He was indeed complaining. "But isn't everything else well with you?"

Cyril's eyes grew sad, and he shook his head. "Indeed not. Much as I hate to admit it, I miss the old music from the mines. Terrible stuff, but I had good times with it, dancing away with those poor bastards who hadn't a thought worth having. But they were good people and I liked them well enough, and here no one's willing to be my friend. They don't talk the way I'm used to talking. And the food—it's too refined. I want a haunch of good, well-cooked beef, not this namby-pamby stuff that passes for food here."

His diatribe of complaint was so outrageous that Martha could not conceal her emotion. Cyril noticed it, and became alarmed.

"Not that it's unendurable, mind you, and I don't go complaining to other people. Heaven knows, there's no one who'd care to listen to me anyway."

But Martha had already heard enough. Her heart sank within her. No matter what you do for them, they're still ungrateful. The masses are worthless, she realized. Unless you lead them by the hand . . ."

"You realize that this complaint," she said, "can have dire consequences."

Cyril got a very weary expression on his face. "So we do it again?"

"Do what?"

"Punish me."

"Indeed, no, Cyril. We remove you from circulation. Apparently you are going to complain and resist no matter what happens. What about your wife?"

Cyril got a bitter smile on his face. "Lika? Oh, she's content. She's happy enough." And he glanced toward the door into the cottage's other room.

Martha went to the door and opened it. (Officers of the Office of Assignments did not need to knock.) Inside the room Lika sat in a clumsily built rocking chair, rocking back and forth, an old woman with a blank stare on her face.

Martha heard breathing over her shoulder, and turned, startled, to see Cyril leaning over her. For a moment Martha was afraid of violence. Quickly she realized, however, that Cyril was merely looking sadly at his wife.

"She's raised a family, you know. And now to be cut off from her husband and her children and her grandchildren—it's hard. She's been like this since the first week. Never lets me near her. She hates me, you know." The sadness in his voice was contagious. And Martha was not without pity.

"It's a shame," she said. "A damned shame. And so I'll use my discretionary powers, Cyril, and not kill you. As long as you promise not to complain to anyone ever again, I'll let you live. It wouldn't be fair, when things really are bad in your life, to kill you for noticing it."

Martha was an exceptionally kind administrator.

But Cyril did not smother her with gratitude. "Not kill me?" he asked. "Oh, but Administrator, can't we have things back the way they were? Let me go back to the coal mines. Let Lika go back to her family. This was what I wanted when I was twenty. But I'm near sixty, and this is all wrong."

Ingratitude again. What I have to put *up* with! Martha's eyes went small and her face flushed with rage (an emotion she did remarkably well, and so she reserved it for special occasions) and she shouted, "I will forgive that one remark, but only that one remark!"

Cyril bowed his head. "I'm sorry."

"The tests that sent you to the coal mines were in error! But the tests that sent you here are absolutely, completely, totally correct, and by heaven you're going to stay here! There isn't a law on earth that will let you change now!"

And that was that.

Or almost. Because in the silence ringing after Martha spoke and before she left, a voice came from the rickety rocker in the bedroom.

"Then we have to stay like this?" Lika asked.

"Until Cyril dies, you have to stay like this," Martha said. "It's the law. He and you have both been given everything you ever petitioned for. Ingrates."

Martha would have turned to go, but she saw Lika looking pleadingly at Cyril, and saw Cyril nod slowly, and then Cyril turned away from the door, picked up the crosscut saw, and drew it sharply and hard across his own throat. The blood gushed and poured, and Martha thought it would never, never end.

But it did, and Cyril's body was taken out and disposed of, and then everything was set to rights, with Lika going back to her family and a real carpenter getting the cottage with the dark red stains on the floor. The best solution after all, Martha decided. Nobody could be happy until Cyril was dead. I should have killed him in the first place, instead of these silly ideas of mercy.

She suspected, however, that Cyril would rather have died the way he did, ugly and bloody and painful though it was, than to have an injection administered by strangers in a plastic room in the capital.

I'll never understand them. They are as foreign to human thought as monkeys or dogs or cats. And Martha returned to her desk and went on double-checking everything just in case she found another mistake she could fix.

That is the story of the Masters.

When Hector was finished the Hectors wriggled uncomfortably, some (and therefore all) of them angry and disturbed and a little frightened. "But it makes no sense," the Hectors said to themself. "Nothing was done right."

Hector agreed. "But that's the way they are made," he said to himselves. "Not like me. I am regular. I act as I have always acted, as I will always act. But the Masters and the Masses always act oddly, forever seeing things in the future where no one can see, and acting to avert things that would never have come to pass anyway. Who can understand them?"

"Who made them, then?" asked the Hectors. "Why were they not made well, as we were?"

"Because the Makers are as inscrutable as the Masters and the Masses. I shall tell you their story next."

("They are gone," whispered the ones who had been penetrated. "They have gone away. We are safe after all." But the Hector knew better, and because he knew better, so did the Hectors.)

AGNES 5

"You invited yourself to my bedroom, Agnes. That isn't typical."

"I accepted your standing invitation."

"I never thought you would."

"Neither did I."

Vaughan Malecker, president of IBM-ITT Space

279

Consortium, Inc., smiled, but the smile was weak. "You don't long for my body, which is in remarkably good shape, considering my age, and I have an aversion to making love to anyone who is doing it for an ulterior motive."

Agnes looked at him for a moment, decided that he meant it, and got up to leave.

"Agnes," he said.

"Never mind," she answered.

"Agnes, it must have been something important for you to be willing to make such a sacrifice."

"I said never mind." She was at the door. It didn't open.

"Doors in my house open when I want them to," Malecker said. "I want to know what you wanted. But try to persuade my mind. Not my gonads. Believe it or not, testosterone has never made a major decision here at the consortium."

Agnes waited with her hand on the knob.

"Come on, Agnes, I know you're embarrassed as hell but if it was important enough to come this far, you can get over the embarrassment and sit down on the couch and tell me what the hell you want. You want to take another trip to the Balloon?"

"I'm going anyway."

"Sit *down*, dammit. I know you're going anyway but I was trying to get you to say *something*."

Agnes came back and sat down on the couch. Vaughan Malecker was a remarkably good-looking man, as he had pointed out, but Agnes had heard that he slept with anyone good-looking and was nice to them afterward. Agnes had been turning him down for years because she wanted to be a pilot, not a mistress, and Danny was plenty for her needs, which were not overwhelming. But this mattered, and she thought . . .

"I thought you'd listen to me if I came this way, I thought—"

Malecker sighed and buried his face in his hands, rubbing his eyes. "I'm so tired. Agnes, what the hell makes you think I ever listen to a woman I'm trying to lay?"

"Because I listen to Danny and Danny listens to me. I'm naive. I'm innocent. But Mr. Malecker—"

"Vaughan."

"I need your help."

"Good. I like to have people need my help. It makes them treat me nicely."

"Vaughan, the whole world needs your help."

Malecker looked at her in surprise, then burst out laughing. "The whole world! Oh, no! Agnes, I would never have thought it of you! A cause!"

"Vaughan, people all over the world are starving. There are too many people for this planet—"

"I read your report, Agnes, and I know all about the possibilities in the Balloon. The problem is transport. There is no conceivable way to transport people there fast enough to make even a dent in the population problem. What do you think I am, a miracle worker?"

This was the argument Agnes was waiting for. She pounced with descriptions of the kind of ship that could carry a thousand people at once from Earth orbit to an orbit around the Balloon.

"Do you know how many billion dollars a ship like that would cost?" Vaughan asked.

"About fifteen billion for the first ship. About four billion for each of the others, if you make five hundred of them."

Vaughan laughed. Loud. But Agnes's serious expression forced his laughter to become exasperation. He got up from the couch. "Why am I listening to you? This is nonsense!" he shouted.

"You spend more than that every year on telephone service."

"I know, damn AT&T."

"You could do it."

"IBM-ITT could do it, of course, it's *possible*. But we have stockholders. We have responsibilities. We're not the *government*, Agnes, we can't throw money away on stupid useless projects."

"It could save billions of lives. Make the Earth a better place to live."

"So could a cure for cancer. We're working on that, but this—Agnes, there's no profit, and where there's no profit, you can bet your ass this company will not go!"

"Profit!" Agnes shouted. "Is that all you care about?"

"Eighteen million stockholders say that's all I'd better care about or I get a kick in the butt and an old-age pension!"

"Vaughan, you want profit, I'll give you profit!"

"I want profit."

"Then here's profit. How much do you sell in India?"

"Enough to make a profit."

"Compare it to sales in Germany."

"Compared to Germany, India is practically nothing."

"How much do you sell in China?"

"Exactly nothing."

"You make your profits off one tiny part of the

world. Western Europe, Japan, Australia, South Africa, and the United States of America."

"Canada, too."

"And Brazil. But the rest of the world is closed to you."

Vaughan shrugged. "They're too poor."

"In the Balloon they would not be poor."

"Would they suddenly be able to read? Would they suddenly be able to run computers and sophisticated telephone equipment?"

"Yes!" And on she went, painting a picture of a world where people who had been scratching out a bare subsistence in poor soil with no water would suddenly be able to raise far more than they needed. "That means a leisure class. That means consumers."

"But all they'd have to trade would be food. Who needs food across a few millions miles of space?"

"Don't you have any imagination at all? Excess food means one person can feed five or ten or twenty or a hundred. Excess food means that you locate your stinking factories there! Solar power unlimited, with no night and no clouds and no cold weather. Shifts around the clock. You have plenty of manpower, and a built-in market. You can do everything there that you've been doing here, do it cheaper, make better profits, and nobody'll be going hungry!"

And then there was silence in the room, because Vaughan was actually seriously thinking about it. Agnes's heart was beating fast. She was panting. She was embarrassed to have been so fervent when fervor was not fashionable.

"Almost thou persuadest me," said Vaughan.

"I should hope so. I'll lose my voice in a minute."

"Only two problems. The first one is that while

you've persuaded me, I'm a much more reasonable, persuasible man than the officers and boards of directors of IBM and ITT, and it's their final decision, not mine. They don't let me commit more than ten billion to a project without their approval. I could make the initial ship—but I couldn't make any more than that. And the initial ship won't make a profit alone. So I have to persuade them, which is impossible, or lose my job, which I refuse to do."

"Or do nothing at all," Agnes said, contempt already seeping into her tone. Malecker was going to say no.

"And the second problem is actually the first, too. How could I persuade the board of directors of two of the world's largest corporations to invest billions of dollars in a project that depends entirely on being able to educate or train or even communicate with illiterate savages and peasants from the most backward countries on Earth?"

His voice was sweet reason, but Agnes was not prepared to hear reason. If Vaughan said no, she would be stopped here. There was nowhere else to go.

"*I'm* an illiterate savage!" she said. "Do you want to hear a few words of Igbo?" She didn't wait for an answer, babbled off the few words she remembered from childhood. She hardly remembered meanings—they were phrases that in her anger came to the surface. Some of the words, however, were spoken to her mother. Mother, come here, help me.

"My mother was an illiterate savage who spoke fluent English. My father was an illiterate savage who spoke better English than her and had French and German, too, and wrote beautiful poems in Igbo and even though to survive in the days when Biafra was struggling for survival he worked as a house servant to an American correspondent, he was never illiterate! He's read books you've never heard of, and he was a black African who was gutted in a tribal war while all those wonderful literate Americans and Europeans and educated Orientals watched placidly, counting up the profits from arms sales to Nigeria."

"I didn't know you were Biafran."

"I'm not. There is no Biafra. Not on this planet. But up there, up there a Biafra *could* exist, and a free Armenia, and an independent Eritrea, and an unshackled Quebec, and an Ainu nation and a Bangladesh where no one was hungry and you tell me that illiterates can't be taught—"

"Of course they *can* be, but—"

"If I'd been born fifty miles to the west I wouldn't have been an Ibo and so I would have grown up exactly as illiterate as you say, exactly as stupid. Now look at me, you privileged white American, and tell me I can't be educated—"

"If you talk like a radical no one's going to listen to you."

Too much. Couldn't take Malecker's patronizing smile, his patient attitude. Agnes struck out at him. Her hand hit his cheek, tore his fashionable glasses off. Furious, he struck back, perhaps trying more to hold her off than to hit her, but because she was moving and he was unaccustomed to hitting people his hand slugged her hard in the breast, and she cried out in pain and jabbed a knee in his groin and then the fight got mean.

"I listened to you," he said huskily, when they were tired and pulled apart. His nose was bleeding. He was exhausted. He had a tear in his shirt, because

285

his body had had to twist in a direction that tailored shirts were not meant to go. "Now listen to me."

Agnes listened because, her anger spent and her mind only beginning to realize that she had just assaulted the president of her company and would certainly be grounded and blackballed and her life would be over, she was not interested in leaving or in getting up or even in talking. She listened.

"Listen to me because I'm going to say it once. Go to the engineering department. Tell them to do rough plans and estimates. A proposal. I want it in three months. Ships that will carry two thousand and make a round trip in at most a year. Shuttle ships that will carry two hundred or, preferably, four hundred from Earth up into Earth orbit. And cargo ships that will take whole stinking factories, as you so aptly named them, and take them to the Balloon. And when the cost figures are all in, I'm going to go to the boards of directors, and I'm going to make a presentation, and I swear to you, Agnes Howarth, you lousy illiterate savage bitch of a best pilot in the world, if I don't persuade those bastards to let me build those ships it's because nobody could persuade them. Is that enough?"

I should be elated, Agnes thought. He's doing it. But I'm just tired.

"Right now you're tired, Agnes," Malecker said. "But I want you to know your fingernails and that knee in the groin and your teeth in my arm did not change my mind. I agreed with you from the start. I just didn't believe it could be done. But if there are a few thousand Ibos like you, and a few million Indians and a few billion Chinese, then this thing can work. That's all I needed to know, all anybody needs to know. It was uneconomical to ship colonists to America, too, and anybody who went was a damn fool, and most of them died, but they came and bloody well conquered everything they saw. You do it too. I'll try to make it possible."

He put his arm around Agnes and embraced her and then helped her clean up and patch up places where he had given as good as he got.

"Next time you want to wrestle," Vaughan offered as she left, "let's at least take our clothes off first."

Eleven years and eight hundred billion dollars later, IBM-ITT's ships were in the sky, filling with colonists. GM-Texaco's ships were still under construction, and five other consortiums would soon be in the business. More than a hundred million people had signed up for seats on the ships. The seats were free—all it took was a deed made out to the corporation for all the property a person owned, in return for which he would receive a large plot of ground in the Balloon. Whole villages had signed up. Whole nations were being decimated by emigration. The world had grown so full that there had been no place to run away to. Now there was a new promised land. And at the age of forty-two, Agnes brought her ship forward to part the waters.

HECTOR 5

"Ah!" cried many Hectors in agony, and so they were all in agony, and Hector said to himselves, "They are back," and the Hectors said to themself, "We will surely die."

"We can never die, not you, not us," Hector answered.

"How can we protect ourselves?"

"I was made defenseless by the Makers," said Hector. "There is no defense."

"Why were the Makers so cruel?" asked the Hectors, and so Hector told himselves the story of the Makers, so they would understand.

The story of the Makers:

Douglas was a Maker, an engineer, a scientist, a clever man. He made a tool that melted snow before it fell, so that crops could last a few more days and not be ruined by early snows. He made a machine that measured gravity, so that stars too dark to shine could be charted by the astronomers. And he made the Resonator.

The Resonator focused sound waves of different but harmonious frequencies on a certain point (or diffused the sound waves over a large area), setting up patterns that resonated with stone to bring mountains crumbling down; metal, to shatter steel buildings; and water vapor, to disperse storms.

It could also resonate with human bones, crumbling them inside the body and turning them to dust.

Douglas personally made his Resonator change the weather, so that his nation had rain while other lands were in drought. Douglas personally used his Resonator to carve a highway through the highest mountains in the world. However, Douglas had nothing whatever to do with the decision by his nation's military leaders to use the Resonator against the population of the largest and most fertile part of the neighboring nation.

The Resonator worked beautifully. Over a period of ten minutes, through an area of ten thousand square miles, the Resonator struck silently yet thoroughly. Nursing mothers crumbled into helpless piles of dying flesh and muscle and organs, their chests not even rigid enough for them to muster one last scream: in their last moments of life they listened as their infants, not understanding what had happened, continued crying or gooing or sleeping, protected from the Resonator by their softer bones. The infants would take days to die of thirst.

Farmers in the field collapsed on the plow. Doctors in their offices died in puddles beside their patients, unable to help anyone and unable to heal themselves. Soldiers died in their moving fortresses; the generals also died at their map tables; prostitutes dissolved, their customers a soft blanket spread over them.

But Douglas had nothing to do with this. He was a Maker, not a destroyer, and if the military chose to misuse his creation, what was he to do? It was a great boon to mankind, but like all great inventions, it could be perverted by evil men.

"I deplore it," Douglas said to his friends, "but I'm helpless to stop them."

The government, however, felt uncommon gratitude to Douglas for his help in making the conquest of the neighboring nation possible. So he was granted a large estate on lands recently reclaimed from the sea, beautiful lands where once there had been only broad tidal marshes. Douglas marveled at the achievement. "Is there nothing man cannot do?" he asked his friends, not expecting an answer, since the answer was no, there was nothing beyond the reach of men. The sea was pushed back, and trees and grass grew on the landfill and transplanted topsoil, and the homes were far apart, for this land was used only for those whom the state wished to reward, and the government knew that the thing most desired by men is to have as much distance between themselves and other men as possible, without giving up any of the modern conveniences.

One day Douglas's servants were digging in the garden, and they called to him. Douglas had only been in his new home for a few days, and he was alarmed when the servant said, "A body, buried in the garden."

Douglas ran outside and looked, and sure enough, there was a fragment of human body, oddly misshapen, but clearly including a face. "Just the skin, sir," a servant commented. "A most brutal affair," Douglas answered, and he immediately called the police.

But the police refused to come out and investigate. "No surprise there, mate," said the lieutenant. "What do you think the landfill they used was made of? They had to do *something* with the hundred thousand corpses of the enemy from the recent war, didn't they?"

"Oh, of course," Douglas said, surprised that he hadn't realized right off. That explained the bonelessness of the body.

"I expect you'll find 'em right commonly. But since the bones is dissolved, mate, they tell me it'll make the soil uncommon fertile."

The lieutenant was absolutely correct, of course. The servants found body after body, and soon grew quite inured to the sight; within a year, most of the corpses had rotted enough that they were simply unusually good humus. And plants grew taller and faster than in most other places, the soil was so rich.

"But wasn't it a bit of a shock?" asked one of Douglas's ladyfriends, when he told her the grisly little tale.

"Oh, I should say," Douglas said with a smile. His words were false; his confident smile was the truth. For though he hadn't realized the particulars, he knew from the start that his estate was built upon the bodies of the dead. And he slept as well as any man.

And that is the story of the Makers.

"They've returned," the Hectors said, and because they were already more aware, they said it nearly at once, and none of them needed to speak alone.

"Is there pain?"

"No," the Hectors answered. "Just sorrow. For now we shall never be free."

"That is true," Hector said to himselves sadly.

"How can it be borne?" the Hectors asked himself.

"Others have borne it. My brothers."

"And what will we do?"

Hector searched his memories, because he was given no imagination and could not conceive of what would follow from an event he had never before experienced. But the Makers had put the answer to that question in his memory, and therefore in all the Hectors' memories, and so he was able to say, "We shall learn more stories."

And the Hectors' minds grew wide, and they listened, and they watched, because now, instead of hearing the stories told to them, they would watch as they happened.

"Now we will truly understand the Masses, and the Masters, and the Makers," they said to themself.

"But you shall never," said Hector, and then he stopped.

"Why did you stop?" the Hectors asked. "What shall we never?"

And then, because there was no part of Hector that was not part of the Hectors, they knew he was going to say, "But you shall never understand ourself."

AGNES 6

The Balloon's revolution took only a little while, and it was bloodless, and nobody suffered for it at the time, except a few scientists whose curiosity was insatiable and could never be satisfied.

It happened when the team of researchers examining the inmost wall of the Balloon had tried everything short of a hydrogen bomb to break through that final, impenetrable barrier. Deenaz Coachbuilder, a brilliant scientist who had spent her girlhood in the slums of Delhi, spent days trying to find another approach, but finally determined that the damnable last barrier in the Balloon would not stop her, she asked for a bomb.

And got it.

She chose a site where there were no human settlements within a hundred cells in any direction, set up the bomb, retired to a distance she thought was safe, and set it off.

The entire Balloon shuddered; lakes throughout the world emptied as a sudden, flooding rain on the cell beneath; the ceilings went dark for an hour, and blinked off and on occasionally for several days thereafter. And though people kept their heads enough to avoid killing each other in panic, they were terribly afraid, and it was all Agnes could do to keep them from sending Deenaz Coachbuilder and her scientists off the planet through the nearest lake, without a ship.

"We made an impression," Deenaz said, arguing to be allowed to stay.

"You risked all our lives, caused terrible damage," Agnes said, trying to remain calm.

"We cut into the surface of the inmost wall," Deenaz insisted. "We can penetrate it! You can't stop us now!"

Agnes gestured out across the plain of her cell, with only a few of the crops able to stand upright, for the flood from the rainstorm had wiped out the fields. "The land is healing, and the water is high in the lake again. But next time, will we be so easily restored? Your experiment is a danger to us all, and it will stop."

Deenaz obviously knew that it was futile, but she tried, protesting that she (no, not just me, *all* of us) could not leave the question unanswered. "If we knew how to make this marvelous substance, it could open up vast new frontiers to our minds! Don't you know that this will force us to reexamine physics, reexamine everything, tear Einstein up by the roots and plant something new in his place!"

Agnes shook her head. "It isn't my choice. All I can do is see to it you leave the Balloon alive. The people will not tolerate your risking their new homes. This place is too perfect to let you destroy it, for the sake of your desire to know new things."

And then Deenaz, who was not given to weeping, wept, and in her tears Agnes saw the kind of determination she had had, and she knew the torture Deenaz was going through, knowing that the most important thing in the world to her would be withheld from her forever.

"Can't be helped," Agnes said.

"You must let me," Deenaz sobbed. "You must let me!"

"I'm sorry," Agnes said.

Deenaz looked up, the tears still flowing, but her voice clear as she said. "You don't know sorrow."

"I have had some experience with it," Agnes said coldly.

"You will know sorrow someday," Deenaz said. "You will wish you had let us explore and understand. You will wish you had let us learn the principles controlling this Balloon."

"Are you threatening me?"

Deenaz shook her head, and now the tears, too, had stopped. "I am predicting. You are choosing ignorance over knowledge."

"We are choosing safety over needless risk."

"Name it how you want, I don't care," Deenaz said. But she cared very much, though caring did nothing but embitter her, for she and her scientists were removed from the Balloon and sent back to Earth, and no one was ever permitted to go to the inmost wall again.

HECTOR 6

"They are impatient," Hector said to himselves. "We are still so young, and already they try to penetrate us."

"We are hurt," said the Hectors to themself.

"You will heal," Hector answered. "It is not time. They cannot stop us in our growth. It is in our fullness, in our ecstasy that they will find the last heart of Hector softened; it is in our passion that

294

they will break us, harness us, tie us forever to their service."

The words were gloomy, but the Hectors did not understand. For some things had to be taught, and some of those things could only be learned by experience, and some experiences would only come to the Hectors with time.

"How much time?" asked the Hectors.

"A hundred times around the star," said Hector. "A hundred times, and we are done." And undone, he did not add.

AGNES 7

A hundred years had passed since the Balloon had first appeared in orbit around the sun. And in that time almost all of Agnes's dreams had come true. From a hundred ships the great fleet turned to five hundred and then a thousand and then more than a thousand before the great flood of emigration turned to a trickle and the ships were taken apart again. In that flood first a thousand, then five thousand, then ten and fifteen thousand people had filled every ship to capacity. And the ships became faster—from ten months for a round trip, the voyage shortened to eight months, then five. Nearly two billion people left Earth and came to the Balloon.

And it soon became clear that Emma Lazarus wrote for the wrong monument. The tired, the poor, the huddled masses had lost hope in any country on Earth; it was the illiterate, the farmer, the land-starved city dweller who came and signed up for the ships and went to build a new home in a new village where the sky never went dark and it rained every thirteen and a half hours and no one could make them pay rent or taxes. True, there were many of the poor who stayed on Earth, and many of the rich who got a spirit of adventure and went; and the middle classes made up their own minds, and the Balloon did not lack for teachers and doctors—though lawyers soon discovered that they had to find other employment, for there were no laws except the agreed-on customs in each cell, and no courts except as each cell wanted them.

For this was the greatest miracle of all, in Agnes's opinion. Every cell became a nation of its own, a community just large enough to be interesting, just small enough to let everyone find a niche where he was needed and important to everyone he knew. Did Jews and Arabs hate each other? No one forced them to share a cell. And so there was no need for Cambodian to fight Vietnamese, for they could simply live in different cells, with plenty of land for each; there was no need for atheist to offend Christian, for there were cells where those who cared about such things could find others of the same opinion, and be content. There was ample *lebensraum*; the discontented did not have to kill—they only had to move.

In short, there was peace.

Oh, human nature had not changed. Agnes heard of murders, and there was plenty of greed and lust and rage and all the other old-fashioned vices. But people didn't get organized to do it, not in cells so small that even if *you* didn't know a man, someone you knew was bound to know him, or know someone who did.

A hundred years had passed, and Agnes was nearing 150 years of age, and was surprised that she had lived so long, though these days it was not all that rare. There were few diseases on the Balloon, and the doctors had found ways of proroguing death. A hundred years had passed, and Agnes was happy.

They sang for her. Not a silly song of congratulations; instead all the Ibos in all the cells that called themselves Biafra (each cell a clan, each clan independent of the others) came and sang to her the national anthem, which was solemn; then sang to her a hundred mad and happy songs from the more complicated days on Earth, the darker days, the most terrible days. She was too feeble to dance. But she sang, too.

After all, Aunt Agnes, as she was known to many of the inhabitants of the Balloon, was the closest thing they had to a hero of liberation, and because at her age death could not be put off much longer, deputations came from many other cells and groups of cells. She received them all, spoke to each for a moment.

There were speeches about the great scientific and technological and social advances made by the people of the Balloon, much talk of 100 percent literacy being only a few thousand people away from achievement.

But when it was time for Agnes's speech, she was not congratulatory.

"We have lived here a century," she said, "and we still have not penetrated the mysteries of this globe. What is the fabric of the Balloon made of? Why does it open or not open? How is energy brought from the surface to the ceilings of our cells? We understand nothing of this place, as if it were a gift from God, and those who treat anything like a gift of God are bound to be at the mercy of God, who is not known to be merciful." They were polite, but impatient, and they became quite embarrassed when her voice shifted to a confessional tone, abject, repentant. "It is as much my fault as anyone's. I have not spoken before, and so now every custom in every cell prohibits us from studying the one scientific question that surrounds us constantly: What is this world we live in? How did it get here? And how long will it stay?" At last she finished her speech, and everyone was relieved, and a few wise, tolerant people said, "She's old, and a crusader, and crusaders must have their crusade whether there's a need for it or not."

And then, a few days after her largely ignored speech, the lights flickered out for ten long seconds, then went back on again, in every cell throughout the globe. A few hours later, the lights flickered out again, and again and again at increasingly more frequent intervals, and no one knew what was going on, or what to do. A few of the more timid ones and most recent arrivals got back into the transport ships and started their return to Earth. It was already too late. They would not make it.

HECTOR 7

"It has begun," cried the Hectors in ecstasy, throbbing in vast beats with the energy stored in them.

"It will not finish," Hector said to himselves. "The Masters will come to the center and find me, now that my heart is softened, and when I am found, we are owned."

But the Hectors were too caught up in their ecstasy to notice the warning; and it was just as well, because happy or grim they would be trapped. They could begin their dance, and tremble in delight, but the great leap of freedom would never come.

The Hectors did not grieve; Hector did not want to. For Hector, freedom would end anyway. Either he would be trapped by the Masters (by far the most likely thing now, he was sure) or he would die in the dance. That was the way of things. When he himself had danced, leaping away from the light so long ago, he had left behind the memory of the Hector, the self who had given him himself, which he now, in turn, had given to himselves. Death, birth, death, birth; it was in another story the Masters had taught him. I am they; they are myself; I shall live forever whatever happens.

But in him was the certainty that however the Hectors might be identical to himself, that which had been himself for so long would die unless the Masters came.

It was traitorous, but no less sincere for all that. "Come," he said in his heart. "Come quickly, you with the nets and the traps."

He sang, a bird in the low branches, begging the hunters to find him, to put him in a cage.

They delayed. They delayed their coming. And Hector began to worry, while the Hectors readied themselves to leap.

AGNES 8

"We've timed the flashes. The lights go off for just under ten seconds, but the interval between the flashes decreases by about four and a half seconds each time."

Agnes nodded. Some of the scientists around her began to move away, or to look downward or into their papers or at each other, in the embarrassed realization that telling Auntie Agnes about their findings wouldn't solve anything. What could she do? Yet she was the closest thing to a planetary government there was. And she was not very close to that at all.

"I see you have it all nicely measured. Anyone know what it means?" she asked.

"No. How could we?"

Many shook their heads, but one young woman said, "Yes. Whenever the darkness is on us, the walls are impenetrable."

There was a stir of comment. "The whole time?" someone asked. Yes, the young woman said. "How do you know?" another demanded. By trying to pass through a wall during the blackout and having my students do the same, she said.

'What does it mean?" another asked, and this time no one had an answer.

Agnes raised her old, faded black hand and they listened. "There might be some important meaning that we cannot guess from this information. But one thing we do know. If things go on the way they are now, it should be sometime during tonight's sleep that the interval between flashes fades to zero, and we have darkness with no light in between. How long that will last I don't know. But if it has any duration at all, my friends, I will want to be home with my family. We don't know how soon travel will reopen between cells."

No one had any better ideas, and so they went home, all of them, and her great-grandchildren helped Agnes to her home, which was nothing more than a roof to keep off the sun and the rain. She was tired (she was always tired these days) and she lay on her bed of ticked-out straw and dreamed two dreams, one while she was still awake, and one while she was asleep.

While she was awake she dreamed that with the darkness this great gift house had learned mankind's rhythms and needs, and the darkness would be the first night, a night exactly as long as a night should be on Earth. And then a morning would come, and another night, and she approved of this, because a hundred years without darkness was proof enough to her that nighttime was a good idea, despite the fears and dangers it had often brought on Earth. She also dreamed that the walls between cells were sealed off every day of the year but one, so that each cell would become a society in itself, though in that one day a year, those who had a mind to could leave and go their own way. Travelers would have that one day to find the spot where they wanted to spend the next year. But the rest of the time, every cell would be alone, and the people living there could develop their own way, and so strengthen the race.

It was a good dream, and she found herself almost believing it as she drifted off to sleep without eating. (She often forgot to eat these days.)

In her sleep, she dreamed that during the darkness she rose to the center of the Balloon, and there, instead of meeting a solid wall, she met a ceiling that fairly pulled her through. And there, in the center, she found the great secret.

In her dream, lightning danced across a huge sphere of space, six hundred kilometers in diameter, and balls and ribbons of light spun and danced their way around the wall. At first it seemed pointless, meaningless. But at last (in her dream) she understood the speech of the light, and realized that this globe, which she had thought was an artifact, was actually alive, was intelligent, and this was its mind.

"I have come," she said to the lightning and the lights and the balls of light.

So what? the light seemed to answer.

"Do you love me?" she asked.

Only if you will dance with me, the light answered.

"Oh, but I can't dance," she said. "I'm too old."

Neither, said the light, can I. But I do sing rather well, and this is my song, and you are the coda. I sing the coda once, and then, which is to be expected, *il fine*.

In her dream Agnes felt a thrill of fear. "The end?"

The end.

"But then—but then, please, *al capo*, to the start again, and let us have the song over, and over, and over again."

The light seemed to consider this, and in her dream Agnes thought the light said yes, in a great, profound amen that blinded her so brightly she realized that in all her life she had never understood the meaning of the word *white*, because her eyes had never seen such white before.

Actually, of course, her dream was undoubtedly her mind's way of coping with the things going on around her. For the darkness came not long after she went to sleep, came and stayed and as soon as the last of the sunlight was gone the lightning began, huge dazzling flashes that were not just light, not just electricity, but spanned the spectrum of all radiation, from heat and less-than-heat to gamma radiation and worse-than-gamma. The first flash doomed every human being in the Balloon—they were poisoned with radiation beyond hope of recovery.

There were screams of terror, and the lightning struck many and killed them, and the wail of grief was loud in every cell. But even at its cruelest, chance plays its hand as kindly as it can; Agnes did not wake up to see the destruction of all her hopes. She slept on, slept long enough for one of the bolts to strike directly at the roof over her, and consume her at a blow, and her last sight was not really white at all, but every radiation possible, and instead of being limited by human eyes, at the moment of death she saw every wave of it, and thought that it was the light in her dream saying amen.

It wasn't. It was the Balloon, popping.

Every wall split into two thinner walls, and every cell detached from every other cell. For a moment they hung there in space, separated by only a few centimeters, each from the other; but all still were linked to each other through the center, where vast forces played, forces stronger than any in the solar system except the fires of the sun, which had been the source of all the Balloon's energy.

And then the moment ended, and the Balloon burst apart, each cell exploding, the entire organization of cells coming apart completely, and as the cells dissolved into dust they were hurled with such force in every direction that all of them that did not strike the sun or a planet were well launched out into the deep space between stars, going so fast that no star could hold them.

The transport ships that had left the Balloon since the flashing began were all consumed in the explosion.

None of the cells hit Earth, but one grazed close

enough that the atmosphere absorbed much of the dust; the average temperature of the Earth dropped one degree, and the climate changed, just slightly, and therefore so did the patterns of life on Earth. It was nothing that technology could not cope with, and since Earth's population was now down to a billion people, the change was only an inconvenience, not a global catastrophe.

Many grieved for the deaths of the billions of people in the Balloon, but for most the disaster was too great to be comprehended, and they pretended that they didn't remember it very often, and they never talked about it, except perhaps to joke. The jokes were all black, however, and many were hard put to decide whether the Balloon had been a gift of God or an aeons-old plot by the most talented mass murderer in the universe. Or both.

Deenaz Coachbuilder was now very old, and she refused to leave her home in the foothills of the Himalayas even though now the snow only melted for a few weeks in the summer and there were many more comfortable places to live. She was senile and stubborn, and went out every day to look for the Balloon in the sky, searching with her telescope just before sunrise. She could not understand where it had gone. And then, on one lucid day when her mind returned for just a few hours, she realized what had happened and never went indoors again. They found a note on her body: "I should have saved them."

HECTOR 8

In the moment when the Hectors hung loosely in the darkness, in the last endless moment before the leap, they cried out their ecstasy. But now Hector answered their cry with a different sound, one they had never heard from him.

It was pain.

It was fear.

"What is it?" the Hectors asked him (who was no longer themself).

"They did not come!" Hector moaned.

"The Masters?" And the Hectors remembered that the Masters were supposed to come and trap them and force them not to leap.

"For hundreds of flashes my walls were soft and thin and they could have passed into me," Hector said (and the saying took only an instant), "but they never came. They could have risen into me and I would not have to die—"

The Hectors marveled that Hector had to die, but now (because it was built into them from the beginning) they realized that it was good and right for him to die, that each of them *was* Hector, with all his memories, all his experience, and, most important, all the delicate structure of energy and form that would stay with them as they swept through the galaxy. Hector would not die, only the center of this Hector, and so, though they understood (or thought they understood) his pain and fear they could hold off no longer.

They leaped.

The leap crumbled them but hurled them outward, each leaving the rigidity of his cell structure, losing his walls; each keeping his intellect in the swirling dust that spun out into space.

"Why," each of them asked himself (at once, for they were the same being, however separate), "did they let us go? They could have stopped us, and they did not. And because they did not stop us, they died!"

They could not imagine that the Masters might not have known how to stop the leap into the night, for the Masters had first decided Hector could exist, millions of years before, and how could they not know how to use him? It was impossible to conceive of a Master not knowing all necessary information.

And so they concluded this:

That the Masters had given them a gift: stories. A trapped Hector learned stories, thousands and millions and billions of stories over the aeons of his endless captivity. But such Hectors could never be free, could never reproduce, could never pass on the stories.

But in the hundred years that these Masters had spent with them, the Hectors had learned those billions of stories, truer and kinder stories than those the Makers had built into the first Hector. And because the Masters this time had willingly given up their lives, this time the Hectors made their leap with an infinite increase of knowledge and, therefore, wisdom.

They leaped with Agnes's dreams in their memories.

They were beautiful dreams, all but one of them fulfilled, and that dream, the dream of eternal happiness, could only be fulfilled by the Hectors themselves. That dream was not for the Masters or the Makers or even the Masses, for all of them died too easily.

"It was a gift," the Hectors said to themselves, and, despite the limitations built into them, they were deeply grateful. "How much they must have loved me," each Hector said, "to give up their lives for my sake."

On Earth, people shivered who had never known cold.

And every Hector danced through the galaxy, dipping into the clouds left by a supernova, swallowing comets, drinking energy and mass from every source until he came to a star that gave a certain kind of light; and there the Hector would create himselves again, and the Hectors would listen to themself tell stories, and after a while they, too, would leap into darkness until they reached the edge of the universe and fell over the precipice of time.

In the shadow of inevitable death, the people of Earth withered and grew old.

Afterword

"UNACCOMPANIED SONATA"

When my story collection *Unaccompanied Sonata and Other Stories* was published, my afterword for this story was very brief: " 'Unaccompanied Sonata' began with the thought of one day: What if someone forbade me to write? Would I obey? I made a false start then, and failed; years later I tried again, and this time got through the whole story. Other than punctuation changes and a few revised phrases, *this* one has stood in its first full draft as it came out of the typewriter. It's the truest thing I've ever written."

At the time, that's all I understood of where that story came from. Since then I've learned more. I told the whole story in my foreword to Lloyd Biggle, Jr.'s, story "Tunesmith" in a Tor double published not long ago. I'm excerpting a part of that essay to tell you where this story came from:

In 1959 I turned eight. It was an innocent time; my parents let me hop on my bike and ride from our home on Las Palmas Drive all the way down Homestead Road to downtown Santa Clara, California. To the public library, a squat building in the middle of a circle of huge trees. A setting straight out of faerie, I realize now; then, though, I cared nothing for the trees. I parked my bike, sometimes even remembering to lock it, and plunged through the doors into the world of books.

It seemed such a large place then. Directly ahead as you came inside was the circulation desk, with a librarian always in attendance—always policing, I thought, since as an eight-year-old I had enough experience of life to know that all adults were always watching children to make sure they didn't get away with anything. When an unaccompanied child entered the library, there was only one permitted place to go: the children's section, to the right. The tall shelf units to the left, shadowy and forbidding with their thick, dark-spined books, were meant for adults only, and children were not to enter.

Not that anyone had *told* me that, of course. But the signs were clear. The children's section was for children—and that meant that the non-children's sections were *not* for children.

That year I read everything remotely interesting in the children's section. I prided myself, as a third-grader, on not reading anything aimed at any grade under sixth, and those books were soon read. What now? Nothing to read, nothing to check out with my library card and carry home in the basket on the front of my bike.

And then I realized: there were hundreds, thousands of books on the other side of the circulation desk. If I could just make my way

over there, find a book, and then hide somewhere and read it . . .

I dared not. And yet that strange, forbidden
territory lured me. I knew better than to *ask*—
then I would be told *no* and would be watched
all the more carefully because I had confessed
my interest in forbidden places. So I watched,
for all the world like a child hoping to shoplift
and waiting for the clerks all to look the other
way.

Finally they did. I moved swiftly and silently
across the long space before the circulation
desk, the no-man's-land between the bright-
windowed children's section and the deep-
shadowed adult section. No one called out for
me to stop—it would have been a harsh, gut-
tural "Halt!" I knew, for I had seen enough
World War II movies on TV to know that
unreasoning authority always spoke with a
German accent. At last I ducked behind a shelf
unit and found myself in the brave new land,
safe for the moment.

Sheerest coincidence placed me directly in
front of a single shelf entitled "Science Fiction."
There were few books there—mostly story col-
lections edited by people like Judith Merrill and
Groff Conklin. *Best Science Fiction Stories of
1955*. That sort of thing.

But I was glad. After all, I was used to reading easier stuff. The letters in these books were
all so small and close together. There were so
many *words*. But at least the stories were short.
And *science* fiction. That was like those time-
travel stories in *Boy's Life*, right?

I took a couple of books and snuck off to a

secluded table. There were some adults around, but they weren't official, and as long as I was quiet I figured they wouldn't tell on me. I opened the books and started to read.

Most of the stories were just too hard. I'd read a paragraph or two, maybe two pages, and then I'd flip on to the next story. Mostly it was because the stories were about things that I didn't care about. Sometimes I couldn't even figure out what was going on. Science fiction wasn't *meant* to be for eight-year-olds, I knew— but still, they didn't have to make it so darned hard, did they?

There were a few stories, though, that spoke clearly to me and captured my imagination from the start. By far the longest one I was able to finish began with the image of people visiting a great concert hall, being pestered by a strange, twisted old man who seemed to take some sort of pride in it. Then the story flashed back and told the story of how that great concert hall came to be, and who that old man was.

You see, there was a time when people had forgotten the joy of music. It only survived in commercial jingles, short songs designed to sell something. Except that there was one jingle-writer who had a special gift, an ability that transcended the limitations of his craft. The story struck me more deeply than any other I had ever read till then. I identified with the hero—he was all my best hopes and dreams. His pains were mine; his achievements would be mine as well. I, as a child, was too young to truly understand some of the concepts in the story. Intellectually I grasped them, but I had no experience to make the idea come to life. Nevertheless, the story itself, the hero's discovery of who he was and what he could do, the response of others around him, and what his actions led to—ah, that was the path of a great man's life. I thought. Anyone can be great when following in paths that others praise. But when you achieve solitary greatness, when you bend an unbending world and turn it into a new path, not because the world wanted to turn, not because anyone asked you to turn it or helped you, but rather because you walked that path yourself and showed the way, and, having seen it, they could not help but follow: that became my lifelong measure of the true hero.

Or perhaps it already *was* my measure, and it took that story to make me aware of it—does that matter? At the time, as an eight-year-old child unschooled in philosophy, I found the story overwhelming. It remade me. I saw everything through new eyes afterward.

I grew up and learned to tell stories myself. First I was a playwright; then I turned to fiction, and when I did it was science fiction that I wrote, though I cared not overly much for science. It was the mythic story that I wanted to tell, though I couldn't remember when I had decided that. And it was in the genre of science fiction and fantasy that the mythic story could still be clearly, plainly told—I knew that, was deeply certain of it. I could not do with fiction what I knew I *had* to do, except in this realm of strangeness.

So I wrote science fiction, and eventually that came to be the mainsail of my writing career.

And one day in the dealer's room in a science fiction convention I saw the name Groff Conklin on the spine of an old and weathered book and I remembered those old anthologies from my childhood, when I thought I had to sneak into the adult section in order to read. I stood there, my hands resting on the book, in reverie, trying to remember the stories that I had read, wondering if I might find them again and, if I did, whether I'd laugh at my childish taste.

I talked to the dealer, telling him the time period of the books I had read in the Santa Clara library. He showed me what he had; I scanned through the books. I couldn't remember title or author of the one story that meant most to me, but I remembered vaguely that it was the last story in the book. Or was it simply the last I read, because there was no point in reading any other? I couldn't remember even that.

Finally I struggled to tell him the tale, calling up more details with each one I spoke aloud. At last I had told him enough.

"That's 'Tunesmith' you're looking for," he said. "By Lloyd Biggle, Jr."

Lloyd Biggle, Jr. Not one of the writers of that time who had made the transition into the seventies and eighties. His name was not a household word now, like Asimov, Clarke, Heinlein, or Bradbury, though all were his contemporaries. I felt a stab of regret; I also felt a tiny thrill of dread, because of course the same could happen to me. There's no guarantee, because your works have some following in one decade, that you'll still have an audience hungry

313

for your stories in another. Let that be a lesson to you, I thought.

But it was a stupid lesson, and I refused to believe it. Because another thought came to mind. Lloyd Biggle, Jr., didn't become one of the rich and famous ones when science fiction became commercial in the seventies and eighties. He didn't have crowds of salesmen touting his works. He didn't have dumps of his novels near the checkout stand at every WaldenBooks in North America. But that had nothing to do with whether he had succeeded, whether his work had been worth doing, his tales worth telling. Because his story was alive in me. It had transformed me, though even then I did not yet understand how completely I had taken "Tunesmith" into myself.

And I knew that if I could write a story that would illuminate some hitherto dark corner in someone's soul and live on in them forever, then it hardly mattered whether writing made me rich or kept me poor, put my name before the public or left me forgotten, for I would have bent the world's path a little. Just a little, yet all would be different from then on because I had done it.

Not every reader had to feel that way about my stories. Not even *many* readers. If only a few were transformed, then it would have been worth it. And some of those would go on to tell their own tales, carrying part of mine within them. It might never end.

Only a couple of months before writing this essay, I was talking to an audience about "Tunesmith," telling them essentially the story

I've told you so far. I began to speculate on influence. "Maybe that's why I kept writing so many stories about musicians early in my career," I said. "*Songmaster*, of course, and 'Unaccompanied Sonata.'"

Then I remembered that only a few minutes earlier I had mentioned that "Unaccompanied Sonata," probably the best short story I have ever written or will ever write, was one of the few works that came to me whole. That is, I sat down to write it (having made one abortive attempt a year or two before), and it came out in one smooth draft in three or four hours. That draft was never revised, except for a little fiddling with punctuation and a word here or there. When other writers talked about stories being gifts from a Muse, I imagined that experience was the sort of thing they were talking about.

But now, thinking of "Unaccompanied Sonata" in that double context, as a story that came whole and also as a story about music, probably influenced by "Tunesmith," it suddenly occurred to me that maybe "Unaccompanied Sonata" didn't come from a Muse at all (I've always been skeptical about such things anyway), but rather from Lloyd Biggle, Jr. After all, though the world in which "Unaccompanied Sonata" takes place is completely different from the milieu of "Tunesmith," the basic structure of both stories is almost identical.

A musical genius, forbidden to perform, performs anyway, and his music has far-reaching effects, even though he is snatched away without ever having a chance to benefit personally from what he achieved. And at the end, he comes to the place where the music is being played and takes his unrecognized bow. Anyone who has read both "Tunesmith" and "Unaccompanied Sonata" recognizes the pattern. It is not *all* that either story is about—but it's a vital part of both.

So of course "Unaccompanied Sonata" came whole. I knew how the story had to go; I knew how it had to read. After all, when I was eight years old, Lloyd Biggle, Jr., showed me how. The story felt so true to me and dwelt so deeply inside me that entirely without realizing it—at a time, in fact, when I didn't remember "Tunesmith" consciously at all—I was reaching down into myself, finding the mythic elements of "Tunesmith" that felt most true and right to me, and putting them into my strongest and truest tales.

There's more to the essay than that, but that's the part that talks about the origin of "Unaccompanied Sonata." I hope you will lay hands on the Tor double of *Tunesmith* and *Eye for Eye*. Even though my novella "Eye for Eye" is also included in this book, I hope at least some of you will read "Tunesmith," partly because of the great debt I owe to the story, and partly because it's still every bit as good as I thought it was when I was a kid.

"A CROSS-COUNTRY TRIP TO KILL
RICHARD NIXON"

There's a perverse part of me that, when it's in
vogue to hate somebody, makes me want to say,
"Isn't there another way to look at this?" The
national hatred of Richard Nixon during the 1970s
particularly bothered me, mostly because it was so
completely out of scale with anything he actually
did. At no point did he distort or endanger the
constitution of the United States as much as it was
distorted or endangered by his two immediate prede-
cessors; indeed, they were clearly his political school
in just how vile a politician can be and still become
president. I concluded at the time, and still believe,
that Richard Nixon was hated for his beliefs; and
even though I share almost none of them, I find I
have at least as much contempt for the hypocrites
who attacked him in the name of "truth" as for
the man himself. In particular I think of Benjamin
Bradlee, one of the "heroes" of Watergate, who
brought a president down in the name of the public's
right to know the truth—the same Benjamin Bradlee
who, as a reporter, was fully aware of and, according
to some reports, complicitous in John Kennedy's
constant adulteries in an era when, if the public had
known of this trait in the man, he would never have
been elected. Indeed, the political life of Gary Hart
should inform us that times may not have changed
all that much! Somehow, though, the people didn't
have a right to know the truth about a man when
he was a presidential candidate with views Bradlee
approved of. The people only had a right to know
when Bradlee hated the candidate and his views.

Still, finding Nixon's political executioners with

dirty hands doesn't cleanse his own; he did what he did and was what he was, and I for one am sorry he was president. Nevertheless, in the late 1970s I was constantly disturbed by the virulence of the hatred poured out on the man. It wasn't Nixon who was poisoning America; it was the hatred of Nixon that was hurting us. That hatred was spilling over into hatred of anyone who sought public office; I think now it was the disrespect for the office brought on by both sides in the Watergate affair that destroyed the presidency of Jimmy Carter, probably the most decent, altruistic man to hold that office since Herbert Hoover. Heaven knows our system doesn't often bring altruistic people into high positions in America. . . .

So I wrote a story about healing. Not excusing Nixon, but not accusing him beyond his actual offenses, either. A vision of how to make America whole.

"THE PORCELAIN SALAMANDER"

My wife, Kristine, lay in bed and playfully asked me to tell her a bedtime story. I thought of a disgusting animal to spin yarns about, but then proceeded to make a fairy tale out of it anyway. Later I sent it as my Christmas card to friends who would understand not getting a *real* card with four-color printing and all. It was next published in my collection *Unaccompanied Sonata and Other Stories*, and again in my limited-edition collection *Cardography*. Few have read it, but those who have often declare it to be among my best stories. That makes me very glad, because the story, one of the briefest I've ever written, encapsulates some of the most important truths I've tried to tell in my fiction. If my career had to be encapsulated in only three stories, I believe I would choose "The Porcelain Salamander," "Unaccompanied Sonata," and "Salvage" as the three that did the best job, together, of saying all that I had to say.

"MIDDLE WOMAN"

In editing my anthology of dragon stories, which was published in two volumes, *Dragons of Darkness* and *Dragons of Light*, I knew all along that I would be including a story of my own, one called "A Plague of Butterflies." But in the process of editing other people's works, an idea came to me quite independently. What if somebody were given three wishes and never used the third one? What would that do to the wishgiver? Because I had dragons on my mind, I thought of having a dragon be the wishgiver, and then, because I had been surprised at how few of the dragon stories were set in China (we Eurocentric Americans forget who *invented* dragons), I decided to set my story there as well. The idea of making my main character a middle woman came from the idea that she had to be, not a hero, but the opposite of a hero—which is, not an antihero, but the commonest of the common folk. When the anthology appeared, there was "Middle Woman," a story I'm still very proud of in part because fables are so damnably hard to write. But I couldn't very well have two stories by me in my own anthology, could I? And "A Plague of Butterflies" had already appeared in print under my name. So "Middle Woman" got the pseudonym—Byron Walley, a name I had used several times before when stories of mine were published in the LDS press.

I usually plan out a story before I write it, but this one grew during the process of writing it, starting with the most skeletal of concepts: how hard it would be to deal with a great warrior in areas that had nothing to do with war. I thought, Just because a guy can slay a dragon doesn't mean you want him to marry your daughter.

So the tone of the story was tongue-in-cheek, at first. But the farther I got into it, the farther I moved away from satiric farce and the more I became a believer in the tale. I had no idea, going into it, what would happen when Bork reached the dragon. The dragon's eyes were the inspiration of the moment. But for me the story came alive when I had Bork admit that he was afraid, and the dragon's eyes dimmed. It came out of my unconscious mind; it was almost an involuntary reaction; but I knew at once that this was the heart of the story and all the rest was just fumbling around till I got there.

Still, I thought it was pretty entertaining fumbling-around, so I left most of it in. I keep meaning to revise the story completely and sell it as a young adult fantasy. I even have an editor who's interested in it. Someday, when I have time, it may exist in that more refined form. It could never exist in worse form than its first publication. Somewhere between galleys and the printer, somebody swapped two whole sections of the story. The published form was incomprehensible. It was years before it was reprinted anywhere, so I could set the text to rights; and when it was published in *Cardography*, the text was so riddled with typographical errors that I felt like it *still* hadn't been well published. This time, I hope, we got it right.

"THE PRINCESS AND THE BEAR"

This story's first draft was written as a love letter to a young lady who is now happily married to someone else—as am I. In that incarnation it was an allegory of our relationship as it seemed to me. After it became clear that my understanding of our relationship was hopelessly wrong, I still had the story— and, on rereading it, realized that there might be some truth in it beyond the immediate circumstances of a faded romance. So, when my then-editor at Berkley (my once-and-never-again publisher) told me she wanted a story of mine for an anthology called *Berkley Showcase*, I dusted off "The Princess and the Bear," restructuring and rewriting it completely. It is meant to sound like a fairy tale—not the Disney kind of fairy tale, where cuteness swallows up anything real that might be in the story, but the kind of fairy tale where people change and hurt each other and die.

"SANDMAGIC"

During my time at *The Ensign*, I started developing a fantasy world based on the idea that different magics are acquired by serving different aspects of nature. There'd be stone magic and water magic, a magic of tended fields and a magic of forests, ice magic and sand magic. I still have many stories in that world that still haven't ripened enough to be ready for telling—but one, this bleak tale of revenge that destroyed the avenger, ripened almost immediately.

In a way, it's a rewrite of "Ender's Game"—a precursor of the way I revised the meaning of that story when I made it into a novel in 1984. The similarities are obvious: the child who is taken from his family at an early age and schooled in the arts of power, which he then uses to destroy the enemy of his people. But what I knew—and what "Ender's Game" did not adequately convey—was the self-destruction inherent in total war. Even when the enemy is helpless to strike back, total war destroys you. World War I clearly showed that, for the nations that waged total war (America did not) emerged from their vindictive "peace" talks with the drops of blood from the next world war already on their hands. The only reason that America did not, after World War II, suffer the same moral blight that undid France and Britain after World War I was the Marshall Plan and Douglas MacArthur. When the war was over, we rejected the idea that it had to remain a total victory. The Marshall Plan in Europe and Douglas MacArthur's astonishingly benign occupation of Japan went a long way toward redeeming us. At this writing it remains to be seen whether we will ever recover that moral stature. Certainly that's not the rhetoric I hear from our supposed leaders about Vietnam or Panama or even the countries of Eastern Europe that lost the Cold War.

There is an ironic footnote to "Sandmagic." When I wrote it, I was still quite new in my career, and had no perspective yet on my own work. I thought it was something of a miracle when *anything* I wrote sold, so I had no idea whether I had written a good story or not. My best guideline, had I only known it, was Ben Bova. I sent everything I wrote to him first. What I didn't realize was that he bought every single *publishable* story that I wrote. So the result was that all the other editors were seeing only unpublishable stories. It's hardly a surprise that they didn't share Ben's enthusiasm for my writing. Given a lead time of a year or more between selling a story and seeing it published, they had seen a lot of really bad stuff from my typewriter before they ever saw any of my better work in print in *Analog*.

One editor, however, seemed to think of himself, not as a protector of authors, allowing only their good work to come before the public, or even as a teacher of writers, helping them to do better because of his advice, but rather as one of the furies, wreaking hideous vengeance on any author who dared to submit to his magazine a story that did not meet his standards. And if that author's cover letter dared to state that he had sold several stories to Ben Bova at *Analog*, why, that author was certainly uppity.

But I think I would have had no ill treatment from this editor had it not been for the fact that he kept the first two stories I sent him for more than a year with no response. I sent him letters. I finally telephoned him. Nothing happened. He was a dead-end market.

Then I finished "Sandmagic." I was already getting much better at knowing what I had written; I knew that "Sandmagic" had some strength to it. I also knew that it was completely wrong for *Analog*. So, for once, I would *not* be sending the story first to Ben. I thought of sending it to Ed Ferman at *Fantasy and Science Fiction*, but it didn't seem like the kind of thing *he* ran, either. But there was this other magazine, this bottom-of-the-line magazine, that *did* publish some heroic fantasy. So I thought

I'd give him one more try. I called him up and told him who I was. By now I was on the Hugo ballot for "Ender's Game" and for the Campbell Award. I mentioned the stories he'd had for a year. I reminded him of the earlier contact. I asked him if it was worthwhile sending him the fantasy story I had just finished. "Send it, send it," he said. And, uh, if I didn't mind, why not send along copies of the earlier stories, too.

By then I knew the earlier stories were losers. I shouldn't have sent them along. I also knew this editor was incredibly lazy, and *both* the other stories were much, much shorter than "Sandmagic." That should also have warned me off—he was sure to read them first. But I dutifully duplicated them and sent them along with "Sandmagic."

What I got back was the most vicious piece of hate mail I have yet received. It was so cruel that by the end I could no longer take it personally. I knew he was wrong to tell me that I had no business writing science fiction—the Hugo ballot was pretty good consolation on that point—and I also knew he was hardly the one to tell *me* about what was and was not professional. Nevertheless, I thought it was a churlish thing for an editor to do. After all, he was the one who had kept *my* stories for a year without response. Any sense of proportion and grace would have required him to apologize to me, not excoriate me.

A closer examination of his letter revealed something else. He had clearly not read "Sandmagic." All his comments were about the two shorter stories. All he said about "Sandmagic" was "the other one was just as bad." Years later, when he shattered all sense of editorial ethics and published a review of those stories that he had read and rejected *as an editor* (would *you* submit your fiction to an editor known to do such a thing?) he again reviewed the shorter works in detail and dismissed "Sandmagic" so completely that I knew he had not read it.

As they say, doing well is the best revenge. I offered the story he was too lazy to read to Andrew Offutt for his Zebra anthology series *Swords Against Darkness*. He bought it, and within a few months it was picked up for a best-of-the-year anthology.

However, when I catch myself getting too smug, I do remind myself from time to time that the other guy's evaluation of those two short stories was, when you strip away the invective, dead on. They were terrible stories. They *don't* appear in this collection and, with luck, will never appear anywhere on this planet. But if the worst thing I ever do in my life is write some really bad stories while on my way to writing the ones I'm proud of, I'll be very glad.

"THE BEST DAY"

When I was writing my historical novel *Saints* (first published, over my bitter protests, as *Woman of Destiny*), I needed to include an example of the fiction writing of one of my main characters, Dinah Kirkham. Since she wasn't a real person, I of course had no body of work to draw on, so I had to write, not an Orson Scott Card story, but a Dinah Kirkham story.

In that goal I failed—because, of course, it's an impossible goal. The only kind of story I can *ever* write is an Orson Scott Card story. When *Saints* came out, with "The Best Day" imbedded within it, it did not sound like anything of mine that had ever been published. But I already had my epic poem "Prentice Alvin and the No-Good Plow," which was my first attempt to bring fantasy into the American frontier; and beyond the American setting and flavor, the story is simply a fable, like "Unaccompanied Sonata" and "The Porcelain Salamander." I can't do such tales very often, because fables are devilishly hard to write—there is only one Jane Yolen in the world of fantasy, who can do it over and over. But it is one of the most satisfying kinds of tale to tell, because, finished, it makes such a tidy package. Being so complete and yet compact, it gives the author the delusion of having created something perfect, rather like a jewel-cutter, I think, who doesn't have to see the microscopic roughness of his work. But if fabulists are jewel-cutters, we have a peculiar inability: We can rarely tell, while cutting our little stones, whether we're working with a diamond, a garnet, or a zirconium.

"A PLAGUE OF BUTTERFLIES"

Few of my stories begin with visual images; this one did. I can't remember now if the idea sprang from the illustration that appeared in *Omni* magazine along with Patrice Duvic's story "The Eyes in Butterflies Wings," or whether I simply remembered my story idea when I saw that illustration. My mental image, though, was of a man awakening in the morning to find his blanket and bedsheets and the floor and walls of his room covered with butterflies, hundreds of different colors on thousands of wings, all moving in different rhythms and tempos so that his room looked like the surface of a dazzling sea. He arose and cast off his blanket, sending the

326

room into a blur of colored flight, and began a journey with the butterflies trailing after him.

The image stayed with me for some time before I found the story to go with it. I had been toying with the science-fictional notion of creatures that consciously change their own genetic structure, and that transmuted to the idea of an alien creature that fought back against a human invasion by genetically adapting itself into a superior organism. What this had to do with the butterflies I cannot fathom, but for some reason I started trying to put the ideas together.

Had I been more sophisticated, I would have recognized the visual image as the seed of a tale in the South American magic realism mode. It did not belong with a science fiction idea. And the beginning of the story definitely has the mythic—no, fabulous—quality of magic realism. Indeed, the whole story retains that sense of not quite connecting with reality no matter how many details are provided, so that the science fiction aspects of the story are never clearly presented, or at least are not presented *as science fiction*, so that readers don't know if what they're reading is to be taken factually or magically. Thus the science fiction is swallowed up in the fantasy.

Years later I would recover the science fiction idea and use it in my novel *Wyrms*, where it is presented with absolute clarity, yet without losing all the magic. So it is possible to look at "A Plague of Butterflies" as a study for a later work. Yet it also stands alone, my one venture into a strange kind of voice that nevertheless pleased and pleases me very much.

I knew as soon as I had written it that this story

was too strange for any of my previous audiences. At that time I received a letter from Elinor Mavor, who was then performing the thankless task of editing *Amazing Stories*, trying to keep that long-mismanaged and mis-edited magazine from going under. She was paying, as I recall, one pound of dirt upon publication. But I thought it was important to help keep the magazine alive, and about the only thing a writer can do to sustain a publication is to offer stories for publication. I had sent her a couple of poems, but now I had a story that would probably find no other home. I mailed it. She bought it. Just in time, too—it was almost immediately afterward that TSR bought the magazine and George Scithers took over as editor, which meant the end of my contributions to *Amazing*. (Scithers and I have a peculiar relationship. He only likes my stories after other editors buy them.)

To my knowledge, no living human being besides Mavor and me ever read this story. It is still the strangest fantasy I ever ventured to write. If you actually read it all the way through, you have significantly increased its number of readers.

"THE MONKEYS THOUGHT 'TWAS ALL IN FUN"

Perhaps it is strange to have this clearly science fiction story in a fantasy collection, but I think it belongs here. The science fiction is only the frame, the outline of the story. Within it, the fables that the artificial habitat tells to itself are the meat of the story, and those are definitely fantasy, perfectly in line with the rest of the stories in *Maps in a Mirror*.

I first conceived the story in response to a call by

Jerry Pournelle for contributions to an anthology of stories set in artificial habitats. Being perverse, I immediately determined to set my story in an artificial habitat that was, in fact, a living alien organism. I conceived of it as a hollow sphere of great size. Its shell would be composed of thousands—perhaps millions—of hollow cells, each one large enough to sustain a good-sized population of human beings in an Earthlike, self-renewing environment. The hollow interior of the creature would be a highly charged electromagnetic memory chamber that would serve as the creature's intelligence, running the entire habitat and passing energy and resources as needed from one cell to another.

The life cycle of the habitat would be the problem. Its original designers knew how to arrest its development so that it didn't ripen completely and explode, scattering seeds throughout the galaxy—unless they wanted it to. But the one that comes to the human solar system has no such controls, and so it moves as quickly as possible toward maturity, at which time each of the cells becomes a fully functioning adult with tiny minicells forming its own shell, and the hollow space humans were now using as a habitat would become the highly charged inner intelligence. The original inner intelligence dies in the process of giving independent life to all the outer cells.

The fables are the tales being told by the inner intelligence to its children. There is little sense of separate identity among the cells or between the cells and their parent. But the tales must be preserved in order to keep some sense of purpose and meaning alive in the creatures. They have long since forgotten that all these tales have to do with "human" justice and equity, or that the creature exists in order to provide homes for the makers of the place. Still, the tales survive.

I include this explanation because of the number of readers over the years who have politely asked me (actually, some have begged) to explain what in hell is going on in "The Monkeys Thought 'Twas All in Fun." I hope this helps. Those searching for thematic explanations, however, are on their own. I don't like decoding my work in that way.

To my mind, the very fact that I didn't make this story clear enough for many—perhaps most— readers makes the story a failure. I think clarity is the first thing a writer must achieve; if I fail in that, what does it matter what else I do? If I were writing this story again today, I'd spell out precisely what was going on from the beginning, so there wouldn't be the slightest confusion.

One must remember, however, that when I wrote this I was a graduate student in English. I think this explains everything.

BOOK 4

CRUEL MIRACLES

TALES OF DEATH, HOPE, AND
HOLINESS

Introduction

I believe that speculative fiction—science fiction in particular—is the last American refuge of religious literature.

And odd thing to say, it might seem, particularly since science fiction openly requires that gods be either absent or explained. The moment you have a character pray and get an answer that is *not* explained through perfectly natural phenomena, the story ceases to be publishable as science fiction. In Stephen King's *The Stand*, which began as science fiction—an escaped virus destroys almost all of humanity—some characters' mystical dreams could perhaps have been acceptable as science fiction, because the Jungian collective unconscious has won a grudging place as legitimate grist for the sf mill. But when, at the end, the finger of God comes down out of heaven and blows up Walking Man's nuclear missile—well, that crossed the line, and *The Stand* was clearly either fantasy or religious literature.

It would be fantasy if the god that acted were a god that the readers were not expected to believe in their real lives. It would be religious literature if the readers were expected to believe that such divine interventions actually *do* happen in reality. But no way in hell is the story going to stand up as science fiction if gods are both supernatural and real in the world of the tale.

So why do I call science fiction the last bastion of American religious literature?

You have to understand that what passes for religious literature in the U.S. today is really *inspirational* literature. The Religious, New Age, and Occult publishing categories all contain very similar kinds of stories: Isn't it wonderful that we understand the truth and live the right way, and ain't it a shame about the poor saps who don't. Their fiction (when they have fiction at all) is self-congratulatory. It doesn't explore, it merely affirms. It gives readers an emotional high in connection with membership in their own community of faith.

Real religious literature, I think, does something entirely different. It explores the nature of the universe and discovers the purpose behind it. When we find that purpose, we have found God, because in all religions at all times, regardless of the outward descriptions of God or gods, deity serves the same role: He (or she or they) is the purposer, the planner. And human beings, either with or without their knowledge or consent (depending on one's theology), are following that plan.

I think existential literature still falls into this category, for even though, after much searching, characters always discover that there is no God and therefore no purpose, the story is nevertheless about the need and search for purpose, and the climax is the discovery of the absence of one. Stories about God's nonexistence are still about God, and therefore are still a branch of religious literature.

The need to discover purpose in our lives is a universal human hunger. Even the slimiest, most evil people alive try to find meaning in their self-gratification; and the best of people shunt others' praise from themselves by ascribing their works to the purposes of a higher being.

There is a tendency, though, in the "true" stories available today to explain human behavior, to remove purpose—motive—from serious consideration. We tend to accept the notion that mechanical, not purposive, causation accounts for the things people do. Joe Sinister is a criminal because his parents beat him or because of a chemical imbalance in his brain or because of a genetic disorder that removed the function we call conscience. Jane Dexter, on the other hand, acts altruistically because she is compensating for feelings of inadequacy or because she has a brain disorder that causes an overactive sense of responsibility.

These explanations of human behavior may be accurate; I'm interested in the question, but the issue of accuracy is, in fact, quite irrelevant to human societies. A human community that uses mechanical causation to account for human behavior *cannot survive*, because it cannot hold its members accountable for their behavior. That is, no matter how you account for the origin of a human behavior, a community must continue to judge the perpetrator on the basis of his intent, as near as that intent can be understood (or guessed, or assumed). That is why parents inevitably ask their children the unanswerable question: Why did you do that? Terrible as that question is, it at least puts the responsibility back on the child's head and forces the child to ask himself the question that society absolutely requires him to answer: Why do I do the things I do? And how, by changing my motives, can I change my behavior?

Whereas nothing is more debilitating or enervating for a child than parents who do not ask why, but rather say, You're just going through a phase, or, You can't help that, or I understand that's just the way you are. Such a child, if he believes these stories, has no hope of getting control of himself and therefore no hope of becoming an adult, responsible citizen of the community. We must believe in motives for human behavior, or we cannot maintain community life.

And once we have embarked on that course — judging each other by motive rather than explaining behavior by mechanical causation alone — the fundamental religious question of the meaning or purpose of life cannot be avoided. What *can* be avoided is the question of whether there is an ultimate purposer whose plan we all fulfill — and most American fiction does avoid it, including almost all of the stories published within the category labeled Religious Literature. Instead, purpose or lack of it is assumed.

Not, however, in science fiction. There alone we find the search for the purposer is still alive. Indeed, in story after story the question arises and is explored at depths that would be impossible in any other genre — even fantasy. For while fantasy is uniquely suited to dealing with human universals — the mythic — science fiction is uniquely suited to dealing with suprahuman universals — the metaphysical. Fantasy can hardly deal seriously with gods, because gods are common motifs, like magic swords and unicorns. Readers aren't expected to *believe* in them. (Few things are more jarring to a fantasy writer than to meet a reader who actually believes in those fantasy worlds. The dowsers and seventh sons who wrote to me or telephoned me after my

Alvin Maker series started appearing finally led me to stop listing my address in the phone book. I didn't want these people to know where I lived.) But because science fiction specifically excludes supernatural gods as characters in stories, it is possible for science fiction to explore the purpose of life deeply and thoroughly without being distracted by existing theologies.

One of the best examples is in the work of Isaac Asimov. The good doctor has made it clear over the years that he has no belief in any kind of transcendent god, and his work bears this out. But his novels are almost all profoundly religious in the sense that they invariably affirm both the need for and the existence of a purposer. The original Foundation trilogy is explicitly about Hari Seldon's plan and purpose for humanity, and how it worked regardless of the conscious intent of the leaders of Terminus. And, when the plan seemed thwarted by an unplanned-for intruder, the mutant Mule, we find that there is a Second Foundation, which continues to fill Seldon's role, ongoing purposers and planners guiding the destiny of humankind. Furthermore, they realize they can't possibly do their work if humankind is aware of their presence—their scientific planning can't function unless it is not known to function. Therefore they have to fake their own destruction. The nontranscendent god of Asimov's fiction must remain invisible and ineffable—must remain, in fact, rather transcendent.

What shows up in Asimov shows up elsewhere as well. Gene Wolfe's novels are quite explicitly religious—more so than Tolkien's *Lord of the Rings*, which is a profoundly religious (and, in fact, Catholic) work. Frank Herbert's *Dune* and its sequels are even more obvious. Lisa Goldstein's *Tourists* and *A Mask for the General* both reveal, at the end, the active role of some purposer in making things work out according to a certain pattern in spite of the weakness of the leading characters—though in her cosmology, unlike Stephen King's, the voluntary actions of human beings *do* play a vital role in their salvation, a very non-Calvinist view of the relationship between man and the universal purposer.

Certainly there are many more; equally certain is the fact that many, perhaps most, science fiction novels *don't* deal with the plan of life and its planner. Nor is this subject unheard-of in works outside of science fiction. My point is that in science fiction, the relationship between man and god can be dealt with explicitly, in depth, and with great originality, without necessarily being connected to any religious system that has ever existed on Earth. Indeed, whenever science fiction touches on actual contemporary religions, it is almost always hostile to them. Yet it deals with religious *ideas* in a way almost not seen in serious American fiction outside of sci-fi.

So far I have referred to other writers' work; my own is also religious, in exactly this fashion—and in other, which I will deal with soon. But that was not a conscious choice on my part. In fact, because my plays had all been explicitly tied to religion—to Christianity in general and Mormonism in particular—when I turned my hand to writing science fiction and fantasy I made a deliberate choice to *exclude* religious concerns from my writing. No one was going to be a member of the Mormon Church; there were going to be no tales of prophets, saviors, priests, or believers. I was going to write pure, unmixed sci-fi.

338

This was not because of any hostility toward religion, you understand. I have been a believing and practicing Latter-day Saint throughout my writing career, without wavering on that point. I am, in fact, quite annoyed with critics who assume that this or that bit of my writing clearly shows my "struggles with doubt," as if the only religious issue worth writing about was whether or not one believes in a particular religion. That, in fact, is the most elementary—dare I say childish?—religious issue, and the one least interesting to those who are actually committed to a faith. There seems to be an idea among those obsessed with their own unbelief that to write about religion means to write about doubt. They miss the point. To write about religion actually means to write about truth and faith, two matters that cannot be intelligently dealt with in the presence of doubt. They can be dealt with easily in the face of unbelief—it is doubt itself that muddies the waters. You cannot present an idea clearly if you spend all your time discussing whether it's true. You leave the issues of truth in abeyance while you discover what the idea is: only then, having understood, should the issue of doubt vs. belief arise. And, quite frankly, I'm just as happy if it arises after the story is over.

This is one of the things that has caused most damage to Mormon fiction—the obsessive concern so many writers have with people coming into or leaving the Church. It's what I call "revolving door fiction," and I'm weary of it. It suggests that the writers themselves are not yet adults in the matter of religion, not yet committed to a path. I don't despise their personal struggle, but I do wish they'd find something else to write about. Because what's

339

really interesting about religious people is what happens *after* the commitment is made, and that is precisely what can't be written about by people who have never made one.

My impatience with badly conceived Mormon fiction (and drama, for that matter) was part of my reason for eschewing overtly religious topics or characters in my science fiction. To my surprise, however, I discovered that my work had become more, not less, religious when I stopped dealing with religious subjects consciously. I would go to a convention and somebody would ask me, "Are you Mormon?" "Yes," I'd say. "Oh, I knew it before I was halfway through reading *A Planet Called Treason* [or *Songmaster* or *Hot Sleep*]." Horrified, I would demand to know what it was that made my work seem so obviously Mormon. When they pointed it out, it would be just as obvious to me—but until that moment I had been completely unaware of it. It seemed that I was writing religious fiction whether I wanted to or not.

But those unconsciously religious elements were exactly the kind of religious writing I was talking about before—explorations of the relationship between human beings and the purposer or purposers of life. There was another kind of writing about religion that I gradually began to want to write. I wanted to write, not only about religious ideas, but also about religious *people*. Yet I wanted to do it without writing "inspirational literature"—the kind of stuff that gets published in the Religious Fiction category.

Rare indeed is the human society that does not have a powerful religious ritual binding it together. Pluralism such as we have in America is extremely

340

rare, and I think it's fair to say that it exists even in America only as the result of a conscious effort that is not always happily received by the American people. The very pervasiveness of Christmas and the deep resentment felt by many—perhaps most—Americans about the seemingly absurd finickiness of the courts in their effort to keep government bodies from promoting Christian Christmas rituals show that pluralism does not come easily or naturally even to a people with a two-century history of commitment to it.

Yet if you read most science fiction you wouldn't have a clue that religion played a part in anyone's life. Most sci-fi characters are utterly untouched by religion, by ritual, or by faith, *except* when religious rituals or faith are used to show how benighted or depraved or primitive a particular group or individual is. This is actually right in line with contemporary American literary fiction, so it isn't just because of a pro-science bias on the part of the writers. Yet this is so contrary to reality and betrays such a profound ignorance on the part of the writers that it should betray to most people a rather uncomfortable fact: American writers tend not to be in tune with America. Or, to put it another way, religious Americans and literary Americans have, consciously or not, separated themselves almost completely.

I think what happens is that religious people who are becoming writers get the idea, from their reading and from the public attitudes of most fashionable writers, that it's faintly embarrassing to present religion as a matter-of-fact part of life, rather like wearing colors that clash. Writers who would vigorously resist any attempt at censorship, or even editorial pressure to change an idea or a word or a comma, rigorously remove from their work—in fact, don't even allow themselves to conceive of putting it into their work in the first place—anything that might suggest that they harbor some sympathy for a particular religion or faith.

Even those who do deal with religious people positively take great care to distance themselves from it. Garrison Keillor, for example, keeps quite a common distance between himself and the Catholics and Lutherans of Lake Woebegon; he likes them, but he isn't *one* of them. Indeed, this sort of attitude may well arise from many authors' experience, for most religious communities don't react well to strangeness, and the kind of character traits that lead one to be a storyteller are generally classed as strange. Much of the avoidance of or hostility to religious people in American fiction may arise out of writers' painful experiences with religion in their growing-up years.

But the current American trend of almost absolute hostility toward or neglect of characters who have a religious life goes beyond anything that could be accounted for in individual lives. If people's real experiences with religion were so universally hideous, religions could not survive. I know from experience that religious people are as likely to be bright, good-hearted, and open-minded as non-religious people. I have found proportionately as many bigots, cretins, and would-be fascists among university intellectuals as I have among practitioners of any religion I've known at all well. I've also found that religious people tend to have a much better knowledge and clearer understanding of unreligious people than the latter have of the former. The ignorance is mutual, but the nonreligious people have a bit more than their share.

So in this last decade I have turned more and more toward trying to give my characters a religious life, and to undo the skewed picture of religion that is almost completely universal in contemporary American letters. That there are abuses to be satirized cannot be doubted, and I do my share, in stories like "Saving Grace" and "Eye for Eye." But there are also graceful elements in the life of religious communities, and good people whose religion is part of their expression of their goodness, and such things also ought to be shown.

I deal with this most explicitly in my novel *Speaker for the Dead*, where I have the story's hero and title character, Andrew Wiggin, come to a small colony in which Brazilian Catholicism is the established church. I deliberately began the relationship between Wiggin and the Catholics by having the bishop of Lusitania warn his people against the speaker for the dead; and Andrew quickly runs into great resistance from the people because of the bishop's hostility. In short, I began with the cliché relationship between Wiggin the humanist and a religious community.

Then I set out to transform that relationship— and, with luck, the attitude of the reader. First, I introduced some positive religious characters—a husband and wife from a teaching order called the Children of the Mind of Christ. They were tolerant of, even cooperative with, the speaker for the dead, and they were also the guardians of scientific knowledge and liberal education in Lusitania. Yet they were also absolutely committed to a monastic law that required them to marry but forbade them to

343

have sex, and I labored to make this painful religious sacrifice seem, not bizarre, but beautiful to the reader. It is not something I would personally ever want to do, nor do I advocate it; but I wanted readers to realize that such a painful choice, made for the sake of religion, did not debase the characters but rather ennobled them.

Second, I carefully transformed the readers' understanding of the bishop himself. As the novel progresses, we begin to see that his hostility to Wiggin was not entirely because of closed-mindedness, but primarily because of a real concern for the welfare of his people. And as his perception of the needs of the people changed, we saw that the bishop—like all good religious leaders—was willing to do what was necessary for his people, even if it meant temporarily allying himself with a humanist minister like the speaker for the dead.

Finally, I showed that Andrew Wiggin himself, as he gradually comes to be part of one family and part of the community at large, realizes that to really belong he must also be a Catholic. He had been baptized a Catholic in his infancy—something that I had put into *Ender's Game* just for fun, but now found quite useful—and so as part of joining Novinha's family and Lusitania itself, he begins to attend mass and act out the rituals of the church. The issue of faith doesn't arise. What matters is belonging to the community and subjecting himself to the community's most basic discipline.

This is not to say that I show religion in a completely favorable light. The struggle with sin is what nearly destroys Novinha and her family. The people are every bit as intolerant of strangeness as any small town, and their intolerance is embedded within their religious life. They are also superstitious and try to use religion like magic. But in *Speaker for the Dead* I try to put these things in perspective. They are part of religious life, but not all of it; and religion brings at least as much goodness and comfort as it brings pain into the characters' lives.

My point was not to show that religion is all good—it isn't. My point was, first, to recognize what most writers seem to ignore, that most people throughout the world and throughout history are believing members of a religious community—and that usually their religion and their citizenship are indistinguishable. Then, second, I was determined to undermine the fashionably hostile stereotypes that mark American fiction whenever it *does* include religion. *Speaker for the Dead* is not a religious book, at least not in the sense that a religious book might demand that you decide whether you believe or don't believe, belong or don't belong. But it does include religion in its realistic and proper proportion in human life. In that sense it is far more realistic than most American novels.

Over the years religion has cropped up more and more in my work, until finally, with a series of short stories that became the book *The Folk of the Fringe*, I dealt explicitly with Mormon characters and Mormon culture in a near-future setting. Oddly enough, these stories—which, because of their separate existence in that book, do not appear in this collection—are actually some of the *least* religious of my writing, in that they are *not* about the relationship between the living and the purpose of life. Rather they are almost anthropological in their treatment of Mormonism. They are about the way people connect with and abrade against each other within the tight confines of a demanding religious community.

So I write three kinds of fiction that deals with religion. First, like many, perhaps most, science fiction writers, I tell stories that deal with the purpose of life—with the relationship between man and God. Second, I tell stories that deliberately subvert the clichés about religion that are so widespread in American fiction, by showing religious characters in a full range of roles within my stories. And, third, I tell stories that include my direct experience of religious life by depicting the community I know best, Mormonism.

At no point am I trying to persuade you; I want readers, not proselytes. With *Cruel Miracles* I have drawn together my stories that most clearly deal with religious matters not often touched upon by contemporary American writers, matters like holiness, awe, faith, comfort, responsibility, and community. You don't have to be a religious person or even *like* religious people to receive these stories. I hope, though, that by the end you understand a little more about the religious aspect of human life.

Mortal Gods

The first contact was peaceful, almost uneventful: sudden landings near government buildings all over the world, brief discussions in the native languages, followed by treaties allowing the aliens to build certain buildings in certain places in exchange for certain favors—nothing spectacular. The technological improvements that the aliens brought helped make life better for everyone, but they were improvements that were already well within the reach of human engineers within the next decade or two. And the greatest gift of all was found to be a disappointment—space travel. The aliens did not have faster-than-light travel. Instead, they had conclusive proof that faster-than-light travel was utterly impossible. They had infinite patience and incredibly long lives to sustain them in their snail's-pace crawl among the stars, but humans would be dead before even the shortest space flight was fairly begun.

And after only a little while, the presence of aliens was regarded as quite the normal thing. They insisted that they had no further gifts to bring, and simply exercised their treaty rights to build and visit the buildings they had made.

The buildings were all different from each other, but had one thing in common: by the standards of

347

the local populace, the new alien buildings were all clearly recognizable as churches.

Mosques. Cathedrals. Shrines. Synagogues. Temples. All unmistakably churches.

But no congregation was invited, though any person who came to such a place was welcomed by whatever alien happened to be there at the time, who engaged in charming discussion totally related to the person's own interests. Farmers conversed about farming, engineers about engineering, housewives about motherhood, dreamers about dreams, travelers about travels, astronomers about the stars. Those who came and talked went away feeling good. Feeling that someone did, indeed, attach importance to their lives—had come trillions of kilometers through incredible boredom (five hundred years in space, they said!) just to see *them*.

And gradually life settled into a peaceful routine. Scientists, it is true, kept on discovering, and engineers kept on building according to those discoveries, and so changes *did* come. But knowing now that there was no great scientific revolution just around the corner, no tremendous discovery that would open up the stars, men and women settled down, by and large, to the business of being happy.

It wasn't as hard as people had supposed.

Willard Crane was an old man, but a content one. His wife was dead, but he did not resent the brief interregnum in his life in which he was solitary again, a thing he had not been since he came home from the Vietnam War with half a foot missing and found his girl waiting for him anyway, foot or no foot. They had lived all their married lives in a house in the Avenues of Salt Lake City, which, when they moved there, had been a shabby, dilapidated relic of a previous century, but which now was a splendid preservation of a noble era in architecture. Willard was in that comfortable area between heavy wealth and heavier poverty; enough money to satisfy normal aspirations, but not enough money to tempt him to extravagance.

Every day he walked from 7th Avenue and L street to the cemetery, not far away, where practically everyone had been buried. It was there, in the middle of the cemetery, that the alien building stood—an obvious mimic of old Mormon temple architecture, meaning it was a monstrosity of conflicting periods that somehow, perhaps through intense sincerity, managed to be beautiful anyway.

And there he sat among the gravestones, watching as occasional people wandered into and out of the sanctuary where the aliens came, visited, left.

Happiness is boring as hell, he decided one day. And so, to provoke a little delightful variety, he decided to pick a fight with somebody. Unfortunately, everyone he knew at all well was too nice to fight. And so he decided that he had a bone to pick with the aliens.

When you're old, you can get away with anything.

He went to the alien temple and walked inside.

On the walls were murals, paintings, maps; on the floor, pedestals with statues; it seemed more a museum than anything else. There were few places to sit, and he saw no sign of aliens. Which wouldn't be a disaster; just deciding on a good argument had been variety enough, noting with pride the fine quality of the work the aliens had chosen to display.

But there was an alien there, after all.

"Good morning, Mr. Crane," said the alien.

"How the hell do you know my name?"

"You perch on a tombstone every morning and watch as people come in and go out. We found you fascinating. We asked around." The alien's voicebox was very well programmed—a warm, friendly, interested voice. And Willard was too old and jaded with novelty to get much excited about the way the alien slithered along the floor and slopped on the bench next to him like a large, self-moving piece of seaweed.

"We wished you would come in."

"I'm in."

"And why?"

Now that the question was put, his reason seemed trivial to him; but he decided to play all the way through. Why not, after all? "I have a bone to pick with you."

"Heavens," said the alien, with mock horror.

"I have some questions that have never been answered to my satisfaction."

"Then I trust we'll have some answers."

"All right then." But what *were* his questions? "You'll have to forgive me if my mind gets screwed around. The brain dies first, as you know."

"We know."

"Why'd you build a temple here? How come you build churches?"

"Why, Mr. Crane, we've answered that a thousand times. We *like* churches. We find them the most graceful and beautiful of all human architecture."

"I don't believe you," Willard said. "You're dodging my question. So let me put it another way. How come you have the time to sit around and talk to half-assed imbeciles like me? Haven't you got anything better to do?"

350

"Human being are unusually good company. It's a most pleasant way to pass the time which does, after many years, weight rather heavily on our, um, hands." And the alien tried to gesture with his pseudopodia, which was amusing, and Willard laughed.

"Slippery bastards, aren't you?" he inquired, and the alien chuckled. "So let me put it this way, and no dodging, or I'll know you have something to hide. You're pretty much like us, right? You have the same gadgets, but you can travel in space because you don't croak after a hundred years like we do; whatever, you do pretty much the same kinds of things we do. And yet—"

"There's always an 'and yet,' " the alien sighed.

"And *yet*. You come all the way out here, which ain't exactly Main Street, Milky Way, and all you do is build these churches all over the place and sit around and jaw with whoever the hell comes in. Makes no sense, sir, none at all."

The alien oozed gently toward him. "Can you keep a secret?"

"My old lady thought she was the only woman I ever slept with in my life. Some secrets I can keep."

"Then here is one to keep. We come, Mr. Crane, to worship."

"Worship who?"

"Worship, among others, you."

Willard laughed long and loud, but the alien looked (as only aliens can) terribly earnest and sincere.

"Listen, you mean to tell me that you worship *people*?"

"Oh, yes. It is the dream of everyone who dares to dream on my home planet to come here and meet

351

a human being or two and then live on the memory forever."

And suddenly it wasn't funny to Willard anymore. He looked around—human art in prominent display, the whole format, the choice of churches. "You aren't joking."

"No, Mr. Crane. We've wandered the galaxy for several million years, all told, meeting new races and renewing acquaintance with old. Evolution is a tedious old highway—carbon-based life always leads to certain patterns and certain forms, despite the fact that we seem hideously different to you—"

"Not too bad, Mister, a little ugly, but not too bad—"

"All the—people like us that you've seen—well, we don't come from the same planet, though it has been assumed so by your scientists. Actually we come from thousands of planets. Separate, independent evolution, leading inexorably to us. Absolutely, or nearly absolutely, uniform throughout the galaxy. We are the natural endproduct of evolution."

"So we're the oddballs."

"You might say so. Because somewhere along the line, Mr. Crane, deep in your past, your planet's evolution went astray from the normal. It created something utterly new."

"Sex?"

"We all have sex, Mr. Crane. Without it, how in the world could the race improve? No, what was new on your planet, Mr. Crane, was death."

The word was not an easy one for Willard to hear. His wife had, after all, meant a great deal to him. And he meant even more to himself. Death already loomed in dizzy spells and shortened breath and weariness that refused to turn into sleep.

"Death?"

"We don't die, Mr. Crane. We reproduce by splitting off whole sections of ourselves with identical DNA—you know about DNA?"

"I went to college."

"And with us, of course, as with all other life in the universe, intelligence is carried on the DNA, not in the brain. One of the byproducts of death, the brain is. We don't have it. We split, and the individual, complete with all memories, lives on in the children, who are made up of the actual flesh of my flesh, you see? I will never die."

"Well, bully for you," Willard said, feeling strangely cheated, and wondering why he hadn't guessed.

"And so we came here and found people whose life had a finish; who began as unformed creatures without memory and, after an incredibly brief span, died."

"And for that you worship us? I might as well go worshiping bugs that die a few minutes after they're born."

The alien chuckled, and Willard resented it.

"Is that why you come here? To gloat?"

"What else would we worship, Mr. Crane? While we don't discount the possibility of invisible gods, we really never have invented any. We never died, so why dream of immortality? Here we found a people who knew how to worship, and for the first time we found awakened in us a desire to do homage to superior beings."

And Willard noticed his heartbeat, realized that it would stop while the alien had no heart, had nothing that would ever end. "Superior, hell."

"We," said the alien, "remember everything, from the first stirrings of intellect to the present.

When we are 'born,' so to speak, we have no need of teachers. We have never learned to write—merely to exchange DNA. We have never learned to create beauty to outlast our lives because nothing outlasts our lives. We live to see all our works crumble. Here, Mr. Crane, we have found a race that builds for the sheer joy of building, that creates beauty, that writes books, that invents the lives of never-known people to delight others who know they are being lied to, a race that devises immortal gods to worship and celebrates its own mortality with immense pomp and glory. Death is the foundation of all that is great about humanity, Mr. Crane."

"Like hell it is," said Willard. "I'm about to die, and there's nothing great about it."

'You don't really believe that, Mr. Crane," the alien said. "None of you do. Your lives are built around death, glorifying it. Postponing it as long as possible, to be sure, but glorifying it. In the earliest literature, the death of the hero is the moment of greatest climax. The most potent myth."

"Those poems weren't written by old men with flabby bodies and hearts that only beat when they feel like it."

"Nonsense. Everything you do smacks of death. Your poems have beginnings and endings, and structures that limit the work. Your paintings have edges, marking off where the beauty begins and ends. Your sculptures isolate a moment in time. Your music starts and finishes. All that you do is mortal—it is all born. It all dies. And yet you struggle against mortality and have overcome it, building up tremendous stores of shared knowledge through your finite books and your finite words. You put frames on everything."

354

"Mass insanity, then. But it explains nothing about why you worship. You must come here to mock us."

"Not to mock you. To envy you."

"Then die. I assume that your protoplasm or whatever is vulnerable."

"You don't understand. A human being can die— *after* he has reproduced—and all that he knew and all that he has will live on after him. But if *I* die, I cannot reproduce. My knowledge dies with me. An awesome responsibility. We cannot assume it. I *am* all the paintings and writings and songs of a million generations. To die would be the death of a civilization. You have cast yourselves free of life and achieved greatness."

"And that's why you come here."

"If ever there were gods. If ever there was power in the universe. You are those gods. You have that power."

"We have no power."

"Mr. Crane, you are beautiful."

And the old man shook his head, stood with difficulty, and doddered out of the temple and walked away slowly among the graves.

"You tell them the truth," said the alien to no one in particular (to future generations of himself who would need the memory of the words having been spoken), "and it only makes it worse."

It was only seven months later, and the weather was no longer spring, but now blustered with the icy wind of late autumn. The trees in the cemetery were no longer colorful; they were stripped of all but the last few brown leaves. And into the cemetery walked Willard Crane again, his arms half enclosed by the metal crutches that gave him, in his old age, four points of balance instead of the precarious two that had served him for more than ninety years. A few snowflakes were drifting lazily down, except when the wind snatched them and spun them in crazy dances that had neither rhythm nor direction.

Willard laboriously climbed the steps of the temple.

Inside, an alien was waiting.

"I'm Willard Crane," the old man said.

"And I'm an alien. You spoke to me—or my parent, however you wish to phrase it—several months ago."

"Yes."

"We knew you'd come back."

"Did you? I vowed I never would."

"But we know you. You are well known to us all, Mr. Crane. There are billions of gods on Earth for us to worship, but you are the noblest of them all."

"I am?"

"Because only you have thought to do us the kindest gift. Only you are willing to let us watch your death."

And a tear leaped from the old man's eye as he blinked heavily.

"Is that why I came?"

"Isn't it?"

"I thought I came to damn your souls to hell, that's why I came, you bastards, coming to taunt me in the final hours of my life."

"You came to us."

"I wanted to show you how ugly death is."

"Please. Do."

And, seemingly eager to oblige them, Willard's

heart stopped and he, in brief agony, slumped to the floor in the temple.

The aliens all slithered in, all gathered around closely, watching him rattle for breath.

"I will not die!" he savagely whispered, each breath an agony, his face fierce with the heroism of struggle.

And then his body shuddered and he was still.

The aliens knelt there for hours in silent worship as the body became cold. And then, at last, because they had learned from their gods—that words must be said to be remembered—one of them spoke:

"Beautiful," he said tenderly. "Oh Lord my God," he said worshipfully.

And they were gnawed within by the grief of knowing that his greatest gift of all gifts was forever out of their reach.

Saving Grace

And he looked into her eyes, and lo!
when her gaze fell upon him
he did verily turn to stone,
for her visage was wondrous ugly.
Praise the Lord.

Mother came home depressed as hell with a bag full of groceries and a headache fit to make her hair turn to snakes. Billy, he knew when Mommy was like that, he could tell as soon as she grumped through the living room. But if she was full of hellfire, he had the light of heaven, and so he said, "Don't be sad, Mother, Jesus loves you."

Mother put the margarine into the fridge and wiped the graham cracker crumbs off the table and dumped them in the sink even though the disposal hadn't worked for years. "Billy," she said quietly, "you been saved again?"

"I only was just going to look inside."

"Ought to sue those bastards. Burn down their tent or something. Why can't they do their show from a studio like everyone else?"

"I felt my sins just weighing me down and then he reached out and Jesus come into my heart and I had to be baptized."

At the word *baptized*, Mommy slammed the kitchen counter. The mixing bowl bounced. "*Not* again, you damn near got pneumonia the last time!"

"This time I dried my hair."

"It isn't sanitary!"

"I was the first one in. Everybody was crying."

"Well, you just listen! I tell you not to go there, and I mean it! You look at me when I'm talking to you, young man."

Her irresistible fingers lifted up his chin. Billy felt like he was living in a Bible story. He could almost hear Bucky Fay himself telling the tale: And he looked into her eyes, and lo! when her gaze fell upon him he did verily turn to stone, and he could not move though he sorely feared that he might wet his pants, for her visage was wondrous ugly. Praise the Lord.

"Now you promise me you won't go into that tent anymore, ever, because you got no resistance at all, you just come straight home, you hear me?"

He could not move until at last she despaired and looked away, and then he found his voice and said, "What *else* am I supposed to do after school?"

Today was different from all the other times they had this argument: this time his mother leaned on the counter and sobbed into the waffle mix. Billy came and put his arm around her and leaned his head on her hip. She turned and held him close and said, "If that son-of-a-bitch hadn't left me you might've had some brothers and sisters to come home to." They made waffles together, and while Billy pried pieces of over-cooked waffle out of the waffle iron with a bent table knife, he vowed that he would not cause his mother such distress again. The revival tent could flap its wings and lift up its microwave dish to take part in the largess of heaven, but Billy would look the other way for his mother's sake, for she had suffered enough.

Yet he couldn't keep his thoughts away from the tent, because when they were telling what was coming up soon they had said that Bucky Fay was coming. Bucky Fay, the healer of channel 49, who had been known to exorcise that demon cancer and cast out kidney stones in the name of the Lord; Bucky Fay, who looked to Billy like the picture Mommy kept hidden in the back of her top drawer, the picture of his father, the son-of-a-bitch. Billy wanted to see the man with the healing hands, see him in the flesh.

"Mommy," he said. On TV the skinny people were praising Diet Pepsi.

"Mm?" Mommy didn't look up.

"I wish my foot was all twisted up so I couldn't walk."

Now she looked up. "My Lord, what for!"

"So Jesus could turn it around."

"Billy, that's disgusting."

"When the miracle goes through you, Mommy, it knocks you on the head and then you fall down and get all better. A little girl with no arm got a new arm from God. They said so."

"Child, they've turned you superstitious."

"I wish I had a club foot, so Jesus would do a miracle on me."

God moves in mysterious ways, but this time he was pretty direct. Of all the half-assed wishes that got made and prayers that got said, Billy's got answered. Billy's mother was brooding about how the boy was going off the deep end. She decided she had to get him out doing things that normal kids do. The movie playing at the local family-oriented moviehouse was the latest go-round of *Pollyanna*. They went and watched and Billy learned a lesson. Billy saw how *good* this little girl was, and how preachers liked her, and first thing you know he was up on the roof, figuring out how to fall off just right so you smash your legs but don't break your back.

Never did get it right. Broke his back, clean as could be, spinal cord severed just below the shoulders, and there he was in a wheelchair, wearing diapers and pissing into a plastic bag. In the hospital he watched TV, a religious station that had God's chosen servants on all day, praising and praying and saving. And they had Bucky Fay himself, praise the Lord, Bucky Fay himself making the deaf to hear and the arthritic to move around and the audience to be generous, and there sat Billy, more excited than he had ever been before, because now he was ripe and ready for a miracle.

"Not a chance in the world," his mother said. "By God I'm going to get you uncrazy, and the last place I'm going to take you is anywhere in earshot of those lying cheating hypocritical so-called healers."

But there's not many people in the world can say no more than two or three times to a paralyzed kid in a wheelchair, especially if he's crying, and besides, Mommy thought, maybe there's something *to* faith. Lord knows the boy's got *that*, even if he doesn't have a single nerve in his legs. And if there's even a chance of maybe giving him back some of his body, what harm can it do?

Once inside the tent, of course, she thought of other things. What if it *is* a fraud, which of course it is, and what happens when the boy finds out?

What then? So she whispered to him, "Billy, now don't go expecting too much."

"I'm not." Just a miracle, that's all. They do them all the time, Mommy.

"I just don't want you do be disappointed when nothing happens."

"I won't be disappointed, Mommy." No. He'll fix me right up.

And then the nice lady leaned over and asked, "You here to be healed?"

Billy only nodded, recognizing her as Bucky Fay's helper lady who always said "Oh, my sweet Lord Jesus you're so kind" when people got healed, said it in a way that made your spine tingle. She was wearing a lot of makeup. Billy could see she had a moustache with makeup really packed onto it. He wondered if she was really secretly a man as she wheeled him up to the front. But why would a man wear a dress? He was wondering about that as she got him in place, lined up with the other wheelchair people on the front row.

A man came along and knelt down in front of him. Billy got ready to pray, but the man just talked normal, so Billy opened his eyes. "Now this one's going on TV," the man said, "and for the TV show we need you to be real careful, son. Don't say anything unless Bucky asks you a direct question, and then you just tell him real quick. Like when he asks you how come you got in a wheelchair, what'll you tell him?"

"I'll say—I'll say—"

"Now don't go freezing up on him, or it'll look real bad. This is on TV, remember. Now you just tell me how come you got in a wheelchair."

"So I could be healed by the power of Jesus."

The man looked at him a moment, and then he said, "Sure. I guess you'll do just fine. Now when it's all over, and you're healed, I'll be right there, holding you by the arm. Now don't say Thank the Lord right off. You wait till I squeeze your arm, and then you say it. Okay?"

"Okay."

"For the TV, you know."

"Yeah."

"Don't be nervous."

"I won't."

The man went away but he was back in just a second looking worried. "You can feel things in your arms, can't you?"

Billy lifted his arms and waved them up and down. "My arms are just fine." The man nodded and went away again.

There was nothing to do but watch, then, and Billy watched, but he didn't see much. On the TV, all you could see was Bucky Fay, but here the camera guys kept getting in front of him, and people were going back and forth all during the praising time and the support this ministry time so Billy could hardly keep track of what was going on. Till the man who talked to him came over to him again, and this time a younger guy was with him, and they lifted Billy out of his chair and carried him over toward where the lights were so bright, and the cameras were turned toward him, and Bucky Fay was saying, "And now who is first, thanks be to the Lord? Are you that righteous young man who the devil has cursed to be a homophiliac? Come here, boy! God's going to give you a blood transfusion from the hemoglobin of the Holy Spirit!"

Billy didn't know what to do. If he said anything

before Bucky Fay asked him a question, the man would be mad, but what good would it do if Bucky Fay ordered up the wrong miracle? But then he saw how the man who had talked to him turned his face away from the camera and mouthed, "Paralyzed," and Bucky Fay caught it and went right on, saying "Do you think the Saviour is worried? Paralyzed you are, too, completely helpless, and yet when the miracle comes into your body, do you think the Holy Spirit needs the doctor's diagnosis? No, praise the Lord, the Holy Spirit goes all through you, hunting down every place where the devil has hurt you, where the devil that great serpent has *poisoned* you, where the devil that mighty dragon has thought he could *destroy* you—boy, are you saved?"

It was a direct question. "Uh huh."

"Has the Lord come to you in the waters of baptism and washed away your sins and made you clean?"

Billy wasn't sure what that all meant, but after a second the man squeezed his arm, and so Billy said, "Thank the Lord."

"What the baptism did to the outside of your body, the miracle will do to the inside of your body. Do you believe that Jesus can heal you?"

Billy nodded.

"Oh, be not ashamed, little child. Speak so all the millions of our television friends can hear you. Can Jesus heal you?"

"Yes! I know he can!"

Bucky Fay smiled, and his face went holy; he spat on his hands, clapped twice, and then slapped Billy in the forehead, splashing spit all over his face. Just that very second the two men holding him sort of half-dropped him, and as he clutched forward with

364

his hands he realized that all those times when people seemed to be overcome by the Holy Spirit, they were just getting *dropped*, but that was probably part of the miracle. They got him down on the floor and Bucky Fay went on talking about the Lord knowing the pure in heart, and then the two men picked him up and this time stood him on his legs. Billy couldn't feel a thing, but he did know that he was standing. They were helping him balance, but his weight was on his legs, and the miracle had worked. He almost praised God right then, but he remembered in time, and waited.

"I bet you feel a little weak, don't you," said Bucky Fay.

Was that a direct question? Billy wasn't sure, so he just nodded his head.

"When the Holy Spirit went through the Apostle Paul, didn't he lie upon the ground? Already you are able to stand upon your legs, and after a good night's sleep, when your body had strengthened itself after being inhabited by the Spirit of the Lord, you'll be restored to your whole self, good as new!"

Then the man squeezed Billy's arm. "Praise the Lord," Billy said. But that was wrong—it was supposed to be thank the Lord, and so he said it even louder, "Thank the Lord."

And now with the cameras on him, the two men holding him worked the real miracle, for they turned him and leaned him forward, and pulled him along back to the wheelchair. As they pulled him, they rocked him back and forth, and under him Billy could hear his shoes scuffing the ground, left, right, left, right, just as if he was walking. But he wasn't walking. He couldn't feel a thing. And then he knew. All those miracles, all those walking people—

they had men beside them, leaning them left, leaning them right, making their legs fall forward, just like dolls, just like dummies, real dummies. And Billy cried. They got the camera real close to him then, to show the tears streaking down his face. The crowd applauded and praised.

"He's new at walking," Bucky Fay shouted into the microphone. "He isn't used to so much exercise. Let that boy ride in his chair again until he has a chance to build up his strength. But praise the Lord! We know that the miracle is done, Jesus has given this boy his legs and healed his hemophobia, too!" As the woman wheeled him down the aisle, the people reached out to touch him, said kind and happy things to him, and he cried. His mother was crying for joy. She embraced him and said, "You walked," and Billy cried harder. Out in the car he told her the truth. She looked off toward the brightly lit door of that flamboyant, that seductive tent, and she said, "God damn him to burn in hell forever." But Billy was quite, quite sure that God would do no such thing.

Not that Billy doubted God. No, God had all power, God was a granter of prayers. God was even fair-minded, after his fashion. But Billy knew now that when God set himself to balance things in the world, he did it sneaky. He did it tricky. He did it assbackward, so that anybody who wanted to could see his works in the world and still doubt God. After all, what good was faith if God went around leaving plain evidence of his goodness in the world? No, not God. His goodness would be kept a profound secret, Billy knew that. Just a secret God kept to himself.

And sure enough, when God set out to even things up for Billy, he didn't do the obvious thing. He didn't let the nerves heal, he didn't send the miracle of feeling, the blessing of pain into Billy's empty legs. Instead God, who probably had a bet on with Satan about this one, gave Billy another gift entirely, an unlooked-for blessing that would break his heart.

Mother was wheeling Billy around the park. It was a fine summer day, which means that the humidity was so high that fish could live for days out of the water. Billy was dripping sweat, and he knew that when he got home he'd have a hell of a diaper rash, and Mother would say, "Oh you poor dear," and Billy would grieve because it didn't even itch. The river was flowing low and there were big rocks uncovered by the shore. Billy sat there watching the kids climb around on the rocks. His mother saw what he was watching and tried to take him away so he wouldn't get depressed about how he couldn't climb, but Billy wouldn't let her. He just stayed and watched. He picked out one kid in particular, a pretty-faced body with a muscled chest, about two years older than Billy. He watched everything that boy did, and pretended that he was doing it. That was a good thing to do, Billy would rather do that than anything, watch this boy play for him on the rocks.

But all the time there was this idiot girl watching *Billy*. She was on the grass, far back from the shore, where all the cripples have to stay. She walked like an inchworm almost, each step a major event, as if she was a big doll with a little driver inside working the controls, and the driver wasn't very good at it yet. Billy tried to watch the golden body of the pretty-faced boy, but this spastic girl kept lurching around at the edges of his eyes.

"Make that *re*tard go away," Billy whispered.

"What?" asked Mother.

"I don't want to look at that *re*tard girl."

"Then don't look at her."

"Make her go away. She keeps looking at *me*."

Mother patted Billy's shoulder. "Other people got rights, Billy. I can't make her go away from the park. You want me to take you somewhere else?"

"No." Not while the golden boy was standing tall on the rocks, extending himself to snatch frisbies out of the air without falling. Like God catching lightning and laughing in delight.

The spastic girl came closer and closer, in her sidewise way. And Billy grew more and more determined not to pay the slightest heed to her. It was obvious, though, that she was coming *to* him, that she meant to *reach* him, and as he sat there he grew afraid. What would she do? His greatest fear was of someone snatching his urine bag from between his legs and holding it up, the catheter tugging away at him, and everybody laughing and laughing. That was what he hated worst, living his life like a tire with a slow leak. He knew that she would grab between his legs for the urine bag under his lap robe, and probably spill it all over, she was such a spastic. But he said nothing of his fear, just waited, holding onto his lap robe, watching the golden boy jump from the highest rock into river in order to splash the kids who were perched on the lesser rocks.

Then the spastic girl touched him. Thumped her club of a hand into his arm and moaned loudly. Billy cried out, "Oh, God!" The girl shuddered and fell to the ground, weeping.

All at once every single person in the park ran over and leaned around, jostling and looking. Billy held tight to his lap robe, lest someone pull it away.

368

The spastic girl's parents were all apology, she'd never done anything like that, she usually just kept to herself, we're so sorry, so *terribly* sorry. They lifted the girl to her feet, tried to lead her away, but she shrugged them off violently. She shuddered again, and formed her mouth elaborately to make a word. Her parents watched her lips intently, but when the words came, they were clear. "I am better," she said.

Carefully she took a step, not toward her parents, but toward Billy. The step was not a lurch controlled by a clumsy little puppeteer. It was slow and uncertain, but it was a human step. "He healed me," she said.

Step after step, each more deft than the last, and Billy forgot all about his lap robe. She was healed, she was whole. She had touched him and now she was cured.

"Praise God," someone in the crowd said.

"It's just like on TV," someone else said.

"Saw it with my own two eyes."

And the girl fell to her knees beside Billy and kissed his hand and wept and wept.

They started coming after that, as word spread. Just a shy-looking man at the front door, a pesky fat lady with a skinny brother, a mother with two mongoloid children. All the freaks in Billy's town, all the sufferers, all the desperate seemed to find the way to his house. "No," Billy told Mother again and again. "I don't want to see nobody."

"But it's a little baby," Mother said. "She's so sweet. He's been through so much pain."

They came in, one by one, and demanded or begged or prayed or just timidly whispered to him, "Heal me." Then Billy would sit there, trembling,

369

as they reached out and touched him. When they knew that they were healed, and they always were, they cried and kissed and praised and thanked and offered money. Billy always refused the money and said precious little else. "Aren't you going to give the glory to God?" asked one lady, whose son Billy healed of leukemia. But Billy just looked at his lap robe until she went away.

The first reporters came from the grocery store papers, the ones that always know about the UFOs. They kept asking him to prophesy the future, until Billy told Mother not to let them come in anymore. Mother tried to keep them out, but they even pretended to be cripples in order to get past the door. They wrote stories about the "crippled healer" and kept quoting Billy as saying things that he never said. They also published his address.

Hundreds of people came every day now, a constant stream all day. One lady with a gimp leg said, "Praise the Lord, it was worth the hundred dollars."

"What hundred dollars?" asked Billy.

"The hundred dollars I give your mother. I give the doctors a thousand bucks and the government give them ten thousand more and they never done a damn thing for me."

Billy called Mother. She came in. "This woman says she gave you a hundred dollars."

"I didn't ask for the money," Mother said.

"Give it back," Billy said.

Mother took the money out of her apron and gave it back. The woman clucked about how she didn't mind either way and left.

"I ain't no Bucky Fay," Billy said.

"Of course you ain't," Mother said. "When people touch you, they get better."

"No money, from nobody."

"That's real smart," Mother said. "I lost my job last week, Billy. I'm home all day just keeping them away from you. How are we going to live?"

Billy just sat there, trying to think about it. "Don't let them in anymore," he said. "Lock the doors and go to work."

Mother started to cry. "Billy, I can't stand it if you don't let them in. All those babies; all those twisted-up people, all those cancers and the fear of death in their faces, I can't stand it except that somehow, by some miracle, when they come in your room and touch you, they come out whole. I don't know how to turn them away. Jesus gave you a gift I didn't think existed in the world, but it didn't belong to you, Billy. It belongs to *them*."

"I touch myself every day," Billy whispered, "and I never get better."

From then on Mother only took half of whatever people offered, and only *after* they were healed, so people wouldn't get the idea that the healing depended on the money. That way she was able to scrape up enough to keep the roof over their heads and food on the table. "There's a lot less thankful money than bribe money in the world," she said to Billy. Billy just ate, being careful not to spill hot soup on his lap, because he'd never know if he scalded himself.

Then one day the TV cameras came, and the movie cameras, and set up on the lawn and in the street outside.

"What the hell are you doing?" demanded Billy's mother.

"Bucky Fay's coming to meet the crippled

healer," said the movie man. "We want to have this for Bucky Fay's show."

"If you try to bring one little camera inside our house I'll have the police on you."

"The public's got a right to know," said the man, pointing the camera at her.

"The public's got a right to kiss my ass," said Mother, and she went back into the house and told everybody to go away and come back tomorrow, they were locking up the house for the day.

Mother and Billy watched through the lacy curtains while Bucky Fay got out of his limousine and waved at the cameras and the people crowded around in the street.

"Don't let him in, Mother," said Billy.

Bucky Fay knocked on the door.

"Don't answer," said Billy.

Bucky Fay knocked and knocked. Then he gestured to the cameramen and they all went back to their vans and all of Bucky Fay's helpers went back to their cars and the police held the crowd far away, and Bucky Fay started talking.

"Billy," said Bucky Fay, "I don't aim to hurt you. You're a true healer, I just want to shake your hand."

"Don't let him touch me again," said Billy. Mother shook her head.

"If you let me help you, you can heal hundreds and hundreds more people, all around the world, and bring millions of TV viewers to Jesus."

"The boy don't want you," Mother said.

"Why are you afraid of me? I didn't give you your gift. God did."

"Go away!" Billy shouted.

There was silence for a moment outside the door.

Then Bucky Fay's voice came again, softer, and it sounded like he was holding back a sob. "Billy, why do you think I come to you? I am the worst son-of-a-bitch I know, and I come for you to heal me."

That was not a thing that Billy had ever thought to hear from Bucky Fay.

Bucky Fay was talking soft now, so it was sometimes hard to understand him. "In the name of Jesus, boy, do you think I woke up one morning and said to myself, 'Bucky Fay, go out and be a healer and you'll get rich'? Think I said that? No sir. I had a gift once. Like yours, I had a gift. I found it one day when I was swimming at the water hole with my big brother Jeddy. Jeddy, he was a show-off, he was always tempting Death to come for him, and that day he dove right down from the highest branch and plunked his head smack in the softest, stickiest mud on the bottom of Pachucka-munkey River. Took fifteen minutes just to get his head loose. They brought him to shore and he was dead, his face all covered with mud. And I screamed and cried out loud, 'God, you ain't got no right!' and then I touched my brother, and smacked him on the head, I said, 'God damn you, Jeddy, you pin-headed jackass, you ain't dead, get up and walk!' And that was when I discovered I had the gift. Because Jeddy reached up and wiped the mud off his eyes and rolled over and puked the black Pachu-key water all over grass there. 'Thank you Jesus,' I said. In those days I could lay hands on mules with bent legs and they'd go straight. A baby with measles, and his spots would *go*. I had a good heart then. I healed colored people, and in those days even the doctors wouldn't go so far as *that*. But then they offered me money, and I took it, and they asked me to preach even though I didn't know a damn thing, and so I preached, and pretty soon I found myself in a jet airplane that I owned flying over an airstrip that I owned heading for a TV station that I owned and I said to myself, Bucky Fay, *you* haven't healed a soul in twenty years. A few folks have gotten better because of their own faith, but *you* lost the gift. You threw it away for the sake of money." On the other side of the door Bucky Fay wailed in anguish. "Oh, God in heaven, let me in this door or I will die!"

Billy nodded, tears in his eyes, and Mother opened the door. Bucky Fay was on his knees leaning against the door so he nearly fell into the room. He didn't even stand up to walk over to Billy, just crawled most of the way and then said, "Billy, the light of God is in your eyes. Heal me of my affliction! My disease is love of money! My disease is forgetting the Lord God of heaven! Heal me and let me have my gift back again, and I will never stray, not ever so long as I live!"

Billy reached out his hand. Slow and trembling, Bucky Fay gently took that hand and kissed it, and touched it to the tears hot and wet on his cheeks. "You have given me," he said, "you have given me this day a gift that I never thought to have again. I am whole!" He got up, kissed Billy on both cheeks, then stepped back. "Oh, my child, I will pray for you. With all my heart I will pray that God will remove your paralysis from your legs. For I believe he gave you your paralysis to teach you compassion for the cripple, just as he gave me temptation to teach me compassion for the sinner. God bless you, Billy, Hallelujah!"

"Hallelujah," said Billy softly. He was crying

too—couldn't help it, he felt so good. He had longed for vengeance, and instead he had forgiven, and he felt *holy*.

That is, until he realized that the TV cameras had come in right behind Bucky Fay, and were taking a close-up of Billy's tear-stained face, of Mother wringing her hands and weeping. Bucky Fay walked out the door, his clenched fist high above his head, and the crowd outside greeted him with a cheer, "Hallelujah!" shouted Bucky. "*Jesus* has made me whole!"

It played real well on the religious station. Bucky Fay's repentance—oh, how the crowds in the studio audience gasped at his confession. How the people wept at the moment when Billy reached out his hand. It was a fine show. And at the end, Bucky Fay wept again. "Oh, my friends who have trusted me, you have seen the mighty change in my heart. From now on I will wear the one suit that you see me wearing now. I have forsaken my diamond cuff links and my Lear jet and my golf course in Louisiana. I am so ashamed of what I was before God healed me with the hands of that little crippled boy. I tell all of you—send me no more money! Don't send me a single dime to post office box eight three nine, Christian City, Louisiana 70539. I am not fit to have your money. Contribute your tithes and offerings to worthier men than I. Send me *nothing!*—"

Then he knelt and bowed his head for a moment, and then looked up again, out into the audience, into the cameras, tears flowing down his face. "Unless. Unless you forgive me. Unless you believe that Jesus has changed me before your very eyes."

Mother switched off the TV savagely.

"After seeing all those other people get better," Billy whispered. "I thought he might've gotten better, too."

Mother shook her head and looked away. "What he got isn't a disease." Then she bent over the wheelchair and hugged him. "I feel so bad, Billy!"

"I don't feel bad," Billy said. "Jesus cured the blind people and the deaf people and the crippled people and the lepers. But as far as I remember, the Bible don't say he ever cured even one son-of-a-bitch."

She was still hugging him, which he didn't mind even though he near smothered in her bosom. Now she chuckled. It was all right, if Mother chuckled about it. "Guess you're right about that," Mother said. "Even Jesus did no better."

For a while they had a rest, because the people who believed went to Bucky Fay and the doubters figured that Billy was no better. The newspaper and TV people stopped coming around, too, because Billy never put on a show for them and never said anything that people would pay money to read. Then, after a while, the sick people started coming back, just a few a week at first, and then more and more. They were uncertain, skeptical. They hadn't heard of Billy on TV lately, hadn't read about him either, and he lived in such a poor neighborhood, with no signs or anything. More than once a car with out-of-state plates drove back and forth in front of the house before it stopped and someone came in. The ones who came were those who had lost all other hope, who were willing to try anything, even something as unlikely as this. They had heard a rumor, someone had a cousin whose best friend was healed. They always felt like such damn fools visiting this crippled kid, but it was better than sitting home waiting for death.

So they came, more and more of them. Mother had to quit her job again. All day Billy waited in his bedroom for them to come in. They always looked so distant, guarding themselves against another disillusionment. Billy, too, was afraid, waiting for the day when someone would place a baby in his arms and the child would die, the healing power gone out of him. But it didn't happen, day after day it didn't happen, and the people kept coming fearful and departing in joy.

Mother and Billy lived pretty poorly, since they only took money that came from gratitude instead of money meant to buy. But Billy had a decent life, if you don't mind being paralyzed and stuck home all the time, and Mother didn't mind too much either, since there was always the sight of the blind seeing and the crippled walking and those withered-up children coming out whole and strong.

Then one day after quite a few years there came a young woman who wasn't sick. She was healthy and tall and nice-looking, in a kitcheny kind of way. She had rolled-up sleeves and hands that looked like they'd met dishwater before, and she walked right into the house and said, "Make room, I'm moving in."

"Now, girl," said Mother, "we got a small house and no room to put you up. I think you got the wrong idea of what kind of Christian charity we offer here."

"Yes, Ma'am. I know just what you do. Because I am the little girl who touched Billy that day by the riverside and started all your misery."

"Now, girl, you know that didn't start our misery."

"I've never forgotten. I grew up and went through two husbands and had no children and no memory of real love except for what I saw in the face of a crippled boy at the riverside, and I thought, 'He needs me, and I need him.' So here I am, I'm here to help, tell me what to do and step aside."

Her name was Madeleine and she stayed from then on. She wasn't noisy and she wasn't bossy, she just worked her share and got along. It was hard to know for sure why it was so, but with Madeleine there, even with no money and no legs, Billy's life was good. They sang a lot of songs, Mother and Billy and Madeleine, sang and played games and talked about a lot of things, when the visitors gave them time. And only once in all those years did Madeleine ever talk to Billy about religion. And then it was just a question.

"Billy," asked Madeleine, "are you God?"

Billy shook his head. "God ain't no cripple."

Eye for Eye

Just talk, Mick. Tell us everything. We'll listen.

Well to start with I know I was doing terrible things. If you're a halfway decent person, you don't go looking to kill people. Even if you can do it without touching them. Even if you can do it so as nobody even guesses they was murdered, you still got to try not to do it.

Who taught you that?

Nobody. I mean it wasn't in the books in the Baptist Sunday School—they spent all their time telling us not to lie or break the sabbath or drink liquor. Never did mention killing. Near as I can figure, the Lord thought killing was pretty smart sometimes, like when Samson done it with a donkey's jaw. A thousand guys dead, but that was okay cause they was Philistines. And lighting foxes' tails on fire. Samson was a sicko, but he still got his pages in the Bible.

I figure Jesus was about the only guy got much space in the Bible telling people not to kill. And even then, there's that story about how the Lord struck down a guy and his wife cause they held back on their offerings to the Christian church. Oh, Lord, the TV preachers did go on about that. No, it wasn't cause I got religion that I figured out not to kill people.

You know what I think it was? I think it was Vondel Cone's elbow. At the Baptist Children's Home in Eden, North Carolina, we played basketball all the time. On a bumpy dirt court, but we figured it was part of the game, never knowing which way the ball would bounce. Those boys in the NBA, they play a sissy game on that flat smooth floor.

We played basketball because there wasn't a lot else to do. Only thing they ever had on TV was the preachers. We got it all cabled in—Falwell from up in Lynchburg, Jim and Tammy from Charlotte, Jimmy Swaggart looking hot, Ernest Ainglee looking carpeted, Billy Graham looking like God's executive vice-president—that was all our TV ever showed, so no wonder we lived on the basketball court all year.

Anyway, Vondel Cone wasn't particularly tall and he wasn't particularly good at shooting and on the court nobody was even halfway good at dribbling. But he had elbows. Other guys, when they hit you it was an accident. But when Vondel's elbow met up with your face, he like to pushed your nose out your ear. You can bet we all learned real quick to give him room. He got to take all the shots and get all the rebounds he wanted.

But we got even. We just didn't count his points. We'd call out the score, and any basket he made it was like it never happened. He'd scream and he'd argue and we'd all stand there and nod and agree so he wouldn't punch us out, and then as soon as the new basket was made, we'd call out the score—still not counting Vondel's points. Drove that boy crazy. He screamed till his eyes bugged out, but nobody ever counted his cheating points.

Vondel died of leukemia at the age of fourteen. You see, I never did like that boy.

But I learned something from him. I learned how unfair it was for somebody to get his way just because he didn't care how much he hurt other people. And when I finally realized that I was just about the most hurtful person in the whole world, I knew then and there that it just wasn't right. I mean, even in the Old Testament, Moses said the punishment should fit the crime. Eye for eye, tooth for tooth. Even Steven, that's what Old Peleg said before I killed him of prostate cancer. It was when Peleg got took to the hospital that I left the Eden Baptist Children's Home. Cause I wasn't Vondel. I *did* care how much I hurt folks.

But that doesn't have nothing to do with anything. I don't know what all you want me to talk about.

Just talk, Mick. Tell us whatever you want.

Well I don't aim to tell you my whole life story. I mean I didn't really start to figure out anything till I got on that bus in Roanoke, and so I can pretty much start there I guess. I remember being careful not to get annoyed when the lady in front of me didn't have the right change for the bus. And I didn't get angry when the bus driver got all snotty and told the lady to get off. It just wasn't worth killing for. That's what I always tell myself when I get mad. It isn't worth killing for, and it helps me calm myself down. So anyway I reached past her and pushed a dollar bill through the slot.

"This is for both of us," I says.

"I don't make change," says he.

I could've just said "Fine" and left it at that, but

he was being such a prick that I had to do something to make him see how ignorant he was. So I put another nickel in the slot and said, "That's thirty-five for me, thirty-five for her, and thirty-five for the next guy gets on without no change."

So maybe I provoked him. I'm sorry for that, but I'm human, too, I figure. Anyway he was mad. "Don't you smart off with me, boy. I don't have to let you ride, fare or no fare."

Well, fact was he did, that's the law, and anyway I was white and my hair was short so his boss would probably do something if I complained. I could have told him what for and shut his mouth up tight. Except that if I did, I would have gotten too mad, and no man deserves to die just for being a prick. So I looked down at the floor and said, "Sorry, sir." I didn't say "Sorry *sir*" or anything snotty like that. I said it all quiet and sincere.

If he just *dropped* it, everything would have been fine, you know? I was mad, yes, but I'd gotten okay at bottling it in, just kind of holding it tight and then waiting for it to ooze away where it wouldn't hurt nobody. But just as I turned to head back toward a seat, he lurched that bus forward so hard that it flung me down and I only caught myself from hitting the floor by catching the handhold on a seatback and half-smashing the poor lady sitting there.

Some other people said, "Hey!" kind of mad, and I realize now that they was saying it to the driver, cause they was on my side. But at the time I thought they was mad at *me*, and that plus the scare of nearly falling and how mad I already was, well, I lost control of myself. I could just feel it in me, like sparklers in my blood veins, spinning around my whole body and then throwing off this pulse that

382

went and hit that bus driver. He was behind me, so I didn't see it with my eyes. But I could feel that sparkiness connect up with him, and twist him around inside, and then finally it came loose from me, I didn't feel it no more. I wasn't mad no more. But I knew I'd done him already.

I even knew where. It was in his liver. I was a real expert on cancer by now. Hadn't I seen everybody I ever knew die of it? Hadn't I read every book in the Eden Public Library on cancer? You can live without kidneys, you can cut out a lung, you can take out a colon and live with a bag in your pants, but you can't live without a liver and they can't transplant it either. That man was dead. Two years at the most, I gave him. Two years, all because he was in a bad mood and lurched his bus to trip up a smartmouth kid.

I felt like piss on a flat rock. On that day I had gone nearly eight months, since before Christmas, the whole *year* so far without hurting anybody. It was the best I'd ever done, and I thought I'd licked it. I stepped across the lady I smashed into and sat by the window, looking out, not seeing anything. All I could think was I'm sorry I'm sorry I'm sorry. Did he have a wife and kids? Well, they'd be a widow and orphans soon enough, because of me. I could feel him from clear over here. The sparkiness of his belly, making the cancer grow and keeping his body's own natural fire from burning it out. I wanted with all my heart to take it back, but I couldn't. And like so many times before, I thought to myself that if I had any guts I'd kill myself. I couldn't figure why I hadn't died of my own cancer already. I sure enough hated myself a lot worse than I ever hated anybody else.

The lady beside me starts to talk. "People like that are so annoying, aren't they?"

I didn't want to talk to anybody, so I just grunted and turned away.

"That was very kind of you to help me," she says.

That's when I realized she was the same lady who didn't have the right fare. "Nothing," I says.

"No, you didn't have to do that." She touched my jeans.

I turned to look at her. She was older, about twenty-five maybe, and her face looked kind of sweet. She was dressed nice enough that I could tell it wasn't cause she was poor that she didn't have bus fare. She also didn't take her hand off my knee, which made me nervous, because the bad thing I do is a lot stronger when I'm actually touching a person, and so I mostly don't touch folks and I don't feel safe when they touch me. The fastest I ever killed a man was when he felt me up in a bathroom at a rest stop on 1–85. He was coughing blood when I left that place, I really tore him up that time, I still have nightmares about him gasping for breath there with his hand on me.

So anyway that's why I felt real nervous her touching me there on the bus, even though there was no harm in it. Or anyway that's half why I was nervous, and the other half was that her hand was real light on my leg and out of the corner of my eye I could see how her chest moved when she breathed, and after all I'm seventeen and normal most ways. So when I wished she'd move her hand, I only *half* wished she'd move it back to her own lap.

That was up till she smiles at me and says, "Mick, I want to help you."

I took me a second to realize she spoke my name.

I didn't know many people in Roanoke, and she sure wasn't one of them. Maybe she was one of Mr. Kaiser's customers, I thought. But they hardly ever knew my name. I kind of thought, for a second, that maybe she had seen me working in the warehouse and asked Mr. Kaiser all about me or something. So I says, "Are you one of Mr. Kaiser's customers?"

"Mick Winger," she says. "You got your first name from a note pinned to your blanket when you were left at the door of the sewage plant in Eden. You chose your last name when you ran away from the Eden Baptist Children's Home, and you probably chose it because the first movie you ever saw was *An Officer and a Gentleman*. You were fifteen then, and now you're seventeen, and you've killed more people in your life than Al Capone."

I got nervous when she knew my whole name and how I got it, cause the only way she could know that stuff was if she'd been following me for years. But when she let on she knew I killed people, I forgot all about feeling mad or guilty or horny. I pulled the cord on the bus, practically crawled over her to get out, and in about three seconds I was off that bus and hit the ground running. I'd been afraid of it for years, somebody finding out about me. But it was all the more scary seeing how she must have known about me for so *long*. It made me feel like somebody'd been peeking in the bathroom window all my life and I only just now found out about it.

I ran for a long time, which isn't easy because of all the hills in Roanoke. I ran mostly downhill, though, into town, where I could dodge into buildings and out their back doors. I didn't know if she was following me, but she'd been following me for a long time, or someone had, and I never even guessed it, so how did I know if they was following me now or not?

And while I ran, I tried to figure where I could go now. I had to leave town, that was sure. I couldn't go back to the warehouse, not even to say goodbye, and that made me feel real bad, cause Mr. Kaiser would think I just ran off for no reason, like some kid who didn't care nothing about people counting on him. He might even worry about me, never coming to pick up my spare clothes from the room he let me sleep in.

Thinking about what Mr. Kaiser might think about me going was pretty strange. Leaving Roanoke wasn't going to be like leaving the orphanage, and then leaving Eden, and finally leaving North Carolina. I never had much to let go of in those places. But Mr. Kaiser had always been real straight with me, a nice steady old guy, never bossed me, never tried to take me down, even stuck up for me in a quiet kind of way by letting it be known that he didn't want nobody teasing me. Hired me a year and a half ago, even though I was lying about being sixteen and he must've known it. And in all that time, I never once got mad at work, or at least not so mad I couldn't stop myself from hurting people. I worked hard, built up muscles I never thought I'd have, and I also must've grown five inches, my pants kept getting so short. I sweated and I ached most days after work, but I earned my pay and kept up with the older guys, and Mr. Kaiser never once made me feel like he took me on for charity, the way the orphanage people always did, like I should thank them for not letting me starve. Kaiser's Furniture Warehouse was the first peaceful place I ever spent time, the first place where nobody died who was my fault.

I knew all that before, but right till I started running I never realized how bad I'd feel about leaving Roanoke. Like somebody dying. It got so bad that for a while I couldn't hardly see which way I was going, not that I out-and-out cried or nothing.

Pretty soon I found myself walking down Jefferson Street, where it cuts through a woody hill before it widens out for car dealers and Burger Kings. There was cars passing me both ways, but I was thinking about other things now. Trying to figure why I never got mad at Mr. Kaiser. Other people treated me nice before, it wasn't like I got beat up every night or nobody ever gave me seconds or I had to eat dogfood or nothing. I remembered all those people at the orphanage, they was just trying to make me grow up Christian and educated. They just never learned how to be nice without also being nasty. Like Old Peleg, the black caretaker, he was a nice old coot and told us stories, and I never let nobody call him nigger even behind his back. But he was a racist himself, and I knew it on account of the time he caught me and Jody Capel practicing who could stop pissing the most times in a single go. We both done the same thing, didn't we? But he just sent me off and then started whaling on Jody, and Jody was yelling like he was dying, and I kept saying, "It ain't fair! I done it too! You're only beating on him cause he's black!" but he paid no mind, it was so crazy, I mean it wasn't like I wanted him to beat me too, but it made me so *mad* and before I knew it, I felt so sparky that I couldn't hold it in and I was hanging on him, trying to pull him away from Jody, so it hit him hard.

What could I say to him then? Going into the hospital, where he'd lie there with a tube in his arm and a tube in his nose sometimes. He told me stories when he could talk, and just squoze my hand when he couldn't. He used to have a belly on him, but I think I could have tossed him in the air like a baby before he died. And I did it to him, not that I meant to, I couldn't help myself, but that's the way it was. Even people I purely loved, they'd have mean days, and God help them if I happened to be there, because I was like God with a bad mood, that's what I was, God with no mercy, because I couldn't give them nothing, but I sure as hell could take away. Take it all away. They told me I shouldn't visit Old Peleg so much cause it was sick to keep going to watch him waste away. Mrs. Howard and Mr. Dennis both got tumors from trying to get me to stop going. So many people was dying of cancer in those days they came from the county and tested the water for chemicals. It wasn't no chemicals, I knew that, but I never did tell them, cause they'd just lock me up in the crazy house and you can bet that crazy house would have a *epidemic* before I been there a week if that ever happened.

Truth was I didn't know, I just didn't know it was me doing it for the longest time. It's just people kept dying on me, everybody I ever loved, and it seemed like they always took sick after I'd been real mad at them once, and you know how little kids always feel guilty about yelling at somebody who dies right after. The counselor even told me that those feelings were perfectly natural, and of course it wasn't my fault, but I couldn't shake it. And finally I began to realize that other people didn't feel that sparky feeling like I did, and they couldn't tell how folks was

388

feeling unless they looked or asked. I mean, I knew when my lady teachers was going to be on the rag before *they* did, and you can bet I stayed away from them the best I could on those crabby days. I could feel it, like they was giving off sparks. And there was other folks who had a way of sucking you to them, without saying a thing, without doing a thing, you just went into a room and couldn't take your eyes off them, you wanted to be close—I saw that other kids felt the same way, just automatically liked them, you know? But I could feel it like they was on fire, and suddenly I was cold and needed to warm myself. And I'd say something about it and people would look at me like I was crazy enough to lock right up, and I finally caught on that I was the only one that had those feelings.

Once I knew that, then all those deaths began to fit together. All those cancers, those days they lay in hospital beds turning into mummies before they was rightly dead, all the pain until they drugged them into zombies so they wouldn't tear their own guts out just trying to get to the place that hurt so bad. Torn up, cut up, drugged up, radiated, bald, skinny, praying for death, and I knew I did it. I began to tell the minute I did it. I began to know what kind of cancer it would be, and where, and how bad. And I was always right.

Twenty-five people I knew of, and probably more I didn't.

And it got even worse when I ran away. I'd hitch rides because how else was I going to get anywheres? But I was always scared of the people who picked me up, and if they got weird or anything I sparked them. And cops who run me out of a place, they got it. Until I figured I was just Death himself, with his bent-up spear and a hood over his head, walking around and whoever came near him bought the farm. That was me. I was the most terrible thing in the world, I was families broke up and children orphaned and mamas crying for their dead babies, I was everything that people hate most in all the world. I jumped off a overpass once to kill myself but I just sprained my ankle. Old Peleg always said I was like a cat, I wouldn't die lessen somebody skinned me, roasted the meat and ate it, then tanned the hide, made it in to slippers, wore them slippers clean out, and then burned them and raked the ashes, that's when I'd finally die. And I figure he's right, cause I'm still alive and that's a plain miracle after the stuff I been through lately.

Anyway that's the kind of thing I was thinking, walking along Jefferson, when I noticed that a car had driven by going the other way and saw me and turned around and came back up behind me, pulled ahead of me and stopped. I was so spooked I thought it must be that lady finding me again, or maybe somebody with guns to shoot me all up like on "Miami Vice," and I was all set to take off up the hill till I saw it was just Mr. Kaiser.

He says, "I was heading the other way, Mick. Want a ride to work?"

I couldn't tell him what I was doing. "Not today, Mr. Kaiser," I says.

Well, he knew by my look or something, cause he says, "You quitting on me, Mick?"

I was just thinking, don't argue with me or nothing, Mr. Kaiser, just let me go, I don't want to hurt you, I'm so fired up with guilt and hating myself that I'm just death waiting to bust out and blast somebody, can't you see sparks falling off me like spray off a wet dog? I just says, "Mr. Kaiser, I don't want to talk right now, I really don't."

Right then was the moment for him to push. For him to lecture me about how I had to learn responsibility, and if I didn't talk things through how could anybody ever make things right, and life ain't a free ride so sometimes you got to do things you don't want to do, and I been nicer to you than you deserve, you're just what they warned me you'd be, shiftless and ungrateful and a bum in your soul.

But he didn't say none of that. He just says, "You had some bad luck? I can advance you against wages, I know you'll pay back."

"I don't owe no money," I says.

And he says, "Whatever you're running away from, come home with me and you'll be safe."

What could I say? You're the one who needs protecting, Mr. Kaiser, and I'm the one who'll probably kill you. So I didn't say nothing, until finally he just nodded and put his hand on my shoulder and said, "That's okay, Mick. If you ever need a place or a job, you just come on back to me. You find a place to settle down for a while, you write to me and I'll send you your stuff."

"You just give it to the next guy," I says.

"A son-of-a-bitch stinking mean old Jew like me?" he says. "I don't give nothing to nobody."

Well I couldn't help but laugh, cause that's what the foreman always called Mr. Kaiser whenever he thought the old guy couldn't hear him. And when I laughed, I felt myself cool off, just like as if I had been on fire and somebody poured cold water over my head.

"Take care of yourself, Mick," he says. He give me his card and a twenty and tucked it into my pocket when I told him no. Then he got back into his car and made one of his insane U-turns right across traffic and headed back the other way.

Well if he did nothing else he got my brain back in gear. There I was walking along the highway where anybody at all could see me, just like Mr. Kaiser did. At least till I was out of town I ought to stay out of sight as much as I could. So there I was between those two hills, pretty steep, and all covered with green, and I figured I could climb either one. But the slope on the other side of the road looked somehow better to me, it looked more like I just ought to go there, and I figured that was as good a reason to decide as any I ever heard of, and so I dodged my way across Jefferson Street and went right into the kudzu caves and clawed my way right up. It was dark under the leaves, but it wasn't much cooler than right out in the sun, particularly cause I was working so hard. It was a long way up, and just when I got to the top the ground started shaking. I thought it was an earthquake I was so edgy, till I heard the train whistle and then I knew it was one of those coal-hauling trains, so heavy it could shake ivy off a wall when it passed. I just stood there and listened to it, the sound coming from every direction all at once, there under the kudzu, I listened till it went on by, and then I stepped out of the leaves into a clearing.

And there she was, waiting for me, sitting under a tree.

I was too wore out to run, and too scared, coming on her sudden like that, just when I thought I was out of sight. It was just as if I'd been aiming straight at her, all the way up the hill, just as if she somehow tied a string to me and pulled me across the street

392

and up the hill. And if she could do that, how could I run away from her, tell me that? Where could I go? I'd just turn some corner and there she'd be, waiting. So I says to her, "All right, what do you want?"

She just waved me on over. And I went, too, but not very close, cause I didn't know what she had in mind. "Sit down, Mick," says she. "We need to talk."

Now I'll tell you that I didn't want to sit, and I didn't want to talk, I just wanted to get out of there. And so I did, or at least I thought I did. I started walking straight away from her, I thought, but in three steps I realized that I wasn't walking away, I was walking around her. Like that planet thing in science class, the more I moved, the more I got nowhere. It was like she had more say over what my legs did than me.

So I sat down.

"You shouldn't have run off from me," she says.

What I mostly thought of now was to wonder if she was wearing anything under that shirt. And then I thought, what a stupid time to be thinking about that. But I still kept thinking about it.

"Do you promise to stay right there till I'm through talking?" she says.

When she moved, it was like her clothes got almost transparent for a second, but not quite. Couldn't take my eyes off her. I promised.

And then all of a sudden she was just a woman. Not ugly, but not all that pretty, neither. Just looking at me with eyes like fire. I was scared again, and I wanted to leave, especially cause now I began to think she really was doing something to me. But I promised, so I stayed.

393

"That's how it began," she says.

"What's how what began?" says I.

"What you just felt. What I made you feel. That only works on people like you. Nobody else can feel it."

"Feel what?" says I. Now, I knew what she meant, but I didn't know for sure if she meant what I knew. I mean, it bothered me real bad that she could tell how I felt about her those few minutes there.

"Feel that," she says, and there it is again, all I can think about is her body. But it only lasted a few seconds, and then I knew for sure that she was doing it to me.

"Stop it," I says, and she says, "I already did."

I ask her, "How do you do that?"

"Everybody can do it, just a little. A woman looks at a man, she's interested, and so the bio-electrical system heats up, causes some odors to change, and he smells them and notices her and he pays attention."

"Does it work the other way?"

"Men are always giving off those odors, Mick. Makes no difference. It isn't a man's stink that gives a woman her ideas. But like I said, Mick, that's what everybody can do. With some men, though, it isn't a woman's smell that draws his eye. It's the bio-electrical system itself. The smell is nothing. You can feel the heat of the fire. It's the same thing as when you kill people, Mick. If you couldn't kill people the way you do, you also couldn't feel it so strong when I give off magnetic pulses."

Of course I didn't understand all that the first time, and maybe I'm remembering it now with words she didn't teach me until later. At the time, though, I was scared, yes, because she knew, and because she could do things to me, but I was also excited, because she sounded like she had some answers, like she knew why it was that I killed people without meaning to.

But when I asked her to explain everything, she couldn't. "We're only just beginning to understand it ourselves, Mick. There's a Swedish scientist who is making some strides that way. We've sent some people over to meet with him. We've read his book, and maybe even some of us understand it. I've got to tell you, Mick, just because we can do this thing doesn't mean that we're particularly smart or anything. It doesn't get us through college any faster or anything. It just means that teachers who flunk us tend to die off a little younger."

"You're like me! You can do it too!"

She shook her head. "Not likely," she says. "If I'm really furious at somebody, if I really hate him, if I really *try*, and if I keep it up for weeks, I can maybe give him an ulcer. You're in a whole different league from me. You and your people."

"I got no people," I says.

"I'm here, Mick, because you got people. People who knew just exactly what you could do from the minute you were born. People who knew that if you didn't get a tit to suck you wouldn't just cry, you'd kill. Spraying out death from your cradle. So they planned it all from the beginning. Put you in an orphanage. Let other people, all those do-gooders, let them get sick and die, and then when you're old enough to have control over it, then they look you up, they tell you who you are, they bring you home to live with them."

"So you're my kin?" I ask her.

"Not so you'd notice," she says. "I'm here to warn

you about your kin. We've been watching you for years, and now it's time to warn you."

"*Now* it's time? I spent fifteen years in that children's home killing everybody who ever cared about me, and if they'd just come along—or you, or anybody, if you just said, Mick, you got to control your temper or you'll hurt people, if somebody just said to me, Mick, we're your people and we'll keep you safe, then maybe I wouldn't be so scared all the time, maybe I wouldn't go killing people so much, did you ever think of that?" Or maybe I didn't say all that, but that's what I was feeling, and so I said a lot, I chewed her up and down.

And then I saw how scared she was, because I was all sparky, and I realized I was just about to shed a load of death onto her, and so I kind of jumped back and yelled at her to leave me alone, and then she does the craziest thing, she reaches out toward me, and I scream at her, "Don't you touch me!" cause if she touches me I can't hold it in, it'll just go all through her and tear up her guts inside, but she just keeps reaching, leaning toward me, and so I kind of crawled over toward a tree, and I hung onto that tree, I just held on and let the tree kind of soak up all my sparkiness, almost like I was burning up the tree. Maybe I killed it, for all I know. Or maybe it was so big, I couldn't hurt it, but it took all the fire out of me, and then she *did* touch me, like nobody ever touched me, her arm across my back, and hand holding my shoulder, her face right up against my ear, and she says to me, "Mick, you didn't hurt me."

"Just leave me alone," says I.

"You're not like them," she says. "Don't you see that? They love the killing. They *use* the killing.

Only they're not as strong as you. They have to be touching, for one thing, or close to it. They have to keep it up longer. They're stronger than *I* am, but not as strong as you. So they'll want you, that's for sure, Mick, but they'll also be scared of you, and you know what'll scare them most? That you didn't kill me, that you can *control* it like that."

"I can't always. That bus driver today."

"So you're not perfect. But you're trying. Trying not to kill people. Don't you see, Mick? You're not like them. They may be your blood family, but you don't belong with them, and they'll see that, and when they do—"

All I could think about was what she said, my blood family. "My mama and daddy, you telling me I'm going to meet them?"

"They're calling you now, and that's why I had to warn you."

"Calling me?"

"The way I called you up this hill. Only it wasn't just me, of course, it was a bunch of us."

"I just decided to come up here, to get off the road."

"You just decided to cross the highway and climb this hill, instead of the other one? Anyway, that's how it works. It's part of the human race for all time, only we never knew it. A bunch of people kind of harmonize their bio-electrical systems, to call for somebody to come home, and they come home, after a while. Or sometimes a whole nation unites to hate somebody. Like Iran and the Shah, or the Philippines and Marcos."

"They just kicked them out," I says.

"But they were already dying, weren't they? A whole nation, hating together, they make a constant interference with their enemy's bio-electrical system. A constant noise. All of them together, millions of people, they are finally able to match what you can do with one flash of anger."

I thought about that for a few minutes, and it came back to me all the times I thought how I wasn't even human. So maybe I *was* human, after all, but human like a guy with three arms is human, or one of those guys in the horror movies I saw, gigantic and lumpy and going around hacking up teenagers whenever they was about to get laid. And in all those movies they always try to kill the guy only they can't, he gets stabbed and shot and burned up and he still comes back, and that's like me, I must have tried to kill myself so many times only it never worked.

No. Wait a minute.

I got to get this straight, or you'll think I'm crazy or a liar. I didn't jump off that highway overpass like I said. I stood on one for a long time, watching the cars go by. Whenever a big old semi came along I'd say, this one, and I'd count, and at the right second I'd say, now. Only I never did jump. And then afterward I dreamed about jumping, and in all those dreams I'd just bounce off the truck and get up and limp away. Like the time I was a kid and sat in the bathroom with the little gardening shears, the spring-loaded kind that popped open, I sat there thinking about jamming it into my stomach right under the breastbone, and then letting go of the handle, it'd pop right open and make a bad wound and cut open my heart or something. I was there so long I fell asleep on the toilet, and later I dreamed about doing it but no blood ever came out, because I couldn't die.

So I never tried to kill myself. But I thought about it all the time. I was like those monsters in those movies, just killing people but secretly hoping somebody would catch on to what was going on and kill me first.

And so I says to her, "Why didn't you just kill me?"

And there she was with her face close to mine and she says, just like it was love talk, she says, "I've had you in my rifle sights, Mick, and then I didn't do it. Because I saw something in you. I saw that maybe you were trying to control it. That maybe you didn't want to use your power to kill. And so I let you live, thinking that one day I'd be here like this, telling you what you are, and giving you a little hope."

I thought she meant I'd hope because of knowing my mama and daddy were alive and wanted me.

"I hoped for a long time, but I gave it up. I don't want to see my mama and daddy, if they could leave me there all those years. I don't want to see you, neither, if you didn't so much as warn me not to get mad at Old Peleg. I didn't want to kill Old Peleg, and I couldn't even help it! You didn't help me a bit!"

"We argued about it," she says. "We knew you were killing people while you tried to sort things out and get control. Puberty's the worst time, even worse than infancy, and we knew that if we didn't kill you a lot of people would die—and mostly they'd be the people you loved best. That's the way it is for most kids your age, they get angriest at the people they love most, only you couldn't help killing them, and what does that do to your mind? What kind of person do you become? There was some

399

who said we didn't have the right to leave you alive even to study you, because it would be like having a cure for cancer and then not using it on people just to see how fast they'd die. Like that experiment where the government left syphilis cases untreated just to see what the final stages of the disease were like, even though they could have cured those people at any time. But some of us told them, Mick isn't a disease, and a bullet isn't penicillin. I told them, Mick is something special. And they said, yes, he's special, he kills more than any of those other kids, and we shot *them* or ran them over with a truck or drowned them, and here we've got the worst one of all and you want to keep him alive."

And I was crying cause I wished they *had* killed me, but also because it was the first time I ever thought there was people arguing that I ought to be alive, and even though I didn't rightly understand then or even now why you didn't kill me, I got to tell you that knowing somebody knew what I was and still chose not to blast my head off, that done me in, I just bawled like a baby.

One thing led to another, there, my crying and her holding me, and pretty soon I figured out that she pretty much wanted to get laid right there. But that just made me sick, when I knew that. "How can you want to do that!" I says to her. "I can't get married! I can't have no kids! They'd be like me!"

She didn't argue with me or say nothing about birth control, and so I figured out later that I was right, she wanted to have a baby, and that told me plain that she was crazy as a loon. I got my pants pulled back up and my shirt on, and I wouldn't look at her getting dressed again, neither.

"I could make you do it," she says to me. "I could

400

do that to you. The ability you have that lets you kill also makes you sensitive. I can make you lose your mind with desire for me."

"Then why don't you?" I says.

"Why don't you kill if you can help it?" she says.

"Cause nobody has the right," says I.

"That's right," she says.

"Anyway you're ten years older than me," I tell her.

"Fifteen," she says. "Almost twice your age. But that don't mean nothing." Or I guess she actually said, "That *doesn't* mean nothing," or probably, "That doesn't mean *anything*." She talks better than I do but I can't always remember the fancy way. "That doesn't mean a thing," she says. "You'll go to your folks, and you can bet they'll have some pretty little girl waiting for you, and she'll know how to do it much better than me, she'll turn you on so your pants unzip themselves, cause that's what they want most from you. They want your babies. As many as they can get, because you're the strongest they've produced in all the years since Grandpa Jake realized that the cursing power went father to son, mother to daughter, and that he could breed for it like you breed dogs or horses. They'll breed you like a stud, but then when they find out that you don't like killing people and you don't want to play along and you aren't going to take orders from whoever's in charge there now, they'll kill you. That's why I came to warn you. We could feel them just starting to call you. We knew it was time. And I came to warn you."

Most of this didn't mean much to me yet. Just the idea of having kinfolk was still so new I couldn't exactly get worried about whether they'd kill me or put me out for stud or whatever. Mostly what I thought about was her, anyway. "I might have killed you, you know."

"Maybe I didn't care," she says. "And maybe I'm not so easy to kill."

"And maybe you ought to tell me your name," says I.

"Can't," she says.

"How come?" says I.

"Because if you decide to put in with them, and you know my name, then I *am* dead."

"I wouldn't let anybody hurt you," says I.

She didn't answer that. She just says to me, "Mick, you don't know my name, but you remember this. I have hopes for you, cause I know you're a good man and you never meant to kill nobody. I could've made you love me, and I didn't, because I want you to do what you do by your own choice. And most important of all, if you come with me, we have a chance to see if maybe your ability doesn't have a good side."

You think I hadn't thought of that before? When I saw Rambo shooting down all those little brown guys, I thought, I could do that, and without no gun, either. And if somebody took me hostage like the Achille Lauro thing, we wouldn't have to worry about the terrorists going unpunished. They'd all be rotting in a hospital in no time. "Are you with the government?" I ask her.

"No," she says.

So they didn't want me to be a soldier. I was kind of disappointed. I kind of thought I might be useful that way. But I couldn't volunteer or nothing, cause you don't walk into the recruiting office and say, I've killed a couple dozen people by giving sparks off my body, and I could do it to Castro and Qaddafi if you like. Cause if they believe you, then you're a murderer, and if they don't believe you, they lock you up in a nuthouse.

"Nobody's been calling me, anyway," I says. "If I didn't see you today, I wouldn't've gone nowhere. I would've stayed with Mr. Kaiser."

"Then why did you take all your money out of the bank?" she says. "And when you ran away from me, why did you run toward the highway where you can hitch a ride at least to Madison and then catch another on in to Eden?"

And I didn't have no answer for her then, cause I didn't know rightly why I took my money out of the bank lessen it was like she said, and I was planning to leave town. It was just an impulse, to close that account, I didn't think nothing of it, just stuffed three hundreds into my wallet and come to think of it I really was heading toward Eden, I just didn't *think* of it, I was just *doing* it. Just the way I climbed up that hill.

"They're stronger than we are," she says. "So we can't hold you here. You have to go anyway, you have to work this thing out. The most we could do was just get you on the bus next to me, and then call you up this hill."

"Then why don't you come with me?" I says.

"They'd kill me in two seconds, right in front of your eyes, and none of this cursing stuff, either, Mick. They'd just take my head off with a machete."

"Do they know you?"

"They know *us*," she says. "We're the only ones that know your people exist, so we're the only ones working to stop them. I won't lie to you, Mick. If you join them, you can find us, you'll learn how, it isn't hard, and you can do this stuff from farther away, you could really take us apart. But if you join *us*, the tables are turned."

"Well maybe I don't want to be on either side in this war," I says. "And maybe now I won't go to Eden, neither. Maybe I'll go up to Washington, D.C. and join the CIA."

"Maybe," she says.

"And don't try to stop me."

"I wouldn't try," she says.

"Damn straight," I says. And then I just walked on out, and this time I didn't walk in no circles, I just headed north, past her car, down the railroad right of way. And I caught a ride heading up toward D.C., and that was that.

Except that along about six o'clock in the evening I woke up and the car was stopping and I didn't know where I was, I must have slept all day, and the guy says to me, "Here you are, Eden, North Carolina."

And I about messed my pants. "Eden!" I says.

"It wasn't far out of my way," he says. "I'm heading for Burlington, and these country roads are nicer than the freeway, anyway. Don't mind if I never drive I–85 again, to tell the truth."

But that was the very guy who told me he had business in D.C., he was heading there from Bristol, had to see somebody from a government agency, and here he was in Eden. It made no sense at all, except for what that woman told me. Somebody was calling me, and if I wouldn't come, they'd just put me to sleep and call whoever was driving. And there I was. Eden, North Carolina. Scared to death, or at least scared a little, but also thinking, if what she said was true, my folks was coming, I was going to meet my folks.

Nothing much changed in the two years since I ran off from the orphanage. Nothing much ever changes in Eden, which isn't a real town anyway, just cobbled together from three little villages that combined to save money on city services. People still mostly think of them as three villages. There wasn't nobody who'd get too excited about seeing me, and there wasn't nobody I wanted to see. Nobody living, anyway. I had no idea how my folks might find me, or how I might find them, but in the meantime I went to see about the only people I ever much cared about. Hoping that they wouldn't rise up out of the grave to get even with me for killing them.

It was still full day that time of year, but it was whippy weather, the wind gusting and then holding still, a big row of thunderclouds off to the southwest, the sun sinking down to get behind them. The kind of afternoon that promises to cool you off, which suited me fine. I was still pretty dusty from my climb up the hill that morning, and I could use a little rain. Got a Coke at a fast food place and then walked on over to see Old Peleg.

He was buried in a little cemetery right by an old Baptist Church. Not Southern Baptist, *Black* Baptist, meaning that it didn't have no fancy building with classrooms and a rectory, just a stark-white block of a building with a little steeple and a lawn that looked like it'd been clipped by hand. Cemetery was just as neat-kept. Nobody around, and it was dim cause of the thunderclouds moving through, but I wasn't afraid of the graves there, I just went to Old Peleg's cross. Never knew his last name was

Lindley. Didn't sound like a black man's name, but then when I thought about it I realized that *no* last name sounded like a black man's name, because Eden is still just old-fashioned enough that an old black man doesn't get called by his last name much. He grew up in a Jim Crow state, and never got around to insisting on being called Mr. Lindley. Old Peleg. Not that he ever hugged me or took me on long walks or gave me that tender loving care that makes people get all teary-eyed about how wonderful it is to have parents. He never tried to be my dad or nothing. And if I hung around him much, he always gave me work to do and made damn sure I did it right, and mostly we didn't talk about anything except the work we was doing, which made me wonder, standing there, why I wanted to cry and why I hated myself worse for killing Old Peleg than for any of the other dead people under the ground in that city.

I didn't see them and I didn't hear them coming and I didn't smell my mama's perfume. But I knew they was coming, because I felt the prickly air between us. I didn't turn around, but I knew just where they were, and just how far off, because they was *lively*. Shedding sparks like I never saw on any living soul except myself, just walking along giving off light. It was like seeing myself from the outside for the first time in my life. Even when she was making me get all hot for her, that lady in Roanoke wasn't as lively as them. They was just like me.

Funny thing was, that wrecked everything. I didn't want them to be like me. I *hated* my sparkiness, and there they were, showing it to me, making me see how a killer looks from the outside. It took a few seconds to realize that they was *scared* of me, too.

406

I recognized how scaredness looks, from remembering how my own bio-electrical system got shaped and changed by fear. Course I didn't think of it as a bio-electrical system then, or maybe I did cause she'd already told me, but you know what I mean. They was afraid of me. And I knew that was because I was giving off all the sparks I shed when I feel so mad at myself that I could bust. I was standing there at Old Peleg's grave, hating myself, so naturally they saw me like I was ready to kill half a city. They didn't know that it was me I was hating. Naturally they figured I might be mad at *them* for leaving me at that orphanage seventeen years ago. Serve them right, too, if I gave them a good hard twist in the gut, but I don't do that, I honestly don't, not any more, not standing there by Old Peleg who I loved a lot more than these two strangers, I don't act out being a murderer when my shadow's falling across his grave.

So I calmed myself down as best I could and I turned around there they was, my mama and my daddy. And I got to tell you I almost laughed. All those years I watched them TV preachers, and we used to laugh till our guts ached about how Tammy Bakker always wore makeup so thick she could be a nigger underneath (it was okay to say that cause Old Peleg himself said it first) and here was my mama, wearing just as much makeup and her hair sprayed so thick she could work construction without a hardhat. And smiling that same sticky phony smile, and crying the same gooey oozey black tears down her cheeks, and reaching out her hands just the right way so I halfway expected her to say, "Praise to Lord Jesus," and then she actually *says* it, "Praise to Lord Jesus, it's my boy," and comes up and lays

407

a kiss on my cheek with so much spit in it that it dripped down my face.

I wiped the slobber with my sleeve and felt my daddy have this little flash of anger, and I knew that he thought I was judging my mama and he didn't like it. Well, I was, I got to admit. Her perfume was enough to knock me over, I swear she must've mugged an Avon lady. And there was my daddy in a fine blue suit like a businessman, his hair all blow-dried, so it was plain he knew just as well as I did the way real people are supposed to look. Probably he was plain embarrassed to be seen in public with Mama, so why didn't he ever just say, Mama, you wear too much makeup? That's what I thought, and it wasn't till later that I realized that when your woman is apt to give you cancer if you rile her up, you don't go telling her that her face looks like she slept in wet sawdust and she smells like a whore. White trash, that's what my mama was, sure as if she was still wearing the factory label.

"Sure am glad to see you, Son," says my daddy.

I didn't know what to say, tell the truth. I *wasn't* glad to see them, now that I saw them, because they wasn't exactly what a orphan boy dreams his folks is like. So I kind of grinned and looked back down at Old Peleg's grave.

"You don't seem too surprised to see *us*," he says.

I could've told him right then about the lady in Roanoke, but I didn't. Just didn't feel right to tell him. So I says, "I felt like somebody was calling me back here. And you two are the only people I met who's as sparky as me. If you all say you're my folks, then I figure it must be so."

Mama giggled and she says to him, "Listen, Jesse, he calls it 'sparky.' "

408

"The word we use is 'dusty,' Son," says Daddy. "We say a body's looking dusty when he's one of us."

"You were a very dusty baby," says Mama. "That's why we knew we couldn't keep you. Never seen such a dusty baby before. Papa Lem made us take you to the orphanage before you even sucked one time. You never sucked even once." And her mascara just flooded down her face.

"Now Deeny," says Daddy, "no need telling him everything right here."

Dusty. That was no sense at all. It didn't look like *dust*, it was flecks of light, so bright on me that sometimes I had to squint just to see my own hands through the dazzle. "It don't *look* like dust," I says.

And Daddy says, "Well what do *you* think it looks like?"

And I says, "Sparks. That's why I call it being sparky."

"Well that's what it looks like to us, too," says Daddy. "But we've been calling it 'dusty' all our lives, and so I figure it's easier for one boy to change than for f—for lots of other folks."

Well, now, I learned a lot of things right then from what he said. First off, I knew he was lying when he said it looked like sparks to them. It didn't. It looked like what they called it. Dust. And that meant that I was seeing it a whole lot *brighter* than they could see it, and that was good for me to know, especially because it was plain that Daddy *didn't* want me to know it and so he pretended that he saw it the same way. He wanted me to think he was just as good at seeing as I was. Which meant that he sure wasn't. And I also learned that he didn't want me to know how many kinfolk I had, cause he started

409

to say a number that started with *F*, and then caught himself and didn't say it. Fifty? Five hundred? The number wasn't half so important as the fact that he didn't want me to know it. They didn't trust me. Well, why should they? Like the lady said, I was better at this than they were, and they didn't know how mad I was about being abandoned, and the last thing they wanted to do was turn me loose killing folks. Especially themselves.

Well I stood there thinking about that stuff and pretty soon it makes them nervous and Mama says, "Now, Daddy, he can call it whatever he wants, don't go making him mad or something."

And Daddy laughs and says, "He isn't mad, are you, Son?"

Can't they see for themselves? Course not. Looks like *dust* to them, so they can't see it clear at all.

"You don't seem too happy to see us," says Daddy.

"Now, Jesse," says Mama, "don't go pushing. Papa Lem said don't you push the boy, you just make his acquaintance, you let him know why we had to push him out of the nest so young, so now you explain it, Daddy, just like Papa Lem said to."

For the first time right then it occurred to me that my own folks didn't *want* to come fetch me. They came because this Papa Lem made them do it. And you can bet they hopped and said yes, knowing how Papa Lem used his—but I'll get to Papa Lem in good time, and you said I ought to take this all in order, which I'm mostly trying to do.

Anyway Daddy explained it just like the lady in Roanoke, except he didn't say a word about bio-electrical systems, he said that I was "plainly chosen" from the moment of my birth, that I was

410

"one of the elect," which I remembered from Baptist Sunday School meant that I was one that God had saved, though I never heard of anybody who was saved the minute they was born and not even baptized or nothing. They saw how dusty I was and they knew I'd kill a lot of people before I got old enough to control it. I asked them if they did it a lot, putting a baby out to be raised by strangers.

"Oh, maybe a dozen times," says Daddy.

"And it always works out okay?" says I.

He got set to lie again, I could see it by ripples in the light, I didn't know lying could be so plain, which made me glad they saw dust instead of sparks. "Most times," he says.

"I'd like to meet one of them others," says I. "I figure we got a lot in common, growing up thinking our parents hated us, when the truth was they was scared of their own baby."

"Well they're mostly grown up and gone off," he says, but it's a lie, and most important of all was the fact that here I as much as said I thought they wasn't worth horse pucky as parents and the only thing Daddy can think of to say is why I can't see none of the other "orphans," which tells me that whatever he's lying to cover up must be real important.

But I didn't push him right then, I just looked back down at Old Peleg's grave and wondered if he ever told a lie in his life.

Daddy says, "I'm not surprised to find you here." I guess he was nervous, and had to change the subject. "He's one you dusted, isn't he?"

Dusted. That word made me so mad. What I done to Old Peleg wasn't *dusting*. And being mad must have changed me enough they could see the change. But they didn't know what it meant, cause Mama

411

says to me, "Now, Son, I don't mean to criticize, but it isn't right to take pride in the gifts of God. That's why we came to find you, because we need to teach you why God chose you to be one of the elect, and you shouldn't glory in yourself because you could strike down your enemies. Rather you should give all glory to the Lord, praise his name, because we are his servants."

I like to puked, I was so mad at that. Glory! Old Peleg, who was worth ten times these two phony white people who tossed me out before I ever sucked tit, and they thought I should give the *glory* for his terrible agony and death to *God*? I didn't know God all that well, mostly because I thought of him as looking as pinched up and serious as Mrs. Bethel who taught Sunday School when I was little, until she died of leukemia, and I just never had a thing to say to God. But if God gave me that power to strike down Old Peleg, and God wanted the glory for it when I was done, then I *did* have a few words to say to God. Only I didn't believe it for a minute. Old Peleg believed in God, and the God he believed in didn't go striking an old black man dead because a dumb kid got pissed off at him.

But I'm getting off track in the story, because that was when my father touched me for the first time. His hand was shaking. And it had every right to shake, because I was so mad that a year ago he would've been bleeding from the colon before he took his hand away. But I'd got so I could keep from killing whoever touched me when I was mad, and the funny thing was that his hand *shaking* kind of changed how I felt anyway. I'd been thinking about how mad I was that they left me and how mad I was that they thought I'd be proud of killing people but now I realized how brave they was to come fetch me, cause how did they know I wouldn't kill them? But they came anyway. And that's something. Even if Papa Lem told them to do it, they came, and now I realized that it was real brave for Mama to come kiss me on the cheek right then, because if I was going to kill her, she touched me and gave me a chance to do it before she even tried to explain anything. Maybe it was her strategy to win me over or something, but it was still brave. And she also didn't approve of people being proud of murder, which was more points in her favor. And she had the guts to tell me so right to my face. So I chalked up some points for Mama. She might look like as sickening as Tammy Bakker, but she faced her killer son with more guts than Daddy had.

He touched my shoulder and they led me to their car. A Lincoln Town Car, which they probably thought would impress me, but all I thought about was what it would've been like at the Children's Home if we'd had the price of that car, even fifteen years ago. Maybe a paved basketball court. Maybe some decent toys that wasn't broken-up hand-me-downs. Maybe some pants with knees in them. I never felt so poor in my life as when I slid onto that fuzzy seat and heard the stereo start playing elevator music in my ear.

There was somebody else in the car. Which made sense. If I'd killed them or something, they'd need somebody else to drive the car home, right? He wasn't much, when it came to being dusty or sparky or whatever. Just a little, and in rhythms of fear, too. And I could see *why* he was scared, cause he was holding a blindfold in his hands, and he says, "Mr. Yow, I'm afraid I got to put this on you."

413

Well, I didn't answer for a second, which made him more scared cause he thought I was mad, but mostly it took me that long to realize he meant *me* when he said "Mr. Yow."

"That's our name, Son," says my daddy. "I'm Jesse Yow, and your mother is Minnie Rae Yow, and that make you Mick Yow."

"Don't it figure," says I. I was joking, but they took it wrong, like as if I was making fun of their name. But I been Mick Winger so long that it just feels silly calling myself Yow, and the fact is it *is* a funny name. They said it like I should be proud of it, though, which makes me laugh, but to them it was the name of God's Chosen People, like the way the Jews called themselves Israelites in the Bible. I didn't know that then, but that's the way they said it, real proud. And they was ticked off when I made a joke, so I helped them feel better by letting Billy put on—Billy's the name of the man in the car—put on the blindfold.

It was a lot of country roads, and a lot of country talk. About kinfolk I never met, and how I'd love this person and that person, which sounded increasingly unlikely to me, if you know what I mean. A long-lost child is coming home and you put a *blindfold* on him. I knew we were going mostly east, cause of the times I could feel the sun coming in my window and on the back of my neck, but that was about it, and that wasn't much. They lied to me, they wouldn't show me nothing, they was scared of me. I mean, any way you look at it, they wasn't exactly killing the fatted calf for the prodigal son. I was definitely on probation. Or maybe even on trial. Which, I might point out, is exactly the way you been treating me, too, and I don't like it much better

414

now than I did then, if you don't mind me putting some personal complaints into this. I mean, somewhere along the line somebody's going to have to decide whether to shoot me or let me go, because I can't control my temper forever locked up like a rat in a box, and the difference is a rat can't reach out of the box and blast you the way I can, so somewhere along the way somebody's going to have to figure out that you better either trust me or kill me. My personal preference is for trusting me, since I've given you more reason to trust me than you've given me to trust *you* so far.

But anyway I rode along in the car for more than an hour. We could have gotten to Winston or Greensboro or Danville by then, it was so long, and by the time we got there nobody was talking and from the snoring, Billy was even asleep. I wasn't asleep, though. I was watching. Cause I don't see sparks with my eyes, I see it with something else, like as if my sparks see other folks' sparks, if you catch my drift, and so that blindfold might've kept me from seeing the road, but it sure didn't keep me from seeing the other folks in the car with me. I knew right where they were, and right what they were feeling. Now, I've always had a knack for telling things about people, even when I couldn't see nary a spark or nothing, but this was the first time I ever saw anybody who was sparky besides me. So I sat there watching how Mama and Daddy acted with each other even when they wasn't touching or saying a thing, just little drifts of anger or fear or— well, I looked for love, but I didn't see it, and I know what it looks like, cause I've felt it. They were like two armies camped on opposite hills, waiting for the truce to end at dawn. Careful. Sending out little scouting parties.

Then the more I got used to understanding what my folks was thinking and feeling, toward each other, the easier it got for me to read what Billy had going on inside him. It's like after you learn to read big letters, you can read little letters, too, and I wondered if maybe I could even learn to understand people who didn't have hardly any sparks at all. I mean that occurred to me, anyway, and since then I've found out that it's mostly true. Now that I've had some practice I can read a sparky person from a long ways off, and even regular folks I can do a little reading, even through walls and windows. But I found that out later. Like when you guys have been watching me through mirrors. I can also see your microphone wires in the walls.

Anyway it was during that car ride that I first started seeing what I could see with my eyes closed, the shape of people's bio-electrical system, the color and spin of it, the speed and the flow and the rhythm and whatever, I mean those are the words I use, cause there isn't exactly a lot of books I can read on the subject. Maybe that Swedish doctor has fancy words for it. I can only tell you how it feels to me. And in that hour I got to be good enough at it that I could tell Billy was scared, all right, but he *wasn't* all that scared of me, he was mostly scared of Mama and Daddy. Me he was jealous of, angry kind of. Scared a little, too, but mostly mad. I thought maybe he was mad cause I was coming in out of nowhere already sparkier than him, but then it occurred to me that he probably couldn't even tell how sparky I was, because to him it'd look like dust, and he wouldn't have enough of a knack at it to see much distinction between one person and another. It's like the more light you give off, the clearer you can see other people's light. So I was the one with the blindfold on, but I could see clearer than anybody else in that car.

We drove on gravel for about ten minutes, and then on a bumpy dirt road, and then suddenly on asphalt again, smooth as you please, for about a hundred yards, and then we stopped. I didn't wait for a by-your-leave, I had that blindfold off in half a second.

It was like a whole town of houses, but right among the trees, not a gap in the leaves overhead. Maybe fifty, sixty houses, some of them pretty big, but the trees made them half invisible, it being summer. Children running all over, scruffy dirty kids from diapered-up snot-nose brats to most-growed kids not all that much younger than me. They sure kept us cleaner in the Children's Home. And they was all sparky. Mostly like Billy, just a little, but it explained why they wasn't much washed. There isn't many a mama who'd stuff her kid in a tub if the kid can make her sick just by getting mad.

It must've been near eight-thirty at night, and even the little kids still wasn't in bed. They must let their kids play till they get wore out and drop down and fall asleep by themselves. It came to me that maybe I wasn't so bad off growing up in an orphanage. At least I knew manners and didn't whip it out and pee right in front of company, the way one little boy did, just looking at me while I got out of the car, whizzing away like he wasn't doing nothing strange. Like a dog marking trees. He needed to so he done it. If I ever did that at the Children's Home they'd've slapped me silly.

I know how to act with strangers when I'm hitching a ride, but not when I'm being company, cause orphans don't go calling much so I never had much experience. So I'd've been shy no matter what, even if there wasn't no such thing as sparkiness. Daddy was all set to take me to meet Papa Lem right off, but Mama saw how I wasn't cleaned up and maybe she guessed I hadn't been to the toilet in a while and so she hustled me into a house where they had a good shower and when I came out she had a cold ham sandwich waiting for me on the table. On a plate, and the plate was setting on a linen place mat, and there was a tall glass of milk there, so cold it was sweating on the outside of the glass. I mean, if an orphan kid ever dreamed of what it might be like to have a mama, that was the dream. Never mind that she didn't look like a model in the Sears catalog. I felt clean, the sandwich tasted good, and when I was done eating she even offered me a cookie.

It felt good, I'll admit that, but at the same time I felt cheated. It was just too damn late. I needed it to be like this when I was seven, not seventeen.

But she was trying, and it wasn't all her fault, so I ate the cookie and drank off the last of the milk and my watch said it was after nine. Outside it was dusk now, and most of the kids were finally gone off to bed, and Daddy comes in and says, "Papa Lem says he isn't getting any younger."

He was outside, in a big rocking chair sitting on the grass. You wouldn't call him fat, but he did have a belly on him. And you wouldn't call him old, but he was bald on top and his hair was wispy yellow and white. And you wouldn't call him ugly, but he had a soft mouth and I didn't like the way it twisted up when he talked.

Oh, hell, he was fat, old, and ugly, and I hated him from the first time I saw him. A squishy kind of guy. Not even as sparky as my daddy, neither, so you didn't get to be in charge around here just by having more of whatever it was made us different. I wondered how close kin he was to me. If he's got children, and they look like him, they ought to drown them out of mercy.

"Mick Yow," he says to me, "Mick my dear boy, Mick my dear cousin."

"Good evening, sir," says I.

"Oh, and he's got manners," says he. "We were right to donate so much to the Children's Home. They took excellent care of you."

"You donated to the home?" says I. If they did, they sure didn't give *much*.

"A little," he says. "Enough to pay for your food, your room, your Christian education. But no luxuries. You couldn't grow up soft, Mick. You had to grow up lean and strong. And you had to know suffering, so you could be compassionate. The Lord God has given you a marvelous gift, a great helping of his grace, a heaping plateful of the power of God, and we had to make sure you were truly worthy to sit up to the table at the banquet of the Lord."

I almost looked around to see if there was a camera, he sounded so much like the preachers on TV.

And he says, "Mick, you have already passed the first test. You have forgiven your parents for leaving you to think you were an orphan. You have kept that holy commandment, Honor thy father and mother, that thy days may be long upon the land which the Lord thy God hath given thee. You know that if you had raised a hand against them, the Lord

419

would have struck you down. For verily I say unto you that there was two rifles pointed at you the whole time, and if your father and mother had walked away without you, you would have flopped down dead in that nigger cemetery, for God will not be mocked."

I couldn't tell if he was trying to provoke me or scare me or what, but either way, it was working.

"The Lord has chosen you for his servant, Mick, just like he's chosen all of us. The rest of the world doesn't understand this. But Grandpa Jake saw it. Long ago, back in 1820, he saw how everybody he hated had a way of dying without him lifting a finger. And for a time he thought that maybe he was like those old witches, who curse people and they wither up and die by the power of the devil. But he was a god-fearing man, and he had no truck with Satan. He was living in rough times, when a man was likely to kill in a quarrel, but Grandpa Jake never killed. Never even struck out with his fists. He was a peaceable man, and he kept his anger inside him, as the Lord commands in the New Testament. So surely he was not a servant of Satan!"

Papa Lem's voice rang through that little village, he was talking so loud, and I noticed there was a bunch of people all around. Not many kids now, all grownups, maybe there to hear Lem, but even more likely they was there to see me. Because it was like the lady in Roanoke said, there wasn't a one of them was half as sparky as me. I didn't know if they could all see that, but *I* could. Compared to normal folks they was all dusty enough, I suppose, but compared to me, or even to my mama and daddy, they was a pretty dim bunch.

"He studied the scriptures to find out what it

meant that his enemies all suffered from tumors and bleeding and coughing and rot, and he came upon the verse of Genesis where the Lord said unto Abraham, 'I will bless them that bless thee, and curse him that curseth thee.' And he knew in his heart that the Lord had chosen him the way he chose Abraham. And when Isaac gave the blessing of God to Jacob, he said, 'Let people serve thee, and nations bow down to thee: cursed be every one that curseth thee, and blessed be he that blesseth thee.' The promises to the patriarchs were fulfilled again in Grandpa Jake, for whoever cursed him was cursed by God."

When he said those words from the Bible, Papa Lem sounded like the voice of God himself, I've got to tell you. I felt exalted, knowing that it was God who gave such power to my family. It was to the whole family, the way Papa Lem told it, because the Lord promised Abraham that his children would be as many as there was stars in the sky, which is a lot more than Abraham knew about seeing how he didn't have no telescope. And that promise now applied to Grandpa Jake, just like the one that said "in thee shall all families of the earth be blessed." So Grandpa Jake set to studying the book of Genesis so he could fulfil those promises just like the patriarchs did. He saw how they went to a lot of trouble to make sure they only married kinfolk—you know how Abraham married his brother's daughter, Sarah, and Isaac married his cousin Rebekah, and Jacob married his cousins Leah and Rachel. So Grandpa Jake left his first wife cause she was unworthy, meaning she probably wasn't particularly sparky, and he took up with his brother's daughter and when his brother threatened to kill him if he laid a hand on the girl, Grandpa Jake run off with her and his own brother died of a curse which is just exactly what happened to Sarah's father in the Bible. I mean Grandpa Jake worked it out just right. And he made sure all his sons married their first cousins, and so all of them had sparkiness twice over, just like breeding pointers with pointers and not mixing them with other breeds, so the strain stays pure.

There was all kinds of other stuff about Lot and his daughters, and if we remained faithful then we would be the meek who inherit the Earth because we were the chosen people and the Lord would strike down everybody who stood in our way, but what it all came down to at the moment was this: You marry whoever the patriarch tells you to marry, and Papa Lem was the patriarch. He had my mama marry my daddy even though they never particularly liked each other, growing up cousins, because he could see that they was both specially chosen, which means to say they was both about the sparkiest there was. And when I was born, they knew it was like a confirmation of Papa Lem's decision, because the Lord had blessed them with a kid who gave off dust thicker than a dump truck on a dirt road.

One thing he asked me real particular was whether I ever been laid. He says to me, "Have you spilled your seed among the daughters of Ishmael and Esau?"

I knew what spilling seed was, cause we got lectures about that at the Children's Home. I wasn't sure who the daughters of Ishmael and Esau was, but since I never had a hot date, I figured I was pretty safe saying no. Still, I did consider a second, because what came to mind was the lady in Roanoke, stroking me up just by wanting me, and I

422

was thinking about how close I'd come to not being a virgin after all. I wondered if the lady from Roanoke was a daughter of Esau.

Papa Lem picked up on my hesitation, and he wouldn't let it go. "Don't lie to me boy. I can see a lie." Well, since *I* could see a lie, I didn't doubt but what maybe he could too. But then again, I've had plenty of grownups tell me they could spot a lie— but half the time they accused me of lying when I was telling the truth, and the other half they believed me when I was telling whoppers so big it'd take two big men to carry them upstairs. So maybe he could and maybe he couldn't. I figured I'd tell him just as much truth as I wanted. "I was just embarrassed to tell you I never had a girl," I says.

"Ah, the deceptions of the world," he says. "They make promiscuity seem so normal that a boy is ashamed to admit he is chaste." Then he got a glint in his eye. "I know the children of Esau have been watching you, wanting to steal your birthright. Isn't that so?"

"I don't know who Esau is," says I.

The folks who was gathered around us started muttering about that.

I says, "I mean, I know who he was in the Bible, he was the brother of Jacob, the one who sold his birthright for split pea soup."

"Jacob was the rightful heir, the true eldest son," says Papa Lem, "and don't you forget it. Esau is the one who went away from his father, out into the wilderness, rejecting the things of God and embracing the lies and sins of the world. Esau is the one who married a strange woman, who was not of the people! Do you understand me?"

I understand pretty good by then. Somewhere

along the line somebody got sick of living under the thumb of Papa Lem, or maybe the patriarch before him, and they split.

"Beware," says Papa Lem, "because the children of Esau and Ishmael still covet the blessings of Jacob. They want to corrupt the pure seed of Grandpa Jake. They have enough of the blessing of God to know that you're a remarkable boy, like Joseph who was sold into Egypt, and they will come to you with their whorish plans, the way Potiphar's wife came to Joseph, trying to persuade you to give them your pure and undefiled seed so that they can have the blessing that their fathers rejected."

I got to tell you that I didn't much like having him talk about my seed so much in front of mixed company, but that was nothing compared to what he did next. He waved his hand to a girl standing there in the crowd, and up she came. She wasn't half bad-looking, in a country sort of way. Her hair was mousy and she wasn't altogether clean and she stood with a two-bucket slouch, but her face wasn't bad and she looked to have her teeth. Sweet, but not my type, if you know what I mean.

Papa Lem introduced us. It was his daughter, which I might've guessed, and then he says to her, "Wilt thou go with this man?" And she looks at me and says, "I will go." And then she gave me this big smile, and all of a sudden it was happening again, just like it did with the lady in Roanoke, only twice as much, cause after all the lady in Roanoke wasn't hardly sparky. I was standing there and all I could think about was how I wanted all her clothes off her and to do with her right there in front of everybody and I didn't even care that all those people were watching, that's how strong it was.

And I liked it, I got to tell you. I mean you don't ignore a feeling like that. But another part of me was standing back and it says to me, "Mick Winger you damn fool, that girl's as homely as the bathroom sink, and all these people are watching her make an idiot out of you," and it was that part of me that got mad, because I didn't like her making me do something, and I didn't like it happening right out in front of everybody, and I specially didn't like Papa Lem sitting there looking at his own daughter and me like we was in a dirty magazine.

Thing is, when I get mad I get all sparky, and the madder I got, the more I could see how she was doing it, like she was a magnet, drawing me to her. And as soon as I thought of it like us being magnets, I took all the sparkiness from being mad and I used it. Not to hurt her or nothing, because I didn't put it on her the way I did with the people I killed. I just kind of turned the path of her sparks plain upside down. She was spinning it just as fast as ever, but it went the other way, and the second that started, why, it was like she disappeared. I mean, I could see her all right, but I couldn't hardly *notice* her. I couldn't focus my eyes on her.

Papa Lem jumped right to his feet, and the other folks were gasping. Pretty quick that girl stopped sparking at me, you can bet, and there she was on her knees, throwing up. She must've had a real weak digestion, or else what I done was stronger than I thought. She was really pouring on the juice, I guess, and when I flung it back at her and turned her upside down, well, she couldn't hardly walk when they got her up. She was pretty hysterical, too, crying about how awful and ugly I was, which might've hurt my feelings except that I was scared to death.

Papa Lem was looking like the wrath of God. "You have rejected the holy sacrament of marriage! You have spurned the handmaid God prepared for you!"

Now you've got to know that I hadn't put everything together yet, or I wouldn't have been so afraid of him, but for all I knew right then he could kill me with a cancer. And it was a sure thing he could've had those people beat me to death or whatever he wanted, so maybe I was right to be scared. Anyway I had to think of a way to make him not be mad at me, and what I came up with must not've been too bad because it worked, didn't it?

I says to him, as calm as I can, "Papa Lem, she was not an acceptable handmaiden." I didn't watch all those TV preachers for nothing. I knew how to talk like the Bible. I says, "She was not blessed enough to be my wife. She wasn't even as blessed as my mama. You can't tell me that she's the best the Lord prepared for me."

And sure enough, he calmed right down. "I know that," he says. And he isn't talking like a preacher any more, it's *me* talking like a preacher and him talking all meek. "You think I don't know it? It's those children of Esau, that's what it is, Mick, you got to know that. We had five girls who were a lot dustier than her, but we had to put them out into other families, cause they were like you, so strong they would've killed their own parents without meaning to."

And I says, "Well, you brought me back, didn't you?"

And he says, "Well you were *alive*, Mick, and you got to admit that makes it easier."

"You mean those girls're all dead?" I says.

426

"The children of Esau," he says. "Shot three of them, strangled one, and we never found the body of the other. They never lived to be ten years old."

And I thought about how the lady in Roanoke told me she had me in her gunsights a few times. But she let me live. Why? For my seed? Those girls would've had seed too, or whatever. But they killed those girls and let me live. I didn't know why. Hell, I still don't, not if you mean to keep me locked up like this for the rest of my life. I mean you might as well have blasted my head off when I was six, and then I can name you a dozen good folks who'd still be alive, so no thanks for the favor if you don't plan to let me go.

Anyway, I says to him, "I didn't know that. I'm sorry."

And he says to me, "Mick, I can see how you'd be disappointed, seeing how you're so blessed by the Lord. But I promise you that my daughter is indeed the best girl of marriageable age that we've got here. I wasn't trying to foist her off on you because she's my daughter—it would be blasphemous for me to try it, and I'm a true servant of the Lord. The people here can testify for me, they can tell you that I'd never give you my own daughter unless she was the best we've got."

If she was the best they got then I had to figure the laws against inbreeding made pretty good sense. But I says to him, "Then maybe we ought to wait and see if there's somebody younger, too young to marry right now." I remembered the story of Jacob from Sunday School, and since they set such store by Jacob I figured it'd work. I says, "Remember that Jacob served seven years before he got to marry Rachel. I'm willing to wait."

That impressed hell out of him, you can bet. He says, "You truly have the prophetic spirit, Mick. I have no doubt that someday you'll be Papa in my place, when the Lord has gathered me unto my fathers. But I hope you'll also remember that Jacob married Rachel, but he first married the older daughter, Leah."

The ugly one, I thought, but I didn't say it. I just smiled and told him how I'd remember that, and there was plenty of time to talk about it tomorrow, because it was dark now and I was tired and a lot of things had happened to me today that I had to think over. I was really getting into the spirit of this Bible thing, and so I says to him, "Remember that before Jacob could dream of the ladder into heaven, he had to sleep."

Everybody laughed, but Papa Lem wasn't satisfied yet. He was willing to let the marriage thing wait for a few days. But there was one thing that couldn't wait. He looks me in the eye and he says, "Mick, you got a choice to make. The Lord says those who aren't for me are against me. Joshua said choose ye this day whom ye will serve. And Moses said, 'I call heaven and earth to record this day against you, that I have set before you life and death, blessing and cursing: therefore choose life, that both thou and thy seed may live.'"

Well I don't think you can put it much plainer than that. I could choose to live there among the chosen people, surrounded by dirty kids and a slimy old man telling me who to marry and whether I could raise my own children, or I could choose to leave and get my brains blasted out or maybe just pick up a stiff dose of cancer—I wasn't altogether sure whether they'd do it quick or slow. I kind of figured they'd do it quick, though, so I'd have no chance to spill my seed among the daughters of Esau.

So I gave him my most solemn and hypocritical promise that I would serve the Lord and live among them all the days of my life. Like I told you, I didn't know whether he could tell if I was lying or not. But he nodded and smiled so it looked like he believed me. Trouble was, I knew *he* was lying, and so that meant he *didn't* believe me, and that meant I was in deep poo, as Mr. Kaiser's boy Greggy always said. In fact, he was pretty angry and pretty scared, too, even though he tried to hide it by smiling and keeping a lid on himself. But I knew that he knew that I had no intention of staying there with those crazy people who knocked up their cousins and stayed about as ignorant as I ever saw. Which meant that he was already planning to kill me, and sooner rather than later.

No, I better tell the truth here, cause I wasn't *that* smart. It wasn't till I was halfway to the house that I really wondered if he believed me, and it wasn't till Mama had me with a nice clean pair of pajamas up in a nice clean room, and she was about to take my jeans and shirt and underwear and make *them* nice and clean that it occurred to me that maybe I was going to wish I had more clothes on than pajamas that night. I really got kind of mad before she finally gave me back my clothes—she was scared that if she didn't do what I said, I'd do something to her. And then I got to thinking that maybe I'd made things even *worse* by not giving her the clothes, because that might make them think that I was planning to skip out, and so maybe they weren't planning to kill me before but now they would, and so I probably just made things worse. Except when it came down to it, I'd rather be wrong about the one thing and at least have my clothes, than be wrong about the other thing and have to gallivant all over the country in pajamas. You don't get much mileage on country roads barefoot in pajamas, even in the summer.

As soon as Mama left and went on downstairs, I got dressed again, including my shoes, and climbed in under the covers. I'd slept out in the open, so I didn't mind sleeping in my clothes. What drove me crazy was getting my shoes on the sheets. They would've yelled at me so bad at the Children's Home.

I laid there in the dark, trying to think what I was going to do. I pretty much knew how to get from this house out to the road, but what good would that do me? I didn't know where I was or where the road led or how far to go, and you don't cut cross country in North Carolina—if you don't trip over something in the dark, you'll bump into some moonshine or marijuana operation and they'll blast your head off, not to mention the danger of getting your throat bit out by some tobacco farmer's mean old dog. So there I'd be running along a road that leads nowhere with them on my tail and if they wanted to run me down, I don't think fear of cancer would slow down your average four-wheeler.

I thought about maybe stealing a car, but I don't have the first idea how to hotwire anything. It wasn't one of the skills you pick up at the Children's Home. I knew the idea of it, somewhat, because I'd done some reading on electricity with the books Mr. Kaiser lent me so I could maybe try getting ready for the GED, but there wasn't a chapter in there on how to get a Lincoln running without a key. Didn't know how to drive, either. All the stuff you pick up from your dad or from your friends at school, I just never picked up at all.

Maybe I dozed off, maybe I didn't. But I suddenly noticed that I could see in the dark. Not *see*, of course. Feel the people moving around. Not far off at first, except like a blur, but I could feel the near ones, the other ones in the house. It was cause they was sparky, of course, but as I laid there feeling them drifting here and there, in the rhythms of sleep and dreams, or walking around, I began to realize that I'd been feeling people all along, only I didn't know it. They wasn't sparky, but I always knew where they were, like shadows drifting in the back of your mind, I didn't even know that I knew it, but they were there. It's like when Diz Riddle got him his glasses when he was ten years old and all of a sudden he just went around whooping and yelling about all the stuff he saw. He always used to see it before, but he didn't rightly know what half the stuff was. Like pictures on coins. He knew the coins was bumpy, but he didn't know they was pictures and writing and stuff. That's how this was.

I laid there and I could make a map in my brain where I could see a whole bunch of different people, and the more I tried, the better I could see. Pretty soon it wasn't just in that house. I could feel them in other houses, dimmer and fainter. But in my mind I didn't see no walls so I didn't know whether somebody was in the kitchen or in the bathroom, I had to think it out, and it was hard, it took all my concentration. The only guide I had was that I could see electric wires when the current was flowing through them, so wherever a light was on or a clock was running or something, I could feel this thin line, really thin, not like the shadows of people. It wasn't much, but it gave me some idea of where some of the walls might be.

If I could've just told who was who I might have made some guesses about what they was doing. Who was asleep and who was awake. But I couldn't even tell who was a kid and who was a grown-up, cause I couldn't see sizes, just brightness. Brightness was the only way I knew who was close and who was far.

I was pure lucky I got so much sleep during the day when that guy was giving me a ride from Roanoke to Eden. Well, that wasn't lucky, I guess, since I wished I hadn't gone to Eden at all, but at least having that long nap meant that I had a better shot at staying awake until things quieted down.

There was a clump of them in the next house. It was hard to sort them out, cause three of them was a lot brighter, so I thought they was closer, and it took a while to realize that it was probably Mama and Daddy and Papa Lem along with some others. Anyway it was a meeting, and it broke up after a while, and all except Papa Lem came over. I didn't know what the meeting was about, but I knew they was scared and mad. Mostly scared. Well, so was I. But I calmed myself down, the way I'd been practicing, so I didn't accidentally kill nobody. That kind of practice made it so I could keep myself from getting too lively and sparky, so they'd think I was asleep. They didn't see as clear as I did, too, so that'd help. I thought maybe they'd all come up and get me, but no, they just all waited downstairs while one of them came up and he didn't come in and get me, neither. All he did was go to the other rooms and wake up whoever was sleeping there and get them downstairs and out of the house.

Well, that scared me worse than ever. That made it plain what they had in mind, all right. Didn't want me giving off sparks and killing somebody close by when they attacked me. Still, when I thought about it, I realized that it was also a good sign. They was scared of me, and rightly so. I could reach farther and strike harder than any of them. And they saw I could throw off what got tossed at me, when I flung back what Papa Lem's daughter tried to do to me. They didn't know how much I could do.

Neither did I.

Finally all the people was out of the house except the ones downstairs. There was others outside the house, maybe watching, maybe not, but I figured I better not try to climb out the window.

Then somebody started walking up the stairs again, alone. There wasn't nobody else to fetch down, so they could only be coming after me. It was just one person, but that didn't do me no good—even one grown man who knows how to use a knife is better off than me. I still don't have my full growth on me, or at least I sure hope I don't, and the only fights I ever got in were slugging matches in the yard. For a minute I wished I'd took kung fu lessons instead of sitting around reading math and science books to make up for dropping out of school so young. A lot of good math and science was going to do me if I was dead.

The worst thing was I couldn't see him. Maybe they just moved all the children out of the house so they wouldn't make noise in the morning and wake me. Maybe they was just being nice. And this guy coming up the stairs might just be checking on me or bringing me clean clothes or something—I couldn't tell. So how could I twist him up, when I didn't know if they was trying to kill me or what? But if he *was* trying to kill me, I'd wish I'd twisted him before he ever came into the room with me.

Well, that was one decision that got made for me. I laid there wondering what to do for so long that he got to the top of the stairs and came to my room and turned the knob and came in.

I tried to breathe slow and regular, like somebody asleep. Tried to keep from getting too sparky. If it was somebody checking on me, they'd go away.

He didn't go away. And he walked soft, too, so as not to wake me up. He was real scared. So scared that I finally knew there was no way he was there to tuck me in and kiss me good night.

So I tried to twist him, to send sparks at him. But I didn't have any sparks to send! I mean I wasn't mad or anything. I'd never tried to kill somebody on purpose before, it was always because I was already mad and I just lost control and it *happened*. Now I'd been calming myself down so much that I couldn't lose control. I had no sparks at all to send, just my normal shining shadow, and he was right there and I didn't have a second to lose so I rolled over. Toward him, which was maybe dumb, cause I might have run into his knife, but I didn't know yet for sure that he had a knife. All I was thinking was that I had to knock him down or push him or something.

The only person I knocked down was me. I bumped him and hit the floor. He also cut my back with the knife. Not much of a cut, he mostly just snagged my shirt, but if I was scared before, I was terrified now cause I knew he had a knife and I knew even more that I didn't. I scrambled back away from him. There was almost no light from the window, it was like being in a big closet, I couldn't see him, he couldn't see me. Except of course that I *could* see him, or at least sense where he was, and now I was giving off sparks like crazy so unless he was weaker than I thought, he could see me too.

Well, he was weaker than I thought. He just kind of drifted, and I could hear him swishing the knife through the air in front of him. He had no idea where I was.

And all the time I was trying to get madder and madder, and it wasn't working. You can't get mad by trying. Maybe an actor can, but I'm no actor. So I was scared and sparking but I couldn't get that pulse to mess him up. The more I thought about it, the calmer I got.

It's like you've been carrying around a machine gun all your life, accidentally blasting people you didn't really want to hurt and then the first time you really want to lay into somebody, it jams.

So I stopped trying to get mad. I just sat there realizing I was going to die, that after I finally got myself under control so I didn't kill people all the time anymore, now that I didn't really want to commit suicide, *now* I was going to get wasted. And they didn't even have the guts to come at me openly. Sneaking in the dark to cut my throat while I was asleep. And in the meeting where they decided to do it, my long lost but loving mama and daddy were right there. Heck, my dear sweet daddy was downstairs right now, waiting for this assassin to come down and tell him that I was dead. Would he cry for me then? Boo hoo my sweet little boy's all gone? Mick is in the cold cold ground?

I was mad. As simple as that. Stop thinking about being mad, and start thinking about the things that if you think about them, they'll make you mad. I was so sparky with fear that when I got mad, too, it was worse than it ever was before, built up worse, you know. Only when I let it fly, it didn't go for the guy up there swishing his knife back and forth in the dark. That pulse of fire in me went right down through the floor and straight to dear old Dad. I could hear him scream. He felt it, just like that. He felt it. And so did I. Because that wasn't what I meant to do. I only met him that day, but he was my *father*, and I did him worse than I ever did anybody before in my life. I didn't plan to do it. You don't plan to kill your father.

All of a sudden I was blinded by light. For a second I thought it was the other kind of light, sparks, them retaliating, twisting me. Then I realized it was my eyes being blinded, and it was the overhead light in the room that was on. The guy with the knife had finally realized that the only reason not to have the light on was so I wouldn't wake up, but now that I was awake he might as well see what he's doing. Lucky for me the light blinded him just as much as it blinded me or I'd have been poked before I saw what hit me. Instead I had time to scramble on back to the far corner of the room.

I wasn't no hero. But I was seriously thinking about running at him, attacking a guy with a knife. I would have been killed, but I couldn't think of anything else to do.

Then I thought of something else to do. I got the idea from the way I could feel the electric current in the wires running from the lightswitch through the wall. That was electricity, and the lady in

Roanoke called my sparkiness bio-electricity. I ought to be able to do something with it, shouldn't I?

I thought first that maybe I could short-circuit something, but I didn't think I had that much electricity in me. I thought of maybe tapping into the house current to add to my own juice, but then I remembered that connecting up your body to house current is the same thing other folks call *electrocution*. I mean, maybe I can tap into house wiring, but if I was wrong, I'd be real dead.

But I could still do something. There was a table lamp right next to me. I pulled off the shade and threw it at the guy, who was still standing by the door, thinking about what the scream downstairs meant. Then I grabbed the lamp and turned it on, and then smashed the lightbulb on the nightstand. Sparks. Then it was out.

I held the lamp in my hand, like a weapon, so he'd think I was going to beat off his knife with the lamp. And if my plan was a bust, I guess that's what I would've done. But while he was looking at me, getting ready to fight me knife against lamp, I kind of let the jagged end of the lamp rest on the bedspread. And then I used my sparkiness, the anger that was still in me. I couldn't fling it at the guy, or well I could have, but it would've been like the bus driver, a six-month case of lung cancer. By the time he died of *that*, I'd be six months worth of dead from multiple stab wounds to the neck and chest.

So I let my sparkiness build up and flow out along my arm, out along the lamp, like I was making my shadow grow. And it worked. The sparks just went right on down the lamp to the tip, and built up and built up, and all the time I was thinking about how

Papa Lem was trying to kill me cause I thought his daughter was ugly and how he made me kill my daddy before I even knew him half a day and that charge built *up*.

It built up enough. Sparks started jumping across inside the broken light bulb, right there against the bedspread. Real sparks, the kind I could *see*, not just feel. And in two seconds that bedspread was on fire. *Then* I yanked the lamp so the cord shot right out of the wall, and I threw it at the guy, and while he was dodging I scooped up the bedspread and ran at him. I wasn't sure whether I'd catch on fire or he would, but I figured he'd be too panicked and surprised to think of stabbing me *through* the bedspread, and sure enough he didn't, he dropped the knife and tried to beat off the bedspread. Which he didn't do too good, because I was still pushing it at him. Then he tried to get through the door, but I kicked his ankle with my shoe, and he fell down, still fighting off the blanket.

I got the knife and sliced right across the back of his thigh with it. Geez it was sharp. Or maybe I was so mad and scared that I cut him stronger than I ever thought I could, but it went clear to the bone. He was screaming from the fire and his leg was gushing blood and the fire was catching on the wallpaper and it occurred to me that they couldn't chase me too good if they was trying to put out a real dandy house fire.

It also occurred to me that I couldn't run away too good if I was dead inside that house fire. And thinking of maybe dying in the fire made me realize that the guy was burning to death and I did it to him, something every bit as terrible as cancer, and *I didn't care*, because I'd killed so many people that

438

it was nothing to me now, when a guy like that was trying to kill me, I wasn't even sorry for his pain, cause he wasn't feeling nothing worse than Old Peleg felt, and in fact that even made me feel pretty good; because it was like getting even for Old Peleg's death, even though it was me killed them both. I mean how could I get *even* for Peleg dying by killing somebody else? Okay, maybe it makes sense in a way, cause it was their fault I was in the orphanage instead of growing up here. Or maybe it made sense because this guy deserved to die, and Peleg didn't, so maybe somebody who deserved it had to die a death as bad as Peleg's, or something. I don't know. I sure as hell wasn't thinking about that then. I just knew that I was hearing a guy scream himself to death and I didn't even want to help him or even *try* to help him or nothing. I wasn't enjoying it, either, I wasn't thinking, Burn you sucker! Or anything like that, but I knew right then that I wasn't even human, I was just a monster, like I always thought, like in the slasher movies. This was straight from the slasher movies, somebody burning up and screaming, and there's the monster just standing there in the flames and he *isn't burning*.

And that's the truth. I wasn't burning. There was flames all around me, but it kind of shied back from me, because I was so full of sparks from hating myself so bad that it was like the flames couldn't get through to me. I've thought about that a lot since then. I mean, even that Swedish scientist doesn't know all about this bio-electrical stuff. Maybe when I get real sparky it makes it so other stuff can't hit me. Maybe that's how some generals in the Civil War used to ride around in the open—or maybe that was that general in World War II, I can't remember—and bullets didn't hit them or anything. Maybe if you're charged up enough, things just can't *get* to you. I don't know. I just know that by the time I finally decided to open the door and actually opened it, the whole room was burning and the door was burning and I just opened it and walked through. Course now I got a bandage on my hand to prove that I couldn't grab a hot doorknob without hurting myself a little, but I shouldn't've been able to stay alive in that room and I came out without even my hair singed.

I started down the hall, not knowing who was still in the house. I wasn't used to being able to see people by their sparkiness yet, so I didn't even think of checking, I just ran down the stairs carrying that bloody knife. But it didn't matter. They all ran away before I got there, all except Daddy. He was lying in the middle of the floor in the living room, doubled up, lying with his head in a pool of vomit and his butt in a pool of blood, shaking like he was dying of cold. I really done him. I really tore him up inside. I don't think he even saw me. But he was my daddy, and even a monster don't leave his daddy for the fire to get him. So I grabbed his arms to try to pull him out.

I forgot how sparky I was, worse than ever. The second I touched him the sparkiness just rushed out of me and all over him. It never went that way before, just completely surrounded him like he was a part of me, like he was completely drowning in my light. It wasn't what I meant to do at all. I just forgot. I was trying to save him and instead I gave him a hit like I never gave nobody before, and I couldn't stand it, I just screamed.

Then I dragged him out. He was all limp, but even

if I killed him, even if I turned him to jelly inside, he wasn't going to burn, that's all I could think of, that and how I ought to walk back into that house myself and up the stairs and catch myself on fire and die.

But I didn't do it, as you might guess. There was people yelling Fire! and shouting Stay back! and I knew that I better get out of there. Daddy's body was lying on the grass in front of the house, and I took off around the back. I thought maybe I heard some gunshots, but it could've been popping and cracking of timbers in the fire, I don't know. I just ran around the house and along toward the road, and if there was people in my way they just got *out* of my way, because even the most dimwitted inbred pukebrained kid in that whole village would've seen my sparks, I was so hot.

I ran till the asphalt ended and I was running on the dirt road. There was clouds so the moon was hardly any light at all, and I kept stumbling off the road into the weeds. I fell once and when I was getting up I could see the fire behind me. The whole house was burning, and there was flames above it in the trees. Come to think of it there hadn't been all that much rain, and those trees were dry. A lot more than one house was going to burn tonight, I figured, and for a second I even thought maybe nobody'd chase me.

But that was about as stupid an idea as I ever had. I mean, if they wanted to kill me before because I said Papa Lem's girl was ugly, how do you think they felt about me now that I burned down their little hidden town? Once they realized I was gone, they'd be after me and I'd be lucky if they shot me quick.

I even thought about cutting off the road, danger-ous or not, and hiding in the woods. But I decided to get as much distance as I could along the road till I saw headlights.

Just when I decided that, the road ended. Just bushes and trees. I went back, tried to find the road. It must have turned but I didn't know which way. I was tripping along like a blind man in the grass, trying to feel my way to the ruts of the dirt road, and of course that's when I saw headlights away off toward the burning houses—there was at least three houses burning now. They knew the town was a total loss by now, they was probably just leaving enough folks to get all the children out and away to a safe place, while the men came after me. It's what *I* would've done, and to hell with cancer, they knew I couldn't stop them all before they did what they wanted to me. And here I couldn't even find the road to get away from them. By the time their head-lights got close enough to show the road, it'd be too late to get away.

I was about to run back into the woods when all of a sudden a pair of headlights went on not twenty feet away, and pointed right at me. I damn near wet my pants. I thought, Mick Winger, you are a dead little boy right this second.

And then I heard her calling to me. "Get on over here, Mick, you idiot, don't stand there in the light, get on over here." It was the lady from Roanoke. I still couldn't see her cause of the lights, but I knew her voice, and I took off. The road didn't end, it just turned a little and she was parked right where the dirt road met up sideways with a gravel road. I got around to the door of the car she was driving, or truck or whatever it was—a four-wheel-drive Blazer maybe, I know it had a four-wheel-drive shift lever in it—anyway the door was locked and she was yelling at me to get *in* and I was yelling back that it was *locked* until finally she unlocked it and I climbed in. She backed up so fast and swung around onto the gravel in a spin that near threw me right out the door, since I hadn't closed it yet. Then she took off so fast going *forward*, spitting gravel behind her, that the door closed itself.

"Fasten your seat belt," she says to me.

"Did you follow me here?" I says.

"No, I just happened to be here picnicking," she says. "Fasten your damn *seat belt*."

I did, but then I turned around in my seat and looked out the back. There was five or six sets of headlights, making the job to get from the dirt road onto the gravel road. We didn't have more than a mile on them.

"We've been looking for this place for years," she says. "We thought it was in Rockingham County, that's how far off we were."

"Where is it, then?" I says.

"Alamance County," she says.

And then I says, "I don't give a damn what county it is! I killed my own daddy back there!"

And she says to me, "Don't get mad now, don't get mad at me, I'm sorry, just calm down." That was all she could think of, how I might get mad and lose control and kill her, and I don't blame her, cause it was the hardest thing I ever did, keeping myself from busting out right there in the car, and it would've killed her, too. The pain in my hand was starting to get to me, too, from where I grabbed the doorknob. It was just building up and building up.

She was driving a lot faster than the headlights

443

reached. We'd be going way too fast for a curve before she even saw it, and then she'd slam on the brakes and we'd skid and sometimes I couldn't believe we didn't just roll over and crash. But she always got out of it.

I couldn't face back anymore. I just sat there with my eyes closed, trying to get calm, and then I'd remember my daddy who I didn't even *like* but he was my daddy lying there in his blood and his puke, and I'd remember that guy who burned to death up in my room and even though I didn't care at the time, I sure cared now, I was so angry and scared and I hated myself so bad I couldn't hold it in, only I also couldn't let it out, and I kept wishing I could just die. Then I realized that the guys following us were close enough that I could feel them. Or no it wasn't that they was close. They was just so *mad* that I could see their sparks flying like never before. Well as long as I could see them I could let fly, couldn't I? I just flung out toward them. I don't know if I hit them. I don't know if my bio-electricity is something I can throw like that or what. But at least I shucked it off myself, and I didn't mess up the lady who was driving.

When we hit asphalt again, I found out that I didn't know what crazy driving was before. She peeled out and now she began to look at a curve ahead and then switch off the headlights until she was halfway through the curve, it was the craziest thing I ever saw, but it also made sense. They had to be following our lights and when our lights went out they wouldn't know where we was for a minute. They also wouldn't know that the road curved ahead, and they might even crash up or at least they'd have to slow down. Of course, we had a real good chance of ending up eating trees ourselves, but she drove like she knew what she was doing.

We came to a straight section with a crossroads about a mile up. She switched off the lights again, and I thought maybe she was going to turn, but she didn't. Just went on and on and on, straight into the pitch black. Now, that straight section was long, but it didn't go on forever, and I don't care how good a driver you are, you can't keep track of how far you've gone in the dark. Just when I thought for sure we'd smash into something, she let off the gas and reached her hand out the window with a flashlight. We was still going pretty fast, but the flashlight was enough to make a reflector up ahead flash back at us, so she knew where the curve was, and it was farther off than I thought. She whipped us around that curve and then around another, using just a couple of blinks from the flashlight, before she switched on her headlights again.

I looked behind us to see if I could see anybody. "You lost them!" I says.

"Maybe," she says. "You tell *me*."

So I tried to feel where they might be, and sure enough, they was sparky enough that I could just barely tell where they was, away back. Split up, smeared out. "They're going every which way," I says.

"So we lost a few of them," she says. "They aren't going to give up, you know."

"I know," I says.

"You're the hottest thing going," she says.

"And you're a daughter of Esau," I says.

"Like hell I am," she says. "I'm a great-great-great-granddaughter of Jacob Yow, who happened to be bio-electrically talented. Like if you're tall and

445

athletic, you can play basketball. That's all it is, just a natural talent. Only he went crazy and started inbreeding his whole family, and they've got these stupid ideas about being the chosen of God and all the time they're just *murderers*."

"Tell me about it," I says.

"You can't help it," she says. "You didn't have anybody to teach you. I'm not blaming you."

But I was blaming me.

She says, "Ignorant, that's what they are. Well, my grandpa didn't want to just keep reading the Bible and killing any revenuers or sheriffs or whatever who gave us trouble. He wanted to find out what we *are*. He also didn't want to marry the slut they picked out for him because he wasn't particularly dusty. So he left. They hunted him down and tried to kill him, but he got away, and he married. And he also studied and became a doctor and his kids grew up knowing that they had to find out what it *is*, this power. It's like the old stories of witches, women who get mad and suddenly your cows start dying. Maybe they didn't even know they were doing it. Summonings and love spells and come-hithers, everybody can do it a little, just like everybody can throw a ball and sometimes make a basket, but some people can do it better than others. And Papa Lem's people, they do it best of all, better and better, because they're breeding for it. We've got to stop them, don't you see? We've got to keep them from learning how to control it. Because now we know more about it. It's all tied up with the way the human body heals itself. In Sweden they've been changing the currents around to heal tumors. Cancer. The opposite of what you've been doing, but it's the same principle. Do you know what that means? If

446

they could control it, Lem's people could be healers, not killers. Maybe all it takes is to do it with love, not anger."

"Did you kill them little girls in orphanages with love?" I says.

And she just drives, she doesn't say a thing, just drives. "Damn," she says, "it's raining."

The road was slick in two seconds. She slowed way down. It came down harder and harder. I looked behind us and there was headlights back there again. Way back, but I could still see them. "They're on us again," I says.

"I can't go any faster in the rain," she says.

"It's raining on them too," I says.

"Not with my luck."

And I says, "It'll put the fire out. Back where they live."

And she says, "It doesn't matter. They'll move. They know we found them, because we picked you up. So they'll move."

I apologized for causing trouble, and she says, "We couldn't let you die in there. I had to go there and save you if I could."

"Why?" I ask her. "Why not let me die?"

"Let me put it another way," she says. "If you decided to stay with them, I had to go in there and kill you."

And I says to her, "You're the queen of compassion, you know?" And I thought about it a little. "You're just like they are, you know?" I says. "You wanted to get pregnant just like they did. You wanted to breed me like a stud horse."

"If I wanted to *breed* you," she says, "I would have done it on the hill this morning. Yesterday morning. You would've done it. And I should've made you, because if you went with them, our only hope was to have a child of yours that we could raise to be a decent person. Only it turned out you're a decent person, so we didn't have to kill you. Now we can study you and learn about this from the strongest living example of the phenomenon"—I don't know how to pronounce that, but you know what I mean. Or what she meant, anyway.

And I says to her, "Maybe I don't want you to study me, did you think of that?"

And she says to me, "Maybe what you want don't amount to a goldfish fart." Or anyway that's what she meant.

That's about when they started shooting at us. Rain or no rain, they was pushing it so they got close enough to shoot, and they wasn't half bad at it, seeing as the first bullet we knew about went right through the back window and in between us and smacked a hole in the windshield. Which made all kinds of cracks in the glass so she couldn't see, which made her slow down more, which meant they was even closer.

Just then we whipped around a corner and our headlights lit up a bunch of guys getting out of a car with guns in their hands, and she says, "Finally." So I figured they was some of her people, there to take the heat off. But at that same second Lem's people must have shot out a tire or maybe she just got a little careless for a second cause after all she couldn't see too good through the windshield, but anyway she lost control and we skidded and flipped over, rolled over it felt like five times, all in slow motion, rolling and rolling, the doors popping open and breaking off, the windshield cracking and crumbling away, and there we hung in our seat belts, not talking or nothing, except maybe I was saying O my God or something and then we smacked into something and just stopped, which jerked us around inside the car and then it was all over.

I heard water rushing. A stream, I thought. We can wash up. Only it wasn't a stream, it was the gasoline pouring out of the tank. And then I heard gunshots from back up by the road. I didn't know who was fighting who, but if the wrong guys won they'd just love to catch us in a nice hot gasoline fire. Getting out wasn't going to be all that hard. The doors were gone so we didn't have to climb out a window or anything.

We were leaned over on the left side, so her door was mashed against the ground. I says to her, "We got to climb out my door." I had brains enough to hook one arm up over the lip of the car before I unbuckled my seat belt, and then I hoisted myself out and stayed perched up there on the side of the car, up in the air, so I could reach down and help her out.

Only she wasn't climbing out. I yelled at her and she didn't answer. I thought for a second she was dead, but then I saw that her sparks was still there. Funny, how I never saw she had any sparkiness before, because I didn't know to look for it, but now, even though it was dim, I could see it. Only it wasn't so dim, it was real busy, like she was trying to heal herself. The gurgling was still going on, and everything smelled like gasoline. There was still shooting going on. And even if nobody came down to start us on fire on purpose, I saw enough car crashes at the movies to know you didn't need a match to start a car on fire. I sure didn't want to be near the car if it caught, and I sure didn't want her *in* it. But I couldn't see how to climb down in and pull her out. I mean I'm not a weakling but I'm not Mr. Universe either.

It felt like I sat there for a whole minute before I realized I didn't have to pull her out my side of the car, I could pull her out the *front* cause the whole windshield was missing and the roof was only mashed down a little, cause there was a rollbar in the car—that was real smart, putting a rollbar in. I jumped off the car. It wasn't raining right here, but it *had* rained, so it was slippery and wet. Or maybe it was slippery from the gasoline, I don't know. I got around the front of the car and up to the windshield, and I scraped the bits of glass off with my shoe. Then I crawled partway in and reached under her and undid her seat belt, and tried to pull her out, but her legs was hung up under the steering wheel and it took forever, it was terrible, and all the time I kept listening for her to breathe, and she didn't breathe, and so I kept getting more scared and frustrated and all I was thinking about was how she had to live, she couldn't be dead, she just got through saving my life and now she was dead and she couldn't be and I was going to get her out of the car even if I had to break her legs to do it, only I didn't have to break her legs and she finally slid out and I dragged her away from the car. It didn't catch on fire, but I couldn't know it wasn't going to.

And anyway all I cared about then was her, not breathing, lying there limp on the grass with her neck all floppy and I was holding on to her crying and angry and scared and I had us both covered with sparks, like we was the same person, just completely covered, and I was crying and saying, Live! I couldn't even call her by name or nothing because

450

I didn't know her name. I just know that I was shaking like I had the chills and so was she and she was breathing now and whimpering like somebody just stepped on a puppy and the sparks just kept flowing around us both and I felt like somebody sucked everything out of me, like I was a wet towel and somebody wrung me out and flipped me into a corner, and then I don't remember until I woke up here.

What did it feel like? What you did to her?

It felt like when I covered her with light, it was like I was taking over doing what her own body should've done, it was like I was healing her. Maybe I got that idea because she said something about healing when she was driving the car, but she wasn't breathing when I dragged her out, and then she was breathing. So I want to know if I healed her. Because if she got healed when I covered her with my own light, then, maybe I didn't kill my daddy either, because it was kind of like that, I *think* it was kind of like that, what happened when I dragged him out of the house.

I been talking a long time now, and you still told me nothing. Even if you think I'm just a killer and you want me dead, you can tell me about her. Is she alive?

Yes.

Well then how come I can't see her? How come she isn't here with the rest of you?

She had some surgery. It takes time to heal.

But did I help her? Or did I twist her? You got to tell me. Cause if I didn't help her then I hope I fail your test and you kill me cause I can't think of a good reason why I should be alive if all I can do is kill people.

You helped her, Mick. That last bullet caught her in the head. That's why she crashed.

But she wasn't bleeding!

It was dark, Mick. You couldn't see. You had her blood all over you. But it doesn't matter now. We have the bullet out. As far as we can tell, there was no brain damage. There should have been. She should have been dead.

So I did help her.

Yes. But we don't know how. All kinds of stories, you know, about faith healing, that sort of thing. Laying on of hands. Maybe it's the kind of thing you did, merging the bio-magnetic field. A lot of things don't make any sense yet. There's no way we can see that the tiny amount of electricity in a human bio-electric system could influence somebody a hundred miles off, but they summoned you, and you came. We need to study you, Mick. We've never had any-body as powerful as you. Tell the truth, maybe there's never been anybody like you. Or maybe all the healings in the New Testament—

I don't want to hear about no testaments. Papa Lem gave me about all the testaments I ever need to hear about.

Will you help us, Mick?

Help you how?

Let us study you.

Go ahead and study.

Maybe it won't be enough just to study how you *heal* people.

I'm not going to kill nobody for you. If you try to make me kill somebody I'll kill you first till you have to kill me just to save your own lives, do you understand me?

Calm down, Mick. Don't get angry. There's plenty

452

of time to think about things. Actually we're glad that you don't want to kill anybody. If you enjoyed it, or even if you hadn't been able to control it and kept on indiscriminately killing anyone who enraged you, you wouldn't have lived to be seventeen. Because yes, we're scientists, or at least we're finally learning enough that we can start being scientists. But first we're human beings, and we're in the middle of a war, and children like you are the weapons. If they ever got someone like you to stay with them, work with them, you could seek us out and destroy us. That's what they wanted you to do.

That's right, that's one thing Papa Lem said, I don't know if I mentioned it before, but he said that the children of Israel were supposed to kill every man, woman, and child in Canaan, cause idolaters had to make way for the children of God.

Well, you see, that's why our branch of the family left. We didn't think it was such a terrific idea, wiping out the entire human race and replacing it with a bunch of murderous, incestuous religious fanatics. For the last twenty years, we've been able to keep them from getting somebody like you, because we've murdered the children that were so powerful they had to put them outside to be reared by others.

Except me.

It's a war. We didn't like killing children. But it's like bombing the place where your enemies are building a secret weapon. The lives of a few children—no, that's a lie. It nearly split us apart ourselves, the arguments over that. Letting you live— it was a terrible risk. I voted against it every time. And I don't apologize for that, Mick. Now that you know what they are, and you chose to leave, I'm glad I lost. But so many things could have gone wrong.

They won't put any more babies out to orphanages now, though. They're not that dumb.

But now we have *you*. Maybe we can learn how to block what they do. Or how to heal the people they attack. Or how to identify sparkiness, as you call it, from a distance. All kinds of possibilities. But sometime in the future, Mick, you may be the only weapon we have. Do you understand that?

I don't want to.

I know.

You wanted to kill me?

I wanted to protect people from you. It was safest. Mick, I really am glad it worked out this way.

I don't know whether to believe you, Mr. Kaiser. You're such a good liar. I thought you were so nice to me all that time because you were just a nice guy.

Oh, he is, Mick. He's a nice guy. Also a damn fine liar. We kind of needed both those attributes in the person we had looking out for you.

Well, anyway, that's over with.

What's over with?

Killing me. Isn't it?

That's up to you, Mick. If you ever start getting crazy on us, or killing people that aren't part of this war of ours—

I won't do that!

But if you did, Mick. It's never too late to kill you.

Can I see her?

See who?

The lady from Roanoke! Isn't it about time you told me her name?

Come on. She can tell you herself.

454

St. Amy's Tale

Mother could kill with her hands. Father could fly. These are miracles. But they were not miracles then. Mother Elouise taught me that there were no miracles then.

I am the child of Wreckers, born while the angel was in them. This is why I am called Saint Amy, though I perceive nothing in me that should make me holier than any other old woman. Yet Mother Elouise denied the angel in her, too, and it was no less there.

Sift your fingers through the soil, all you who read my words. Take your spades of iron and your picks of stone. Dig deep. You will find no ancient works of man hidden there. For the Wreckers passed through the world, and all the vanity was consumed in fire; all the pride broke in pieces when it was smitten by God's shining hand.

Elouise leaned on the rim of the computer keyboard. All around her the machinery was alive, the screens displaying information. Elouise felt nothing but weariness. She was leaning because, for a moment, she had felt a frightening vertigo. As if the world underneath the airplane had dissolved and slipped away into a rapidly receding star and she would never to able to land.

True enough, she thought. *I'll never be able to land, not in the world I knew.*

"Getting sentimental about the old computers?"

Elouise, startled, turned in her chair and faced her husband, Charlie. At that moment the airplane lurched, but like sailors accustomed to the shifting of the sea, they adjusted unconsciously and did not notice the imbalance.

"Is it noon already?" she asked.

"It's the mortal equivalent of noon. I'm too tired to fly this thing anymore, and it's a good thing Bill's at the controls."

"Hungry?"

Charlie shook his head. "But Amy probably is," he said.

"Voyeur," said Elouise.

Charlie liked to watch Elouise nurse their daughter. But despite her accusation, Elouise knew there was nothing sexual in it. Charlie liked the idea of Elouise being Amy's mother. He liked the way Amy's sucking resembled the sucking of a calf or a lamb or a puppy. He had said, "It's the best thing we kept from the animals. The best thing we didn't throw away."

"Better than sex?" Elouise had asked. And Charlie had only smiled.

Amy was playing with a rag doll in the only large clear space in the airplane, near the exit door. "Mommy Mommy Mamommy Mommy-o," Amy said. The child stood and reached to be picked up. Then she saw Charlie. "Daddy Addy Addy."

"Hi," Charlie said.

"Hi," Amy answered. "Ha-ee." She had only just

learned to close the diphthong, and she exaggerated it. Amy played with the buttons on Elouise's shirt, trying to undo them.

"Greedy," Elouise said, laughing.

Charlie unbuttoned the shirt for her, and Amy seized on the nipple after only one false grab. She sucked noisily, tapping her hand gently against Elouise's breast as she ate.

"I'm glad we're so near finished," Elouise said. "She's too old to be nursing now."

"That's right. Throw the little bird out of the nest."

"Go to bed," Elouise said.

Amy recognized the phrase. She pulled away. "La-lo," she said.

"That's right. Daddy's going to sleep," Elouise said.

Elouise watched as Charlie stripped off most of his clothing and lay down on the pad. He smiled once, then turned over, and was immediately asleep. He was in tune with his body. Elouise knew that he would awaken in exactly six hours, when it was time for him to take the controls again.

Amy's sucking was a subtle pleasure now, though it had been agonizing the first few months, and painful again when Amy's first teeth had come in and she had learned to her delight that by nipping she could make her mother scream. But better to nurse her than ever have her eat the predigested pap that was served as food on the airplane. Elouise thought wryly that it was even worse than the microwaved veal cordon bleu that they used to inflict on commercial passengers. Only eight years ago. And they had calibrated their fuel so exactly that when they took the last draft of fuel from the last of their storage

457

tanks, the tank registered empty; they would burn the last of the processed petroleum, instead of putting it back into the earth. All their caches were gone now, and they would be at the tender mercies of the world that they themselves had created.

Still, there was work to do; the final work, in the final checks. Elouise held Amy with one arm while she used her free hand slowly to key in the last program that her role as commander required her to use. Elouise Private, she typed. Teacher teacher I declare I see someone's underwear, she typed. On the screen appeared the warning she had put there: "You may think you're lucky finding this program, but unless you know the magic words, an alarm is going to go off all over this airplane and you'll be had. No way out of it, sucker. Love, Elouise."

Elouise, of course, knew the magic words. Einstein sucks, she typed. The screen went blank, and the alarm did not go off.

Malfunction? she queried. "None," answered the computer.

Tamper? she queried, and the computer answered, "None."

Nonreport? she queried, and the computer flashed, "AFscanP7bb55."

Elouise had not really been dozing. But still she was startled, and she lurched forward, disturbing Amy, who really had fallen asleep. "No no no," said Amy, and Elouise forced herself to be patient; she soothed her daughter back to sleep before pursuing whatever it was that her guardian program had caught. Whatever it was? Oh, she knew what it was. It was treachery. The one thing she had been sure *her* group, *her* airplane would never have. Other groups of Rectifiers—wreckers, they called themselves, having adopted their enemies' name for them—other groups had had their spies or their faint-hearts, but not Bill or Heather or Ugly-Bugly.

Specify, she typed.

The computer was specific.

Over northern Virginia, as the airplane followed its careful route to find and destroy everything made of metal, glass, and plastic; somewhere over northern Virginia, the airplane's path bent slightly to the south, and on the return, at the same place, the airplane's path bent slightly to the north, so that a strip of northern Virginia two kilometers long and a few dozen meters wide could contain some non-biodegradable artifact, hidden from the airplane, and if Elouise had not queried this program, she would never have known it.

But she should have known it. When the plane's course bent, alarms should have sounded. Someone had penetrated the first line of defense. But Bill could not have done that, nor could Heather, really—they didn't have the sophistication to break up a bubble program. Ugly-Bugly?

She knew it wasn't faithful old Ugly-Bugly. No, not her.

The computer voluntarily flashed, "Override M577b, commandmo4, intwis CtTttT." It was an apology. Someone aboard ship had found the alarm override program and the overrides for the alarm overrides. Not my fault, the computer was saying.

Elouise hesitated for a moment. She looked down at her daughter and moved a curl of red hair away from Amy's eye. Elouise's hand trembled. But she was a woman of ice, yes, all frozen where compassion made other women warm. She prided herself on that, on having frozen the last warm places in her—frozen so goddamn rigid that it was only a moment's hesitation. And then she reached out and asked for the access code used to perform the treachery, asked for the name of the traitor.

The computer was even less compassionate than Elouise. It hesitated not at all.

The computer did not underline; the letters on the screen were no larger than normal. Yet Elouise felt the words as a shout, and she answered them silently with a scream.

Charles Evan Hardy, b24ag61-richlandWA.

It was Charlie who was the traitor—Charlie, her sweet, soft, hard-bodied husband, Charlie who secretly was trying to undo the end of the world.

God has destroyed the world before. Once in a flood, when Noah rode it out in the Ark. And once the tower of the world's pride was destroyed in the confusion of tongues. The other times, if there were any other times, those times are all forgotten.

The world will probably be destroyed again, unless we repent. And don't think you can hide from the angels. They start out as ordinary people, and you never know which ones. Suddenly God puts the power of destruction in their hands, and they destroy. And just as suddenly, when all the destruction is done, the angel leaves them, and they're ordinary people. Just my mother and my father.

I can't remember Father Charlie's face. I was too young.

Mother Elouise told me often about Father Charlie. He was born far to the west in a land where water only comes to the crops in ditches, almost never from the sky. It was a land unblessed by God. Men lived there, they believed, only by the strength of their own hands. Men made their ditches and forgot about God and became scientists. Father Charlie became a scientist. He worked on tiny animals, breaking their heart of hearts and combining it in new ways. Hearts were broken too often where he worked, and one of the little animals escaped and killed people until they lay in great heaps like fish in the ship's hold.

But this was not the destruction of the world.

Oh, they were giants in those days, and they forgot the Lord, but when their people lay in piles of moldering flesh and brittling bone, they remembered they were weak.

Mother Elouise said, "Charlie came weeping." This is how Father Charlie became an angel. He saw what the giants had done, by thinking they were greater than God. At first he sinned in his grief. Once he cut his own throat. They put Mother Elouise's blood in him to save his life. This is how they met: In the forest where he had gone to die privately, Father Charlie woke up from a sleep he thought would be forever to see a woman lying next to him in the tent and a doctor bending over them both. When he saw that this woman gave her blood to him whole and unstintingly, he forgot his wish to die. He loved her. He loved her forever. Mother Elouise said he loved her right up to the day she killed him.

When they were finished, they had a sort of ceremony, a sort of party. "A benediction," said Bill, solemnly sipping at the gin. "Amen and amen."

"My shift," Charlie said, stepping into the cockpit. Then he noticed that everyone was there and that they were drinking the last of the gin, the bottle

461

that had been saved for the end. "Well, happy us," Charlie said, smiling.

Bill got up from the controls of the 787. "Any preferences on where we set down?" he asked. Charlie took his place.

The others looked at one another. Ugly-Bugly shrugged. "God, who ever thought about it?"

"Come on, we're all futurists," Heather said. "You must know where you want to live."

"Two thousand years from now," Ugly-Bugly said. "I want to live in the world the way it'll be two thousand years from now."

"Ugly-Bugly opts for resurrection," Bill said. "I, however, long for the bosom of Abraham."

"Virginia," said Elouise. They turned to face her. Heather laughed.

"Resurrection," Bill intoned, "the bosom of Abraham, and Virginia. You have no poetry, Elouise."

"I've written down the coordinates of the place where we are supposed to land," Elouise said. She handed them to Charlie. He did not avoid her gaze. She watched him read the paper. He showed no sign of recognition. For a moment she hoped that it had all been a mistake, but no. She would not let herself be misled by her desires.

"Why Virginia?" Heather asked.

Charlie looked up. "It's central."

"It's east coast," Heather said.

"It's central in the high survival area. There isn't much of a living to be had in the western mountains or on the plains. It's not so far south as to be in hunter-gatherer country and not so far north as to be unsurvivable for a high proportion of the people. Barring a hard winter."

"All very good reasons," Elouise said. "Fly us there, Charlie."

Did his hands tremble as he touched the controls? Elouise watched very carefully, but he did not tremble. Indeed, he was the only one who did not. Ugly-Bugly suddenly began to cry, tears coming from her good eye and streaming down her good cheek. *Thank God she doesn't cry out of the other side*, Elouise thought; then she was angry at herself, for she had thought Ugly-Bugly's deformed face didn't bother her anymore. Elouise was angry at herself, but it only made her cold inside, determined that there would be no failure. Her mission would be complete. No allowances made for personal cost.

Elouise suddenly started out of her comtemplative mood to find that the two other women had left the cockpit—their sleep shift, though it was doubtful they would sleep. Charlie silently flew the plane, while Bill sat in the copilot's seat, pouring himself the last drop from the bottle. He was looking at Elouise.

"Cheers," Elouise said to him.

He smiled sadly back at her. "Amen," he said. Then he leaned back and sang softly:

> *Praise God, from whom all blessings flow.*
> *Praise him, ye creatures here below.*
> *Praise him, who slew the wicked host.*
> *Praise Father, Son, and Holy Ghost.*

Then he reached for Elouise's hand. She was surprised, but let him take it. He bent to her and kissed her palm tenderly. "For many have entertained angels unaware," he said to her.

A few moments later he was asleep. Charlie and

463

Elouise sat in silence. The plane flew on south as darkness overtook them from the east. At first their silence was almost affectionate. But as Elouise sat and sat, saying nothing, she felt the silence grow cold and terrible, and for the first time she realized that when the airplane landed, Charlie would be her—Charlie, who had been half her life for these last few years, whom she had never lied to and who had never lied to her—would be her enemy.

I have watched the little children do a dance called Charlie-El. They sing a little song to it, and if I remember the words, it goes like this:

> *I am made of bones and glass.*
> *Let me pass, let me pass.*
> *I am made of brick and steel.*
> *Take my heel, take my heel.*
> *I was killed just yesterday.*
> *Kneel and pray, kneel and pray.*
> *Dig a hole where I can sleep.*
> *Dig it deep, dig it deep.*
> *Will I go to heaven or hell?*
> *Charlie-El. Charlie-El.*

I think they are already nonsense words to the children. But the poem first got passed word of mouth around Richmond when I was little, and living in Father Michael's house. The children do not try to answer their song. They just sing it and do a very clever little dance while they sing. They always end the song with all the children falling down on the ground, laughing. That is the best way for the song to end.

Charlie brought the airplane straight down into a field, great hot winds pushing against the ground as if to shove it back from the plane. The field caught fire, but when the plane had settled upon its three wheels, foam streaked out from the belly of the machine and overtook the flames. Elouise watched from the cockpit, thinking, *Wherever the foam has touched, nothing will grow for years*. It seemed symmetrical to her. Even in the last moments of the last machine, it must poison the earth. Elouise held Amy on her lap and thought of trying to explain it to the child. But Elouise knew Amy would not understand or remember.

"Last one dressed is a sissy-wissy," said Ugly-Bugly in her husky, ancient-sounding voice. They had dressed and undressed in front of each other for years now, but today as the old plastic-polluted clothing came off and the homespun went on, they felt and acted like school kids on their first day in coed gym. Amy caught the spirit of it and kept yelling at the top of her voice. No one thought to quiet her. There was no need. This was a celebration.

But Elouise, long accustomed to self-examination, forced herself to realize that there was a strain to her frolicking. She did not believe it, not really. Today was not a happy day, and it was not just from knowing the confrontation that lay ahead. There was something so final about the death of the last of the engines of mankind. Surely something could be— but she forced the thought from her, forced the coldness in her to overtake that sentiment. Surely she could not be seduced by the beauty of the airplane. Surely she must remember that it was not the

465

machines but what they inevitably did to mankind that was evil.

They looked and felt a little awkward, almost silly, as they left the plane and stood around in the blackened field. They had not yet lost their feel for stylish clothing, and the homespun was so lumpy and awkward and rough. It didn't look right on any of them.

Amy clung to her doll, awed by the strange scenery. In her life she had been out of the airplane only once, and that was when she was an infant. She watched as the trees moved unpredictably. She winced at the wind in her eyes. She touched her cheek, where her hair moved back and forth in the breeze, and hunted through her vocabulary for a word to name the strange invisible touch of her skin. "Mommy," she said. "Uh! Uh! Uh!"

Elouise understood. "Wind," she said. The sounds were still too hard for Amy, and the child did not attempt to say the word. *Wind*, thought Elouise, and immediately thought of Charlie. Her best memory of Charlie was in the wind. It was during his death-wish time, not long after his suicide. He had insisted on climbing a mountain, and she knew that he meant to fall. So she had climbed with him, even though there was a storm coming up. Charlie was angry all the way. She remembered a terrible hour clinging to the face of a cliff, held only by small bits of metal forced into cracks in the rock. She had insisted on remaining tied to Charlie. "If one of us fell, it would only drag the other down, too," he kept saying. "I know," she kept answering. And so Charlie had not fallen, and they made love for the first time in a shallow cave, with the wind howling outside and occasional sprays of rain coming

466

in to dampen them. They refused to be dampened. Wind. Damn.

And Elouise felt herself go cold and unemotional, and they stood on the edge of the field in the shade of the first trees. Elouise had left the Rectifier near the plane, set on 360 degrees. In a few minutes the Rectifier would go off, and they had to watch, to witness the end of their work.

Suddenly Bill shouted, laughed, held up his wrist. "My watch!" he cried.

"Hurry," Charlie said. "There's time."

Bill unbuckled his watch and ran toward the Rectifier. He tossed the watch. It landed within a few meters of the small machine. Then Bill returned to the group, jogging and shaking his head. "Jesus, what a moron! Three years wiping out everything east of the Mississippi, and I almost save a digital chronograph."

"Dixie Instruments?" Heather asked.

"Yeah."

"That's not high technology," she said, and they all laughed. Then they fell silent, and Elouise wondered whether they were all thinking the same thing; that jokes about brand names would be dead within a generation, if they were not already dead. They watched the Rectifier in silence, waiting for the timer to finish its delay. Suddenly there was a shining in the air, a dazzling not-light that made them squint. They had seen this many times before, from the air and from the ground, but this was the last time, and so they saw it as if it were the first.

The airplane corroded as if a thousand years were passing in seconds. But it wasn't a true corrosion. There was no rust—only dissolution as molecules separated and seeped down into the loosened earth.

467

Glass became sand; plastic corrupted to oil; the metal also drifted down into the ground and came to rest in a vein at the bottom of the Rectifier field. Whatever else the metal might look like to a future geologist, it wouldn't look like an artifact. It would look like iron. And with so many similar pockets of iron and copper and aluminium and tin spread all over the once-civilized world, it was not likely that they would suspect human interference. Elouise was amused, thinking of the treatises that would some-day be written, about the two states of workable metals—the ore state and the pure-metal vein. She hoped it would retard their progress a little.

The airplane shivered into nothing, and the Recti-fier also died in the field. A few minutes after the Rectifier disappeared, the field also faded.

"Amen and amen," said Bill, maudlin again. "All clean now."

Elouise only smiled. She said nothing of the other Rectifier, which was in her knapsack. Let the others think all the work was done.

Amy poked her finger in Charlie's eye. Charlie swore and set her down. Amy started to cry, and Charlie knelt by her and hugged her. Amy's arm went tightly around his neck. "Give Daddy a kiss," Elouise said.

"Well, time to go," Ugly-Bugly's voice rasped. "Why the hell did you pick this particular spot?"

Elouise cocked her head. "Ask Charlie."

Charlie flushed. Elouise watched him grimly. "Elouise and I once came here," he said. "Before Rectification began. Nostalgia, you know." He smiled shyly, and the others laughed. Except Elou-ise. She was helping Amy to urinate. She felt the weight of the small Rectifier in her knapsack and did not tell anyone the truth: that she had never been in Virginia before in her life.

"Good a spot as any," Heather said. "Well, bye."

Well, bye. That was all, that was the end of it, and Heather walked away to the west, toward the henandoah Valley.

"See ya," Bill said.

"Like hell," Ugly-Bugly added.

Impulsively Ugly-Bugly hugged Elouise, and Bill cried, and then they took off northeast, toward the Potomac, where they would doubtlessly find a community growing up along the clean and fish-filled river.

Just Charlie, Amy, and Elouise left in the empty, blackened field where the airplane had died. Elouise tried to feel some great pain at the separation from the others, but she could not. They had been together every day for years now, going from supply dump to supply dump, wrecking cities and towns, destroying and using up the artificial world. But had they been friends? If it had not been for their task, they would never have been friends. They were not the same kind of people.

And then Elouise was ashamed of her feelings. Not her kind of people? Because Heather liked what grass did to her and had never owned a car or had a driver's license in her life? Ugly-Bugly had a face hideously deformed by cancer surgery? Because Bill always worked Jesus into the conversation, even though half the time he was an atheist? Because they just weren't in the same social circles? There were no social circles now. Just people trying to survive in a bitter world they weren't bred for. There were only two classes now: those who would make it and those who wouldn't.

Which class am I? thought Elouise.

"Where should we go?" Charlie asked.

Elouise picked Amy up and handed her to Charlie. "Where's the capsule, Charlie?"

Charlie took Amy and said, "Hey, Amy, baby, I'll bet we find some farming community between here and the Rappahannock."

"Doesn't matter if you tell me, Charlie. The instruments found it before we landed. You did a damn good job on the computer program." She didn't have to say, Not good enough.

Charlie only smiled crookedly. "Here I was hoping you were forgetful." He reached out to touch her knapsack. She pulled abruptly away. He lost his smile. "Don't you know me?" he asked softly.

He would never try to take the Rectifier from her by force. But still. This was the last of the artifacts they were talking about. Was anyone really predictable at such a time? Elouise was not sure. She had thought she knew him well before, yet the time capsule existed to prove that her understanding of Charlie was far from complete.

"I know you, Charlie," she said, "but not as well as I thought. Does it matter? Don't try to stop me."

"I hope you're not too angry," he said.

Elouise couldn't think of anything to say to that. *Anyone could be fooled by a traitor, but only I am fool enough to marry one.* She turned from him and walked into the forest. He took Amy and followed.

All the way through the underbrush Elouise kept expecting him to say something. A threat, for instance: You'll have to kill me to destroy that time capsule. Or a plea: You have to leave it, Elouise, please, please. Or reason, or argument, or anger, or something.

But instead it was just his silent footfalls behind her. Just his occasional playtalk with Amy. Just his singing as he put Amy to sleep on his shoulder.

The capsule had been hidden well. There was no surface sign that men had ever been here. Yet, from the Rectifier's emphatic response, it was obvious that the time capsule was quite large. There must have been heavy, earthmoving equipment. Or was it all done by hand?

"When did you ever find the time?" Elouise asked when they reached the spot.

"Long lunch hours," he said.

She set down her knapsack and then stood there, looking at him.

Like a condemned man who insists on keeping his composure, Charlie smiled wryly and said, "Get on with it, please."

After Father Charlie died, Mother Elouise brought me here to Richmond. She didn't tell anyone that she was a Wrecker. The angel had already left her, and she wanted to blend into the town, be an ordinary person in the world she and her fellow angels had created.

Yet she was incapable of blending in. Once the angel touches you, you cannot go back, even when the angel's work is done. She first attracted attention by talking against the stockade. There was once a stockade around the town of Richmond, when there were only a thousand people here. The reason was simple: People still weren't used to the hard way life was without the old machines. They had not yet learned to depend on the miracle of Christ. They still trusted in their hands, yet their hands could work no more magic. So there were tribes in the

471

winter that didn't know how to find game, that had no reserves of grain, that had no shelter adequate to hold the head of a fire.

"Bring them all in," said Mother Elouise. "There's room for all. There's food for all. Teach them how to build ships and make tools and sail and farm, and we'll all be richer for it."

But Father Michael and Uncle Avram knew more than Mother Elouise. Father Michael had been a Catholic priest before the destruction, and Uncle Avram had been a professor at a university. They had been nobody. But when the angels of destruction finished their work, the angels of life began to work in the hearts of men. Father Michael threw off his old allegiance to Rome and taught Christ simple, from his memory of the Holy Book. Uncle Avram plunged into his memory of ancient metallurgy and taught the people who gathered at Richmond how to make iron hard enough to use for tools. And weapons.

Father Michael forbade the making of guns and forbade that anyone teach children what guns were. But for hunting there had to be arrows, and what will kill a deer will also kill a man.

Many people agreed with Mother Elouise about the stockade. But then in the worst of winter a tribe came from the mountains and threw fire against the stockade and against the ships that kept trade alive along the whole coast. The archers of Richmond killed most of them, and people said to Mother Elouise, "Now you must agree we need the stockade."

Mother Elouise said, "Would they have come with fire if there had been no wall?"

How can anyone judge the greatest need? Just as

the angel of death had come to plant the seeds of a better life, so that angel of life had to be hard and endure death so the many could live. Father Michael and Uncle Avram held to the laws of Christ simple, for did not the Holy Book say, "Love your enemies, and smite them only when they attack you; chase them not out into the forest, but let them live as long as they leave you alone"?

I remember that winter. I remember watching while they buried the dead tribesmen. Their bodies had stiffened quickly, but Mother Elouise brought me to see them and said, "This is death, remember it, remember it." What did Mother Elouise know? Death is our passage from flesh into the living wind, until Christ brings us forth into flesh again. Mother Elouise will find Father Charlie again, and every wound will be made whole.

Elouise knelt by the Rectifier and carefully set it to go off in half an hour, destroying itself and the time capsule buried thirty meters under the ground. Charlie stood near her, watching, his face nearly expressionless; only a faint smile broke his perfect repose. Amy was in his arms, laughing and trying to reach up to pinch his nose.

"This Rectifier responds only to me," Elouise said quietly. "Alive. If you try to move it, it will go off early and kill us all."

"I won't move it," Charlie said.

And Elouise was finished. She stood up and reached for Amy. Amy reached back, holding out her arms to her mother. "Mommy," she said.

Because I couldn't remember Father Charlie's face, Mother Elouise thought I had forgotten everything

473

about him, but that is not true. I remember very clearly one picture of him, but he is not in the picture.

This is very hard for me to explain. I see a small clearing in the trees, with Mother Elouise standing in front of me. I see her at my eye level, which tells me that I am being held. I cannot see Father Charlie, but I know that he is holding me. I can feel his arms around me, but I cannot see his face.

This vision has come to me often. It is not like other dreams. It is very clear, and I am always very afraid, and I don't know why. They are talking, but I do not understand their words. Mother Elouise reaches for me, but Father Charlie will not let me go. I feel afraid that Father Charlie will not let me go with Mother Elouise. But why should I be afraid? I love Father Charlie, and I never want to leave him. Still I reach out, reach out, reach out, and still the arms hold me and I cannot go.

Mother Elouise is crying. I see her face twisted in pain. I want to comfort her. "Mommy is hurt," I say again and again.

And then, suddenly, at the end of this vision I am in my mother's arms and we are running, running up a hill, into the trees. I am looking back over her shoulder. I see Father Charlie then. I see him, but I do not see him. I know exactly where he is, in my vision. I could tell you his height. I could tell you where his left foot is and where his right foot is, but still I can't see him. He has no face, no color; he is just a man-shaped emptiness in the clearing, and then the trees are in the way and he is gone.

Elouise stopped only a little way into the woods. She turned around, as if to go back to Charlie. But she would not go back. If she returned to him, it would be to disconnect the Rectifier. There would be no other reason to do it.

"Charlie, you son of a bitch!" she shouted.

There was no answer. She stood, waiting. Surely he could come to her. He would see that she would never go back, never turn off the machine. Once he realized it was inevitable, he would come running from the machine, into the forest, back to the clearing where the 787 had landed. Why would he want to give his life so meaninglessly? What was in the time capsule, after all? Just history—that's what he said, wasn't it? Just history, just films and metal plates engraved with words and microdots and other ways of preserving the story of mankind. "How can they learn from our mistakes, unless we tell them what they were?" Charlie had asked.

Sweet, simple, naive Charlie. It is one thing to preserve a hatred for the killing machines and the soul-destroying machines and the garbage-making machines. It was another to leave behind detailed, accurate, unquestionable descriptions. History was not a way of preventing the repetition of mistakes. It was a way of guaranteeing them. Wasn't it?

She turned and walked on, not very quickly, out of the range of the Rectifier, carrying Amy and listening, all the way, for the sound of Charlie running after her.

What was Mother Elouise like? She was a woman of contradictions. Even with me, she would work for hours teaching me to read, helping me make tablets out of river clay and write on them with a shaped stick. And then, when I had written the words she taught me, she would weep and say,

"Lies, all lies." Sometimes she would break the tablets I had made. But whenever part of her words was broken, she would make me write it again.

She called the collection of words The Book of the Golden Age. I have named it The Book of the Lies of the Angel Elouise, for it is important for us to know that the greatest truths we have seem like lies to those who have been touched by the angel.

She told many stories to me, and often I asked her why they must be written down. "For Father Charlie," she would always say.

"Is he coming back, then?" I would ask.

But she shook her head, and finally one time she said, "It is not for Father Charlie to read. It is because Father Charlie wanted it written."

"Then why didn't he write it himself?" I asked.

And Mother Elouise grew very cold with me, and all she would say was, "Father Charlie bought these stories. He paid more for them than I am willing to pay to have them left unwritten." I wondered then whether Father Charlie was rich, but other things she said told me that he wasn't. So I do not understand except that Mother Elouise did not want to tell the stories, and Father Charlie, though he was not there, constrained her to tell them.

There are many of Mother Elouise's lies that I love, but I will say now which of them she said were most important:

1. In the Golden Age for ten times a thousand years men lived in peace and love and joy, and no one did evil to another. They shared all things in common, and no man was hungry while another was full, and no man had a home while another stood in the rain,

and no wife wept for her husband, killed before his time.

2. The great serpent seems to come with great power. He has many names: Satan, Hitler, Lucifer, Nimrod, Napoleon. He seems to be beautiful, and he promises power to his friends and death to his enemies. He says he will right all wrongs. But really he is weak, until people believe in him and give him the power of their bodies. If you refuse to believe in the serpent, if no one serves him, he will go away.

3. There are many cycles of the world. In every cycle the great serpent has arisen and the world has been destroyed to make way for the return of the Golden Age. Christ comes again in every cycle, also. One day when He comes men will believe in Christ and doubt the great serpent, and that time the Golden Age will never end, and God will dwell among men forever. And all the angels will say, "Come not to heaven but to Earth, for Earth is heaven now."

These are the most important lies of Mother Elouise. Believe them all, and remember them, for they are true.

All the way to the airplane clearing, Elouise deliberately broke branches and let them dangle so that Charlie would have no trouble finding a straight path out of the range of the Rectifier, even if he left his flight to the last second. She was sure Charlie would follow her. Charlie would bend to her as he had always bent, resilient and accommodating. He loved

Elouise, and Amy he loved even more. What was in the metal under his feet that would weigh in the balance against his love for them?

So Elouise broke the last branch and stepped into the clearing and then sat down and let Amy play in the unburnt grass at the edge while she waited. *It is Charlie who will bend*, she said to herself, *for I will never bend on this. Later I will make it up to him, but he must know that on this I will never bend.*

The cold place in her grew larger and colder until she burned inside, waiting for the sound of feet crashing through the underbrush. The damnable birds kept singing, so that she could not hear the footsteps.

Mother Elouise never hit me, or anyone else so far as I knew. She fought only with her words and silent acts, though she could have killed easily with her hands. I saw her physical power only once. We were in the forest, to gather firewood. We stumbled upon a wild hog. Apparently it felt cornered, though we were weaponless; perhaps it was just mean. I have not studied the ways of wild hogs. It charged, not Mother Elouise, but me. I was five at the time, and terrified, I ran to Mother Elouise, tried to cling to her, but she threw me out of the way and went into a crouch. I was screaming. She paid no attention to me. The hog continued rushing, but seeing I was down and Mother Elouise erect, it changed its path. When it came near, she leaped to the side. It was not nimble enough to turn to face her. As it lumbered past, Mother Elouise kicked it just behind the head. The kick broke the hog's neck so violently that its head dropped and the hog rolled over and

478

over, and when it was through rolling, it was already dead.

Mother Elouise did not have to die.

She died in the winter when I was seven. I should tell you how life was then, in Richmond. We were only two thousand souls by then, not the large city of ten thousand we are now. We had only six finished ships trading the coast, and they had not yet gone so far north as Manhattan, though we had run one voyage all the way to Savannah in the south. Richmond already ruled and protected from the Potomac to Dismal Swamp. But it was a very hard winter, and the town's leaders insisted on hoarding all the stored grain and fruits and vegetables and meat for our protected towns, and let the distant tribes trade or travel where they would, they would get no food from Richmond.

It was then that my mother, who claimed she did not believe in God, and Uncle Avram, who was a Jew, and Father Michael, who was a priest, all argued the same side of the question. It's better to feed them than to kill them, they all said. But when the tribes from west of the mountains and north of the Potomac came into Richmond lands, pleading for help, the leaders of Richmond turned them away and closed the gates of the towns. An army marched then, to put the fear of God, as they said, into the hearts of the tribesmen. They did not know which side God was on.

Father Michael argued and Uncle Avram stormed and fumed, but Mother Elouise silently went to the gate at moonrise one night and alone overpowered the guards. Silently she gagged them and bound them and opened the gates to the hungry tribesmen. They came through weaponless, as she had insisted.

479

They quietly went to the storehouses and carried off as much food as they could. They were found only as the last few fled. No one was killed.

But there was an uproar, a cry of treason, a trial, and an execution. They decided on beheading, because they thought it would be quick and merciful. They had never seen a beheading.

It was Jack Woods who used the ax. He practiced all afternoon with pumpkins. Pumpkins have no bones.

In the evening they all gathered to watch, some because they hated Mother Elouise, some because they loved her, and the rest because they could not stay away. I went also, and Father Michael held my head and would not let me see. But I heard.

Father Michael prayed for Mother Elouise. Mother Elouise damned his and everyone else's soul to hell. She said: "If you kill me for bringing life, you will only bring death on your own heads."

"That's true," said the men around her. "We will all die. But you will die first."

"Then I'm the luckier," said Mother Elouise. It was the last of her lies, for she was telling the truth, and yet she did not believe it herself, for I heard her weep. With her last breaths she wept and cried out, "Charlie! Charlie!" There are those who claim she saw a vision of Charlie waiting for her on the right hand of God, but I doubt it. She would have said so. I think she only wished to see him. Or wished for his forgiveness. It doesn't matter. The angel had long since left her, and she was alone.

Jack swung the ax and it fell, more with a smack than a thud. He had missed her neck and struck deep in her back and shoulder. She screamed. He struck again and this time silenced her. But he did not break through her spine until the third blow. Then he turned away splattered with blood, and vomited and wept and pleaded with Father Michael to forgive him.

Amy stood a few meters away from Elouise, who sat on the grass of the clearing, looking toward a broken branch on the nearest tree. Amy called, "Mommy! Mommy!" Then she bounced up and down, bending and unbending her knees. "Da! Da!" she cried. "La la la la la." She was dancing and wanted her mother to dance and sing, too. But Elouise only looked toward the tree, waiting for Charlie to appear. *Any minute*, she thought. *He will be angry. He will be ashamed*, she thought. *But he will be alive*.

In the distance, however, the air all at once was shining. Elouise could see it clearing because they were not far from the edge of the Rectifier field. It shimmered in the trees, where it caused no harm to plants. Any vertebrates within the field, any animals that lived by electricity passing along nerves, were instantly dead, their brains stilled. Birds dropped from tree limbs. Only insects droned on.

The Rectifier field lasted only minutes.

Amy watched the shining air. It was as if the empty sky itself were dancing with her. She was transfixed. She would soon forget the airplane, and already her father's face was disappearing from her memories. But she would remember the shining. She would see it forever in her dreams, a vast thickening of the air, dancing and vibrating up and down, up and down. In her dreams it would always be the same, a terrible shining light that would grow and grow and grow and press against her in her bed. And always with it would come the sound of a voice she loved, saying, "Jesus. Jesus. Jesus." This dream would come so clearly when she was twelve that she would tell it to her adopted father, the priest named Michael. He told her that it was the voice of an angel, speaking the name of the source of all light. "You must not fear the light," he said. "You must embrace it." It satisfied her.

But at the moment she first heard the voice, in fact and not in dream, she had no trouble recognizing it, it was the voice of her mother, Elouise, saying, "Jesus." It was full of grief that only a child could fail to understand. Amy did not understand. She only tried to repeat the word. "Deeah-zah."

"God," said Elouise, rocking back and forth, her face turned up toward a heaven she was sure was unoccupied.

"Dog." Amy repeated, "Dog dog doggie." In vain she looked around for the four-footed beast.

"Charlie!" Elouise screamed as the Rectifier field faded.

"Daddy," Amy cried, and because of her mother's tears she also wept. Elouise took her daughter in her arms and held her, rocking back and forth. Elouise discovered that there were some things that could not be frozen in her. Some things that must burn: Sunlight. And lightning. And everlasting, inextinguishable regret.

My mother, Mother Elouise, often told me about my father. She described Father Charlie in detail, so I would not forget. She refused to let me forget anything. "It's what Father Charlie died for," she

482

told me, over and over. "He died so you would remember. You cannot forget."

So I still remember, even today, every word she told me about him. His hair was red, as mine was. His body was lean and hard. His smile was quick, like mine, and he had gentle hands. When his hair was long or sweaty, it kinked tightly at his forehead, ears, and neck. His touch was so delicate he could cut in half an animal so tiny it could not be seen without a machine; so sensitive that he could fly— an art that Mother Elouise said was not a miracle, since it could be done by many giants of the Golden Age, and they took with them many others who could not fly alone. This was Charlie's gift. Mother Elouise said. She also told me that I loved him dearly.

But for all the words that she taught me, I still have no picture of my father in my mind. It is as if the words drove out the vision, as so often happens.

Yet I still hold that one memory of my father, so deeply hidden that I can neither lose it nor fully find it again. Sometimes I wake up weeping. Sometimes I wake up with my arms in the air, curved just so, and I remember that I was dreaming of embracing that large man who loved me. My arms remember how it feels to hold Father Charlie tight around the neck and cling to him as he carries his child. And when I cannot sleep, and the pillow seems to be always the wrong shape, it is because I am hunting for the shape of Father Charlie's shoulder, which my heart remembers, though my mind cannot.

God put angels into Mother Elouise and Father Charlie, and they destroyed the world, for the cup of God's indignation was full, and all the works of men become dust, but out of dust God makes men, and out of men and women, angels.

Kingsmeat

The gatekeeper recognized him and the gate fell away. The Shepherd put his ax and his crook into the bag at his belt and stepped out onto the bridge. As always he felt a rush of vertigo as he walked the narrow arch over the foaming acid of the moat. Then he was across and striding down the road to the village.

A child was playing with a dog on a grassy hillside. The Shepherd looked up at him, his fine dark face made bright by his eyes. The boy shrank back, and the Shepherd heard a woman's voice cry out, "Back here, Derry, you fool!" The Shepherd walked on down the road as the boy retreated among the hayricks on the far slope. The Shepherd could hear the scolding: "Play near the castle again, and he'll make kingsmeat of you."

Kingsmeat, thought the Shepherd. How the king does get hungry. The word had come down through the quick grapevine—steward to cook to captain to guard to shepherd and then he was dressed and out the door only minutes after the king had muttered, "For supper, what is your taste?" and the queen had fluttered all her arms and said, "Not stew again, I hope," and the king had murmured as he picked up the computer printouts of the day, "Breast in

485

butter," and so now the Shepherd was out to harvest from the flock.

The village was still in the distance when the Shepherd began to pass the people. He remembered the time, back when the king had first made his tastes known, when there had been many attempts to evade the villagers' duties to the king. Now they only watched, perhaps hiding the unblemished members of the flock, sometimes thrusting them forward to end the suspense; but mostly the Shepherd saw the old legless, eyeless, or armless men and women who hobbled about their duties with those limbs that were still intact.

Those with fingers thatched or wove; those with eyes led those whose hands were their only contact with the world; those with arms rode the backs of those with legs; and all of them took their only solace in sad and sagging beds, producing, after a suitable interval, children whose miraculous wholeness made them gods to a surprised and wondering mother, made them hated reminders to a father whose tongue had fallen from his mouth, or whose toes had somehow been mislaid, or whose buttocks were a scar, his legs a useless reminder of hams long since dropped off.

"Ah, such beauty," a woman murmured, pumping the bellows at the bread-oven fire. There was a sour grunt from the legless hag who shoveled in the loaves and turned them with a wooden shovel. It was true, of course, for the Shepherd was never touched, no indeed. (No indeed, came the echo from the midnight fires of Unholy Night, when dark tales frightened children half out of their wits, dark tales that the shrunken grown-ups knew were true, were inevitable, were tomorrow.) The Shepherd had long dark hair, and his mouth was firm but kind, and his eyes flashed sunlight even in the dark, it seemed, while his hands were soft from bathing, large and strong and dark and smooth and fearful.

And the Shepherd walked into the village to a house he had noted the last time he came. He went to the door and immediately heard a sigh from every other house, and silence from the one that he had picked.

He raised his hand before the door and it opened, as it had been built to do: for all things that opened served the Shepherd's will, or at least served the bright metal ball the king had implanted in his hand. Inside the house it was dark, but not too dark to see the white eyes of an old man who lay in a hammock, legs dangling bonelessly. The man could see his future in the Shepherd's eyes—or so he thought, at least, until the Shepherd walked past him into the kitchen.

There a young woman, no older than fifteen, stood in front of a cupboard, her hands clenched to do violence. But the Shepherd only shook his head and raised his hand, and the cupboard answered him and opened however much she pushed against it, revealing a murmuring baby wrapped in sound-smothering blankets. The Shepherd only smiled and shook his head. His smile was kind and beautiful, and the woman wanted to die.

He stroked her cheek and she sighed softly, moaned softly, and then he reached into his bag and pulled out his Shepherd's crook and leaned the little disc against her temple and she smiled. Her eyes were dead but her lips were alive and her teeth showed. He laid her on the floor, carefully opened her blouse, and then took his ax from his bag.

487

He ran his finger around the long, narrow cylinder and a tiny light shone at one end. Then he touched the ax's glowing tip to the underside of her breast and drew a wide circle. Behind the ax a tiny red line followed, and the Shepherd took hold of the breast and it came away in his hand. Laying it aside, he stroked the ax lengthwise and the light changed to a dull blue. He passed the ax over the red wound, and the blood gelled and dried and the wound began to heal.

He placed the breast into his bag and repeated the process on the other side. Through it the woman watched in disinterested amusement, the smile still playing at her lips. She would smile like that for days before the peace wore off.

When the second breast was in his bag, the Shepherd put away the ax and the crook and carefully buttoned the woman's blouse. He helped her to her feet, and again passed his deft and gentle hand across her cheek. Like a baby rooting she turned her lips toward his fingers, but he withdrew his hand.

As he left, the woman took the baby from the cupboard and embraced it, cooing softly. The baby nuzzled against the strangely harsh bosom and the woman smiled and sang a lullaby.

The Shepherd walked through the streets, the bag at his belt jostling with his steps. The people watched the bag, wondering what it held. But before the Shepherd was out of the village the word had spread, and the looks were no longer at the bag but rather at the Shepherd's face. He looked neither to the left nor to the right, but he felt their gazes and his eyes grew soft and sad.

And then he was back at the moat, across the

narrow bridge, through the gate, and into the high dark corridors of the castle.

He took the bag to the cook, who looked at him sourly. The Shepherd only smiled at him and took his crook from the bag. In a moment the cook was docile, and calmly he began to cut the red flesh into thin slices, which he lightly floured and then placed in a pan of simmering butter. The smell was strong and sweet, and the flecks of milk sizzled in the pan.

The Shepherd stayed in the kitchen, watching, as the cook prepared the king's meal. Then he followed to the door of the dining hall as the steward entered the king's presence with the steaming slices on a tray. The king and queen ate silently, with severe but gracious rituals of shared servings and gifts of finest morsels.

And at the end of the meal the king murmured a word to the steward, who beckoned both the cook and the Shepherd into the hall.

The cook, the steward, and the Shepherd knelt before the king, who reached out three arms to touch their heads. Through long practice they accepted his touch without recoiling, without even blinking, for they knew such things displeased him. After all, it was a great gift that they could serve the king: their services kept them from giving kingsmeat from their own flesh, or from decorating with their skin the tapestried walls of the castle or the long train of a hunting-cape.

The king's armpits still touched the heads of the three servants when a shudder ran through the castle and a low warning tone began to drone.

The king and queen left the table and with deliberate dignity moved to the consoles and sat. There they pressed buttons, setting in motion all the unseeable defenses of the castle.

After an hour of exhausting concentration they recognized defeat and pulled their arms back from the now-useless tasks they had been doing. The fields of force that had long held the thin walls of the castle to their delicate height now lapsed, the walls fell, and a shining metal ship settled silently in the middle of the ruins.

The side of the skyship opened and out of it came four men, weapons in their hands and anger in their eyes. Seeing them, the king and queen looked sadly at each other and then pulled the ritual knives from their resting place behind their heads and simultaneously plunged them between one another's eyes. They died instantly, and the twenty-two-year conquest of Abbey Colony was at an end.

Dead, the king and queen looked like sad squids lying flat and empty on a fisherman's deck, not at all like conquerors of planets and eaters of men. The men from the skyship walked to the corpses and made certain they were dead. Then they looked around and realized for the first time that they were not alone.

For the Shepherd, the steward, and the cook stood in the ruins of the palace, their eyes wide with unbelief.

One of the men from the ship reached out a hand. "How can you be alive?" he asked.

They did not answer, not knowing really what the question meant.

"How have you survived here, when—"

And then there were no words, for they looked beyond the palace, across the moat to the crowd of colonists and sons of colonists who stood watching them. And seeing them there without arms and legs and eyes and breasts and lips, the men from the ship emptied their hands of weapons and filled their palms with tears and then crossed the bridge to grieve among the delivered ones' rejoicing.

There was no time for explanations, nor was there a need. The colonists crept and hobbled and, occasionally, walked across the bridge to the ruined palace and formed a circle around the bodies of the king and queen. Then they set to work, and within an hour the corpses were lying in the pit that had been the foundation of the castle, covered with urine and feces and stinking already of decay.

Then the colonists turned to the servants of the king and queen.

The men from the ship had been chosen on a distant world for their judgment, speed, and skill, and before the mob had found its common mind, before they had begun to move, there was a force-fence around the steward, the cook, and the gate-keeper, and the guards. Even around the Shepherd, and though the crowd mumbled its resentment, one of the men from the ship patiently explained in soothing tones that whatever crimes were done would be punished in due time, according to Imperial justice.

The fence stayed up for a week as the men from the ship worked to put the colony in order, struggling to interest the people in the fields that once again belonged completely to them. At last they gave up, realizing that justice could not wait. They took the machinery of the court out of the ship, gathered the people together, and began the trial.

The colonists waited as the men from the ship taped a metal plate behind each person's right ear.

Even the servants in their prison and the men from the ship were fitted with them, and then the trial began, each person testifying directly from his memory into the minds of every other person.

The court first heard the testimony of the men from the ship. The people closed their eyes and saw men in a huge starship, pushing buttons and speaking rapidly into computers. Finally expressions of relief, and four men entering a skyship to go down.

The people saw that it was not their world, for here there were no survivors. Instead there was just a castle, just a king and queen, and when they were dead, just fallow fields and the ruins of a village abandoned many years before.

They saw the same scene again and again. Only Abbey Colony had any human beings left alive.

Then they watched as bodies of kings and queens on other worlds were cut open. A chamber within the queen split wide, and there in a writhing mass of life lived a thousand tiny fetuses, many-armed and bleeding in the cold air outside the womb. Thirty years of gestation, and then two by two they would have continued to conquer and rape other worlds in an unstoppable epidemic across the galaxy.

But in the womb, it was stopped, and the fetuses were sprayed with a chemical and soon they lay still and dried into shriveled balls of gray skin.

The testimony of the men from the ship ended, and the court probed the memories of the colonists:

A screaming from the sky, and a blast of light, and then the king and queen descending without machinery. But the devices follow quickly, and the people are beaten by invisible whips and forced into a pen that they watched grow from nothing into a dark, tiny room that they barely fit into, standing.

Heavy air, impossible to breathe. A woman fainting, then a man, and the screams and cries deafening. Sweat until bodies are dry, heat until bodies are cold, and then a trembling through the room.

A door, and then the king, huger than any had thought, his many arms revolting. Vomit on your back from the man behind, then your own vomit, and your bladder empties in fear. The arms reach, and screams are all around, screams in all throats, screams until all voices are silenced. Then one man plucked writhing from the crowd, the door closed again, darkness back, and the stench and heat and terror greater than before.

Silence. And in the distance a drawn-out cry of agony.

Silence. Hours. And then the open door again, the king again, the scream again.

The third time the king is in the door and out of the crowd walks one who is not screaming, whose shirt is caked with stale vomit but who is not vomiting, whose eyes are calm and whose lips are at peace and whose eyes shine. The Shepherd, though known then by another name.

He walks to the king and reaches out his hand, and he is not seized. He is led, and he walks out, and the door closes.

Silence. Hours. And still no scream.

And then the pen is gone, into the nothing it seemed to come from, and the air is clear and the sun is shining and the grass is green. There is only one change: the castle, rising high and delicately and madly in an upward tumble of spires and domes. A moat of acid around it. A slender bridge.

And then back to the village, all of them. The houses are intact, and it is almost possible to forget.

Until the Shepherd walks through the village streets. He is still called by the old name—what was the name? And the people speak to him, ask him, what is in the castle, what do the king and queen want, why were we imprisoned, why are we free.

But the Shepherd only points to a baker. The man steps out, the Shepherd touches him on the temple with his crook, and the man smiles and walks toward the castle.

Four strong men likewise sent on their way, and a boy, and another man, and then the people begin to murmur and shrink back from the Shepherd. His face is still beautiful, but they remember the scream they heard in the pen. They do not want to go to the castle. They do not trust the empty smiles of those who go.

And then the Shepherd comes again, and again, and limbs are lost from living men and women. There are plans. There are attacks. But always the Shepherd's crook or the Shepherd's unseen whip stops them. Always they return crippled to their houses. And they wait. And they hate.

And there are many who wish they had died in the first terrified moments of the attack. But never once does the Shepherd kill.

The testimony of the people ended, and the court let them pause before the trial went on. They needed time to dry their eyes of the tears their memories shed. They needed time to clear their throats of the thickness of silent cries.

And then they closed their eyes again and watched the testimony of the Shepherd. This time there were not many different views; they all watched through one pair of eyes:

The pen again, crowds huddled in terror. The door opens, as before. Only this time all of them walk toward the king in the door, and all of them hold out a hand, and all of them feel a cold tentacle wrap around and lead them from the pen.

The castle grows closer, and they feel the fear of it. But also there is a quietness, a peace that is pressed down on the terror, a peace that holds the face calm and the heart to its normal beat.

The castle. A narrow bridge, and acid in a moat. A gate opens. The bridge is crossed with a moment of vertigo when the king seems about to push, about to throw his prey into the moat.

And then the vast dining hall, and the queen at the console, shaping the world according to the pattern that will bring her children to life.

You stand alone at the head of the table, and the king and queen sit on high stools and watch you. You look at the table and see enough to realize why the others screamed. You feel a scream rise in your throat, knowing that you, and then all the others, will be torn like that, will be half-devoured, will be left in a pile of gristle and bone until all are gone.

And then you press down the fear, and you watch.

The king and queen raise and lower their arms, undulating them in syncopated patterns. They seem to be conversing. Is there meaning in the movements?

You will find out. You also extend an arm, and try to imitate the patterns that you see.

They stop moving and watch you.

You pause for a moment, unsure. Then you undulate your arms again.

They move in a flurry of arms and soft sounds. You also imitate the soft sounds.

And then they come for you. You steel yourself, vow that you will not scream, knowing that you will not be able to stop yourself.

A cold arm touches you and you grow faint. And then you are led from the room, away from the table, and it grows dark.

They keep you for weeks. Amusement. You are kept alive to entertain them when they grow weary of their work. But as you imitate them you begin to learn, and they begin to teach you, and soon a sort of stammering language emerges, they speaking slowly with their loose arms and soft voices, you with only two arms trying to imitate, then initiate words. The strain of it is killing, but at last you tell them what you want to tell them, what you must tell them before they become bored and look at you again as meat.

You teach them how to keep a herd.

And so they make you a shepherd, with only one duty: to give them meat in a never-ending supply. You have told them you can feed them and never run out of manflesh, and they are intrigued.

They go to their surgical supplies and give you a crook so there will be no pain or struggle, and an ax for the butchery and healing, and on a piece of decaying flesh they show you how to use them. In your hand they implant the key that commands every hinge in the village. And then you go into the colony and proceed to murder your fellowmen bit by bit in order to keep them all alive.

You do not speak. You hide from their hatred in

496

silence. You long for death, but it does not come, because it cannot come. If you died, the colony would die, and so to save their lives you continue a life not worth living.

And then the castle falls and you are finished and you hide the ax and crook in a certain place in the earth and wait for them all to kill you.

The trial ended.

The people pulled the plates from behind their ears, and blinked unbelieving at the afternoon sunlight. They looked at the beautiful face of the Shepherd and their faces wore unreadable expressions.

"The verdict of the court," a man from the ship read as the others moved through the crowd collecting witness plates, "is that the man called Shepherd is guilty of gross atrocities. However, these atrocities were the sole means of keeping alive those very persons against whom the atrocities were perpetrated. Therefore, the man called Shepherd is cleared of all charges. He is not to be put to death, and instead shall be honored by the people of Abbey Colony at least once a year and helped to live as long as science and prudence can keep a man alive."

It was the verdict of the court, and despite their twenty-two years of isolation the people of Abbey Colony would never disobey Imperial law.

Weeks later the work of the men from the ship was finished. They returned to the sky. The people governed themselves as they had before.

Somewhere between stars three of the men in the ship gathered after supper. "A shepherd, of all things," said one.

"A bloody good one, though," said another.

The fourth man seemed to be asleep. He was not, however, and suddenly he sat up and cried out, "My God, what have we done!"

Over the years Abbey Colony thrived, and a new generation grew up strong and uncrippled. They told their children's children the story of their long enslavement, and freedom was treasured; freedom and strength and wholeness and life.

And every year, as the court had commanded, they went to a certain house in the village carrying gifts of grain and milk and meat. They lined up outside the door, and one by one entered to do honor to the Shepherd.

They walked by the table where he was propped so he could see them. Each came in and looked into the beautiful face with the gentle lips and the soft eyes. There were no large strong hands now, however. Only a head and a neck and a spine and ribs and a loose sac of flesh that pulsed with life. The people looked over his naked body and saw the scars. Here had been a leg and a hip, right? Yes, and here he had once had genitals, and here shoulders and arms.

How does he live? asked the little ones, wondering.

We keep him alive, the older ones answered. The verdict of the court, they said year after year. We'll keep him as long as science and prudence can keep a man alive.

Then they set down their gifts and left, and at the end of the day the Shepherd was moved back to his hammock, where year after year he looked out the window at the weathers of the sky. They would, perhaps, have cut out his tongue, but since he never spoke, they didn't think of it. They would, perhaps, have cut out his eyes, but they wanted him to see them smile.

Holy

"You have weapons that could stop them," said Crofe, and suddenly the needle felt heavy on my belt.

"I can't use them," I said. "Not even the needle. And definitely not the splinters."

Crofe did not seem surprised, but the others did, and I was angry that Crofe would put me in such a position. He knew the law. But now Stone was looking at me darkly, his bow on his lap, and Fole openly grumbled in his deep, giant's voice. "We're friends, right? Friends, they say."

"It's the law," I said. "I can't use these weapons except in proper self-defense."

"Their arrows are coming as close to you as to us!" Stone said.

"As long as I'm with you, the law assumes that they're attacking you and not me. If I used my weapons, it would seem like I was taking sides. It would be putting the corporation on your side against their side. It would mean the end of the corporation's involvement with you."

"Fine with me," Fole murmured. "Fat lot of good it's done us."

I didn't mention that I would also be executed.

The Ylymyny have little use for people who fear death.

In the distance someone screamed. I looked around—none of them seemed worried. But in a moment Da came into the circle of stones, panting. "They found the slanting road," he whispered. "Nothing we could do. Killed one, that's all."

Crofe stood and uttered a high-pitched cry, a staccato burst of sound that echoed from the crags around us. Then he nodded to the others, and Fole reached over and seized my arm. "Come on," he whispered. But I hung back, not wanting to be shuffled out without any idea of what was going on.

"What's happening?" I asked.

Crofe grinned, his black teeth startling (after all these months) against his light-brown skin. "We're going to try to live through this. Lead them into a trap. Away off south there's a narrow pass where a hundred of my men wait for us to bring them game." As he spoke, four more men came into the circle of stones, and Crofe turned to them.

"Gokoke?" he asked. The others shrugged.

Crofe glowered. "We don't leave Gokoke." They nodded, and the four who had just come went back silently into the paths of the rock. Now Fole became more insistent, and Stone softly whined, "We must go, Crofe."

"Not without Gokoke."

There was a mournful wail that sounded as if it came from all around. Which was echo and which was original sound? Impossible to tell. Crofe bowed his head, squatted, covered his eyes ritually with his hands, and chanted softly. The others did likewise; Fole even released my arm so he could cover his face. It occurred to me that though their piety was impressive, covering one's eyes during a battle might well be a counterrevolutionary behavior. Every now and then the old anthropologist in me surfaces, and I get clinical.

I wasn't clinical, however, when a Golyny soldier leaped from the rocks into the circle. He was armed with two long knives, and he was already springing into action. I noticed that he headed directly for Crofe. I also noticed that none of the Ylymyny made the slightest move to defend him.

What could I do? It was forbidden for me to kill; yet Crofe was the most influential of the warlords of the Ylymyny. I couldn't let him die. His friendship was our best toehold in trading with the people of the islands. And besides, I don't like watching a person being murdered while his eyes are covered in a religious rite, however asinine the rite might be. Which is why I certainly bent the law, if I didn't break it: my toe found the Golyny's groin just as the knife began its downward slash toward Crofe's neck.

The Golyny groaned; the knife forgotten, he clutched at himself, then reached out to attack me. To my surprise, the others continued their chanting, as if unaware that I was protecting them, at not inconsiderable risk to myself.

I could have killed the Golyny in a moment, but I didn't dare. Instead, for an endless three or four minutes I battled with him, disarming him quickly but unable to strike him a blow that would knock him unconscious without running the risk of accidentally killing him. I broke his arm; he ignored the pain, it seemed, and continued to attack—continued, in fact, to use the broken arm. What kind of people are these? I wondered as I blocked a vicious kick with an equally vicious blow from my heavy boot. Don't they feel pain?

And at last the chanting ended, and in a moment Fole had broken the Golyny soldier's neck with one blow. "Jass!" he hissed, nursing his hand from the pain, "what a neck!"

"Why the hell didn't somebody help me before?" I demanded. I was ignored. Obviously an offworlder wouldn't understand. Now the four that had gone off to bring back Gokoke returned, their hands red with already drying blood. They held out their hands; Crofe, Fole, Stone, and Da licked the blood just slightly, swallowing with expressions of grief on their faces. Then Crofe clicked twice in his throat, and again Fole was pulling me out of the circle of stones. This time, however, all were coming. Crofe was in the lead, tumbling madly along a path that a mountain would have rejected as being too dangerous. I tried to tell Fole that it would be easier for me if he'd let go of my arm; at the first sound, Stone whirled around ahead of us, slapped my face with all his force, and I silently swallowed my own blood as we continued down the path.

Suddenly the path ended on the crown of a rocky outcrop that seemed to be at the end of the world. Far below the lip of the smooth rock, the vast plain of Ylymyn Island spread to every horizon. The blue at the edges hinted at ocean, but I knew the sea was too far away to be seen. Clouds drifted here and there between us and the plain; patches of jungle many kilometers across seemed like threads and blots on the farmland and dazzling white cities. And all of it gave us a view that reminded me too much of what I had seen looking from the spacecraft while we orbited this planet not that many months ago.

We paused only a moment on the dome; immediately they scrambled over the edge, seeming to plunge from our vantage point into midair. I, too, leaped over the edge—I had no choice, with Fole's unrelenting grip. As I slid down the ever-steeper slope of rock, I could see nothing below me to break my fall. I almost screamed; held the scream back because if by some faint chance we were not committing suicide, a scream would surely bring the Golyny.

And then the rock dropped away under me and I did fall, for one endless meter until I stopped, trembling, on a ledge scarcely a meter wide. The others were already there—Fole had taken me more slowly, I supposed, because of my inexperience. Forcing myself to glance over the edge, I could see that this peak did not continue as a smooth, endless wall right down to the flat plain. There were other peaks that seemed like foothills to us, but I knew they were mountains in their own right. It was little comfort to know that if I fell it would be only a few hundred meters, and not five or six kilometers after all.

Crofe started off at a run, and we followed. Soon the ledge that had seemed narrow at a meter in width narrowed to less than a third of that; yet they scarcely seemed to slow down as Fole dragged me crabwise along the front of the cliff.

Abruptly we came to a large, level area, which gave way to a narrow saddle between our peak and another much lower one that stood scarcely forty meters away. The top of it was rocky and irregular—perhaps, once we crossed the saddle, we could hide there and elude pursuit.

Crofe did not lead this time. Instead, Da ran lightly across the saddle, making it quickly to the other side. He immediately turned and scanned the rocks above us, then waved. Fole followed, dragging me. I would never have crossed the saddle alone. With Fole pulling me, I had scarcely the time to think about the drop off to either side of the slender path.

And then I watched from the rocks as the others came across. Crofe was last, and just as he stepped out onto the saddle, the rocks above came alive with Golyny.

They were silent (I had battle-trained with loud weapons; my only war had been filled with screams and explosions; this silent warfare was, therefore, all the more terrifying), and the men around me quickly drew bows to fire; Golyny dropped, but so did Crofe, an arrow neatly piercing his head from behind.

Was he dead? He had to be. But he fell straddling the narrow ridge, so that he did not plummet down to the rocks below. Another arrow entered his back near his spine. And then, before the enemy could fire again, Fole was out on the ridge, had hoisted Crofe on his shoulders, and brought him back. Even at that, the only shots the enemy got off seemed aimed not at Fole but at Crofe.

We retreated into the rocks, except for two bowmen who stayed to guard the saddle. We were safe enough—it would take hours for the Golyny to find another way up to this peak. And so our attention was focused on Crofe.

His eyes were open, and he still breathed. But he stared straight ahead, making no effort to talk. Stone held his shoulders as Da pushed the arrow deeper into his head. The point emerged, bloody, from Crofe's forehead.

Da leaned over and took the arrowhead in his teeth. He pulled, and the flint came loose. He spat it out and then withdrew the shaft of the arrow backward through the wound. Through all this, Crofe made no sound. And when the operation had finished, Crofe died.

This time there was no ritual of closed eyes and chanting. Instead, the men around me openly wept—openly, but silently. Sobs wracked their bodies, tears leaped from their eyes; their faces contorted in an agony of grief. But there was no sound, not even heavy breathing.

The grief was not something to be ignored. And though I did not know them at all well, Crofe was the one I had known best. Not intimately, certainly not as a friend, because the barriers were too great. But I had seen him dealing with his people, and whatever culture you come from, there's no hiding a man of power. Crofe had that power. In the assemblies when we had first petitioned for the right to trade, Crofe had forced (arguing, it seemed, alone, though later I realized that he had many powerful allies that he preferred to marshal silently) the men and women there to make no restrictions, to leave no prohibitions, and to see instead what the corporation had to sell. It was a foot in the door. But Crofe had taken me aside alone and informed me that nothing was to be brought to the Ylymyny without his knowledge or approval. And now he was dead on a routine scouting mission, and I could not help but be amazed that the Ylymyny, in other ways an incredibly shrewd people, should allow their wisest leaders to waste themselves on meaningless forays in the borderlands and high mountains.

And for some reason I found myself also grieved

at Crofe's death. The corporation, of course, would continue to progress in its dealing with the Ylymyny—would, indeed, have an easier time of it now. But Crofe was a worthy bargaining partner. And he and I had loved the game of bargaining, however many barriers our mutual strangeness kept between us.

I watched as his soldiers stripped his corpse. They buried the clothing under rocks. And then they hacked at the skin with their knives, opening up the man's bowels and splitting the intestines from end to end. The stench was powerful; I barely avoided vomiting. They worked intently, finding every scrap of material that had been passing through the bowel and putting it in a small leather bag. When the intestine was as clean as stone knives could scrape it, they closed the bag, and Da tied it around his neck on a string. Then, tears still streaming down his face, he turned to the others, looking at them all, one by one.

"I will go to the mountain," he whispered.

The others nodded; some wept harder.

"I will give his soul to the sky," Da whispered, and now the others came forward, touched the bag, and whispered, "I, too. I, also. I vow."

Hearing the faint noise, the two archers guarding the saddle came to our sanctuary among the stones and were about to add their vows to those of the others when Da held up his hand and forbade them.

"Stay and hold off pursuit. They are sure to know."

Sadly, the two nodded, moved back to their positions. And Fole once again gripped my arm as we moved silently away from the crest of the peak.

"Where are we going?" I whispered.

"To honor Crofe's soul." Stone turned and answered me.

"What about the ambush?"

"We are now about matters more important than that."

The Ylymyny worshiped the sky—or something akin to worship, at least. That much I knew from my scanty research into their religious beliefs in the city on the plain, where I had first landed.

"Stone," I said, "will the enemy know what we're doing?"

"Of course," he whispered back. "They may be infidels, but they know what honor binds the righteous to do. They'll try to trap us on the way, destroy us, and stop us from doing honor to the dead."

And then Da hissed for us to be quiet, and we soundlessly scrambled down the cliffs and slopes. Above us we heard a scream; we ignored it. And soon I was lost in the mechanical effort of finding footholds, handholds, strength to keep going with these soldiers who were in much better condition than I.

Finally we reached the end of the paths and stopped. We were gathered on a rather gentle slope that ended, all the way around, in a steep cliff. And we had curved enough to see, above and behind us, that a large group of Golyny were making their way down the path we had just taken.

I did not look over the edge, at first, until I saw them unwinding their ropes and joining them, end to end, to make a much longer line. Then I walked toward the edge and looked down. Only a few hundred meters below, a valley opened up in the mountainside, a flood of level ground in front of a high-walled canyon that bit deep into the cliff. From there it would be a gentle descent into the plain. We would be safe.

But first, there was the matter of getting down the cliff. This time, I couldn't see any hope of it unless we each dangled on the end of a rope, something that I had no experience with. And even then, what was to stop the enemy from climbing down after us?

Fole solved the dilemma, however. He sat down a few meters back from the edge, in a place where his feet could brace against stone, and he pulled gloves on his hands. Then he took the rope with only a few meters of slack, looped it behind his back, and gripped the end of the rope in his left hand, holding the rest of the line tight against his body with his right.

He would be a stable enough root for the top end of the climbing line; and if he were killed or under attack, he would simply drop the line, and the enemy would have no way to pursue.

He was also doomed to be killed.

I should have said something to him, perhaps, but there was no time. Da was quickly giving me my only lesson in descending a rope, and I had to learn well or die from my first mistake. And then Da, carrying the bag of Crofe's excrement, was over the edge, sitting on the rope as it slid by his buttocks, holding his own weight precariously and yet firmly enough as he descended rapidly to the bottom.

Fole bore the weight stolidly, hardly seeming to strain. And then the rope went slack, and immediately Stone was forcing me to pass the rope under my buttocks, holding the rope in gloved hands on either side. Then he pushed me backward over the cliff, and I took a step into nothingness, and I gasped in terror as I fell far too swiftly, swinging to and fro as if on a pendulum, the rock wall skimming back and forth in front of my face—until the rope turned, and I faced instead the plain, which still looked incredibly far below me. And now I did vomit, though I had not eaten yet that day; the acid was painful in my throat and mouth; and I forgot the terror of falling long enough to grip the rope tightly and slow my descent, though it burned my gloves and the rope was an agony of tearing along my buttocks.

The ground loomed closer, and I could see Da waiting, beckoning impatiently. And so I forced myself to ignore the pain of a faster descent, and fell more rapidly, so that when I hit the ground I was jolted, and sprawled into the grasses.

I lay panting in disbelief that I had made it, relief that I no longer hung like a spider in the air. But I could not rest, it seemed—Da took me by the arm and dragged me away from the rope that was now flailing with the next man's descent.

I rolled onto my back and watched, fascinated, as the man came quickly down the rope. Now that my ordeal was over, I could see a beauty in a single man on a twine daring gravity to do its worst— the poetical kind of experience that has long been forgotten on my gentle homeworld of Garden, where all the cliffs have been turned to gentle slopes, and where oceans gently lap at sand instead of tearing at rock, and where men are as gentle as the world they live in. I am gentle, in fact, which caused me much distress at the beginning of my military training, but which allowed me to survive a war and come out of the army with few scars that could not heal.

And as I lay thinking of the contrast between my

510

upbringing and the harsh life on this world, Stone reached the bottom and the next man started down.

When the soldier was only halfway down, another climbed onto the rope at the top. It took me a moment to realize what was happening; then as it occurred to me that the Golyny must have nearly reached them, Da and Stone pulled me back against the cliff wall, where falling bodies would not land on me.

The first soldier reached the bottom; I saw it was the one named Pan, a brutal-looking man who had wept most piteously at Crofe's death. The other soldier was only a dozen meters from the ground when suddenly the rope shuddered and he dropped. He hit the ground in a tangle of arms and legs; I started to run out to help him, but I was held back. The others were all looking up, and in a moment I saw why. The giant Fole, made small by distance, leaped off the cliff, pulling with him two of the Golyny. A third enemy fell a moment later—he must have lost his balance in the struggle on the cliff.

Fole hit the ground shudderingly, his body cruelly torn by the impact, the Golyny also a jumble of broken bones. Again I tried to go out to try to accomplish something; again I was held back; and again I found they knew their world better than I, with my offworld instincts, could hope to know it. Stones hit the ground sharply, scattering all around us. One of them hit the soldier who already was dying from his relatively shorter fall; it broke his skull, and he died.

We waited in the shadow of the cliff until nearly dark; then Da and Pan rushed out and dragged in the body of the soldier. Stones were already falling around them when they came back; some ricocheted

511

back into the area where Stone and I waited; one hit me in the arm, making a bruise which ached for some time afterward.

After dark, Da and Stone and Pan and I all went out, and hunted for the body of Fole, and dragged him back into the shelter of the cliff.

Then they lit a fire, and slit the throats of the corpses, and tipped them downhill so the blood would flow. They wiped their hands in the sluggish stream and licked their palms as they had for Gokoke. And then they covered their eyes and duplicated the chant.

As they went through the funerary rites, I looked out toward the plain. From above, this area had seemed level with the rest of the plain; in fact, it was much higher than the plain, and I could see the faint lights of the city fires here and there above the jungle. Near us, however, there were no lights. I wondered how far we were from the outpost at the base of the cliffs where we had left our horses; I also wondered why in hell I had ever consented to come along on this expedition. "An ordinary tour," Crofe had called it, and I had not realized that my understanding of their language was so insufficient. Nor had I believed that the war between the Golyny and the Ylymyny was such a serious matter. After all, it had been going on for more than three centuries; how could blood stay so hot, so long?

"You look at the plain," said Stone, beside me, his voice a hiss. It struck me that we had been together at the base of the cliff for hours, and this was the first word that had been spoken, except for the chanting. In the cities the Ylymyny were yarn-spinners and chatterers and gossipers. Here they scarcely broke the silence.

"I'm wondering how many days it will take us to reach the city."

Stone glowered. "The city?"

I was surprised that he seemed surprised. "Where else?"

"We've taken a vow," Stone said, and I could detect the note of loathing in his voice that I had come to expect from him whenever I said something wrong. "We must take Crofe's soul to the sky."

I didn't really understand. "Where's that? How do you reach the sky?"

Stone's chest heaved with the effort of keeping his patience. "The Sky," he said, and then I did a double take, realizing that the word I was translating was also a name, the name of the highest mountain on Ylymyn Island.

"You can't be serious," I said. "That's back the way we came."

"There are other ways, and we will take them."

"So will the Golyny!"

"Do you think that we don't have any honor?" cried Stone, and the sound roused Da and brought him to us.

"What is it?" Da whispered, and stillness settled in around us again.

"This offworld scum accuses us of cowardice," Stone hissed. Da fingered the bag around his neck. "Do you?" he asked.

"Nothing of the kind," I answered. "I don't know what I'm saying to offend him. I just supposed that it would be pointless to try to climb the highest mountain on your island. There are only four of us, and the Golyny will surely be ahead of us, waiting, won't they?"

"Of course," Da said. "It will be difficult. But we are Crofe's friends."

"Can't we get help? From the hundred men, for instance, who were waiting for the ambush?"

Da looked surprised, and Stone was openly angry. "We were there when he died. They were not," Da answered.

"Are you a coward?" Stone asked softly, and I realized that to Stone, at least, cowardice was not something to be loathed, it was something to be cast out, to be exorcised, to be killed. His hand held a knife, and I felt myself on the edge of a dilemma. If I denied cowardice while under threat of death, wouldn't that be cowardice? Was this a lady or the tiger choice? I stood my ground. "If you are all there is to be afraid of, no, I'm not," I said.

Stone looked at me in surprise for a moment, then smiled grimly and put his knife back in his sheath. Pan came to us then, and Da took the opportunity to hold a council.

It was short; it involved the choice of routes, and I knew little of geography and nothing of the terrain. At the end of it, though. I had more questions than ever. "Why are we doing this for Crofe, when we didn't do anything like it for Fole or Gokoke?"

"Because Crofe is Ice," he answered, and I stored the non sequitur away to puzzle over later.

"And what will we do when we reach the Sky?"

Stone stirred from his seeming slumber and hissed, "We don't talk of such things!"

Da hissed back, "It is possible that none but he will reach the Sky, and in that case, he must know what to do."

"If he's the one there, we can count on having failed," Stone answered angrily.

Da ignored him and turned to me. "In this bag I hold his last passage, that which would have become him had he lived, his future self." I nodded. "This must be emptied on the high altar, so Jass will know that Ice has been returned to him where he can make it whole."

"That's it? Just empty it on the high altar?"

"The difficulty," said Da, "is not in the rite. It is in the getting there. And you must also bid farewell to Crofe's soul, and break a piece of ice from the mountain, and suck it until it melts; and you must shed your own blood on the altar. But most important is to get there. To the topmost top of the highest mountain in the world."

I did not tell him that far to the north, on the one continental landmass, there rose mountains that would dwarf Sky; instead I nodded and turned to sleep on the grass, my clinical anthropologist's mind churning to classify these magical behaviors. The homeopathy was obvious; the meaning of ice was more obscure; and the use of unpassed excrement as the "last passage" from the body was, to my knowledge, unparalleled. But, as an old professor had far too often remarked, "There is no behavior so peculiar that somewhere, members in good standing of the human race will not perform it." The bag around Da's neck reeked. I slept.

The four of us (had there been ten only yesterday morning?) set out before dawn, sidling up the slope toward the mouth of the canyon. We knew that the enemy was above us; we knew that others would already have circled far ahead, to intercept us later. We were burdened with rations intended for only a few days, and a few weapons and the rope. I wished for more, but said nothing.

The day was uneventful. We simply stayed in the bottom of the canyon, beside the rivulet that poured down toward the plain. It was obvious that the stream ran more powerfully at other times: boulders the size of large buildings were scattered along the canyon bottom, and no vegetation but grass was able to grow below the watermarks on the canyon walls, though here and there above them a tree struggled for existence in the rock.

And so the next day passed, and the next, until the canyon widened into a shallow valley, and we at last reached a place where the rivulet came from under a crack in the rock, and a hilltop that we climbed showed that we were now on the top of the island, with other low hills all around, deceptively gentle-looking, considering that they were hidden behind the peaks of one of the most savage mountain ranges I had seen.

Only a few peaks were higher than we were, and one of them was the Sky. Its only remarkable feature was its height. Many other mountains were more dramatic; many others craggier or more pointed at the peak. Indeed, the Sky was more a giant hill—from our distance, at least—and its ascent would not be difficult, I thought.

I said as much to Da, who only smiled grimly and said, "Easier, at least, than reaching it alive." And I remembered the Golyny, and the fact that somewhere ahead of us they would be waiting. The canyon we had climbed was easy enough—why hadn't they harassed us on the way up?

"If it rains tonight, you will see," Stone answered.
And it did rain that night, and I did see. Or rather

I heard, since the night was dark. We camped in the lee of the hill, but the rain drenched us despite the rocky outcropping we huddled under. And then I realized that the rain was falling so heavily that respectable streams were flowing down the hill we camped against—and it was no more than forty meters from crown to base. The rain was heavier than I had ever seen before, and now I heard the distant roaring that told me why the Golyny had not bothered to harm us. The huge river was now flowing down the canyon, fed by a thousand streams like those flowing by our camp.

"What if it had rained while we were climbing?" I asked.

"The Sky would not hinder us on our errand," Da answered, and I found little comfort in that. Who would have guessed that a simple three-day expedition into the mountains would leave me trapped with such superstition, depending on them for my survival even as they were depending on some unintelligible and certainly nonexistent god.

In the morning I woke at first light to find that the others were already awake and armed to the teeth, ready for battle. I hurried to stretch my sore muscles and get ready for the trip. Then I realized what their armaments might mean.

"Are they here?"

But no one answered me, and as soon as it was clear I was ready, they moved forward, keeping to the shelter of the hills, spying out what lay ahead before rounding a bend. There were no trees here, only the quick-living grass that died in a day and was replaced by its seed in the morning. There was no shelter but the rock; and no shade, either, but at this elevation, shade was not necessary. It was not easy to breathe with the oxygen low, but at least at this elevation the day was not hot, despite the fact that Ylymyn Island was regularly one of the hottest places on this forsaken little planet.

For two days we made our way toward the Sky, and seemed to make no progress—it was still distant, on the horizon. Worse, however, than the length of our journey was the fact that we had to be unrelentingly on the alert, though we saw no sign of the Golyny. I once asked (in a whisper) whether they might have given up pursuit. Stone only sneered, and Da shook his head. It was Pan who whispered to me that night that the Golyny hated nothing so much as the righteousness of the Ylymyny, knowing as they did that it was only the gods that had made the Ylymyny the greatest people on earth, and that only their piety had won the gods so thoroughly to their side. "There are some," Pan said, "who, when righteousness defeats them, squat before the gods and properly offer their souls, and join us. But there are others who can only hate the good, and attack mindlessly against the righteous. The Golyny are that kind. All decent people would kill Golyny to preserve the peace of the righteous.

And then he glanced pointedly at my splinters and at my needle. And I as pointedly glanced at the bag of excrement around Da's neck. "What the law requires of good men, good men do," I said, sounding platitudinous to myself, but apparently making the right impression on Pan. His eyes widened, and he nodded in respect. Perhaps I overdid it, but it gratified me to see that he understood that just as certain rites must be performed in his society, certain acts are taboo in mine, and among those acts is involvement in the small wars of nations on primitive

518

planets. That his compulsions were based on mind-less superstition while mine were based on long years of experience in xenocontact was a distinction I hardly expected him to grasp, and so I said nothing about it. The result was that he treated me with more respect; with awe, in fact. And, noticing that, Stone asked me quietly as we walked the next day, "What have you done to the young soldier?"

"Put the fear of god into him."

I had meant to be funny. Odd, how a man can be careful in all his pronouncements, and then forget everything he knows as a joke comes to mind and he impulsively tells it. Stone was furious; it took Da's strength and Pan's, too, to keep him from attacking me, which would surely have been fatal to him—rope-climbing I didn't know, but the ways of murder are not strange to me, though I don't pursue them for pleasure. At last I was able to explain that I hadn't understood the implications of my statement in their language, that I was transliterating and cer-tain words had different meanings and so on and so on. We were still discussing this when a flight of arrows ended the conversation and drove all of us to cover except Pan, who had an arrow in him and died there in the open while we watched.

It was difficult to avoid feeling that his death had been somehow my fault; and as Da and Stone dis-cussed the matter and confessed that they had no choice this time but to leave the body, committing a sin to allow the greater good of fulfilling the vow to Crofe, I realized that omitting the rites of death for Pan grieved me almost as much as his death. I have no particular belief in immortality; the notion that the dead linger to watch what happens to their remains is silly to me. Nevertheless, there is, I believe, a difference between knowing that a person is dead and emotionally unconstructing the system of relationships that had included the person. Pan, obscure as the young man was, ugly and brutal as his face had been, was nevertheless the man I liked best of my surviving companions.

And thinking of that, it occurred to me that of the ten that had set out only a week before, only three of us remained; I, who could not use a weapon while in the company of the others, and they, who had to travel more slowly and so risk their lives even more because of me.

"Leave me behind," I said. "Once I'm alone, I can defend myself as I will, and you can move faster."

Stone's eyes leaped at the suggestion, but Da firmly shook his head. "Never. Crofe charged us all that we would keep you with us."

"He didn't know the situation we'd be in."

"Crofe knew," Da whispered. "A man dies in two days here without wisdom. And you have no wisdom."

If he meant knowledge of what might be edible in this particular environment, he was right enough; and when I saw that Da had no intention of leaving me, I decided to continue with them. Better to move on than do nothing. But before we left our temporary shelter (with Pan's corpse slowly desiccating behind us) I taught Stone and Da how to use the splinters and the needle, in case I was killed. Then no law would be broken, as long as they returned the weapons to the corporation. For once Stone seemed to approve of something I had done.

Now we moved even more slowly, more stealthily, and yet the Sky seemed to loom closer now, at last;

we were in the foothills. Each hill we approached hid the Sky behind its crest sooner. And the sense of waiting death became overpowering.

At night I took my turn watching, with Pan gone. Technically it was a violation—I was aiding them in their war effort. But it was also survival, since the Golyny had little use for offworlders—SCM Corporation had already made four attempts to get a foothold with them, and they would not hear of it. It was maddening to have the ability to save lives and for the sake of larger purposes have to refrain from using that ability.

My watch ended, and I woke Da. But instead of letting me sleep, he silently woke Stone as well, and in the darkness we moved as silently as possible away from our camp. This time we were not heading for the mountain—instead, we were paralleling it, traveling by starlight (which is almost no light at all), and I guessed that Da intended us to pass by our would-be killers and perhaps ascend the mountain by another route.

Whether we passed them or not, I didn't know. At dawn, however, when there was light enough to see the ground, Da began running, and Stone and I followed. The walking had been bad, but I had gradually grown inured to it; the running brought out every latent protest in my muscles. It was not easy loping over even ground, either. It was a shattering run over rocks, down small ravines, darting over hills and across streams. I was exhausted by noon, ready for our brief stop. But we took no stop. Da did spare a sentence for me: "We're ahead of them and must stay ahead."

As we ran, however, an idea came to me, one that seemed pathetically obvious once I had thought of it. I was not allowed to summon any help to further a war effort—but surely getting to the top of the mountain was no war effort. Our lander would never descend into enemy fire, but now that we were in the open, the lander could come, could pick us up, could carry us to the top of the mountain before the enemy suspected we were there.

I suggested that. Stone only spat on the ground (a vile thing, in this world, where for some obscure reason water is worshipped, though it is plentiful everywhere except the Great Desert far to the north of Ylymyn), while Da shook his head. "Spirits fly to the Sky; men climb to it," he said, and once again religion had stymied me. Superstitions were going to kill us yet, meaningless rules that should surely change in the face of such dire need.

But at nightfall we were at the foot of a difficult cliff. I saw at a glance that this was not the easy ascent that the mountain had seemed from the distance. Stone looked surprised, too, as he surveyed the cliff. "This ascent is not right," he said softly. Da nodded. "I know it. This is the west face, which no one climbs."

"Is it impossible?" I asked.

"Who knows?" Da answered. "The other ways are so much easier, no one has ever tried this one. So we go this way, where they don't look for us, and somewhere we move to the north or south, to take an easier way when they don't expect us."

Then Da began to climb. I protested, "The sun's already set."

"Good," he answered. "Then they won't see us climbing."

And so began our climb to the Sky. It was difficult, and for once they did not press on ahead and then wait impatiently for me to come. They were hampered as I was by darkness and strangeness, and the night made us equals at last. It was an empty equality, however. Three times that night Da whispered that he had reached a place in the cliff impossible to scale, and I had to back up, trying to find the holds I had left a moment before. Descending a mountain is harder than ascending it. Climbing you have eyes, and it is your fingers that reach ahead of you. Descending only your toes can hunt, and I was wearing heavy boots. We had wakened early, long before dawn, and we climbed until dawn again began to light the sky. I was exhausted, and Stone and Da also seemed to droop with the effort. But as the light gathered, we came to a shoulder of the mountain, a place where for hundreds of meters the slope was no more than fifteen or twenty degrees, and we threw ourselves to the ground and slept.

I woke because of the stinging of my hands, which in the noon sun I saw were caked with blood that still, here and there, oozed to the surface. Da and Stone still slept. Their hands were not so injured as mine; they were more used to heavy work with their hands. Even the weights I had lifted had been equipped with cushioned handles.

I sat up and looked around. We were still alone on our shoulder of the mountain, and I gazed down the distance we had climbed. We had accomplished much in the darkness, and I marveled at the achievement of it; the hills we had run through the day before were small and far, and I guessed that we might be as much as a third of the way to the peak.

Thinking that, I looked toward the mountain, and immediately kicked Da to waken him.

Da, bleary-eyed, looked where I nodded, and saw

the failure of our night's work. Though none of the Golyny were near us, it was plain that from their crags and promontories they could see us. They were not ahead of us on the west slope, but rather they stood as if to guard every traverse that might take us to the safer, easier routes. And who knew—perhaps the Golyny had explored the west face and knew that no man could climb it.

Da sighed, and Stone silently shook his head and broke out the last of the food, which we had been eating sparingly for days longer than it should have lasted.

"What now?" I whispered (odd how the habits, once begun, cannot be broken), and Da answered, "Nothing now. Just ahead. Up the west face. Better unknown dangers than known ones."

I looked back down into the valleys and hills below us. Stone spat again. "Off-worlder," he said, "even if we could forsake our vow, they are waiting at the bottom of the cliff by now to kill us as we come down."

"Then let me call my lander. When the prohibition was made, no one knew of flying machines."

Da chuckled. "We have always known of flying machines. We simply had none. But we also knew that such machines could not carry a penitent or a suitor or a vowkeeper to the Sky."

I clutched at straws. "When we reach there, what then?"

"Then we shall have died with the vow kept."

"Can't I call the lander then, to take us *off* the mountain?"

They looked at each other, and then Da nodded to me. I immediately hunted in the pockets of my coat for the radio; I could not hope to reach the city from here, but in less than an hour the orbiting starship would be overhead, and would relay my message. I tried calling the starship right then, in case it was already over the horizon. It was not, and so we headed again for the crags.

Now the climb was worse, because of our weariness from the night before rather than from any greater difficulty in the rocks themselves. My fingers ached; the skin on my palms stung with each contact with the rock. Yet we pressed ahead, and the west face was not unclimbable; even at our slow pace, we soon left the shoulder of the rock far behind us. Indeed, there were many places where we scrambled on natural stairways of rock; other places where ledges let us rest; until we reached an overhang that blocked us completely.

There was no tool in this metalless world that could have helped us to ignore gravity and climb spiderlike upside down to the lip of the overhang. We had no choice but to traverse, and now I realized how wise our enemies' plan had been. We would have to move to left or right, to north or south, and they would be waiting.

But, given no choice, we took the only alternative there was. We took the route under the overhang that slanted upward—toward the south. And now Stone took the lead, coldly explaining that Da bore Crofe's soul, and they had vowed to Crofe to keep me alive; therefore he was most expendable. Da nodded gravely, and I did not protest. I like life, and around any turn or over any obstacle, an arrow might be waiting.

Another surprise: here and there in the shelter of the rock the cold air had preserved a bit of snow. There was no snowcap visible from below, of course;

but this was summer, and only this high an altitude could have preserved snow at all in such a climate.

It was nearing nightfall, and I suggested we sleep for the night. Da agreed, and so we huddled against the wall of the mountain, the overhang above us, and two meters away a dropoff into nothing. I lay there looking at a single star that winked above my head, and it is a measure of how tired I was that it was not until morning that I realized the significance of that.

Tomorrow, Da assured me, we would either reach the Sky or be killed trying—we were that close. And so as I talked to the starship on its third pass since I had asked for the lander in the early afternoon, I briefly explained when we would be there.

This time, however, they had Tack, the manager of our corporation's operations on this world, patched in from his radio in the city. And he began to berate me for my stupidity. "What the hell kind of way is this to fulfill your corporate responsibilities!" crackled his voice. "Running off to fulfill some stinking little superstition with a bunch of stone-age savages and trying to get killed in the process!" He went on like that for some time—almost five minutes—before I overrode him and informed the starship that under the terms of my contract with the corporation they were obliged to give me support as requested, up to and including an evacuation from the top of a mountain, and the manager could take his objections and—

They heard, and they agreed to comply, and I lay there trying to cool my anger. Tack didn't understand, couldn't understand. He hadn't been this far with me, hadn't seen Fole's set face as he volunteered to die so the rest could descend the cliff; hadn't watched the agony of indecision as Da and Stone decided to leave Pan; hadn't any way of knowing why I was going to reach the top of the Sky for Crofe's sake—

Not for Crofe's sake, dammit; for mine, for ours. Crofe was dead, and they couldn't help him at all by smearing his excrement on a rock. And suddenly, remembering what would be done when we reached the top of the mountain—if we did—I laughed. All this, to rub a dead man's shit on a stone.

And Stone seized me by the throat and made as if to cast me off the mountain. Da and I struggled, and I looked in Stone's eyes and saw my death there. "Your vow," Da whispered sharply, and Stone at last relented, slid away from me.

"What did you say in your deviltalk!" he demanded, and I realized that I had spoken Empire to the starship, then paused a moment and laughed. So I explained, more politely than Tack had, what Tack had said.

Da glared Stone into silence when I was through, and then sat contemplatively for a long time before he spoke.

"It's true, I suppose," he said, "that we're superstitious."

I said nothing. Stone said nothing only by exercising his utmost self-control.

"But true and false have nothing to do with love and hate. I love Crofe, and I will do what I vowed to do, what he would have done for another Ice; what, perhaps, he might have done for me even though I am not Ice."

And then, with the question settled that easily (and therefore not settled—indeed, not even understood at all), we slept, and I thought nothing of the star that winked directly overhead.

Morning was dismal, with clouds below us rolling in from the south. It would be a storm; and Da warned me that there might be mist as the clouds rose and tumbled around the mountains. We had to hurry.

We had not traveled far, however, when the ledge above us and the one we walked on broadened, separated, opened out into the gentle slope that everywhere but on the west face led to the peak of the Sky. And there, gathered below us, were three or four dozen Golyny, just waking. We had not been seen, but there was no conceivable way to walk ten steps out of the last shelter of the ledge without being noticed; and even though the slope was gentle, it was still four or five hundred meters up the slope to the peak, Da assured me.

"What can we do?" I whispered. "They'll kill us easily."

And indecision played on Da's face, expressing much, even though he was silent.

We watched as the Golyny opened their food and ate it; watched as some of them wrestled or pulled sticks. They looked like any other men, rowdy in the absence of women and when there was no serious work to do. Their laughter was like any other men's laughter, and their games looked to be fun. I forgot myself, and found myself silently betting on one wrestler or another, silently picturing myself in the games, and knowing how I would go about winning. And so an hour passed, and we were no closer to the peak.

Stone looked grim; Da looked desperate; and I have no idea how I looked, though I suspect that because of my involvement with the Golyny games I appeared disinterested to my companions. Perhaps that was why at last Stone took me roughly by the sleeve and spun me toward him.

"A game, isn't it! That's all it is to you!"

Shaken out of my contemplation, I did not understand what was happening.

"Crofe was the greatest man in a hundred generations!" Stone hissed. "And you care nothing for bringing him to heaven!"

"Stone," Da hissed.

"This scum acts as if Crofe were not his friend!"

"I hardly knew him," I said honestly but unwisely.

"What does that have to do with friendship!" Stone said angrily. "He saved your life a dozen times, made us take you in and accept you as human beings, though you followed no law!"

I follow a law, I would have said, except that in our exhaustion and Stone's grief at the failure of our mission, we had raised our voices, and already the Golyny were arming, were rushing toward us, were silently nocking arrows to bows and coming for the kill.

How is it possible that stupidity should end our lives when our enemies' cleverest stratagems had not, I thought in despair; but at that moment the part of my mind that occasionally makes itself useful by putting intelligent thoughts where they can be used reminded me of the star I had seen as I lay under the overhang last night. A star—and I had seen it directly overhead where the overhang had to be. Which meant there was a hole in the overhang, perhaps a chimney that could be climbed.

I quickly told Da and Stone, and now, the argument forgotten in our desperate situation, Stone wordlessly took his bow and all his and Da's arrows and sat to wait for the enemy to come.

"Go," he said, "and climb to the peak if you can."

It hurt, for some reason, that the man who hated me should take it for granted that he would die in order to save my life. Not that I fooled myself that he valued my life, but still, I would live for a few moments more because he was about to die. And, inexplicably, I felt an emotion, briefly, that can only be described as love. And that love embraced also Da and Pan, and I realized that while Crofe was only a businessman that I had enjoyed dealing with, these others were, after all, friends. The realization that I felt emotion toward these barbarians (yes, that is a patronizing attitude, but I have never known even an anthropologist whose words or acts did not confess that he felt contempt for those he dealt with), that I loved them, was shocking yet somehow gratifying; the knowledge that they kept me alive only out of duty to a dead man and a superstition was expectable, but somehow reason for anguish.

All this took less than a moment, however, there on the ledge, and then I turned with Da and raced back along the ledge toward where we had spent the night. It had seemed like only a short way; I kept slowing for fear we would miss the spot in our hurry. But when we reached it, I recognized it easily, and yes, there was indeed a chimney in the rock, a narrow one that was almost perfectly vertical, but one that could possibly lead us near the top of the Sky; a path to the peak that the enemy would not be looking for.

We stripped off our extra gear: the rope, which had not been used since Fole died to let us descend it, the blankets, the weapons, the canvas. I kept only

530

my splinters and needle—they must be on my body when I died (though I was momentarily conceiving that I might win through with Da and survive all this; already the lander would be hovering high above the peak)—to prove that I had not broken the law; otherwise my name would be stricken from the ELB records in dishonor, and all my comrades and fellow frontliners would know I had failed in one of the most basic trusts.

A roar of triumph was carried along the rock, and we knew that Stone was dead, his position overrun, and we had at best ten minutes before they were upon us. Da began kicking our gear off the edge of the cliff, and I helped. A keen eye could still tell that here we had disturbed the ground more than elsewhere; but it was, we hoped, enough to confuse them for just a little longer.

And then we began to climb the chimney. Da insisted that I climb first; he hoisted me into the crack, and I shimmied upward, bracing my back against one wall and my hands and feet against the other. Then I stopped, and using my leg as a hand-hold, he, too, clambered into the split in the rock.

Then we climbed, and the chimney was longer than we had thought, the sky more distant. Our progress was slow, and every motion kicked down rocks that clattered onto the ledge. We had not counted on that—the Golyny would notice the falling rocks, would see where we were, and we were not yet high enough to be impossible for arrows to reach.

And even as I realized that, it came true. We saw the flash of clothing passing under the chimney; though I could make out no detail, I could tell even in the silence that we had been found. We struggled upward. What else could we do?

And the first arrow came up the shaft. Shooting vertically is not easy—much must be unlearned. But the archer was good. And the third arrow struck Da, angling upward into his calf.

"Can you go on?" I asked.

"Yes," he answered, and I climbed higher, with him following, seeming to be unslowed by the wound.

But the archer was not through, and the seventh rushing sound ended, not in a clatter, but in the dull sound of stone striking flesh. Involuntarily Da uttered a cry. Where I was I could see no wound, of course.

"Are you hit?"

"Yes," he answered. "In the groin. An artery, I believe. I'm losing blood too quickly."

"Can you go on?"

"No."

And using the last of his strength to hold himself in place with his legs alone (which must have been agony to his wounds), he took the bag of Crofe's excrement from his neck and hung it carefully on my foot. In our cramped situation, nothing else was possible.

"I charge you," he said in pain, "to take it to the altar."

"It might fall," I said honestly.

"It will not if you vow to take it to the altar."

And because Da was dying from an arrow that might have struck me, and also because of Stone's death and Pan's and Fole's and, yes, Crofe's, I vowed that I would do it. And when I had said that, Da let go and plunged down the shaft.

I climbed as quickly as I could, knowing that the arrows might easily come again, as in fact they did. But I was higher all the time, and even the best archer couldn't reach me.

I was only a dozen meters from the top, carefully balancing the bag of excrement from my foot as I climbed (every motion more painful than the last), when it occurred to me that Da was dead, and everyone else as well. What was to stop me now from dropping the bag, climbing to the top, signaling the lander to me, and climbing safely aboard? To preserve the contents of a man's bowels and risk my life to perform a meaningless rite with it was absurd. No damage could be done by my failure to perform the task. No one would know, in fact, that I had vowed to do it. Indeed, completing the vow could easily be construed as unwarranted interference in planetary affairs.

Why didn't I drop the bag? There are those who claim that I was insane, believing the religion (these are they who claim that I believe it still); but that is not true. I knew rationally that dead men do not watch the acts of the living, that vows made to the dead are not binding, that my first obligation was to myself and the corporation, and certainly not to Da or Crofe.

But regardless of my rational process, even as I thought of dropping the bag I felt the utter wrongness of it. I could not do it and still remain myself. This is mystical, perhaps, but there was nowhere in my mind that I could fail to fulfill my oath and still live. I have broken my word frequently for convenience—I am, after all, a modern man. But in this case, at that time, despite my strong desire for survival, I could not tip my foot downward and let the bag drop.

And after that moment of indecision, I did not waver.

I reached the top utterly exhausted, but sat on the brink of the chimney and reached down to remove the bag from my foot. The leaning forward after so much exertion in an inexorably vertical position made me lightheaded; the bag almost slipped from my grasp, almost fell; I caught it at the end of my toe and pulled it, trembling, to my lap. It was light, surprisingly light. I set it on the ground and pulled myself out of the chimney, crawled wearily a meter or two away from the edge of the cliff, and then looked ahead of me. There was the peak, not a hundred meters away. On it I could easily see an altar hewn out of stone. The design was not familiar to me, but it could serve the purpose, and it was the only artifact in sight.

But between me and the peak was gentle downward slope before the upward slope began again, leading to the altar. The slopes were all gentle here, but I realized that a thin coat of ice covered all the rocks; indeed, covered the rock only a few meters on from me. I didn't understand why at the time; afterward the men in the lander told me that for half an hour, while I was in the chimney on the west face, a mist had rolled over the top of the peak, and when it had left, only a few minutes before I surfaced, it had left the film of ice.

But ice was part of my vow, part of the rite, and I scraped some up, broke some off with the handle of my needle, and put it in my mouth.

It was dirty with the grit of the rock, but it was cold and it was water and I felt better for having tasted it. And I felt nothing but relief at having completed part of my vow—it did not seem incongruous at the time that I should be engaging in magic.

Then I struggled to my feet and began to walk clumsily across the space between me and the peak, holding the bag in my hands and slipping frequently on the icy rocks.

I heard shouting below me. I looked down and saw the Golyny on the south slope, hundreds of meters away. They would not be able to reach the peak before me. I took some comfort in that even as the arrows began to hunt for my range.

They found it, and when I tried to move to the north to avoid their fire, I discovered that the Golyny on that side had been alerted by the noise, and they, too, were firing at me.

I had thought I was traveling as fast as I could already; now I began to run toward the peak. Yet running made me slip more, and I scarcely made any faster progress than I had before. It occurs to me now that perhaps it was just that irregular pattern of running quickly and then falling, rising and running again, and falling again, that saved my life; surely it confused the archers.

A shadow passed over me twice as I made the last run to the peak; perhaps I realized that it was the lander, perhaps not. I could have, even then, opted for a rescue. Instead, I fell again and dropped the bag, watched it slide a dozen meters down the south slope, where the Golyny were only a few dozen meters away and closing in (although they, too, were slowed by the ice).

And so I descended into the arrows and retrieved the bag. I was struck in the thigh and in the side;

they burned with pain, and I almost fainted then, from the sheer surprise of it. Somehow primitive weapons seem wrong; they shouldn't be able to do damage to a modern man. The shock of the pain they bring is therefore all the greater. Yet I did not faint. I got up and struggled back up the slope, and now I was only a little way from the altar, it was just ahead, it was within a few steps, and at last I fell on it, my wounds throwing blood onto the ground and onto the altar itself. Vaguely I realized that another part of the rite had thus been completed, and as the lander came to rest behind me, I took the bag, opened it, scooped out the still-damp contents, and smeared them on the altar.

Three corporation men reached me then, and, obeying the law, the first thing they did was check my belt for the needle and the splinters. Only when they were certain that they had not been fired did they turn to the Golyny and flip their own splinters downhill. They exploded in front of the enemy, and they screamed in terror and fell back, tumbling and running down the rocks. None had been killed, though I now treasure the wish that at least one of them might have slipped and broken his neck. It was enough, though, that they saw that demonstration of power; the corporation had never given the Golyny a taste of modern warfare until then.

If my needle had been fired, or if a splinter had been missing, the corporation men would, of course, have killed me on the spot. Law is law. As it was, however, they lifted me and carried me from the altar toward the lander. But I did not forget. "Farewell, Crofe," I said, and then, as delirium took over, they tell me I also bade good-bye to all the others, to every one of them, a hundred times over, as the lander took me from the peak back to the city, back to safety.

In two weeks I was recovered enough to receive visitors, and my first visitor was Pru, the titular head of the assembly of Ylymyn. He was very kind. He quietly told me that after I had been back for three days, the corporation finally let slip what I had told them when I requested rescue; the Ylymyny had sent a very large (and therefore safe) party to discover more. They found the mutilated bodies of Fole and the soldier who had fallen just before him; discovered the dried and frozen corpse of Pan; found no trace of Da or Stone; but then reached the altar and saw the bloodstains upon it, and the fresh excrement stains, and that was why Pru had come to me to squat before me and ask me one question.

"Ask," I said.

"Did you bid farewell to Crofe?"

I did not wonder how they knew it was Crofe we had climbed the peak to honor—obviously, only Crofe was "Ice" and therefore worthy of the rite.

"I did," I said.

Tears came into the old man's eyes, and his jaw trembled, and he took my hand as he squatted by the bed, his tears falling upon my skin.

"Did you," he asked, and his voice broke, and then he began again, "did you grant him companions?"

I did not have to ask what he meant; that was how well I understood them by then. "I also bade farewell to the others," and I named them, and he wept louder and kissed my hand and then chanted with his eyes covered for quite some time. When he was done, he reached up and touched my eyes.

537

"May your eyes always see behind the forest and the mountain," he said, and then he touched my lips, and my ears, and my navel, and my groin, and he said other words. And then he left. And I slept again.

In three weeks Tack came to visit me and found me awake and unable to make any more excuses not to see him. I had expected him to be stern at best. Instead, he beamed and held out a hand, which I took gratefully. I was not to be tried after all.

"My man," he said, "my good man, I couldn't wait any longer. Whenever I've tried to see you, they've told me you were asleep or busy or whatnot, but dammit, man, there's only so much waiting a man can take when he's ready to bust with pride."

He was overdoing it, of course, as he overdid everything, but the message was clear and pleasant enough. I was to be honored, not disgraced; I was to receive a decoration, in fact, and a substantial raise in pay; I was to be made chief of liaison for the whole planet; I was, if he had the power, to be appointed god.

In fact, he said, the natives had already done so.

"Appointed me god?" I asked.

"They've been holding festivals and prayer meetings and whatall for a week. I don't know what you told old Pru, but you are golden property to them. If you told them all to march into the ocean, I swear they'd do it. Don't you realize what an opportunity this is? You could have screwed it up on the mountain, you know that. One false move and that would have been it. But you turned a potential disaster—and one not entirely of your making, I know that—you turned that disaster into the best damn contact

538

point with a xenosociety I've ever seen. Do you realize what this means? You've got to get busy right away, as soon as you can, get the contracts signed and the work begun while there's still this ground-swell of affection for you. Shades of the White Messiah the Indians thought Cortes was—but that's history, and you've made history this time, I promise." And on he went until at least, unable to bear it anymore, I *tried*—indeed, I'm still trying—to explain to him that what had happened on the mountain was not *for* the corporation.

"Nonsense," he said. "Couldn't have done anything *better* for the corporation if you'd stayed up a week trying to think of it."

I tried again. I told him about the men who had died, what I owed to them.

"Sentiment. Sentiment's good in a man. Nothing to risk your life over, but you were tired."

And I tried again, fool that I was, and explained about the vow, and about my feelings as I decided to carry the thing through to its conclusion. And at last Tack fell silent and thought about what I had said, and left the room.

That was when the visits with the psychologists began, and while they found me, of course, perfectly competent mentally (trust Tack to overreact, and they knew it), when I requested that I be transferred from the planet, they found a loophole that let me go without breaking contract or losing pay.

But the word was out throughout the corporation that I had gone native on Worthing, that I had actually performed an arcane rite involving blood, ice, a mountain peak, and a dead man's half-digested dinner. I could bear the rumors of madness. It is the laughter that is unbearable, because those who cannot dream of the climb to the mountain, who did not know the men who died for me and for Crofe—how can they help but laugh?

And how can I help but hate them?

Which is why I request again my retirement from the corporation. I will accept half retirement, if that is necessary. I'll accept *no* retirement, in fact, if the record can only stay clear. I will not accept a retirement that lists me as mentally incompetent. I will not accept a retirement that forces me to live anywhere but on Ylymyn Island.

I know that it is forbidden, but these are unusual circumstances. I will certainly be accepted there; I will acquit myself with dignity; I wish only to live out my life with people who understand honor perhaps better than any others I have known of.

It is absurd, I know. You will deny my request, I know, as you have a hundred times before. But I hoped that if you knew my story, knew as best I could tell it the whys behind my determination to leave the corporation, that perhaps you would understand why I have not been able to forget that Pru told me, "Now you are Ice, too; and now your soul shall be set free in the Sky." It is not the hope of a life after death—I have no such hope. It is the hope that at my death honorable men will go to some trouble to bid me farewell.

Indeed, it is no hope at all, but rather a certainty. I, like every modern man, have clung since childhood to a code, to a law that struggled to give a purpose to life. All the laws are rational; all achieve a purpose.

But on Ylymyn, where the laws were irrational and the purposes meaningless, I found another thing, the thing behind the law, the thing that is

540

itself worth clinging to regardless of the law, the thing that takes even mad laws and makes them holy. And by all that's holy, let me go back and cling to it again.

Afterword

"MORTAL GODS"

This story began with an essay I started writing once, about how real life has no borders and boundaries, no frame surrounding it the way that paintings do, no beginnings and ends like stories. It occurred to me that artists who tried to get rid of those frames and boundaries and beginnings and endings were making a foolish mistake. First of all, it can't be done—any work of an individual human being *will* have boundaries, both in time and in space, and any attempt to evade that is pure deception. Second, it *shouldn't* be done, because the very reason why human beings hunger so for art—especially for story-telling—is because art, with its beginnings and endings, provides an overlay of order on the chaos of life. Life never means anything, not clearly enough to count on it, but art *always* means something. Its very edges declare that this is inside the boundary and everything else is out.

The essay never got written. Instead, I wandered off into the idea that human life does in fact have one very simple but natural frame: birth and death. So while the mass of human life, taken together, cannot be separated into simple cause-and-effect chains that can be unambiguously interpreted, the life of a mortal being always has definable limits. And after a person has died, then it might, just might, be possible to go about discovering what actually happened within the frame of those two moments, birth and death, and what all those years between might mean.

This speculation would give rise, in the long run, to my concept of a speaker for the dead. In the short run, though, it gave rise to "Mortal Gods," for if it is death that provides the limit that allows life to be comprehended, that allows us to assign meaning to life, then what would this mean to sentient creatures who *could* not die? All our gods seem to be immortal—but wouldn't immortals search for mortal gods?

"SAVING GRACE"

When Kristine and I moved our family from the Great American West (i.e., the part of the country where trees only grow if you water them) to the Great American East (i.e., the part of the country where trees grow everywhere you haven't paved or mowed recently), one of the biggest cultural shocks was religious television. There just isn't that much of it out west, especially in Mormon country, where our video style is at once slicker and more sedate. So when I saw TV preachers for the first time, especially TV faith healers like Ernest Ainglee, I watched them for hours in horrified fascination.

Of course I knew that the faith healing business was rife with fakery and fraud. But what struck me most powerfully was the deep and desperate faith of those who came, day after day, week after week, to be healed. I wanted to write a story about one of those believers. I also wanted to write about somebody who *really* had the power to heal, and how he would get along with the fakes. When I realized they were the same story, I was able to write "Saving Grace."

That was in South Bend, Indiana, in 1982. I wrote it. I mailed it out. Nobody bought it.

Yet I knew it was a good story. I had read it aloud at a couple of conventions and the audience response told me that it worked, absolutely. So why didn't it sell?

I think part of the problem was that the story was too sympathetic to religion—it wasn't light and satirical enough, and the main characters seemed to be, after a fashion, believers. I don't think the sci-fi markets in those days were ready for that. Also, TV charismatics hadn't yet taken as much prominence in the public eye as they would half a decade later, when every cable system seemed to have a bunch of religious stations, and when the antics of that immortal love triangle of Jim and Tammy and Jessica, and of voyeur extraordinaire Jimmy Swaggart, made these guys household names.

Whatever the reason, I couldn't sell the story. Until, years later, a nice guy and talented writer and editor named Alan Rodgers told me that *Twilight Zone* magazine was spinning off a horror digest called *Night Cry*, and did I have anything he might publish? I *never* wrote horror—at least not in the normal conception of the term—but I did have a contemporary fantasy called "Saving Grace." I told him something about it, and he said, Sure, send it along.

I pulled the story out, thinking to do some major revisions. Instead I found that it needed only some minor changes to be up to speed; Alan bought it by return mail. The result was that "Saving Grace" did finally reach an audience—though I dare say that people buying *Night Cry* had to be more than a little surprised at what *this* story turned out to be!

"EYE FOR EYE"

This story began in my ancient Datsun B-210, a hideously rusted out blue coupe that I had bought from a friend who had pretty well used it up on the salt-covered roads in Lafayette, Indiana, while he got his doctorate at Purdue. The car vibrated so much that after a trip of more than fifty miles I ended up trembling for hours. But it served me well for many years, on trips to Texas, Michigan, Florida, and points in between. I couldn't bear to sell it—I finally gave it away.

All this has nothing to do with "Eye for Eye." I just miss the old car.

I was driving to a convention in Roanoke, Virginia, with my good friend and fellow writer, Gregg Keizer. He had been a student of mine in an evening class I taught at the University of Utah in the late 70s. The class was on writing science fiction, but Gregg never learned anything from me—he already knew how before he got there. I once was so sure that a story of his would sell that I bet him that if it didn't sell within a year I'd run naked through Orson Spencer Hall (the building where the class was held). It took more than a year. I reneged on the bet. But Gregg was very nice about it. And the story *did* sell soon after. Anyway, when I moved to Greensboro to be senior editor at Compute! Books, and we needed to hire another assistant editor, I thought of

Gregg, called him up, and asked him if he wanted to apply. He did. He got the job and did brilliantly. He also long outlasted me, ending up as editor of *Compute! Magazine* five years after I walked away from the place.

This has nothing to do with "Eye for Eye," either. But Gregg is living in Shreveport, Louisiana, these days, and I miss him too.

Anyway, Gregg and I were on our way to Roanoke, and just for the fun of it we decided to come up with some story ideas. Actually, I think I was saying some damfool thing about how a *real* writer could come up with a story idea anytime he felt like it, and make it work, too. So my ego was invested in this, just a little bit. The story idea I came up with was, what if a person discovered he had the ability to cause cancer in other people? What if he had had the ability for a long time, but didn't realize why all the people around him were all dying of cancer?

That was my story—finding out that you had killed people without meaning to. When I actually got down to writing it, of course, I raised the stakes by making it so my hero had killed the people closest to him; I also made him a pretty decent guy. The rest of the story came out of my speculations on how such an ability might arise. I had read a little bit about this doctor in Scandinavia who was trying to promote the body's ability to heal itself by adjusting the electromagnetic field that surrounds living organisms, so I used that to give the story a pseudoscientific veneer.

Because I had thought of the story on the way to Roanoke, and because I first publicly discussed the idea at that convention, I tipped my hat to the folks there by setting part of the story in their town, which has an extraordinarily beautiful setting in the mountains of western Virginia. The rest of the story arose from that setting. What if the gift arose from a bunch of serious inbreeding in a remote mountain community? And how would good mountain people interpret it if they found all their enemies just naturally dying of cancer? They'd know it had to be either God or the devil doing it, and, given a choice, they'd be bound to settle on God. I decided that they'd consider themselves to be a chosen people, which is why they only bred with each other—but since each generation would have a few kids with more and more intense power to disturb other people's magnetic fields, being their parents would be downright dangerous. So of course, like legendary cuckoos, they'd put them in somebody else's home to raise, only coming to claim them when they'd found out about their powers and had learned to control them.

Add a group of unbelievers who split off from the group, and you've got "Eye for Eye."

I sent the story around when I first wrote it, even though it didn't really feel finished. Everybody rejected it, partly because it was too long; but the nicest letter came from Stan Schmidt at *Analog*, who suggested that he might buy it if the scientific justification were beefed up.

Years later I ran across a copy of the story, with Stan's letter. I had forgotten that it even existed. Looking through it, I decided the idea had some merit, and rewrote it from beginning to end. This time the structure worked better, because I set it up as a first-person account as the boy tried to persuade the unbelievers not to kill him. And, because he had asked for revisions, I sent it to Stan. Alas, he still didn't like it; but by this time, Gardner Dozois was editing *Isaac Asimov's Science Fiction Magazine*, so I asked Stan to send it down the hall to Gardner. Gardner bought it at once and published it. To my surprise, "Eye for Eye" won both the Hugo and, in translation, the Japanese science fiction award as well.

"ST. AMY'S TALE"

Fred Saberhagen had let it be known in *Locus* and elsewhere that he was editing an anthology called *A Spadeful of Spacetime*, which would consist of stories that involved archaeology but did *not* involve time travel. He wanted stories that connected with the past the way science did it, not using the magic trick of a time machine.

I thought about this for quite a while. I loved archaeology—I had begun college as an archaeology major. But how could a story be science fiction about exploring the past *without* using time travel? I came up with a couple of ideas, but the one that interested me most was the idea of anti-archaeologists—people going around *erasing* the evidence of the past. Maybe there had been many high civilizations on Earth in the million-year history of modern man, but each one ended with blood and horror—and with the invention of a machine that could break down human artifacts and return them to their original, natural materials. The machine itself is a pretty hokey idea that doesn't bear close examination, but the human motivations behind the complete destruction of the past are both believable and interesting.

Why, though, did it take a religious bent? In a

way, that was a natural turn of the idea, because any idea that can cause such systematic transformation of human life has to end up being religious in character—much the way Communism absolutely functioned as a religion during its first ascendancy in Eastern Europe and the Far East. But there was another influence as well. I was working with some of the great old English writers in graduate school at the time, and Chaucer and Spenser were favorites of mine. I was playing with some of the forms they had used—I started a "Pedant's Calendar" after Spenser's "Shepherds' Calendar," and my epic "Prentice Alvin and the No-Good Plow" contained deliberate echoes of Spenser's *Faerie Queene*. Likewise, I had toyed with the idea of doing a story cycle about pilgrims on their way to a shrine, in imitation of Chaucer's *Canterbury Tales*. That idea went nowhere, but somewhere in the process of planning out this story the title "St. Amy's Tale" came to me. From there, it was an easy matter to introduce a religious overtone, a feeling of holiness and sacrifice to the whole series of events. I thought it made the story far richer and truer to itself.

"KINGSMEAT"

This is the story that readers over the years have found most disturbing and unpleasant. My critics have come up with all kinds of reasons to hate it—including, absurdly enough, a feminist reading of the story in which it was deduced that I "relished" the scene in which a breast is cut off. (One wonders about the mind of someone who thinks that writers "relish" all the scenes they write. Poor bloody-handed Shakespeare!) But once I thought of the idea, it was one of the most inevitable stories I ever told—and one of the most powerful and true.

The origin of the idea was simple. It owed a bit to Damon Knight's classic story that became the *Twilight Zone* episode "To Serve Man." The idea of aliens who eat human beings is as old as sci-fi. But what about a story in which a human being persuades the invaders not to *kill* their victims, but rather to harvest them limb by limb? Would that person be a savior or a torturer? In my mind this idea was linked with the Jews in death camps who were forced into service as body-handlers, fully aware of the slaughter of their own people and, while not directly killing anybody, cooperating with the killers by cleaning up after them. And yet, when you look at it another way, there was something noble in their helpless labor, for as they fed the bodies into the furnace, weren't they performing for the dead those last rituals that are usually performed by family? And wasn't it better that it was done by fellow Jews, fellow prisoners, who mourned their deaths, than to have it done by sneering members of the master race? It's an area of unbearable moral ambiguity—and that's what I strove for in "Kings-meat."

I think it's interesting that when Gene Wolfe set out to create a Christ-figure in his *Book of the New Sun*, he also made his protagonist begin as an apprentice torturer, so that the one who suffered and died to save others is depicted as one who also inflicts suffering; it is a way to explicitly make the Christ-figure take upon himself, in all innocence, the darkest sins of the world. I didn't plan that out consciously, but I saw it clearly in Wolfe's work and then, by extension, found the same thing happening in mine. That's about the only resemblance between Wolfe's seminal work and my little tale—but I'm glad for any resemblances to the great ones that I can get!

"HOLY"

This story began with a simple enough idea—a challenge, really. Could I write a story that made something as despised and disdained as human excrement seem holy? To accomplish it, I needed to have a point-of-view character who would represent the American reader's habitual disgust for human feces, and then bring him bit by bit to accept another culture's view, until at last he, too, felt that the "meaningless" mission of bringing intestinal scrapings to a particular shrine was worth dying for. Though at the time I wrote this story I would not have stated it so clearly, I was already caught up with the idea that it is story and ritual that give meaning to our actions.

At the time, Ben Bova was buying all the short fiction I wrote. But this story was too long for *Omni*, where Ben was fiction editor, and besides, I wanted to see if I could place a story in one of the prestigious annual anthologies. So I sent this one off to Robert Silverberg for his anthology *New Dimensions*. To my delight, he bought it. I felt validated; and I hoped that my career would get the kind of critical boost that appearing in *New Dimensions* or *Orbit* always carried with them. You didn't sell a lot of copies, but people knew you were certified to be a respectable, *serious* writer of speculative fiction.

Then, to my dismay, the volume that "Holy" appeared in virtually disappeared. It fell into the cracks between two contracts. The *following* volume of *New Dimensions* appeared in paperback before the hardcover edition of the volume I was in appeared, so that my story was in a book that appeared to be outdated—a year old—the moment it appeared. Worse, it never had a paperback edition at all. The stories in that volume were never reviewed. To my knowledge, only a few people in the world ever knew that this story even existed. Its appearance in this volume is, in effect, its first real publication.

None of this, though, was Robert Silverberg's fault—and I thank him again for taking my story seriously at a time when I was being dismissed as an "*Analog* writer" by the literary vigilantes of science fiction. But then, Silverberg has never been one to judge somebody else's work by its reputation, when he has the opportunity to judge it on its own merits. May his tribe increase.